To my sister, Shelly. You were my lullaby singer, my mac and cheese maker, and my second mama. You've never been afraid to be exactly who you are, and you've always accepted me just as I am. Thank you for all the support over the years. A-weema-weh, a-weema-weh…

Courage is fear holding on a minute longer.

—General George S. Patton

Prologue

Chicago, Illinois
Thursday, 5:38 p.m.

Someone was trying to kill her.

As Eve Edens squeezed the brakes on her classic 1966 Vespa motor scooter and felt absolutely zero response, it occurred to her that all the misfortune she'd suffered lately could no longer be chalked up to coincidence. The mugging, the fire, and now this? Even *she* wasn't *this* unlucky.

So, it was official; someone wanted her dead…

Of course, she'd have to worry about who that could be later. Right now, she had to find a way to stop the scooter from plowing into the stalled traffic fifty feet in front of her.

Her breath punched from her lungs, and her brain buzzed with terror as she thumbed the button for the horn. But the pathetic *meep, meep, meep* didn't do a thing to catch the attention of the motorists parked on the roadway ahead. And even if it did, it's not as if they could get out of the way or anything. Traffic was at a standstill in all lanes. There was no place to go except…

Oh, geez. She was going to have to try for the lake.

Yanking the handlebars hard to the right, she

gritted her teeth as she bounced over the curb on Lake Shore Drive with head-whipping force. In a flash, she was on the grassy area separating the road from the jogging path and the greenbelt that ran the length of the city. Then, she was zooming across the trail at forty miles per hour, nearly plowing into a man wearing bright red running shorts. Missing him by no more than a hairsbreadth, she careened down the steep embankment on the opposite side. Dodging trees and gathering speed—which she *so* didn't need—she braced herself for the inevitable.

Sweet Lord, help me!

And then the inevitable happened. She was airborne.

The smell of car exhaust and hot asphalt was replaced by the aroma of freshwater algae and fish as she flew past the high, man-made marina wall and over the cobalt blue of Lake Michigan. The Vespa whined beneath her, its engine revving uselessly, and she only had a split second to think, a split second to gather her scattered wits. Letting go of the handlebars, she kicked the scooter away right before she slammed into the water. *Sploosh!*

Oh, God! It was like hitting a brick wall. A *cold* brick wall. Because even in late summer, the lake's temperature remained in the forties. For a moment, the hard jolt and shock of the frigid water paralyzed her, and she drifted down into the dark abyss. Then, her stalled synapses started firing like crazy, giving her the cranial version of a kick-in-the-pants, and she swam toward the surface with everything she had. But no matter how hard she scissored her legs or pulled with her arms, the sunlight glittering on the rippling waves above grew fainter and fainter, and the cold pressing in on her from all sides grew ragged, icy teeth that bit into the exposed skin of her arms and face.

She was drowning.

The woman who'd grown up on the water, knowing how to set a sail before she could read, was drowning. The woman who'd spent her entire adult life studying marine animals from both above and below the water's surface was drowning. The woman who was mere weeks away from delivering her doctoral thesis on the effects of tourist snorkeling and diving on the world's great reefs was drow—

Doctoral thesis?

Her books!

Her backpack was filled with her research material. All however-many-umpteen pounds of it. And it was dragging her down to a watery grave.

Reaching for the clip around her waist, she managed to squeeze the locking mechanism with fingers gone numb from the frosty water. Then she shrugged out of the shoulder straps and immediately kicked toward the surface. Her lungs were burning for oxygen, her blood pounding in her head with every thundering heartbeat, and the urge to take a breath was as instinctual as it was overwhelming. But to do so would mean death. So she bit into her bottom lip and beat back that desire even as she clawed her way through the water.

So close, so close. Stars danced before her eyes; darkness closed in on the edge of her vision. *No! No! I'm not gonna make it!* And then…

"Uhhhhhh!" she raked in life-giving air the instant

she broke the surface, coughing and sputtering as she sucked droplets of water into her lungs along with all that beautiful, delicious oxygen.

She could hear people yelling to her from the top of the marina wall, asking if she was okay, but she was too busy restoring her body's air supply to answer. Once she hacked up the liquid from her heaving lungs, she flipped onto her back, concentrating everything she had on simply floating and slowing her frantic heartbeat. As the water closed over her ears, drowning out the sound of the concerned crowd, she let her gaze linger on the white, puffy clouds lazily drifting across the powder-blue sky.

For a few seconds, she found comfort in the quietness of the lake's embrace, in the weightlessness that permitted her thoughts to drift with the tide. But the seconds were fleeting. Because the taste of blood from her bitten lip quickly brought her slamming back to reality. Like it or not—and she most certainly did *not*—she could no longer overlook the fact that someone was out to get her…

And if the police ignored this latest incident like they'd ignored the first two, if they blew it off as bad luck, or being in the wrong place at the wrong time, or flippin' faulty wiring or something, she was going to be left with no recourse but to turn to the one man she'd sworn to avoid like a skin-diving expedition with tiger sharks. She was going to have to ask "Wild Bill" Reichert and his band of merry-covert-operative-men over at Black Knights Inc. for help.

Crap.

Chapter One

Black Knights Inc. Headquarters on Goose Island
Saturday, 3:54 p.m.

"It appears that Chicago's reigning socialite has had another accident."

The shammy Bill Reichert was using to polish the chrome exhaust on Phoenix, his custom Harley chopper, dropped from his nerveless fingers to the grease-stained concrete floor.

Swallowing the unexpected lump in his throat, he quickly skirted the bike, crossing his arms over his chest in order to hold his galloping heart in check. "Is she…" He had to lick his dry lips and take a deep breath, sucking in the familiar scents of motor oil, fresh paint, and strong coffee. The smells grounded him enough to manage, "Is she o-okay?"

Bryan "Mac" McMillan, lounging on the leather sofa they'd dragged into the shop and pushed against the side of the staircase that led to the loft space on the second floor, folded one corner of the *Chicago Tribune* back. He lifted a brow at what Bill assumed was his bloodless face. Because despite the fact that the ol' ticker wasn't simply ticking but hammering like crazy, he didn't think any of the red stuff was actually making it to his brain. He felt faint.

"Now don't go off with your pistol half-cocked," Mac replied in his slow, Texas drawl. "She's fine." The relief that poured through Bill was so overwhelming he had to lean back against Phoenix's hand-tooled leather seat or risk taking a header straight onto the shop floor. "Says here," Mac continued, "she plowed her motor scooter off the marina wall somewhere between Museum Campus and Buckingham Fountain on Thursday evening. She nearly drowned because she was weighed down by her backpack." The thought had the hairs on Bill's arms and neck standing on end. "Had to be scary as hell."

A million half-formed questions buzzed haphazardly through his under-oxygenated cerebral cortex. He grasped the first one to take any sort of solid shape. "What the fuck was she doing riding a scooter? Those things are dangerous, especially in traffic and—" He slammed to a stop when Mac once again glanced at him over the top of the paper with that annoying eyebrow raised. "What?" he demanded.

"*Those things are dangerous?*" Mac snorted. "Says the man who rides a quarter ton of hand-rolled steel."

Bill made a face, briefly glancing down at Phoenix's large gas tank with its intricate, almost whimsical paint job: a mythical firebird rising from the flames. "Okay," he admitted grudgingly. "Point taken. But the difference between me and her is that I can *handle* my bike where she, obviously, *can't*. What happened anyway? How did she manage to ditch the thing in the lake? Let me guess, she was texting."

Bill could totally see it. The woman had a social life

that, more often than not, made the society pages. One of the main reasons he avoided perusing the local news...

I mean, come *on*, it was bad enough he had to occasionally stomach her company because she happened to be his kid sister's best friend. But to read about some ooh-la-la party she'd attended on the arm of whichever rich-as-Croesus ass-hat happened to be Chicago's newest and brightest? *Yeah, no thanks*. He'd rather stand in the middle of a daisy-chained set of IEDs with the timer on the whole mess ticking down to *Boom*sville.

"Accordin' to this," Mac lowered the paper to his lap, flicking a finger at it, "after the police fished her scooter from the lake, they discovered one of the couplings on her brake lines had rusted and come loose. Apparently, Eve didn't realize she was in trouble until she was almost at top speed. Then, with traffic stalled in front of her, she had to shoot for the lake or risk killin' herself or someone else."

Shit. Bill swallowed uncomfortably, the scene playing out very vividly before his eyes.

Too vividly...

And here he'd accused her of negligence when, in fact, she'd made the smartest decision possible given her pathetically few options at the time.

Well, smarts had never been something Eve Edens lacked. Loyalty? Sincerity? Fidelity? Now *those* were entirely different matters.

"The police are sayin' it was an accident," Mac continued, frowning.

Uh-oh. Bill knew that look. He cocked his head, eyes narrowed. "But your Spidey sense is telling you something different?"

Mac was a former all-star FBI agent, and if the man said something smelled fishy, you could bet your left nut there was a goddamned blue whale in the room. And, yeah, so Bill realized that wasn't *technically* a fish, but the point was still valid.

"Just seems awfully coincidental, that's all. Nobody's *that* unlucky, are they?"

He frowned, considering Mac's words and remembering all the drama Eve seemed to trail behind her like a not-so-invisible tail. But before he could voice his opinion one way or the other, his cell phone sprang to life in his hip pocket. Pulling it out, the number for BKI's guardhouse lit the screen.

"What's up, Toran?" he asked after thumbing on the phone.

"A taxi just pulled up out front. Eve Edens is here," replied the guard. Well, speak of the devil. Bill's heart, which had just returned to its normal rate, kicked itself into overdrive again.

Holy moly. Eve felt the need to whistle and shake her head as she glanced around the second-story loft with its multiple office doors and bank of state-of-the-art computers. She'd never get used to the fact that Billy and her best friend Becky operated a covert government defense firm—that's right; a real life James Bond-type enterprise—under the guise of a custom motorcycle shop. But that probably had a lot to do with the fact that she'd known them back in the day. Back when Becky was little more than a sullen teenager with a chip the size of Texas on her shoulder, and Billy was just a fresh-faced petty officer with pie-in-the-sky dreams of becoming a spec-ops warrior.

Although, as it turned out, those dreams hadn't been pie-in-the-sky at all. Because he *had* become a spec-ops warrior. He'd become one of the big, bad Navy SEALs who were so popular in the media nowadays. And as she let her gaze travel across the conference table to his face, she tried to see the young man who'd stolen her heart so long ago.

Um, yes, and that'd be what the Black Knights referred to as a no-go. Because his ready smile and easy laugh were gone. Gone like the woolly mammoths. Gone like the homing pigeons. Long, *long* gone. Now his brutally handsome face was unyielding, fixed in grim lines of determination and impatience. His jaw was wider than she remembered, looking like it'd been shaped by a hatchet strike. His lips were harder and his tan skin was tougher. The corners of his dark chocolate-colored eyes were creased from spending years out in the elements, squinting against some far-away desert sun. And yes. It was official. There was nothing even remotely youthful about him now, save for the lush fan of his thick lashes and the plump curve of his lower lip.

This Billy Reichert—this hard, world-weary soldier—no longer resembled the young man who'd patiently and gently guided her toward the discovery of passion. No longer resembled the young man who'd teased her, laughed with her, loved her, and made her feel like she was…*the only girl in the world.*

Okay, and great, she was channeling Rihanna. Which meant she'd mentally stalled as long as she could.

"I think I'm in trouble," she blurted, and the words reverberated around the cavernous space of the chopper shop/super-secret-spy shop like fog-horns echoing across open water. It was then she realized the place was unusually quiet. "Where is everybody? Where's Becky?"

"What kind of trouble?" Billy ignored her questions as his eyes narrowed dangerously.

There was a time she'd have laughed in the face of *anyone* who described Billy Reichert as menacing. But she wasn't laughing now. Because his expression was that of an executioner. Cold. Hard. Unyielding. Talk about *brrrr.* She tried to disguise her shiver as a half-shrug.

"Um," she bit her lip and let her gaze swing over to Mac, seated at the head of the conference table. *That's better. At least he doesn't look like he ate babies for breakfast.* "I…I think someone might be trying to hurt me."

Hurt? *Yeah, right.* More like annihilate. But she was taking this one step at a time…

"Unless you're the kind who's so clumsy you'd trip over a cordless phone, you *do* seem to have run into a whole lotta bad luck recently," Mac drawled, his dark hair falling across his wide forehead, accentuating the deep, friendly blue of his eyes. And even though his expression was kind and his words sympathetic, Eve felt her cheeks heat.

Stupid fair complexion. And stupid nosy reporters!

Her entire life she'd been plagued by journalists who thought to capture for posterity—on film and in print—every folly, mishap, and humiliation she suffered. But she supposed that's what she got for being born the daughter of an East Coast heiress and Midwestern real estate mogul. Big buckets of money brought their own fame…of a sort.

"I guess you've been keeping up with the news," she muttered, shaking her head, the skin on her scalp prickling with embarrassment at the thought of Billy reading those articles. Because, talk about catching a girl *not* at her best.

Like the picture that'd run in the *Tribune* this morning? The one captured as a still from the video someone had shot with their smart phone? Well, it'd shown her and her Vespa flying over Lake Michigan, which was…so *very* flattering…*Not!* Of course, the snapshot wasn't nearly as mortifying as the full-length video clip that some fine, upstanding citizen had been kind enough to upload to YouTube—along with the *Wizard of Oz*, Mrs.-Gulch-on-her-Bicycle music playing in the background. So far, the video had fifty thousand hits. And that was…pretty perfect. Par for the course, really, considering how her life had been going since she was about, oh, say eighteen or so.

But even as humiliating as the YouTube video was, the fact remained that it wasn't nearly as awful as the picture that'd run in the paper last month after she barely managed to escape the fire that engulfed her apartment. In *that* particular shot, she'd sported a crazy, wide-eyed look, made even more delightful by the smudge of soot under her nose in the exact shape of Hitler's mustache. The caption had read: Heil Heiress and Her Amazing Death Defying Fire Act!

Geez Louise. Maybe whoever was out to do her in wasn't actually trying to kill her with bullets, fire, or cut brake lines but was, in fact, attempting to embarrass her to death.

"You want to explain to us exactly what's been going on?" Mac pressed, and she looked up to find his expression gently encouraging. But when she glanced over at Billy?

Nada. No encouragement there. Just a squint-eyed look of contemplation and was that…? Yep. That looked infuriatingly close to disbelief.

Oh, no he di-int! She did a mental headshake, frowning fiercely as she vehemently declared, "I'm not making any of this up, Billy."

One of his dark brows quirked, and it was like a lit match touching the fuel of her temper. She was instantly on the defensive—which really wasn't anything new. He tended to have that effect on her most days because he blamed her for…well, *everything*. But that didn't change the fact that she'd been nervous enough about coming here without having to deal with his enmity and snarky, high-handed attitude. "I'm not, dangit!" She slammed a palm down on the table, fighting not to wince at the resounding *crack* that echoed around the large space. "Where's Becky? She'll believe me!"

Or at least Eve *thought* Becky would believe her. Because, truth be told, there was a teensy, tiny, ever-so-miniscule seed of doubt planted back in the far reaches of her brain. The explanations the police gave *seemed* logical…

But, no. *No.* She wasn't crazy, and she wasn't paranoid. Someone wanted her dead. Period. End of story. *Alert the gosh-darned presses!*

"You haven't said anything for me to believe or not believe, Eve," Billy explained evenly, leaning back in his chair and crossing his arms over his chest. His biceps bulged, stretching the thin fabric of his gray T-shirt with its Black Knights Inc. Custom Motorcycles logo, emphasizing the hard planes of his pectoral muscles.

"Oh." She shook her head, quickly looking away from the masculine temptation that was Billy Reichert lest her cheeks turn the color of vintage Cabernet. "Yep. I guess that's true, huh?"

Curses. Billy had always managed to muddle her thinking. And it'd only gotten worse since they'd been reunited fourteen months ago after more than a decade apart. He'd blasted back into her life when he'd, you know, done her the itsy-bitsy favor of saving her from a band of bloodthirsty Somali pirates. She'd been doing research for her doctoral thesis out on the Indian Ocean when she and Becky found themselves the captives of a band of gun-toting, sea-faring desperados. It was then she'd been allowed in on the little secret of Black Knights Inc. Then when she'd been made to understand that Billy, and all the men who worked with him, were a whole heck of a lot more than simple motorcycle mechanics.

And since that day, she and Billy had done their best to avoid each other.

Ha! Understatement of the century! Because people *avoided* dog poop on the sidewalk. They *avoided* standing under a tree during a thunderstorm. They *avoided* mayonnaise-based salads that'd been left sitting out in the sun for more than an hour. What she and Billy had been doing? Well, that fell more into the turn-tail-and-run-for-your-life category.

Unfortunately, her current predicament precluded that particular status quo, so it was time to wrangle her wayward thoughts and lay it all on the line. Then again, this would all be so much easier with Becky in her corner.

Where is the woman, anyway?

She voiced the question again, and added, "And where is everyone else? This place is like a tomb." Usually, Black Knights Inc. was filled with the sounds of blaring music, whining tools, a gurgling coffee pot, and heavy boots clomping up and down metal stairs—not to mention, Becky's husband, Frank "Boss" Knight, could generally be relied upon to be bellowing at someone to pull their head out of their ass.

"Becky and Boss are taking a long weekend," Bill informed her abruptly, clearly ready to get back to the question of why she thought someone would want to hurt her. And, yes, now that he mentioned it, she did remember receiving a text from Becky saying that very thing.

Shoot. If she'd recalled that this morning after the police report came in, she might've thought twice about making this trek out to Goose Island. Then again…there was nowhere else for her to turn. The Black Knights… er, Billy and Mac it seemed, were her last hope.

"Everyone else is out on a mission or dealing with personal business," Billy continued when he mistook her distracted silence as her waiting for him to answer the rest of her question. "Except for Ace, who'll be here soon. So now that we've covered the niceties, you want to tell us just what the hell has been going on with you? Why you've suddenly been thrown into the role of Violet Jessop?"

"Who?" she asked, her nose wrinkling, her brain reeling with too many thoughts to catch.

"You know," he made a face, "the unluckiest woman in the history of the world? The one who was onboard the *Olympic*, *Titanic*, and *Brittanic* during all three disastrous voyages?"

She glanced over at Mac, distracted yet again by the turn of the conversation. And okay, maybe she was allowing it to happen on purpose. Because even though she knew she needed to answer Billy's question, the fact remained that she was scared to death he wasn't going to believe her when she did. Come on, he didn't think too highly of her to begin with—second understatement of the century—so why would he give her paranoid ramblings credence when the Chicago police hadn't? "Have you ever heard of this woman?" she asked Mac.

"Nope," the big Texan shrugged. "But I don't question this guy on much," he hooked a thumb at Billy, "considering he usually has his nose buried in a book."

She swung her gaze back across the conference table, reading the calm certainty in Billy's eyes.

"Wow," she shook her head. "And here I thought *I* had it bad. Sounds like this poor Violet Whats-Her-Name was the reason Murphy wrote his law. Somehow that makes me feel marginally better about everything I've been going through." Then Mac's words sunk in and, in the spirit of continuing to avoid having to discuss her suspicions and fears—her personal defense instructor, who'd been telling her for months she needed to "*grow a set of balls and stop avoiding tense situations*," would've been so disappointed—she cocked her head and said, "I don't remember you reading a lot before. In fact, you used to tease me incessantly about having *my* nose pressed into a book all the time, and—"

She stumbled to a stop because Billy's eyes sharpened, like those of a hawk spotting its prey. She swallowed, her level of discomfort—because, hey, after their sordid history and Billy's obvious disdain for her, there wasn't a moment she *wasn't* uncomfortable when he was in the room—shot through the three-story roof. And when he opened his mouth? Boy, oh boy, you better believe she had every right to feel that way. Because his words were saber strikes, slicing into her already sadly lacking confidence, and making her regret not only her cowardice at not addressing the main issue head-on, but also in coming out to BKI at all. "And I don't remember you being a scooter-riding divorcee with a taste for skimpy dresses, fancy parties, and rich men," he snarled. "I guess things change, huh?"

Holy shit fire.

Mac glanced back and forth between Bill and Eve, and the tension vibrating in the air caused the hairs on his arms and neck to lift. He ran a hand over the back of his head and opened his mouth to try to defuse the situation just as the rear door to the shop banged open and Ace yelled, "Hey, Lucy! I'm home!"

"Up here!" Mac called down, unaccountably glad for the distraction because, *damn*, these two were twitchier around each other than a couple of rattlesnakes. And all the not-so-subtle animosity flowing back and forth between them was making *him* feel twitchy.

He hated feeling twitchy.

Ace's boots clomped up the metal stairs. "And like Big Gay Al," he continued, oblivious to the electric atmosphere sizzling around the place that was threatening to singe everyone's eyebrows off, "I've brought along some chocolate salty balls from that new chocolate shop across the street and, I must say, they are fantast… Oh, Eve," Ace smiled when he topped the stairs, "what brings you out to our fine establishment this sunny Saturday afternoon?"

"It's Chef," Eve said, her voice a little shaky, no doubt from having withstood the poison-tipped barbs Wild Bill had just thrown her way.

Mac didn't know what the history was with these two, but it was obviously ugly and painful, and it made him intensely thankful to have learned early on the lesson about that crazy little thing called love when it was combined with a beautiful woman. And Eve was certainly beautiful. Prettier than a speckled pup, as Mac's dearly departed, born-and-bred-Texan father would say. But given her raven hair, clear blue eyes, and milky skin, Mac was more inclined to agree with Bill's assessment that she looked more like one of those expensive china dolls than any pup, speckled or not.

"What did you say, love?" Ace asked, setting the box of chocolate truffles on the conference table and glancing around the group. He picked up on the strained emotions and frowned.

"It's Chef on *South Park* who makes the chocolate salty balls, not Big Gay Al," Eve said, her voice only marginally stronger.

"I knew there was a reason I loved you besides your smashing fashion sense and front-row tickets to all the best shows," Ace chuckled, bending to smack a kiss on her cheek before pulling out the chair beside hers. Lowering his lanky frame into it, he hooked an arm around her shoulders. "Anyone who can appreciate the vulgarity and offensiveness of *South Park* is A-okay in my book." The guy gave her a hard squeeze and, from the corner of Mac's eye, he thought he saw Bill shift uncomfortably. Turning to lift a brow, he discovered that, sure as shit, the muscle in Bill's jaw was ticking fast enough to beat the band.

Dude, what the hell do you think? That Ace is suddenly gonna stop *likin' long and hard and* start *likin' soft and wet?*

Jesus. And once again Mac congratulated himself on having the good sense to avoid these types of sticky situations. Quickly, he filled Ace in on Eve's belief that someone was out to harm her. This also gave Bill a moment to get his sorry self under control—and the fact that he needed to get his sorry self under control was just too weird because usually, even in the middle of an all-out shit-storm, Wild Bill Reichert was cool as a cucumber.

"But who in the world would want to hurt you, love?" Ace asked, giving her another squeeze. This time Bill actually growled.

Mac rolled in his lips, glancing pointedly at the man, the look he gave was all about the *pull your shit together*. When Bill ignored him, Mac kicked him under the table and was rewarded with a look that promised retribution. Ace, unaware of the little scuffle, continued, "Do you have any suspicions?"

"That's the thing," Eve said, voice steadier now. Obviously she was unaware that Bill was a ticking time bomb, and with every one of Ace's squeezes, kisses, and endearments, he was getting closer and closer to blowing sky high. "There's only one person who comes to mind. But I don't think he's capable of violence."

"What do you mean?" Bill demanded, sitting up straighter, his expression just this side of a death-squad. *Oh, my God. You've got it bad, my friend.* Mac mentally shook his head. "Who the hell comes to mind?"

"Dale Pennyworth," Eve muttered, a sharp V forming between her sleek, black eyebrows. "He was my stalker."

Chapter Two

Stalker.

The room did a fast tilt, and Bill grabbed onto the edge of the conference table to steady himself. "You have a stalker? Why in God's name didn't you mention that in the beginning?"

"*Had* a stalker," Eve emphasized, eyes flashing, chin raised. "*Had.* I haven't seen Dale nor had any contact with him in over a year. And, like I said, I don't think he's a violent man. Crazy and a little bit obsessive, but not violent."

Was she nuts or just naïve? Because stalking very rarely ended with a bouquet of flowers and a touching good-bye letter.

"I hate to break it to you, sweetheart," he said, and then felt like biting his lip when her nostrils flared delicately. He'd used that endearment with her years ago, and to pull it out now caused memories to burn as harsh and fresh as the bile climbing up the back of his throat. In an instant, a kaleidoscope of images skittered across his brain. The way she used to look at him, with such faith and conviction and...*adoration* glowing in her wide, blue eyes. The way she used to touch him, tentatively and curiously and so freakin' sexily that he'd been hard-pressed not to throw her down on a horizontal surface every chance he got. The way she used to...

Damnit. With a hard shove, he stuffed everything back into a mental closet and slammed the door shut before continuing, "But stalkers aren't known to just give up and go about their business. Once you're someone's obsession, you *remain* someone's obsession."

Lord knew he could personally vouch for that. Because for over a decade, a day hadn't gone by when he didn't think of Eve, a night hadn't gone by when he didn't dream about her...

"Can we back up a minute here?" Mac cut in, his lazy Texas twang belying his tack-sharp mind. "Before we start discussin' suspects, we need to figure out why Eve disagrees with the police reports claiming these events are nothin' more than a string of bad luck."

Eve made a face, one of self-doubt, and it took everything Bill had not to reach across the table and squeeze her hand. Then Ace did the deed for him, and an angry shade of red edged into his vision. He started grinding his molars hard enough to crack his tooth enamel and figured chances were pretty good that any second now he'd be spitting out his fillings. And, yeah, it was ridiculous to be jealous of a man who made no secret about being gay. Ace was about as far out of the closet as you could get. We're talking shock-your-grandma, jazz-hands, out-as-in-*way*-out.

But that was definitely jealousy Bill was feeling. Because Ace got to touch Eve, kiss Eve, comfort Eve...

And though Bill didn't want to do those things...*he didn't!*...he still remembered how good it felt when he'd been twenty-one, stupid, and horny—the most common and most dangerous trifecta amongst human males—and he *had* wanted to do them. And, it was a goddamned Charlie Foxtrot—otherwise known as a clusterfuck—but he missed that. There! He admitted it!

He should've felt better afterward.

He didn't.

Shit.

"It's not that I don't believe you, Eve," Mac was quick to add. "But I want to make sure I have my facts straight."

"I'm afraid you'll all think I'm just being paranoid or something," Eve mumbled, studying the nails on one hand like they might hold the answer to the origins of man. Bill wasn't going to think about the fact that her *other* hand was still held tightly in Ace's. No, he wasn't. *Sonofabitch!* Now he was staring at their entwined fingers. Hers were so pale and delicate compared to BKI's resident helicopter pilot's. "That's what the police thought when I told them someone's out to kill me."

And *that* was enough to snap his attention away from Eve and Ace's interlaced hands. Because those last two words had all the blood in his body rushing to his head until it was hard to hear past the pulsing roar in his ears.

Kill her? That was a damn sight more specific than her earlier declaration that someone was out to hurt her. *Sonofa*—Stars skipped behind his lids when he blinked, and he realized he was holding his breath. Sucking in a slow, steady gulp of oxygen, he tried to convince himself that maybe she *was* just being paranoid.

Yeah, perhaps it's just a figment of her overly sheltered imagination.

Unfortunately, the part of him that'd been honed to

a razor's edge in too many high-stakes operations to count argued that, when it came to three life-threatening "accidents" in close succession, there was no such thing as paranoia.

"According to the fire marshal," Eve explained softly, "the blaze in my apartment started when a strong breeze through my open living room window blew my curtains onto a lit candle. But, I *always* make sure to blow out my candles before going to bed. And I distinctly remember doing it that night. Then again, perhaps it's possible the wick relit itself somehow, but..." She shook her head and lifted her hand to chew a hangnail.

Bill knew it for the sign of agitation it was. Sometimes, he thought he knew her *too* well even though they'd only spent three measly months together. Then again, there were other times he regretted the fact that he didn't know her well enough...

Of their own accord, his eyes drifted down her slender throat, past her little pearl pendant necklace—Yes, the woman actually wore pearls. And it drove him crazy, because the jewelry was so delicate, so feminine and classy, and it reminded him of everything about her that he'd initially been attracted to, was *still* attracted to as a matter of fact, *goddamnit*—to the gentle slope of her breasts beneath her demure, pastel blouse.

Yeah, there were a lot of things about her he still didn't know. Like the way she'd arch beneath him when he drove into her, or sigh with completion after he'd pushed her to the pinnacle of physical release, or taste when she—

Christ, man! Get a hold of yourself.

He shifted in his chair, trying to rearrange the hard-on

that seemed to be part of his SOP—standard operating procedure—whenever Eve was in the same room with him. Well that, along with a heaping helping of wariness and, okay, let's stop beating around the bush and admit he also suffered from a pretty decent amount of *hurt*. Yes, he was still *hurt* by what had happened with her. By the *way* it'd all happened.

There! He admitted that, too!

And why the hell his little revelations weren't making him feel better today, he'd never know. Wasn't honesty supposed to be the best policy, especially when it came to being honest with oneself?

Well, so far, his personal epiphanies were only piling on the shit topping to what was turning out to be a craptastically awful day. And that was just about perfect.

"What about the mugging?" Mac's question interrupted his ill-tempered musings.

Eve stopped chewing on her nail and shrugged. It caused her breasts to press against the delicate fabric of her top until he could see the imprint of the lace along the upper edge of her bra. But he wasn't going to stare. No, he absolutely was *not* going to stare.

Ace kicked him under the table, and he realized he was staring. *Jesus!* And what was *with* everybody today? Did his shins have bull's-eyes painted on them or something?

"It was strange," Eve admitted, unaware of the under-the-table byplay. "I worked late at the Shedd Aquarium, and as I was crossing the parking lot to my Vespa, a masked man hopped out of the bushes and pointed his gun at me."

That was just the thing Bill needed cool his ardor. Because the thought of the girl who'd been so painfully shy it'd taken him almost three weeks just to coax a kiss from her staring down the business end of a loaded weapon was absolutely, positively terrifying.

Then she proved how far she'd come from that quiet, self-conscious young woman he'd first fallen in love with when she continued, "I told him to take my purse. I was going to throw it away, to the side, and run in the opposite direction like you're supposed to do. But the man just stared at me, the gun shaking until it rattled. And that's when my training kicked in, and I executed a roundhouse that knocked the weapon from his hand. I bolted for my scooter, gunned it, and didn't look back."

Every single thought in Bill's head came to a screaming stop. He fancied he could hear the *errrrtttt* of tires squealing between his ears because...Eve? Training? Roundhouse kick?

He knew he was gaping, jaw unhinged and hanging somewhere in the vicinity of his chest, when Eve looked at him and lifted her chin. "Ever since the pirate episode, I've been taking personal defense classes and shooting lessons. I've gotten pretty good," she boasted, though the effect was somewhat ruined when her lower lip trembled ever so slightly.

"Hot damn," Ace whistled. "You're one kick-ass broad, you know that?"

Eve blushed, dropping her eyes back to the surface of the table. Now *that* was more like the old Eve. "No," she jerked her chin from side to side. "It was just instinct brought on by good training. I was shaking so badly by the time I made it out to Lake Shore Drive that I had to pull over. I still shake when I think back on it."

To prove it, she held up her hand, palm down. And, sure enough, the thing was quivering like a dry leaf in a stiff breeze.

Bill felt the overwhelming urge to get up and go pound on this Dale Who-The-Fuck-Ever's door in order to put the guy in a nice, tidy chokehold. Even if he *wasn't* the person who'd jumped out of the bushes to hold a gun on Eve, the fact remained the man had stalked her and Bill needed an outlet for all the violence that was suddenly and unexpectedly coursing through his veins.

Fortunately, Mac's cooler head prevailed. "So you don't think this man was simply after your purse?"

Eve shook her head, then hesitated, gnawing her bottom lip—another sign of agitation Bill knew well—and shrugged. "But maybe he was, you know? Maybe that was his first robbery and what I took to be indecision about killing me was really just nerves about pulling off the heist in the first place. That's what the police suggested. Well," she frowned, "except Jeremy. Jeremy doesn't buy that explanation, but what can he do about it? It's not his case. And he's just about gotten himself fired multiple times because he continues to hound the higher ups in the CPD to look into these incidents again."

"Jeremy?" Mac inquired, leaning forward on the conference table and cocking his head.

"He's my cousin," Eve explained. "Our mothers

were identical twins. After my mom died when I was seven, Aunt Betty sort of acted like a surrogate. So, really, Jeremy is more like a brother to me." And Bill remembered the man very clearly. Well, he remembered the man's overgrown superiority complex, that is. "He works vice for the CPD," Eve continued. "And I've been staying with him since the fire in my condo."

Now *that* surprised Bill. Because when he'd known her, she always run to Daddy Dearest when things got dicey.

"You're not staying with your father?" he asked, closely watching her pretty face to catch any snippet of emotion. Eve's expressions usually came in two forms. One was the open book form. And two was the *wide*-open book form.

"No," she shook her head, not meeting his gaze. "Dad and I haven't exactly been getting along recently. He doesn't approve of some of the...uh...*changes* I've been making in my life or in myself." Her subtle frown told him it was a little more than that. And, bastard that he was, he couldn't say he was sorry Eve had had a falling out with her world-class prick of a father. Then, she added quietly, "I think he wanted me to stay his shy little girl forever."

Because you're easy to control that way, he thought. *And Patrick Edens is the most controlling sonofabitch ever to have been born of woman.*

"Let's move on to the Vespa," Mac said, interrupting Bill's astringent thoughts and the vitriol they inspired. Which was a good thing. Because he felt his stomach fill with acid, and he knew if he didn't put a check on his emotions soon, he'd be swilling Pepto-Bismol like a drunkard swilling boxed wine. "The newspaper said it was a rusted coupling on your brake line."

And all the uncertainty that'd been in Eve's face as she was recounting the details of the first two episodes disappeared. Her jaw firmed, her eyes sparked, and she withdrew her hand from Ace's—*praise be*—and used it to plant a firm finger onto the tabletop. "No," she shook her head adamantly. "No way. Four months ago when I bought that scooter, I had Becky inspect it from top to bottom. If there'd been a rusty coupling, she'd have found it. Someone sabotaged it. They *had* to have."

And okay, now Bill was completely, totally, unequivocally convinced. Because his mechanic-extraordinaire baby sister didn't make mistakes. "I believe you, Eve," he blurted before he realized he even opened his mouth.

She stared at him, peach-colored lips slightly open, surprise flickering in her eyes. "You do?" There was such a note of hope in her voice and it went all through him.

Jesus. Sometimes he wanted to kick his own ass for the way he'd been treating her since their reintroduction. Was it her fault she'd done what many young girls her age and from her socio-economic station did, which was become fascinated by the poor boy from the wrong side of the tracks? Was it her fault that once he was out of the picture at BUD/S training and she was away at college that she began to realize her daddy was right about a guy like him—a guy who didn't know the difference between a dinner fork, salad fork, and dessert fork—not belonging in her life? Was it her fault that her head had been turned by a Ralph Lauren-wearing, fancy-talking Ivy Leaguer who epitomized everything that was familiar and safe to her?

No. If he was honest with himself, no, it wasn't her fault. After all, she'd been so very young. So very young and so very naïve. Really, looking back on it now, he realized he shouldn't have been shocked when she cut him loose.

Then again, the *way* she'd cut him loose was another matter entirely…

Sighing, he pushed all that old pain and disappointment aside and allowed his expression to soften as he nodded. "Yes, Eve, I believe you. Something about this whole mess stinks."

"And this time," Ace smirked, "it isn't your attitude."

Bill frowned. "You're really pushing my buttons today, Ace-hole." Usually the nickname was guaranteed to wipe the smile from Ace's face.

Unfortunately, this time it had the opposite effect. The pilot's grin only widened. "So I've noticed."

Eve glanced back and forth between the two of them, blinking in confusion.

Then, Mac cut in, distracting her from the testosterone-laden staring contest with, "I'm gonna make a call to Washington and see if I can get my hands on your case files."

"Washington?" she asked.

"Chief Washington of the CPD," Mac explained.

"Oh, you don't have to do that. Jeremy's made copies of everything. He'd be happy to share anything he has with you."

"Okay, then." Mac nodded, and Bill couldn't help but doubt just how *happy* Jeremy Buchanan would be to share *anything*, much less his police files. "In the meantime, I think it's probably best if you move out of your cousin's place and move in here with us."

At this little announcement, Bill's ulcer, the one he'd been so sure he'd finally beaten once and for all, raised its ugly head and took a bite out of his stomach lining. Pressing a hand below his breastbone, he grimaced and tried to ignore the uncertainty in Eve's eyes when she slowly, hesitantly searched his face. And as much as this was going to suck gargantuan donkey balls, he said, "Mac's right. I'll take you over to your cousin's so you can pack a bag. And then, once you're back here and we've looked over your files, we can decide how to proceed."

She swallowed, her eyes bright with gratitude, and he remembered the first time he ever saw her. He'd been home on an extended leave from the Navy, waiting for the time he'd be called up for the SEAL training, and he'd gone to one of his sister's summer league track meets to pass the time…

There'd she'd been, Evelyn Rose Edens, crossing the finish line after running the women's 3000 meters. She'd looked like a gazelle, all lithe and sleek, legs a mile and a half long. He'd asked Becky to introduce him, and Eve had been so shy she'd barely been able to meet his gaze. But when she finally did look up at him?

Total gut check.

Her flushed, delicate face had been pure perfection, and her eyes? Well, they were the deepest, most amazing blue he'd ever seen. And he'd fallen. Right then and there it was game over for him, because her expression, so sweet and innocent, so sheltered, had all his protective instincts surging to the surface. He'd wanted nothing more than to throw an arm around her shoulders and keep her safe. Forever…

Well, forever had turned out to be a remarkably short length of time. The span of one sultry, sun-and-blue-ball-filled summer.

"Th-thank you, Billy," she stuttered, dragging his mind back to the present. She was twelve years older now. A divorcee. A well-respected and renowned marine biologist. A self-defense prodigy, by the sounds of it. And, yet…she still appeared so sweet and innocent. And, with one look, she still made everything inside him want to stand up, chest-beating, spear-waving, and protect her from the big, bad world.

How does she do *that?*

He shook his head, at himself, at this clusterfuck of a situation, and murmured, "You're welcome." Then, lest she get the wrong idea and think he was doing this out of the goodness of his heart—because, come on, when it came to her and his heart, there wasn't much goodness left—he added, "Becky'd never forgive me if I turned you away in your hour of need."

Whatever light had been in her eyes dimmed. She nodded jerkily before saying, "I'm going to run to the restroom. Then I'll be ready to go to Jeremy's to pack a bag."

Watching her disappear down the long hall, he wondered how the hell he was going to handle the next few days when Mac looked over at him, heavy brow furrowed. "What's that look for?" he demanded.

"You want to tell us why you turn into a total Neanderthal whenever she's around?" Mac hooked a thumb in the general direction of the hallway.

"Now, why in the world would I do that? What are we? Girlfriends or something?"

Ace leaned across the table and patted Bill's fingers, batting his blond lashes fervently. "Only if you want to be, handsome."

Bill snatched his hand away but couldn't quite control the smile that tugged at his lips. "Cut it out," he grumbled, trying and failing to paste on a fierce frown. "Don't you have bon-bons to eat and an episode of *Glee* to watch?"

"As a matter of fact..." Ace snatched up the box of chocolates, winking dramatically before sauntering over to the stairs leading to the living area on the third floor. But he stopped on the first tread, turning, his expression suddenly somber. "Seriously, though" he nodded, "if you guys need me for anything, you know where to find me. And Bill?"

Bill sighed, because he knew what was coming. It was written all over Ace's face. "Yeah?"

"You be nice to Eve. That poor woman is starved for affection. So why don't you try a little tenderness, huh?"

"And who the hell are you, now?" he groused. "Otis Redding?"

"No, I'm just saying from the way you amble around this place on all fours, you're probably not one for a gentle touch."

"Oh, yeah?" Bill asked. "Well, I've got some advice for you, too. I've written it down. It's right here in my pocket." He dug into the hip pocket of his jeans and came out with an empty fist and a raised middle finger.

Ace laughed, then immediately sobered. "Let me put it to you this way. If you're mean to Eve, I might have to rearrange that pearly white smile of yours, *capiche*?"

And the threat would've been funny except for the fact that Ace was a master at Muay Thai, the most brutal form of hand-to-hand combat in the world. The guy might come off as intimidating as a glitter unicorn sitting under a rainbow at a Justin Bieber concert, but Bill wouldn't want to find himself on the man's bad side.

"I'll be nice to her," he promised through clenched teeth, because as much as he hated to admit it, Ace was right. It was time to let bygones be bygones. For Christ's sake, it'd been *twelve years!*

The Knights' resident flyboy turned his head, eyeing Bill suspiciously.

"Look," Bill huffed with exasperation, "the thing is, I've never been good when it comes to lobbing around sugar and spice and everything nice. But I'm telling you I'm going to *try*, okay?"

Ace's smile was victorious as he nodded once before turning to clomp up the stairs.

Then Eve reappeared at the end of the hallway, looking as beautiful as he remembered—scratch that; looking even *more* beautiful than he remembered—and all the old hurts came rushing back with brutal force. It made him realize just how difficult it was going to be to keep his word.

Chapter Three

Jeremy Buchanan's Condo
5:33 p.m.

"I COULD KEEP YOU SAFE," JEREMY DECLARED, HUGGING her tightly, and Eve felt her lower lip quiver. "I could hire bodyguards. I could take some time off work. You name it, Cuz, and I'll do it."

"No," she shook her head, stepping from Jeremy's fierce embrace, taking comfort in the unwavering look of support on his face. "I'm going to go stay at Black Knights Inc. until we can either find out who's doing this, or at the very least convince your associates in the police department that I'm not crazy. I promise you, I'll be safer there."

Jeremy snorted, glancing past her shoulder at Billy, who was standing sentry at the balcony door in faded jeans, clunky biker boots, and that skin-tight BKI T-shirt that emphasized his washboard belly and made her internal temperature jump about ten degrees.

Ten degrees? Okay, so it was more like ten *thousand*. But who was counting anyway? Not her. No, sir. No how. She was *not* counting.

All right, so maybe she was counting a little bit. It was hard not to when he was caught in a ray of sunlight, looking for all the world like something out of a *Sons of Anarchy* episode—just with far less facial hair and pinky rings, and a far more deadly determination gleaming in his dark eyes—as he scanned the street below.

"You'll be safer with a bunch of bikers?" Jeremy's incredulity was palpable. "You've got to be kidding me."

Oh...*that.*

Okay, so she couldn't very well tell him the truth about Black Knights Inc.; she'd been sworn to secrecy. Which meant she was left with no recourse but to give him just enough information to assuage his fears. "They have a ten-foot-high brick wall surrounding the place and twenty-four hour surveillance. It's like a flippin' fort there. So don't worry."

"I'm not so worried about somebody breaking into the place," Jeremy's lips pursed. "I'm more worried about what you'll have to put up with in regards to Mr. No-Neck over there." He tilted his chin toward Billy. "I see the years haven't improved his manners any."

She shook her head. "You never liked him, did you?"

"He was never worthy of you, Eve."

She searched her cousin's eyes, so much like her own, and frowned. "You've been listening to Dad too much, Jeremy. Elitism doesn't suit you."

"It's not elitism, Cuz. It's pure, unadulterated fact. And I'd have known that with or without your father's input. That man's a grade-A prick. Pardon my language."

"No pardon necessary," Billy piped up from his position by the balcony door. Eve blushed from the soles of her feet to the roots of her hair. So much for what she'd thought was a private conversation. *Note to self: Billy has the hearing of a bat.* "Assuming," Billy continued, "that you're using grade-A prick as a technical term."

"When I'm speaking of you," Jeremy raised his voice, although it was apparent there was no need, "I most certainly am. And if you so much as look sideways at my cousin, I promise you I'll—"

"Yeah, yeah," Billy's tone was bored. "You'll beat me longer and harder than you beat that gherkin-sized dick of yours. I get it."

Jeremy took a step in Billy's direction, but Eve stopped him with a hand on his arm. "Remember you insulted him first," she whispered.

"He's a dickwad," Jeremy hissed.

"More technical terminology, I'm assuming," Billy mused, brow raised, sardonic grin on his lips.

Eve decided it was time to get the heck out of Dodge. Which brought her around to the *second* reason why she'd stopped by Jeremy's condo. "I, uh..." She hesitated. Because her dear, sweet cousin was already upset by her decision to leave his protection in favor of the Knights' and she didn't want to prick his ego further with her next request—he was big and cocky and all about playing the hero, which made it sort of funny that he and Billy didn't get along because they were so very much alike—but she didn't see any way around it. Jeremy had done everything he could to prove she wasn't just being paranoid about her growing list of "accidents." Now it was time to let someone else take a stab at it. "I need my case files," she finally blurted.

Jeremy's chin jerked back. "What? Why?"

"Because we've got an ex-FBI agent working for us," Billy answered, still staring out the balcony door in narrow-eyed concentration. "And he might be able to see something in her files that you and your fellow CPD boys couldn't."

"Yeah, and I might be onboard with that except the part where this guy is an *ex*," he stressed the word, frowning, "FBI agent."

Eve stepped in before the two of them could start slinging insults again. Grabbing her cousin's arm, she looked up at him imploringly, "Please, Jeremy. You've done everything you know to do and—"

"I could try to talk to my captain again," he interrupted. "I could—"

"Get yourself fired," Eve said, shaking her head. "Your captain has had enough. He agrees with the fire department and the investigator on the case. There's no evidence. You can't keep harping on him. You can't keep questioning his judgment. He's the only true friend you've got down at that station. Believe me, you don't want to mess with that."

The fact that Jeremy had chosen to become a police officer when he'd inherited enough money to keep him footloose and fancy free for life had caused more than a few problems for him at work. Most cops, who struggled to get by from paycheck to paycheck, couldn't understand why Jeremy chose to risk his life on the force every day instead of whiling away his hours on a beach. But Eve understood. A person needed a purpose, something worth waking up for every morning. And Jeremy's purpose was to be a hero…

She watched his cheeks hollow and his chin twitch from side to side as he considered her words. Then he cursed, and she knew she'd won.

"Fine," he grumbled. "I'll go get them."

"Thank you," she whispered, going up on tiptoe to kiss his cheek, his expensive cologne tickling her nose. "And I'll call you tomorrow to let you know how things are going."

"You sure you want to do this?" he pressed, searching her face.

Um, no? She didn't *want* to do any of it. What she *wanted* was a char-free condo and a Vespa that had brakes, but those two things were no longer options.

"I'll be fine," she assured him, avoiding his question. "I trust the Black Knights to keep me safe. Plus," and she was going to go straight to hell for this lie, but she knew it would go a long way in easing her cousin's misgivings, "Becky will there."

A hint of relief flashed behind his eyes. "Okay," he nodded. "But if things change, or if you catch too much flak from that one," again he jerked his chin toward Billy, "then you call me."

"I will." She smiled, squeezing his arm and taking a deep breath before shouldering her purse and overnight bag.

A warm breeze wafted into the condo when Billy opened the balcony door, bringing with it the hot smell of summer, of fresh-cut grass, heavily blooming flowers, and steaming pavement. It ruffled Billy's thick, dark hair like playful fingers. But somehow he still managed to pull off that whole mean and menacing thing. Which was good, she supposed. Because mean and menacing was exactly the kind of man she needed right now. And, perhaps, if she was honest with herself, it was the kind of man she'd needed all along. Or more specifically, *he* was the kind of man she'd needed all along. It crushed her to think about all she'd lost that night during her freshman year in college when she finally caved to her father's wishes and agreed to go out with Robert Parish's son, Blake.

One night out with the big-time land-developer's pride-and-joy had changed her life. Forever…

"When we reach the street, I want you to stay behind me," Billy murmured once she'd crossed the room to him, wrenching her from her unpleasant thoughts.

"Why?" When she glanced up into his hard, handsome face, she didn't like what she saw there. She figured this was probably the expression he wore during those times he was knee-deep inside the wiry innards of an IED.

And, yes, it still blew her mind to know that Billy'd spent nearly a decade either making things go *kaboom* or disarming things that went *kaboom*.

Talk about having a set of brass balls. *Geez Louise.*

"There's a car parked on the street out front," he said, his voice disconcertingly calm, especially when compared to his I-eat-metal-shavings-for-lunch expression. "There's someone in the front seat…watching this condo." A chill snaked up her spine despite the heat of the day. "I can't make out who it is. Jeremy," he raised his voice when Jeremy reentered the room with a manila file folder tucked up under his arm, "you carrying?"

"Of course." Her cousin jogged over to them, instantly on alert. *See*, they were so much alike. "What's up?"

"See that black SUV parked across the street?"

"Yeah," Jeremy nodded after craning his head through the open door. "What's the score?"

The atmosphere was vibrating with masculine tension, and Eve fancied she could actually *taste* the testosterone hanging in the air like a mist.

"The score is someone's real interested in this place, and I want to make sure whoever it is doesn't get a shot at Eve," Billy said. The last part of his sentence made her dizzy.

A shot at her…

He was afraid someone was out there ready to take a *shot* at her!

Holy *crap*, this was just too surreal. She'd never done anything to anyone. At least not something that would warrant an extra hole in her head. In fact, the only instance where she could recall being purposefully mean to someone was that time in kindergarten when she ripped up Curtis Forsythe's Thanksgiving craft project—the turkey made from his handprint and construction paper—because he kept pulling her pigtails.

But, surely *that* wasn't enough to deserve a bullet in the brain…

"Once we're downstairs, we're going to edge out the front door, keeping Eve behind us until we make the Hummer," Billy instructed. "When we're on our way, if that Chevy takes off after us, which I'm pretty sure it will, I want you to use your connections with the CPD to run the plates."

"You don't think it'd be better to leave Eve up here? Let you and me go down there and question this fucker?"

"Nope," Billy shook his head, causing a dark brown lock to fall across his wide forehead.

And, great. Now was *not* the time to be thinking of how incredibly sexy he was, to be remembering what it felt like to run her fingers through his silky hair after it'd been warmed by the summer sun and tousled by a friendly breeze, but there you go. Because those were the exact thoughts scrolling through her head.

For Pete's sake, Eve. Even after all the nasty things he's said to you in the past year, you still get all gooey-bellied and jelly-kneed around him? What the heck is the matter with you?

She refused to contemplate the answer to that question. She had enough on her plate right now without dealing with her ever-present feelings for one William Wesley Reichert.

Case in point..."I want to find out who this is without them knowing we're on to them," Billy told Jeremy. "So we're going to stroll out there, calm as you please, like you're just seeing us out. Savvy?"

"Aye, aye, Captain," Jeremy snorted, playing off Billy's Jack Sparrow jargon as they turned for the door.

And, *huzzah!* Eve mentally patted herself on the back for picking up on that reference, because she wasn't much of a moviegoer. As a girl, her father hadn't liked the idea of her sitting in a darkened theater where anyone and everyone with an eye toward ransom could sneak up and grab her. And then, after she'd become an adult, a *single* adult, sitting alone in the gloom, eating too-salty popcorn while being surrounded by all those starry-eyed couples just reminded her of everything she'd lost when she'd lost Billy.

But in *this* case, she was well-schooled on Johnny Depp's Captain Jack lingo because after having been held hostage by Somali pirates, Becky'd thought it would be a hoot to hold a *Pirates of the Caribbean* movie marathon—complete with eye patches, fake parrots, and little chocolates in the shape of gold coins. So Eve could "who drank all the rum?" and "I've got a jar of dirt!" right along with the best of them.

Of course, not even good ol' Johnny Depp could bring more than a short-lived smile to her lips right then because the fact remained that she was in danger. Maybe *imminent* danger. She gnawed on her bottom lip during the too-short elevator ride to the bottom floor. Then, after they'd shuffled across the well-appointed lobby, it was time for the show. Or maybe the show*down* was the better way to put it.

Oh geez. Oh geez...

She repeated the mantra like a pathetic prayer when they edged out the front door as a unit, Jeremy and Billy creating a wall of living flesh in front of her. She instinctively grabbed the back of Billy's waistband, hooking her fingers into a belt loop and marveling at the warmth of him, at the sheer strength of the muscles in his lower back as they bunched with his steps and brushed across her knuckles. It was the first time she'd touched him in months. And, okay, so she could admit she'd missed his nearness *waayyy* more than she should have, especially considering how things stood between them. But she could also admit that while the sensation of his hard flesh against the back of her hand was titillating, it was also comforting. Giving her the strength to keep from faltering as they crossed the street to the parked Hummer.

"Get ready to open the door, Eve," Billy instructed quietly once they'd made it to the vehicle. He and Jeremy body-blocked her from the suspicious SUV's direct line of sight. Then, a *chirp-chirp* emanated from the big Hummer, and she knew he'd unlocked the door and disarmed the alarm system with the key fob in the hand that *wasn't* snaked behind his hip, palming the handgun he kept hidden there. *Gulp.* "Okay, now jump on in there, and don't be shy about it."

She wished she could say she hopped-to without hesitation. Unfortunately, that wasn't the case. For some reason she couldn't explain, maybe it was momentary panic or a bout of fleeting hysteria or…the fact that she didn't want to let go of Billy and the comfort his nearness provided, but she froze. For just a second. But it was long enough for Billy turn to her, his expression so soft, the light in his eyes so warm that she almost forgot how precarious her situation was and melted into a puddle of hormonal slop right there on the pavement.

"It's okay, sweetheart," he crooned in a low voice, the endearment jolting her like a shock from an electric eel. "Go ahead and hop in."

It took a second more for her to snap out of her trance—*I really am a sad sack, aren't I?*—but then she hurried to do as she was instructed. Heaving open the heavy door and jumping up into the mammoth vehicle, she quickly tossed her bags onto the back seat. The heat inside the Hummer had sweat popping out all over her skin and trickling in an itchy line between her breasts, but that was nothing compared to the fire in her heart.

*Sweetheart...*Oh, how she'd loved to hear that word on his lips that summer and—

For the love of all that's holy, pull your head out of your butt! Someone might be waiting back there to kill you!

Okay, and that was the voice of sanity yanking her from her reverie. And, yep, perhaps she should listen to it.

Shaking her head at herself, she watched as Billy skirted the front of the vehicle before wrenching open the driver's side door and hopping inside, bringing with him the smell of sunshine, leather, Irish Spring soap, and man.

Before she had a chance to utter one word, he leaned over, yanked her seatbelt tight across her lap and started the big engine. Throwing the monster vehicle into gear, he slowly—*slowly?*—pulled out onto Jeremy's street as adrenaline coursed through her system, making her brain fizz. At the stop light on the corner, she swiveled in her seat and tried to peer out the heavily tinted back window to see behind them. But there was something strapped there. Narrowing her eyes against the dimness of the hot interior, she wondered if that was a....? Yep, that was most definitely a gun rack. A gun rack with two short-barreled shotguns attached to it.

Double gulp.

Facing forward once again, she scooted down in her seat to try to use the side rearview to see—

"You're gonna give yourself whiplash if you keep flopping around like that," Billy commented, cool as can be over there, which only managed to redline her own anxiety.

"Is it behind us? That black Chevy? Is it following us?" she asked breathlessly. The air conditioner was blowing full blast on her heated cheeks, but it did little to mitigate the stagnant air inside the Hummer.

"Indeed it is," Bill said like one might say *indeed the sun is shining.*

What the huh? How could he remain so unruffled when there was a mysterious black SUV following them? Possibly being driven by the very person who'd been trying to eighty-six her for months?

Oh yeah, because he did this sort of thing for a living. Which was the whole reason why she'd run to him in the first place.

Okay Eve, she coached herself, taking a deep, cleansing breath, *get it under control. You're in good hands.*

And just the thought had her glancing over at the steering wheel, where Bill's broad, tan hands handled the huge Hummer as gently and as easily as a little girl handles a puppy.

She'd always loved his hands. So big, so…capable looking. With long, knobby fingers, square nail beds, and tough calluses, his hands had always made her feel safe, secure…*protected.* Looking at them now reminded her of the first time he kissed her…

They'd just come back from a day on the water where

she'd taught him how to captain the little Daysailer her father had given her for her eighteenth birthday. She'd been feeling awfully proud of herself for having instructed the big, handsome petty officer on anything. But after they'd stepped off the boat and onto the dock and he'd turned to her? You better believe she'd known by the look in his eyes that her time as teacher was over. His expression had clearly conveyed that *he* had a thing or two to show *her*.

And, boy, oh boy, had he ever…

Even now she could recall the exact feel of his broad, callused palms cupping her cheeks, remember the sensation of his rough thumb hooked gently beneath her jaw, guiding her head this way and that as his tongue learned the secrets of her mouth, licked and laved and sucked until she forgot her own name and—

"Calm down, Eve," Billy instructed, and she realized not only was she staring at his hands, she was also panting like she'd just surfaced from a skin dive. "This vehicle is armored and the glass is bulletproof. You're safe in here."

And curses! There she'd gone again. Completely forgetting the critical nature of her situation because she was overcome by a combination of painfully hot memories and Billy's nearness.

Sheesh. Too much more of that, and she should seriously consider getting her head examined. Maybe that launch into the air back at the marina and the resultant splashdown in Lake Michigan had flash-frozen her gray matter.

"That's not—" She abruptly stopped herself and

shook her head. "I'm fine. I just don't understand why you're not trying to lose them?" They were creeping along at a snail's pace, like they were out taking a flippin' Sunday drive as opposed to trying to shake the person tailing them. "Do you need me to drive?"

She wasn't good a lot of things. She couldn't draw or sing or hold her liquor. She sucked at baking cakes—they never seemed to rise—and public speaking scared the ever-lovin' crap out of her. But when her father signed her up for defensive driving lessons with an ex-Hollywood stuntman after she'd started having issues with Dale the Stalker? Well, not to toot her own horn or anything—*toot, toot*—but she'd taken to the endeavor like she'd been born an Andretti.

However, the look Billy sent her questioned the validity of her most recent IQ test.

Indignation burned. "Didn't Becky tell you how good I was down in Costa Rica?" she demanded. And, yes, a little more than six months ago she'd helped Billy and the rest of the Black Knights clear the name of one of their own by leading the CIA on a wild car chase. Which, let's face it, still felt more like a dream set in Bizarro Land than an actual series of events…

But it *had* happened and she *had* done her part—*huzzah!*—and it was beyond irritating that even after all of that, Billy still didn't give her the credit she so richly deserved. And when he refused to wipe that disbelieving smirk from his face, she slapped a palm against the hot dashboard. "Stop looking at me like that! I'm an excellent driver!"

He rolled in his lips as he casually—oh-so-flippin' *casually*—stopped at a red light. "I know you are, Rain Man," he said, and it only irked her more when she *didn't* get that particular reference. "But I don't *want* to lose them. I want them to stick with us until your cousin calls to let us know who they are. *Then* we can decide how to handle the situation."

Oh...well. That made sense. Sort of...

As if on cue, her cell phone jangled out the opening bars of Styx's "Come Sail Away," and she unbuckled her seatbelt in order to swivel around and grab her purse.

"Jeremy?" she answered after frantically scrounging around in her oversized handbag. Her phone had the annoying habit of making its way to the very bottom of the thing. "Who is it? Who's following us?"

Her blood sizzled through her veins like she'd ascended too quickly from a deep dive because this could be it. Right here, right now, she might hear the name of whomever was trying to kill her.

"It's Samantha Tate," Jeremy informed her, his irritation evident.

Her heart sank along with all her momentary hopes, because Samantha Tate was the *Chicago Tribune*'s most persistent, most *annoying* investigative reporter. "Thanks, Jeremy," she muttered. "I'll let you know how things shake out."

"Take care, Cuz," he said before cutting the connection.

"So?" Billy asked, turning to her briefly, a question in his lovely brown eyes.

"Samantha Tate," she supplied. "She's a—"

"I know exactly who she is," he cut in, frowning. "And *what* she is."

"You mean besides a serious pain the ass?" Eve submitted and felt a warm rush of pleasure flood her chest when his crack of surprised laughter echoed against the roof of the Hummer.

"That too," he said, lips twitching. "And since she already knows who *we* both are, I see no reason to try to lose her. We'll just let her follow us out to Goose Island."

"She's been leaving messages for me for two days," Eve groused, glancing into the side view mirror and discovering that, sure enough, inside that black Chevy Tahoe was the vague outline of a woman with puffy hair. "I haven't called her back because…well, for one thing I hate talking to the press. And for another thing, I'm sure she wants to sensationalize everything that's been happening to me so she can snag herself another front-page byline. I'm sorry she's sticking her big nose in the middle of this. I know how much you super-secret spy guys despise journalists."

"We don't despise journalists," Billy clarified with a half shrug. "It's just that *their* job is usually directly opposed to *our* job. But don't worry. You won't have to talk to her. She'll never get past BKI's front gates."

And, just like that, Eve was reminded she'd be spending an indeterminate amount of time under one roof with Billy "Wild Bill" Reichert and all his brooding looks, sharp words, and menacing, smoldering sex appeal…

Triple gulp.

Chapter Four

Black Knights Inc. Headquarters, Front Gate
7:15 p.m.

"I DEMAND TO SEE MY DAUGHTER! I KNOW SHE'S HERE!"

Mac glared at the salt-and-pepper-haired man raving on the other side of BKI's tall, wrought-iron gate and wondered if he'd ever despised anyone on first sight as much as he despised Eve's father.

Patrick Edens was wearing a cream-colored linen suit like he was freakin' Colonel Sanders or something. Though Mac would lay two-to-one odds that Edens had never set foot inside a Kentucky Fried Chicken in his entire pampered life. A long black limousine was parked at the curb, and a gold Rolex glinted on Edens's wrist when he lifted a hand to point a manicured finger at Mac. "You filthy, lecherous bikers can't hold her prisoner here! I'll—"

"Sir," Mac cut in, and it was only his gentlemanly Southern upbringing that allowed him to address the raving ass-hat in such a polite fashion, "I can assure you we're not holdin' your daughter prisoner here. She—"

"Dad?"

Mac lifted his eyes toward the sunset sky with its streaks of pink and orange and sent up a small prayer of gratitude. Too much more of that and he'd be tempted to shove a fist straight into Edens's mouth, ruining the man's expensively capped teeth. And since Edens had the look of a guy who wouldn't take a punch—a punch he damn well deserved because, seriously? Filthy, lecherous bikers?—without raising a big ol' stink and getting a bunch of stuffy lawyers involved, that would be very, *very* bad.

Lord knows a lawsuit is the dead last thing any of us need right now...

"What are you doing here?" Eve asked, still towel-drying her hair.

She'd been in the shower when Toran buzzed from the front gate to say her father had arrived on the scene. And Bill and Ace had been in the middle of coordinating an emergency exfiltration for Ozzie and Steady who, like always, had managed to make trouble for themselves in some bug-infested South American hellhole. Which meant—*oh, goody, goody gumdrops*—he'd been the only one left to run interference on their unwelcome guest.

"I should ask *you* the same!" the elder Edens thundered. "What are *you* doing here? It's like you enjoy getting yourself into situations that titillate the press!"

Mac turned to see Eve's face fall, and he wondered if, perhaps, he'd still be forced to plant one in Edens's kisser after all.

"Dad—" she tried, but her father just cut her off.

"I was contacted by Samantha Tate. And imagine my surprise when she asked me why my daughter had decided to shack up with a bunch of greasy motorcycle mechanics."

"I'm not shacking—"

"Get your stuff. You're coming home with me." Edens threw his nose in the air, adjusting his baby blue silk tie. "And that's final."

Mac lifted a brow, sliding a surreptitious glance toward Eve. The poor woman's face was so red it was almost purple, and she was chewing on her bottom lip so hard he was surprised she didn't just gnaw the sucker right off. It was obvious that, even as a grown woman, she was used to doing as her father instructed. So it surprised him when she lifted her chin against the warm evening breeze and said, "No, Dad. I'm staying here."

Well, look at you, honey. Way to go...

"Wh-what?" Edens sputtered, his face taking on a similar hue to his daughter's. Only his wasn't fueled by timidity or humiliation; it was fueled by fury. Patrick Edens obviously wasn't a man used to hearing the word "no."

"I'm staying here," Eve repeated. "It's safe here. Now, I know you don't believe I'm in trouble, but—"

"You're *not* in any trouble!" Edens spat. "Why do you keep insisting that you are when the police have assured you time and time again that it's nothing more than a string of bad luck?" Edens pursed his lips, narrowing his eyes. "It's because of Jeremy, isn't it? I knew it was a mistake for you to move in with him instead of coming home to me. Well, we can remedy that tonight and—"

"No." This time when Eve said the word there was some power behind it. Mac crossed his arms over his chest, content to let her handle the situation because she appeared to have it well under control.

Edens on the other hand? The man looked like he was about to blow a gasket. And sure enough, his face contorted into an ugly snarl, and he hissed, "Don't you do this again!" His upper lip curled. "Haven't you had enough of the press? Haven't your recent mishaps and your new personal endeavors brought enough disgrace to our family?"

Eve stumbled back as if Edens's words had gut-punched her, and Mac was just about to step in when she rallied, dragging in a deep breath and squaring her shoulders. "None of that was my fault, and you know it. Now go home, Dad." Before Edens could answer, she spun on her heel and started marching back toward the warehouse.

"Eve!" Edens shouted at her back, but she ignored him, her chin held high.

Mac turned a considering eye on Edens, sucking in a breath through his nose. The air smelled like warm pavement, blooming flowers, and Edens's top-shelf cologne. "Well," he said, "I think that about does it." Eve's father opened his mouth to object, but Mac yelled to Toran who was watching all the commotion through the open window of the gatehouse. "Escort Mr. Edens here off our private property." Edens sputtered like a kinked garden hose. "And if he puts up a fight, call the police."

Then, he turned to follow Eve into the shop. And as he watched her long, determined strides, he couldn't help but wonder if Wild Bill had misjudged the woman.

Black Knights Inc. Headquarters, 2nd Floor
8:20 p.m.

No, no, no. Something isn't right. How the hell did the arson investigator miss this?

"You gonna invite us?" Mac asked, dragging Bill's attention away from the high-resolution photos Jeremy Buchanan had provided. They showed Eve's blackened, gutted condo, and if Bill was being honest, Buchanan had really come through for them in a couple of ways. First, he'd held his own as they escorted Eve to the Hummer—Bill had recognized that kill-or-be-killed look in the man's eye, the look that said Buchanan had been willing to do whatever needed to be done in order to keep his cousin safe. And second, these files were straight-up cherry. Comprehensive and detailed.

He wondered if maybe, just maybe, he'd jumped to the wrong conclusion about the guy. Not that Buchanan wasn't still an asshole. He was. No question. But there were quite a few people who thought *Bill* was an asshole, so that particular moniker didn't hold a hell of a lot of water. Plus, the dude worked vice. He was a multimillionaire, trust-fund baby who preferred to get his hands dirty in the trenches to make the world a better place rather than sitting in some high rise celebrating the high life. So, yeah, maybe Buchanan wasn't as ginormous a tool as Bill'd initially thought.

"Hey. I said, you want to invite us?" Mac repeated.

"Huh?" he frowned, his eyes darting back to the photo in his hand, his thoughts racing along with his heart. Most of the guys he worked with had metronome-steady pulse rates, but not him. Nope. He'd never perfected that little trick. Then again, unlike other operators, the adrenaline didn't make him weaker or less logical. Hell, no. It did just the opposite, focusing him, sharpening his world and everything in it to a fine point. Except, for the life of him, he couldn't guess what in the world Mac was talking about. "Invite you to what?"

"That party you got going on in your head," Mac drawled. "You've been sitting over there making noises for the last five minutes."

He had?

Bill glanced at the other two people seated around the conference table. Eve was gnawing her thumb down to what had to be a bloody stump, and Ace, holding the report on the condition of Eve's Vespa, was frowning at him over the top of it.

Okay, so obviously he had. But that's because he was onto something big, *huge*. And the only thing that tempered his excitement at having made this particular discovery was the knowledge that Eve had been right all along…

Someone *was* trying to kill her. *Sonofabitch.*

"The fire department used the old method of locating the fire's point of origin by relying on lowest burn and deepest char pattern," he said, shaking his head in disbelief. That method had been proven faulty more than five years ago. "Which points to the drapes on Eve's living room window. But what they didn't take into account was that the fire burned for over six minutes after the initial flashover and before the CFD put it out. And *that* means it had time to change from a fuel-controlled fire to a ventilation-controlled fire."

He glanced around at the faces looking back at him, expecting something more than a series of wide-eyed blinks. Then he reminded himself not everyone—very few people, in fact—understood the mechanisms by which explosions, and the resulting flames, operated, and he tried to put it in layman's terms.

"It means the fire didn't originate from the curtains lit by the candle. It means the fire originated by the front door and spread toward the air coming in *through* the open window. See," he slapped the photo he'd been examining down on the conference table and turned it around so the others could see, tapping the image with his finger. "Whoever started this did so with a quick-burning and, my guess would be, brutally hot accelerant that was poured under the door and lit. It turned the place into a tinderbox in minutes. But it burned the longest and hottest by the open window where the air could fuel it, which is why the arson investigator mistook that for the point of origin."

"So I was right," Eve whispered, her eyes as round as hand grenades. "Someone wants me dead."

"Jesus, Eve." Ace scooted his chair closer to hers and threw a muscled arm around her shoulders. Bill tried very hard to ignore it this time, but when Eve reached over and clutched Ace's hand, he recognized the green-eyed monster sitting on his shoulder for what it was.

For Christ's sake, man! Cut that shit out!

Although, honestly, he wasn't sure if he was mentally yelling at himself or Ace. And for a brief moment he was thrown back to earlier that afternoon, when Eve'd curled her delicate fingers into his waistband and the simple feel of her knuckles brushing his back had damn near lit him on fire. That small touch had been more erotic than some of his more memorable full-on make-out sessions, which just proved how far he *hadn't* come in his long, oh-so-long, *too*-damn-long journey to forgetting about one Miss Evelyn Edens.

Well, shit on a stick…

"How in the world did you manage to get out of there alive?" Ace asked gently, giving Eve a squeeze and jerking Bill from his unwelcome thoughts.

"One of the fire escapes is beneath my bedroom window," she said, her voice hoarse, which was just what Bill needed to crank down the heat on his ill-timed burst of libido. Well, that and the pictures that flashed through his head of how she'd been forced to make her escape. He grabbed the travel-sized bottle of Pepto-Bismol he'd shoved in his pocket and sucked back a healthy chug.

Come on, you sweet, pink elixir. Work your wonders…

"When the fire alarm woke me up, flames were already licking under my bedroom door." She shook her head, her inky black hair swishing across her shoulders and Ace's arm. Bill remembered how soft it had once felt swishing against *his* arm. And *goddamnit!* He gulped another chug of Pepto. "So I threw open my window, and…and climbed out," she swallowed, her dry throat making a sticky sound in the relative silence of the big room.

Yeah, climbed out onto a rickety iron fire escape from the friggin' eighteenth floor. *Jesus.*

"It was smart," he admitted, wiping a drop of the pink medicine from his lips.

"What was?" Mac asked, brow furrowed.

"The way the fire was set. It's almost like whoever did it knew the CFD was still employing the old investigative techniques. Or they just got lucky."

"What do you mean?"

"Well, the Internet lists all sorts of ways to get past arson investigators," he explained, moving to point a finger at the photo again, but Becky's unbelievably ugly and unconscionably fat tomcat had hopped up on the conference table at some point and was now lying on the pile of photos, reclined back like a raja on a bed of pillows.

"Damnit, Peanut," he groused, regretting the fact that he'd told Becky he would feed the bastard, not to mention consenting to scooping giant turds out of the litter box. Talk about a job no self-respecting man should ever agree to. Shoving an impatient hand under Peanut's big fuzzy butt, he retrieved the photo. The tomcat's crooked tail flicked once, but other than that, he didn't move a muscle.

Damn scurvy feline. Walks around like he owns the place...

"As I was saying," he flicked a couple of gray cat hairs off the photo, "the Internet lists ways to get past arson investigators, but most of those rely on the old point-of-origin dog-and-pony show. Could be whoever did this didn't know there are more precise investigative methods out there today and—"

He stopped because Eve's face, naturally pale, had turned as white as the potassium perchlorate he used when making explosive primers.

"What?" he asked. "What is it?"

"D-Dale," she said, her pulse hammering at the base of her throat. Seeing it caused every cell in Bill's body to go on high alert. Somewhere inside him a red light was flashing and an alarm was blaring.

"What about the bastard?" he demanded, sitting up straighter, barely recognizing his own voice.

"He's a..." She licked her lips. "He's a volunteer firefighter. And he...he does a lot of training with the CFD."

And just like that, rage exploded inside Bill with the force of a bunker buster. Because even though he and Eve weren't exactly simpatico, the fact remained that nobody, and he meant *nobody,* got away with attempting to turn her into a crispy critter.

"Let's go get him," he said, his molars aching with the force of his grinding jaw.

"But...but..." Eve blinked rapidly when he pushed up from the table, ready to put an extra hole in Dale WhoTheFuck's head. "Shouldn't we bring this to the police? Or...or the fire department? Or—"

"You mean the same police who've already closed the files on your cases?" he snarled, blowing like a raging bull. Luckily no one at the table was wearing red. "Or the CFD that incorrectly identified your condo fire's point of origin? You think they're going to listen to a couple of motorcycle mechanics?"

"Oh," Eve said, clueing in to their perilous situation. "I see." Then she shook her head. "But you're friends with the police chief, right? Couldn't you—"

"Yeah," this time it was Mac who cut in, "and we

want to *stay* friends with him. Which means we can't have him orderin' his subordinates to reinvestigate closed cases based simply on the hunches of a couple of guys from the local motorcycle club."

"Okay," she admitted, "but maybe Jeremy—"

"Love, your cousin would be as useless now as he has been all along," Ace interrupted, and a delicate muscle began to tick in Eve's jaw. "These aren't his cases. Hell, this isn't even his department."

Used to be, Bill didn't think Eve *owned* a temper. Now he'd go so far as to describe it as, not necessarily hot, but certainly warm. And after Mac told him how she'd stood up to her father earlier? Well, for some reason it just made her all the more desirable. Like he *needed* any more reasons. *Damnit all to hell...*

"We're just going to go watch Dale for a while. See if he does anything hinky, anything that we can give Chief Washington as ammunition to reopen your cases," Bill assured her, even though there was a large part of him that would've preferred storming into the man's house and shoving a pistol against his temple until he spilled his guts. Then again, he wasn't on the battlefield. This was a civilian issue that required a civilian response. Although...even in a civilian situation there was still some room for a little shock and awe if the need arose.

The anticipation of getting his mitts on Dale caused a smile to curve to his lips.

"Oh, goody." Ace rubbed his hands together gleefully. "Anytime you get that look I know there are fun times ahead..."

Chapter Five

Dale Pennyworth's Townhouse
9:35 p.m.

"What do you mean I'm staying here?" Eve demanded, glaring out the rear passenger side window of the Hummer at Dale's broad back as he lumbered down the sidewalk. There he was, pretty as you please, probably strolling down to the corner market to pick up milk or beer or cheese puffs like he hadn't tried to kill her on three separate occasions.

Well…maybe. She still had trouble picturing Dale pouring fuel under her door and setting a match to it. Because, sure, he was mustache creepy, but he'd never really come off as *murderer* creepy.

Then again, she'd been wrong about people before. Her ex-husband for one…

"The restraining order you have against him specifies a fifty-foot buffer," Billy said, fiddling with something in the mid-sized black duffel bag on his lap.

"That says *he* can't come within fifty feet of *me*," she insisted as Mac checked the clip on a…she squinted from backseat…it looked like a Glock 22 .40 caliber. And rock on! Her shooting instructor would be so proud of her! "It doesn't say anything about *me* staying away from *him*."

"Same difference," Billy muttered, tossing the bag into the back seat with her. Whatever was inside made a clanking noise when it landed, rattling her already frayed nerves.

"But I want to see what he's up to just the same as you," she declared, scowling at Billy when he swiveled in the driver's seat to frown back at her. "I think I deserve that much after all he's put me through."

That, and the fact that she was *trying* to be tough. And as far as she could figure, being "tough" meant she couldn't very well sit out here while Billy and Mac ran around doing the dirty work. That's what the *old* Eve would've done, and she'd been vigorously endeavoring to leave that milksop of a woman behind.

"Did you miss the part where we're loading our weapons?" Bill demanded. "This guy could be headed out to catch a movie, or he could be headed out to light another fire in some woman's house. In which case, we'll be required to apprehend him. And at that point, since we'll have already gotten our hands dirty with him, we might as well take the opportunity to make him confess."

"By *make* him confess I'm assuming you mean *force* him to confess," she said, her lips pursed.

"Naturally," Billy nodded, thumbing off the safety on his weapon. "After all, we're the ones with the guns."

"Ever think of just asking him?" she inquired, batting her lashes.

Billy stopped fiddling with the Glock to look up and gape at her, one brow climbing steadily up his forehead. "Just *asking* him? What are you? Canadian?"

She pursed her lips. "I just don't want to see you guys get into any trouble over this. If he does something *hinky*, as you put it, couldn't you just turn him over to the police and have him arrested for suspicious activity or something? They could question him, detain him, and keep him from being a threat to me or anyone else."

"You mean the same CPD who have had their heads shoved up their asses since day one where you're concerned?" His tone was bland. "The same CPD that botched the fire's point of origin?"

"That was the C*F*D," she stressed.

"Whatever," he waved a hand. "The fact remains that they've dismissed the attempts on your life without even questioning your stalker, and—"

"Yes," she harrumphed. "Jeremy was pretty upset about that."

"And I can see why. It's shoddy work. So, to say my faith in doing this thing by the books is at a rock-bottom low would be putting it mildly. In case you haven't noticed, your life is on the line here, Eve. Which means I'm not just willing to *bend* the rules; I'm willing to *break* every last one."

His words sent a surge of warmth through her entire body. "But what if Dale sees you guys? Or what if you *do* wind up questioning him—*illegally*, I might add—and he has you arrested?"

"Never going to happen," Bill shook his head, smiling. "We've got the Chicago Police Chief on our side."

Yep, they'd mentioned this Washington person on more than one occasion. "What's your relationship with him?" she asked, wrinkling her nose. Visions of Mac and Billy being loaded into a paddy wagon and carted off to the clink ran through her head. Although…were paddy wagons even a thing anymore?

"Let's just say he's one of the *very* few people living here in Chicago who is privy to BKI's true calling, and he owes us a couple of favors. So stop worrying. Sit tight. Stay quiet. And let us take care of this, will you? You know, you're lucky I let you come at all. I should've made you stay with Ace."

And, boy, oh boy, all the warmth brought on by his earlier words was instantly replaced by ice-cold indignation. Because if he thought Ace had put up a good fight when he'd been required to stay back at BKI headquarters to answer any calls that might come in from the Knights currently out in the field, he'd have been shocked to his core by the fit she'd have thrown had he tried to make *her* hang back. "Oh, yeah?" she nodded, channeling a little of her best friend, Becky, and smiling sarcastically, "over my dead body."

His face hardened, and a muscle started ticking in his wide jaw. "Yes, Eve," he said, his voice quiet. *Deadly* quiet. "Your dead body, or the fact that we're trying to keep you from being one, is exactly why we're here. Now, you stay in the Hummer until we get back. You got me?"

She glared at him, nostrils flaring, breath sawing from her lungs. She wasn't the same girl she'd been twelve years ago. She could *do* this. She *could*. But he'd never see her as anything more than that shy, bumbling, backbone-less eighteen-year-old. And *that* bothered her even more than all the things Dale Pennyworth had done to her.

"Nod your head so I know you understand," he demanded, reaching back to grab her knee, his dark eyes, even in the dimly lit interior of the vehicle, were diamond bright, flashing with conviction.

All the bravado she'd donned threatened to abandon her—especially with his warm palm burning a hole straight through her jeans—but she refused to let him see it. Instead, she narrowed her eyes and jerked her chin in a quick nod. And even though she was conceding—what other choice did she have?—she made very sure the look on her face called him a stubborn, autocratic, tyrannical A-hole.

He lifted a brow, withdrawing his hand and—*dangit!*—why did she suddenly feel bereft? "Something more you want to say to me?" he asked.

"Oh, I figure you understand this expression well enough." She pointed to her face, ignoring the tingling of her kneecap. "No reason to gild the lily."

She thought she saw one corner of his mouth twitch, and her eyes narrowed further.

"Silence about a thing just magnifies it," he murmured.

And where had she heard that phrase before? Where had she…Then it hit her. "Really? You're quoting *Cat on a Hot Tin Roof* at me right now?"

"Payback's a bitch," he smiled, his big, square teeth blazing white in his tan face. "You used to love to sling literary quotes at my head."

She had?

"I did?" She lifted a brow, thinking back. She *had* gone through a rather annoying pedantic phase at the end of her teens. "And did you find it as irritating then as I do right now?"

"Nah," he lifted a muscled shoulder, and she could see he was biting the inside of his cheek. "I thought you were adorable. So full of love for books, head bursting with knowledge. It was quite endearing, really."

All her hot air left her like his words were pins and she was a balloon. Because what did a girl say to something like that? *Thank you for being nice to me... for once?* Or maybe...*please forgive me for not being stronger back then, for letting my dad push me around*?

But no. That last one was sure to go over like a thunderstorm at an outdoor wedding. Because Billy and her father were as compatible as oil and water. And bringing up either one in front of the other usually resulted in muttered curses and questions regarding each other's paternity.

So she said nothing. And the silence filling the Hummer grew more strained with each passing second...until Mac democratically cleared his throat. "If we're gonna do this thing, the time is now," he said. "Dale is turnin' the corner up there, and we're gonna lose him."

Billy held her gaze for a moment longer, and she so wished she could read whatever was written all over his face. But then he turned away, and the opportunity was lost. In the next instant, Billy and Mac were exiting the vehicle, and she had no recourse but to watch them jog across the dark street—Dale didn't exactly live in the nicest part of town and most of the street lights weren't functioning—and up the block.

They looked very professional in their pseudo-SWAT team get-ups: black body armor, black cargo pants, black combat boots, just black on black. Not to mention the matte black guns they carried at the smalls of their backs. And yes, even though Billy had told her they were just coming here to watch Dale, the outfits emphasized the fact that he and Mac had both been banking on Dale giving them a reason to jump him. And talk about *wowza*. If Dale Pennyworth caught a glimpse of them following him, he wasn't going to know what to do first, crap his pants or spill his guts. And, dangit! She was going to miss it!

She was supposed to have grown a shiny set of brass ladyballs by now, but she'd caved to Billy's domineering *stay put* decree after only five seconds. Which meant she hadn't *really* grown that set of ladyballs after all.

Crap.

But just as she began mentally chastising herself, movement down the block snagged her attention.

What the...?

You shouldn't have touched her, an annoying little voice whispered through Bill's head as he slunk around the corner, quiet as a whisper, blending into the blackness of the shadows cast by the surrounding apartment buildings.

Mac was across the street doing a pretty stellar job of disappearing into the darkness himself. Bill could only make out the whites of the man's eyes and the motion of his hand as he tapped two fingers against his cheeks and pointed up the block, the signal for *I've got a bead on the target.*

Bill nodded, advancing up the ill-lit street one silent step at a time, skirting around an overturned trashcan that smelled of dirty diapers, warm beer, and moldy Indian food. For a moment he wished he was back in the Hummer, breathing in Eve's subtle scent. That is until that pesky voice spoke up again. *Touching Eve always messes with your head, man.*

And, yeah, so the sonofabitching voice had a point. Although, the reality was, it wasn't necessarily his *head* that got messed with. Unless, of course, one was talking about his *little* head.

Damn, what a goatscrew.

Okay, and *that* was more like it. *That* sentiment he could agree with. Because no matter how often he reminded himself of the hurt she'd caused him, no matter how many times he assured himself he was right in his assessment of her character, there'd inevitably be a moment, like the one back there in the Hummer when she looked up at him with such conviction, such tenaciousness, that he began to doubt anything and everything he'd held true about her these past dozen years.

Uh-huh. Goatscrew about summed it up and—

Whoa. What the hell?

Farther up the block, the dark green door on a four-flat apartment building opened, and a young woman in scrubs stepped out. Bill watched in consternation as

Eve's stalker, heretofore referred to as Dale Fuckwad, jumped behind a lamp post.

Uh, can you say Creepy McCreepster, boys and girls? And, just like that, his mission went from a simple tail and observe to a full-on apprehend and secure. Because that sick sonofabitch was obviously going to try to off another innocent woman.

Instincts on high alert, Bill glanced across the street to find Mac's eyes turned in his direction. He nodded—*yeah, I'm seeing what you're seeing*—as a hard punch of adrenaline blasted through his veins, increasing his heart rate from a steady *lub, dub* into a fast-paced *thumpety, thumpety, thumpety.* The world around him snapped into crystalline focus, and the night was no longer so dark; the sounds of the city around him—a distant siren, a dog barking, and the bass of a nearby car stereo—no longer so muffled.

Motioning with his hand, he silently indicated Mac should take a position farther up the street. And once his partner was in place, Bill moved in for the kill. Or, in this case, the capture.

His combat boots made no noise as he hurriedly advanced to the next corner, keeping low and sticking to the shadows, blending into his surroundings like a specter. Then, just as he reached to unsecure his weapon, the young woman—a nurse?—skipped down the stairs of her apartment building and started off toward the bus stop on the next block.

Dale Fuckwad waited a beat before following the woman, and Bill could almost feel the asshole's neck in his hands as he silently stalked up behind the scumbag.

This man. This...*vile*, despicable man was responsible for nearly getting Eve killed not once, but three times.

And we're gonna make the sonofabitch pay, that little voice whispered gleefully. Now Bill was more than happy to have the bugger banging around inside his head, because they were finally working in complete harmony. Yessir, he was going to do it. He was going to catch Eve's would-be murderer in less than seven hours and, *hell yeah*, it was times like this he had the overwhelming desire to go all ape-man and beat his chest while yelling out victory.

Black Knights Inc. to the rescue! Hoo-ah!

Of course, it was an internal celebration because when the young nurse sat down on the bench at the bus stop, Fuckwad once more darted behind a light post and Bill saw his opportunity. He leapt forward the last foot, slapping a hand over Dale's mouth while simultaneously shoving the scary end of his pistol into the dude's squishy kidney with just enough force to make any future possibility of a transplant questionable.

"Don't move, asshole," he breathed in the man's ear, ignoring the foul smell of unwashed armpits and greasy pepperoni pizza.

Dale instinctively struggled in his grip. That is until Mac materialized out of the darkness like the Grim Reaper himself. Then Dale went limp in Bill's arms, and Bill wondered if the bastard had fainted. But soon, a pathetic whimper assured him the chubby psycho was still with them, and he sent a small prayer of thanks heavenward—*thank you, sweet baby Jesus*—because he couldn't quite envision he and Mac carting the tubby sonofabitch back the four and a half blocks to the dude's townhouse wherein the interrogation could commence.

"Now, Dale," the man whimpered at the sound of his name, but Bill ignored it as he hauled the guy back to his feet, forcing him to support his own substantial weight, "my partner and I have a few questions for you. And we want to ask them in private." Dale shook his head vigorously, so Bill oh-so-subtly—okay, it wasn't subtle at all—reminded the guy of the Glock shoved into his back. Again a pitiful whimper slipped between the fingers he held over Dale's mouth. Bill barely resisted rolling his eyes. "And if you come with us willingly, if you don't put up a fight, I can promise you, you won't get hurt. Now, be a good boy and nod your head so I know you understand me."

The man was shaking so hard he was pulling a Santa Claus and jiggling in Bill's arms like a bowl full of jelly. Still, Bill was able to feel the guy jerkily nod his head. "That's good. Now, let's turn around, real easy like, and head on back to your place."

What had snagged Eve's attention was the sight of Billy and Mac coming up the block, frog-marching Dale between them. And the poor man looked like he was about to have a heart attack.

Wait...*poor man? Poor. Man?* Had she really just had that thought? Good Lord, she should really have her head examined. Because the only reason Billy and Mac would grab Dale as opposed to simply watching him was if he'd been up to no good which, *oh, crap*, meant she'd *once again* been incredibly wrong in her assessment of someone.

It's strike number two for you tonight, Eve ol' girl! And strike number one thousand and thirty two in the grand ballgame of her life.

Curses. Shaking her head at herself, lamenting her terrible judgment when it came to the characters of men, she watched as the trio climbed the steps leading to Dale's front door. Okay, so they were going *inside* to question him? She shivered at the thought, imagining canisters of gasoline stacked against the walls, as well as all other manner of crazy, scary equipment that might be used by the mentally deranged stalker-y sort. Then again, she supposed interrogating Dale inside the privacy of his own home made a lot more sense than continuing to restrain the guy at gunpoint on the street.

Holding her breath, she saw Billy lean in close to Dale, probably issuing instructions for the man to unlock the door. Dale shook his head, struggling to step back until Mac was forced to wrench Dale's arms up high behind his back. *Oooh, ouchy.* That looked like it hurt. Still, Dale shook his head vigorously, and Eve had to give the guy credit. He was obviously smart enough to realize his chances of escaping whatever lay in store for him once they entered that townhouse dropped from *not likely* all the way down to *not a snowball's chance in hell.*

Billy said something to Mac, his teeth flashing white when Mac nodded. She squinted through the tinted window, trying to figure out what he was doing when he reached into a zippered pocket on his cargo pants, pulling out something that he attached to the hinges and locks on Dale's front door. A second later, a muted *hiss* echoed down the street accompanied by a shower of sparks from the door's metal hardware. And, just like that, Billy grabbed the big slab of solid wood and edged it aside, the whole thing having been neatly removed from its frame.

Uh…can you say *holy schnikes*?

Okay, so simply digging in Dale's pocket for the keys would've been easier, but it also would've been far less impressive. And Billy was obviously trying to make a very clear impression on Dale. The impression that Dale had better cooperate, because they had the ways, the means, and the *intent* to get past any and all of his resistance.

It must've worked, because Dale stopped whipping around in Mac's arms and allowed himself to be pushed over the threshold. In a flash, Mac and Billy followed him in, and Eve was left with no recourse but to sit there like a good girl while the big bad men took all the risks.

Um, yes. *So* not going to happen. Because there was an opportunity here. An opportunity to prove to herself and *Billy* just how far she'd come. A chance to take control of her own life and stop being a victim…

Snatching the duffel bag from the seat beside her, she heaved it onto her lap. It was heavier than it looked, and when she dug inside she could see why. The thing was filled with rolls of wire, canisters of powder, and cellophane-covered blocks of sticky stuff that looked like putty but smelled more like industrial cleaning products.

*Come on, come on...*She glanced over her shoulder at the back window and the shotguns mounted there. If left with no other option, she supposed she could use one of those. But since she hadn't had any training with shotguns, that wouldn't be her first choice. Then, in the side pocket of the duffel...victory!

With a triumphant laugh, she un-holstered the little snub-nosed Smith & Wesson revolver from its leather case and flipped out the cylinder to make sure all six chambers were loaded.

"Score," she whispered into the silence of the Hummer's interior before easing open the door. She slipped quietly from the vehicle, careful to keep the weapon tight against her thigh so as not to draw the attention of anyone who might happen to look out their window.

Scurrying across the street, her heart pounding with fear and, yes, a little bit of anticipation—*woo-hoo! Ladyballs in the ha-yowse!*—she stepped over the crushed body of an empty beer can lying in the middle of the sidewalk and hustled up the stairs. And before she could second guess her decision, or think about how unbelievably *pissed* Billy was going to be, she held her revolver at the ready—just like her shooting instructor had taught her: one hand curled loosely around the grip while the other supported the edge of her shooting hand and the bottom of the weapon—and ran inside.

Chapter Six

Dale Pennyworth was wearing some sort of weird bodysuit and an expression of abject horror as Mac watched Bill push him down into a recliner before lowering a Glock at the guy's bulbous nose. Mac actually thought the dude might shit a kidney—a rather *bruised* kidney by the way Bill had had his gun shoved in the dude's back—and wouldn't *that* add the final touch to the stench of cold pizza, stale beer, and inch-thick dust hovering about the place?

Taking at quick glance around, Mac saw shelf after shelf packed with action figures, comic books, the occasional used tissue, and a shitload of empty Bud Light cans. Obviously, it was the maid's week off…Year off? Maybe decade off?

"So, Dale," Bill growled, looking like nothing less than death on two feet. BKI's explosives expert loomed over the poor schmuck who was now reclined in his leather chair, trying to put as much distance between himself and the terrifying black eye of Bill's Glock as he possibly could. "You want to tell us what you were doing following that poor woman?"

"Wh-who are you?" Pennyworth stammered, swallowing loudly. The man was a day or two past his last shower, sweating like a whore in church, and when he opened his mouth, his breath smelled like a horse fart.

Oh, joy. And Mac had hoped for a quiet, uneventful Saturday. Although he should've known better. His life had been the opposite of quiet and uneventful since the morning he agreed to wave sayonara to the FBI and instead throw his hat in with the badass boys of BKI.

"Let's just say," Bill grumbled, "that we're acquainted with Eve Edens and—"

"Eve?" Pennyworth interrupted and tried to push into a seated position. When his nose ran into the barrel of Bill's gun, he decided to stay exactly where he was. *Smart man.* "Is…is she okay?" Dale wheezed, holding his hands up in front of him, watery blue eyes wide and unblinking.

"She is. No thanks to you," Bill snarled, and Mac could tell by the tension in Bill's jaw that he'd rather just plug Pennyworth with a couple of slugs and be done with it. Fortunately, Wild Bill was a soldier. And there was a vast difference between a soldier and a killer.

"I t-tried to keep her safe," Dale blubbered, shaking his balding blond head. "She's so innocent. So gentle and good. But she didn't understand. She took out that restraining order against me, and…Eve? What are you doing here?"

Oh, no. No, Lord, please don't let her be there when I turn around.

Mac peeked over his shoulder, and…*sure as shit*… there she was, pointing a snub-nosed revolver straight at Pennyworth and looking like one of Charlie's Angels as she advanced into the room.

"Goddamnit, Eve!" Bill roared, and Mac winced as

the words echoed around the space, bouncing off the wood-paneled walls and against all the clutter. "I told you to stay in the vehicle!"

"Yes," she barely spared him a glance, keeping her eyes and her weapon trained on Pennyworth like maybe the pudgy guy was about to perform some sort of magic trick that would miraculously make Mac and Bill's weapons disappear. It was quite funny when Mac thought about it. Although...he cocked his head... she *was* handling that snubbie like a pro. "And I've decided," she licked her lips, stepping over the feet of a life-sized Captain America doll as she continued to move toward them, " to *stop* doing everything people tell me to do."

"Well, you picked a hell of a time to start that!" Bill shouted, and Mac worried the dude might burst an aneurism. "Jesus! Put down the gun before you accidently shoot me or Mac."

"Or *me*," Pennyworth added, his Adam's apple bobbing beneath his double chin.

"Oh, for Pete's sake!" Eve stomped her foot. "I know what I'm doing, so will you just..." she made a little waving motion with the revolver, "get on with it?"

Bill hesitated, his jaw ticking. Then he rolled his eyes and turned his attention back to Pennyworth. "Okay, *Dale*," he sneered the man's name. "I'm going to ask you a series of questions. If you don't answer them honestly, I'll end you. If you try anything funny, I'll end you. If you so much as twitch in Eve's direction, I'll end you. And lest you think I'm bluffing, let me first inform you that I did two tours in Iraq and three in Afghanistan. I killed and maimed my enemies, and I did it all with a song in my heart. So rest assured, I have no problem pulling this trigger and turning your greasy head into nothing more than spatter patterns."

And holy crow! After that little speech even *Mac* was ready to spill his guts. He glanced over to find Eve blinking rapidly and gaping at Bill. Pennyworth just swallowed, nodding eagerly.

"That's good," Bill smiled, but the gesture didn't reach his eyes. His eyes said he was tempted to beat the information from the man like candy from a piñata. "Now, you want to tell us where you were the night of August 28th?"

"You mean the night Eve's apartment caught fire?" Pennyworth asked, his gaze not on Bill, but on Eve, a deep frown making his chubby face wrinkle like a Shar Pei's.

"That's the one," Bill confirmed, the promise of slow death in his tone.

"I'm sorry I wasn't there, Eve," Pennyworth's eyes were pleading. "I was away at a comic book conference, but if I'd been here, I would've—"

"You weren't in the city that night?" Bill cut him off.

"No," Pennyworth shook his head. "I was in Detroit, but I—"

"Do you have proof?"

"I—" Pennyworth made a face then pointed toward the messy coffee table. "I think I still have my Amtrak ticket and my hotel receipt. But I don't understand... Wh-what is this all about?"

"Hey, partner," Bill motioned with his chin toward

the papers strewn across the coffee table, "see if our odiferous friend here is telling the truth, will you?"

"On it," Mac said, grabbing the pen lying on top of the mess—no way was he touching *anything* in this place with his bare hands—in order to dig through the various documents and trash that passed as Pennyworth's filing system. Ten years as a federal agent had given him a bullshit gauge that was damn near unerring. And right now the thing was pointing firmly in the green. Then his instincts were proved correct when he located the railway stub right before he found the receipt for the MGM Grand Hotel in downtown Detroit. He squinted at the dates. "He's not lying." He shook his head at Bill. "He was in the Motor City the night the fire was set."

"Wait a second," Pennyworth said. "I thought the blaze was an accident. I thought—"

"Thoughts?" Bill raised an eyebrow, ignoring Pennyworth.

Mac shook his head and voiced four words Bill *didn't* want to hear, "He's not our guy."

"Then what the hell was he doing stalking that pretty little nurse?"

"I wasn't *stalking* her," Dale insisted with a whine. "Why does everyone always *think* that? I was just making sure she made it to the bus stop all right. This isn't the best neighborhood, you know?"

Bill glanced down at the man's perspiring face, looking as if he was trying to see the truth in his words. He must've found whatever he was looking for because he blew out a frustrated breath before holstering his weapon. Digging into his hip pocket, he pulled out a wad of hundred dollar bills and thumbed off a couple of Benjamins.

"For getting your door fixed," he told Pennyworth, dropping the bills on the overflowing coffee table. But when Pennyworth pushed into a seated position, Bill slapped a hand on the man's shoulder and shoved him back in the recliner, leaning down until they were nose-to-nose.

Lord almighty, dude, you better hold your breath, Mac thought.

"I don't want to hear about you following Eve anymore, you got me?" Bill growled. "If I do, I'm going to come back here to plant a boot in your ass and a fist in your teeth."

"I-I won't," Pennyworth breathed, and Mac wrinkled his nose, wondering how Bill could stand being so close to the man. "I thought she needed my protection. She seemed so fragile, so..." Pennyworth's eyes rolled toward Eve who continued to draw down on him, somehow despite her frilly blouse, managing to look tougher than a one-eared alley cat. "But she's not. I can see that now. She doesn't need my guardianship."

"Guardianship?" Bill straightened, eyes narrowed at Pennyworth.

In response, the man pointed at his weird body suit then toward the corner of the room where a rubber face mask that resembled Batman's without the pointy ears sat on a wire rack. "That's what I call myself when I patrol the streets at night."

"Jesus Christ," Bill shook his head like a dog

shaking off water. Then he dragged in a breath like he was praying for patience…or maybe just perseverance…and slowly spread his lips in a smile that Mac figured was *supposed* to put Pennyworth at ease. Unfortunately, in Mac's opinion, all those white, shiny teeth just looked feral. Pennyworth must've agreed with his assessment, because the man shrank farther into his recliner. "I'm going to give you some free advice," Bill told Pennyworth. "You going to listen to what I have to say?"

Pennyworth hesitated then vehemently nodded.

"What you're doing, your *intentions* are good," Bill stressed. "Misguided, but good."

Pennyworth sat up a little straighter, his chest puffing out with hope and maybe a touch of pride.

Then Bill's next words deflated him quicker than a tire punctured by a five-inch nail. "But you're liable to get yourself and these women you think you're protecting killed."

"But, I—"

"No." Bill held up his hand. "No buts. You don't have the training or the physical stamina to fight off an attacker if one were to actually go after any of these women. If you tried, you'd undoubtedly just make a bad situation worse. You want to be a real superhero?"

Again Pennyworth nodded.

"Then lose some weight. Take some defense classes. And volunteer at a shelter for abused women."

Pennyworth recoiled, frowning fiercely. "But I want to wear the suit," he pointed down at his ridiculous outfit. "And I want to—"

Bill cut him off by shaking his head exasperatedly, turning to Mac and saying, “I tried.”

“I know you did,” Mac replied, fighting a smile.

“Now let’s get the hell out of here before I sock him one just for being a smelly moron.”

Mac rolled in his lips, nodding for Eve to precede them out the front door. He’d just stepped over the threshold when he heard Bill add, “And if I were you, Dale, I wouldn’t waste my time calling this in and reporting it. Not only am I best buds with some pretty powerful folks in the police department, but I also have a clean record. The same can’t be said for you. So let’s not get into a your-word-against-my word thing, huh?”

“N-no,” Mac heard Pennyworth sputter. “O-of course not.”

Tromping down the stairs and piling into the Hummer took barely a minute, but the three of them were silent for a long time after Bill cranked over the big engine and put the vehicle in gear. Then, finally, while stopped a red light, Bill muttered, “For shit’s sake, is it just me, or is that guy more than a French fry or two short of a McDonald’s Happy Meal?”

And Mac couldn’t hold it in any longer. He started laughing so hard he had to grab his stomach. “No, no,” he shook his head when he could finally speak, wiping away a tear. “It’s not you. I have a feeling there’s a manifesto hidden somewhere in all his junk, but instead of rantings and ravings, it’s filled with stories of him roaming the streets of Chicago, saving helpless damsels in distress from imagined fiends.”

“It’s not funny,” Eve muttered from the back seat.

"Yeah," Mac nodded. "It really is."

"No, it's not," she insisted. "Because this means my would-be killer is still out there."

And *that* sobered him instantly.

Black Knights Inc. Headquarters
10:24 p.m.

"What fresh hell is this?" Bill grumbled as he pulled up to BKI's big iron gates only to find a Chicago Fox News van blocking the way.

Why in God's name hadn't Toran warned them of the waiting ambush so they could reenter the compound through the secret river tunnel? He glared at the man sitting in the guardhouse even though he knew Toran couldn't see him through the Hummer's tinted windows. And then it occurred to him…

He and Mac had set their phones to "silent" before following Delusional Dale down the block. Digging into his hip pocket, he yanked out his iPhone and…sure enough. He had three missed calls and two waiting text messages. All from Toran…

Can't a guy catch one friggin' break today! Is that too much to ask?

Apparently. Because Kristin Avery, Fox's bottle-blond news reporter turned in their direction and began marching toward the Hummer with a microphone in hand and cameraman following close on her designer heels.

"I thought you said Samantha Tate gave up when

she couldn't convince you to have Eve come out and answer her questions," Mac muttered, as Bill slammed a palm down on the Hummer's horn. The loud *hooonnnkkk* didn't do much in motivating the news van to move.

"I guess she was just gathering the troops," he growled, suppressing the urge to jump out of the SUV and shove that microphone straight into Kristin Avery's ear. Rolling down the window, he yelled at the approaching television reporter. "Get the hell out of the way! You can't block entry to a place of residence!"

"I just have a few questions for Eve Edens!" Ms. Avery called breathlessly when she crossed the final few feet. She didn't hesitate to stick the mic through the open window, angling it toward the back seat. "Bernard, can you get a shot?" she asked the bulky black behemoth who was her cameraman.

"Getting a partial," Bernard responded, his camera lens jutting through the open window, barely an inch from Bill's cheek.

Bill had never considered himself necessarily bloodthirsty—yes, he'd killed in the name of the flag and freedom, but, despite what he'd boasted to Dale, he'd taken no joy in it—but he would be surprised if the smile that spread across his lips at that moment didn't come complete with a set of fangs.

"You better get that goddamned camera out of my face before I shove the entire thing up your ass," he growled. And even though Bernard must've been used to threats in his line of work, his expression said he knew *this* particular warning wasn't an idle one.

Kristin Avery missed it though, as she was too busy shouting questions at Eve. "Are you seeing one of the mechanics who works here, Miss Edens? Is there romance in the air? Or have all your recent misfortunes led you to seek the comfort of a place that boasts twenty-four-hour surveillance? And, if so, what does your father have to say about that?"

"No, no, no, and who the fuck cares what Patrick Edens thinks?" Bill answered for Eve as his ulcer began spewing acid. He ignored the urge to reach for his travel-sized bottle of Pepto. "She's simply here visiting friends. Friends who are sick and tired of watching her get hounded by the motherfucking press at every motherfucking turn!"

And, yes. He'd used the foul language intentionally. *Let them try to put* that *on the evening news.*

"Is that true, Eve?" Ms. Avery persisted, shooting Bill a look hot enough to fry his eyebrows.

"Of course it's true," he growled, having reached—um, no; that'd be more like *surpassed*—the limit of his patience. He shoved at the microphone while simultaneously hitting the power button for the window. Bernard was left with a choice: either remove his camera or risk having it crushed by the rising glass. Bernard chose the first option.

Good man.

"Now *move* your van!" Bill yelled through the window. When Kristin Avery hesitated, he threw the Hummer into gear and began inching forward. The hulking SUV wasn't only bulletproof, it also came with a tempered-steel grill guard that could ram a hole into the side of a brick building. The flimsy sheet metal that made up the body of the news van didn't stand a chance.

Ms. Avery must've realized this, because she squealed and began running toward the van with Bernard lumbering behind her. Bill was about five seconds away from giving the van a little kiss with the Hummer's grill guard, when the reporter and cameraman jumped inside the open cargo door. A heartbeat later, the van's driver shoved the vehicle into reverse, and Bill was left with a clear shot through BKI's quickly opening iron gates. He gunned it, the Hummer growling delightedly at the sudden injection of fuel. But once he'd passed into the interior of the compound, he glanced into his rearview mirror and—*sweet Mother Mary*—he was forced to slam on the brakes. *Errrttt!* The SUV's big tires left rubber on the blacktop.

"What the hell?" Mac asked, turning to him with a brow raised in question.

"That woman is either shithouse crazy or dumb as a box of rocks," he grumbled, barely believing what his eyes were telling him. Samantha Tate was slipping into the compound through the closing gates.

"Huh?" Mac said, cocking his head.

In answer, Bill punched the Hummer into park and threw open his door. In ten steps he was nose-to-nose with Chicago's own rising-star investigative reporter. "I suppose I have you to thank for the circus out there." He pointed toward the news van that was once more parked in front of the gates.

"I know how you motorcycle guys dislike the limelight," Samantha purred, throwing her heavy, dark tresses over her shoulder. "Probably has something to do with all the military training, huh?"

Bill's eyes narrowed.

"Oh, yes," Samantha chuckled. "I've done my research. And, believe me, I intend to do more."

God, please keep me from strangling her.

"But that's not why I'm here tonight" she continued, oblivious to the fact that Bill had curled his hands into fists lest she find them wrapped around her pale, slim throat. "I'm here tonight to pose a few questions to Eve Edens about her most recent mishap. And if you don't help me make that happen, I'll ask Kristin and her news crew to set up camp out here. She's a good friend of mine. I'm sure she'll agree."

The light in the woman's eyes was sharp and hungry, and Bill remembered one of the Knights comparing Samantha Tate to a barracuda. Only instead of smelling blood in the water, she smelled brewing news stories.

"You've got serious moxie, lady," he growled, grabbing her elbow and hustling her toward the gate despite her protests. "I'll give you that."

"Let go of me, you big brute!" Ms. Tate thundered, slapping ineffectually at his restraining hand.

Lifting his chin at Toran, the two halves of the gate slid open again. Only this time, they stopped when there was just enough room for him to shove the nosy reporter through the opening. "Loiter around out here all you want. It's no skin off my ass," he told her, as the gate snapped shut with a loud *clang*. "All you'll see is us protecting a good friend from having her life flayed open once again by the press..." He hoped he wasn't struck down by a bolt of lightning for that lie, because Eve Edens? A good friend? Ha! "…and building motorcycles. Have a good night," he finished before stomping back toward the Hummer.

Sliding into the driver's seat, he glanced over to find Mac chuckling.

"What?" he demanded, reaching into his hip pocket and pulling out the bottle of pink salvation. He took a healthy swig.

"What was that last thing Ms. Tate hollered at you?" Mac asked, eyes glinting with humor.

Bill wiped a hand over his mouth, willing the Pepto to work its magic. "I didn't catch it all, but there was something in there about an acid enema."

Mac hooted with laughter, but when Bill looked into the rearview mirror and saw the humiliation and fear on Eve's face, he couldn't join in the hilarity.

I'm sorry, she mouthed, her perfectly shaped, china doll lips quivering.

Those silent words went all through him, touching a soft spot inside he'd thought callused over long ago by the horrors of battle and the pain of a broken heart.

"Forgive me." This time, the soft words were spoken aloud. And for a moment he wasn't sure if she was asking him to forgive her for bringing the press down on their heads or if she was asking him to forgive her for the way she'd treated him all those years ago.

And in that moment, as he looked at her, sitting back there, so beautiful and vulnerable, he found himself wanting to do just that. To forgive her for…for all of it. But then an image of her and that ass-hat, Blake Parish, smiling at each other as they recited their wedding vows, flashed through his head. And whatever internal softening he'd felt once more hardened to stone.

"It's fine," he said, his voice gruff, his expression very clearly stating exactly the opposite.

Her big, blue eyes dropped to her lap and, if he wasn't mistaken, that was the glint of a teardrop trickling down her pale cheek.

Jesus, Bill, you're a dickhead.

He waited for something inside himself, his pride, his conscience, one small inner voice to disagree with him. Unfortunately, all he heard was radio-silence.

Damn it all to hell...

Chapter Seven

Black Knights Inc. Headquarters, 2nd Floor
10:45 p.m.

EVE GLANCED AROUND AT THE THREE MEN SEATED at the conference table, trying and failing to forget the look on Billy's face when she asked him to forgive her.

She hadn't known at the time that she'd posed a broader question than the one urging him to except her apology for the appearance of the press, but the expression in his eyes told her she had. And then she'd waited with bated breath for his response, hope and longing exploding inside her like a punctured scuba tank. Because for a moment there she'd thought…

But no. How could she possibly expect Billy's forgiveness for the way things had happened when she couldn't even forgive herself?

"So what now?" Ace asked, dragging her from her bleak thoughts. She watched him take a sip of coffee and wrinkled her nose. She'd learned long ago it was best to avoid the stuff they brewed at BKI, since it had the consistency of motor oil and tasted about the same…not to mention the smell. The smell was like a combination of burned rubber and hot dirt, and it seemed to hover over the whole place in a caustic cloud.

"Now, we explore other avenues," Mac said, using a stir-stick on his own mug of caffeinated sludge.

"Which would be?" Billy asked, his handsome face determined.

Okay, and *why* did he have to be so darned good-looking? Why couldn't he have gone bald, or grown fat, or rotted all his teeth from his head?

Would any of those things have changed the way you feel about him?

Grrr. She told the pesky little voice that posed the question to go suck a bowl of turds, because...what the heck? She was *trying* to distance herself from Billy and the feelings she still had for him, and *that* kind of questioning wasn't helping matters in the least.

For Pete's sake! It was a sad day when a girl couldn't depend on her own conscience to have her back.

"We get copies of the employment files at the Shedd Aquarium to see if any of Eve's coworkers have black marks on their records," Mac said. "We do the same with the people at her yacht club and the charity for the preservation of the wetlands she co-chairs."

Her heart plummeted to her toes. "You think it's someone I know?" she asked, willing him to give her a different answer than the one she fully expected him to offer.

"It would make sense," Mac said, and so much for the force of her will. "Someone knew where you lived. Someone knew where you worked. Someone knew what you drove. So, can you think of anyone who might want to hurt you or get revenge on you? Have you had any problems at work? Any run-ins at the club or the charity? Have you had a recent fallin' out with any friends or..." Mac slid a sidelong glance at Billy. "Or any jilted lovers?"

"Don't look at me," Billy held up his hands. "I'm not one of her jilted lovers. Not for lack of trying, mind you. But back when I knew her, she was saving it for *the one*." He made quote marks with his fingers. "Which, as everybody sitting here knows, wasn't me."

"What's that I'm tasting?" Ace said, making smacking noises. "Is that sour grapes?"

"Shut the hell up," Billy growled.

Eve was no longer listening. Because Billy's not-so-subtle reminder of those hot and heavy petting sessions in the back of his Camaro blazed through her mind. The wet kisses and fervent touches—he'd had magic hands even back then—the ache that'd built and built but never found any release. Because she'd stopped it...

Oh, *why* had she stopped it? And did he know how much she regretted that her first time—and all the times after that—hadn't been with him?

No. No, he didn't. And it was probably just as well...

"No, Mac," she shook her head, unaccountably tired all of a sudden. On top of the strain she'd been under by being around Billy, she'd been wracking her brain for two days over who could possibly hate her enough to want her dead. And so far? Well, so far she'd come up with a big handful of nothing, nada, zilch. And as much as she hated to admit it, to admit to *another* weakness, the truth was, all the stresses were beginning to wear her down. It felt like someone had dropped an anvil on each of her shoulders, not to mention the ten-pound weights some sadistic sonofagun had decided to attach to her eyelids. "I can't think of a single person who'd fall into any of the categories you just mentioned."

"How about that douchebag ex-husband of yours?" Billy sneered.

Eve felt her face turn beet red at the mention of Blake. Blake…the man she'd betrayed Billy with. Blake…the man who'd been trying for over a decade to win her back. "He wouldn't do this," she said quietly, staring at the table.

"How can you be so sure?"

"Because…" she swallowed before admitting, "he still loves me. He's always loved me. And he wants me back, not *dead*."

Billy snorted and rolled his eyes. Mac frowned at him before reaching across the table to pat her hand. "It's okay," he reassured her. "We'll figure this out."

"I know we will," was what she said. But what she felt? Well, it was the polar opposite. Unfortunately, all the wide-eyed hope she'd had earlier in the day had up and decided to abandon her. Now, she was left feeling nothing but drained and disheartened. She tried to offer Mac a smile but figured the gesture fell short when his brow furrowed. But she was saved from attempting to give the smile another go when the opening bars to "Come Sail Away" sounded from her purse. It was hooked over the back of her chair, so she had to swivel in order to dig inside and locate her cell phone. She glanced at the name on the screen and closed her eyes, sucking in a deep breath before pressing a button and sending the call directly to voice mail. She couldn't deal with him right now.

"Your dad again?" Mac asked, because her phone

had been going off every half hour since she'd left her father standing behind BKI's big front gates.

"Yes," she nodded, not quite meeting the man's gaze. She was humiliated that Mac'd had to stand there and listen to her father cast aspersions on his character and the characters of all the Knights. It wasn't that her father was a *bad* man. It's just that he was opinionated and elitist and very, *very* set in his ways. Which hadn't really been a problem for her until she started exercising her independence, and then their relationship had quickly gone downhill. But she hoped, oh, how she *hoped*, he'd come around. And *soon*. Because his constant nagging was only adding to her exhaustion.

"He's certainly...uh..." Mac cocked his head, "persistent."

"That's one word for it," she said, snorting and rubbing a thumb against her pounding temple.

Ace hooked an arm around her shoulders, giving her a quick squeeze. "You look completely beat, love," he murmured in her ear. "How about you head upstairs and snuggle into bed. I'll bring you a nice hot chocolate, we can gossip about boys, and you can forget about this whole mess for a while. How does that sound?"

How did it sound? "Like heaven," she sighed, glancing up into his angelic face and kind eyes. Ace was going to make some man very happy one day.

"Good." He planted a kiss on her cheek. From the corner of her eye, she thought she saw Billy clench his hands into fists. "It's all settled then." Ace stood and pulled her up by her elbows. "You go get into your PJs and I'll be right up." For good measure, after she'd turned toward the stairs leading to the loft-style bedrooms on the third floor, he gave her ass a resounding smack.

She squealed, swinging around to glare at him, but a slow smile ruined the expression.

"That's more like it," Ace grinned. "You've got a beautiful smile, love. And it breaks my heart when you don't use it. Now, up you go," he said, shooing her toward the stairs. She turned to do as instructed, but when her foot landed on the first tread, any momentary lightheartedness she felt disappeared like a catamaran in the Bermuda Triangle. It just…vanished. Because, oh, the look in Billy's eyes out in that Hummer. The memory flashed through her mind, ripped at her heart.

It's over, Eve. You ruined it.

And great. Now, not only was she exhausted, but she was on the verge of a crying jag guaranteed to last half the night. Without a backward glance, she sprinted up the stairs, wrenched open the door to the guest room, and threw herself down on the bed face-first, burying her head in the pillows lest the men downstairs hear the uncontrollable sobbing that shook her from head to toe.

"What is *that* look for?" Bill growled at Ace after Eve disappeared upstairs. BKI's flyboy was standing there, arms crossed, head cocked, a narrowed-eyed glare plastering his face.

"Remember what I told you I'd do to you if you

weren't nice to Eve?" Ace smiled, all teeth and no emotion, though he did bat his girlishly long lashes.

"What the hell?" Bill threw his hands in the air, feeling his frustration mount to precarious levels. If he didn't simmer down soon, his ulcer would wake up and go in for a second...third?...helping. "I *have* been nice to her. I friggin' went and interrogated her stalker. I made sure he leaves her the hell alone from now on. I kept those damned meddling reporters from getting to her. And I—"

"And you were a big, snide, ass-clown with that little speech about her saving herself for *the one*." Ace uncrossed his arms so he could sarcastically make the quote marks with his fingers.

Bill winced. Yeah, okay, so that hadn't exactly been one of his bright, shining moments, but...

Still, after everything, he thought he'd done a pretty bang-up job of keeping his more cynical feelings to himself. So he'd appreciate it if his fellow Knights, specifically Ace, would cut him a little goddamned slack. He told the guy as much.

"Slack?" Ace asked, his expression telegraphing his annoyance louder than a WWII sticky bomb taking out a German Panzer. "You don't need any slack. What you need is an old-fashioned ass-whooping." Okay, and now Bill was good and pissed. He pushed up from the table, but Ace ignored the killing gleam in his eye and just kept on. "Because your ticket on the Poor-Me-I-Got-Dumped train has long expired. You need to hop off at the next stop, my friend. It's at the intersection of Suck-It-Up and Get-The-Hell-Over-It."

Whoa. Bill felt like he'd just been kicked in the sprouts, and red edged into his vision for about the zillionth time that night.

"What. The. *Fuck.* Would you know about it?" he hissed, skirting the table.

Mac's, "Come on now, guys, let's just take a T.O. here before things get out of hand," went ignored.

"I know that you dated for three months back when you were both too young and too dumb to know your assess from holes in the ground. I know you went off to big, bad BUD/S training, leaving your eighteen-year-old girlfriend at college with all the accompanying temptations inherent therein. I know you went weeks, sometimes *months*, without calling her because of your training. I know she did what many young girls her age do and allowed her head to be turned by a good-looking, fancy-talking rich boy. I know—"

"How do you know all this?" Bill demanded, feeling the vein next to his temple pulse in warning as his ulcer sat up to lick its chops. He didn't want to sock Ace in the kisser. Well…he kind of did. He'd been wanting to hit someone or something all evening.

"Becky told me," Ace said, re-crossing his arms and jutting out his chin. Bill had never hated a perfectly groomed five-o'clock shadow so much in his life. "And before you go thinking your kid sister is telling tales out of school, I want you to know that I *asked* her what the deal was between you and Eve. I mean, come on, the wall of tension between you two is so high and tight you could bounce a grenade off it."

"You gossip like a girl, Ace-hole," he grumbled,

staring down at his worn black combat boots. Any time he wore them, he was reminded of Iraq and Afghanistan. Of the garbage bags that'd passed as roadside trash but were, in fact, IEDs gnarly enough to take out entire sections of military convoys.

He'd spent years combing those desert roads, safely exploding this device and not-so-safely disarming that one. And all that time, even through all the danger, through all the sweat and tears, he'd never stopped thinking of Eve, never stopped wondering and agonizing over why she'd done what she'd done. Never stopped despising and blaming her for *how* she'd done it.

But maybe Ace was right. Maybe it was time to let it go. Just…let it *all* go. She'd been so young…so young and so very naïve…

"I gossip like a girl?" Ace queried, dragging Bill from his ruminations. A shit-eating grin was spread across the man's pretty-boy face. "Why thank you, Bill. I take that as a compliment."

"Yeah, well, the next time you think of opening your mouth to discuss my private life," he grunted, and it occurred to him then that he was emotionally exhausted, bone-tired of holding on to scorn and hostility that was more than a decade old. It was time to move on, "why don't you try counting your teeth instead, huh?"

"I'll take that under advisement," Ace winked, but Bill knew they were only words. Ace would continue to butt into everybody's business with impunity. Just like he always had. "And now," Ace continued, reading the surrender on Bill's face, "why don't you go up and talk to Eve. If I'm right, and I always am, she could use a little comforting right now."

Now *that* made Bill's chin jerk back on his neck like he'd been the recipient of a five-finger sandwich. "I thought that's what *you* were going to do."

Ace rolled his eyes, heaving a long-suffering, overly dramatic sigh. "She'd much rather that comfort come from you, you nitwit."

No, she wouldn't. No way. No how. "She would?"

"Without a doubt," Ace stated with conviction. "So get to it."

"But..." He glanced back at Mac who was still seated at the conference table.

All right, it was confession time. Because in all honesty, the thought of going upstairs to comfort Eve scared the living shit out of him. He may never be able to forget what had happened, he may never be able to trust her again, but that didn't mean he didn't still want her more than he wanted his next sunrise. If he lived to be a hundred years old, he figured he'd never stop wanting Eve. And that meant, in order to save himself more grief and misery, he had to stay away from her whenever he possibly could.

Now being the perfect example.

"Don't we still have things to discuss?" he asked Mac, and it was only partly a stalling tactic. Because Bill hadn't missed the flicker in Mac's eyes when Eve asked if he really thought whoever was doing this was someone she knew. Mac smelled a rat. Bill was certain of it. "Like, who you suspect is *really* behind these attempts on her life?"

"I don't know who's behind them," Mac said, his expression contemplative.

"There," Bill pointed a finger at the guy's face. "That look right there tells me you know more than you're saying."

Mac shrugged. "Here's what I know. There are usually two reasons people commit premeditated murder."

"And those are?"

"Love and money."

"Jesus," Bill swiped a hand over the back of his neck where a patch of goose bumps had suddenly erupted. Love and money, huh? Well, shit. That could mean only one thing. "So you suspect it's someone *very* close to her," he murmured, unconsciously shooting a worried glance toward the stairs leading to the third floor.

"Let's rule out everything else first," Mac stated. Then he added, "But let's do it in the morning. Because right now, I'm tired as a cactus."

Ace snorted. "You've been hanging around with the ragin' Cajun too long, Mac my man."

"Hey," Mac frowned, "I'm from Texas. We have our own expressions and—"

Bill stopped listening, instead turning his full attention toward the staircase.

Did he dare?

"Go," Ace came up beside him, giving him a little shove even as Mac continued to rant about the superiority of Texans when it came to the inventiveness of Southern colloquialisms. "But I warn you, you better just talk to her, just comfort her. I don't want to hear you up there smudging her cookies."

"Smudging her what?" Bill asked, only half listening since all his attention was focused on those stairs. Was it a stairway to heaven or hell?

"You know what I'm talking about," Ace insisted. "Eating her cake, flicking her bean, smudging her cookies. None of that."

And, *shit*, had his thoughts been plastered all over his face?

He turned to lift a brow at Ace who flattened his mouth and narrowed his eyes. "Yeah, I can see the gerbils spinning the wheels in your head. But I trust you to keep them, and yourself, in check. Can you do that for me?"

"Of course I can," Bill said, but he wondered who he was trying to convince more, Ace or himself. Then he decided there was no use standing there pondering imponderable thoughts, so he pulled his determination around himself like a steely mantle and stomped across the room to the metal steps.

Chapter Eight

Somewhere on Lake Shore Drive
11:02 p.m.

She needed to die. It was the only way…

And it broke his heart that's how it had to be. But there was a law in the jungle: Eat or be eaten. And, as sad as it might sound, it didn't matter what the relationship was. The female praying mantis ate her lover. The chimpanzee was known to eat his enemy. Even polar bear fathers had been filmed killing and eating their young.

He didn't make the rules, by God. But he'd certainly learned to live by them. And the only way he could see to get free of his current predicament was for Eve to meet her maker.

Unfortunately, she was proving far more difficult to kill than he ever imagined…

Tough. That's what she was. Tough and smart and beautiful. And there was a part of him that was so damned proud of her and how far she'd come from that young woman who'd suffered nearly paralyzing shyness and self-doubt. A part of him that *adored* her and scorned himself and the decisions he'd made that necessitated her death.

No. He shook his head, gazing out of his living room

window at the cars zooming past on Lake Shore Drive, and beyond, to the calming blue of the lake itself. *You've made your decision.*

As always, the inner pep talk steadied him. And he could admit that he no longer had the time to stage her death, to orchestrate another accident. The clock was ticking down to the final hour, and he had to act fast. It needed to be quick. It needed to be dirty. And it needed to be soon.

Which meant it was time to call in the cavalry, otherwise known as the lowlife Chicago thugs who were threatening to break his knees before breaking his neck…

Picking up a cheap, plastic pre-paid phone, he dialed a number he knew by heart. One quick string of words later, and it was done. Eve's life—or the *end* of her life—was no longer in his hands.

It's just as well, he thought, sighing. It'd been obvious that night when he hesitated in putting a bullet in her brain that he really didn't have the stomach to see this kind of nasty business through. He *loved* her, after all. But he hadn't been able to countenance the thought of the half million dollars he'd have to pay that seedy Chicago gangster—on top of the wad of money he already owed the man—for services rendered.

Then again, time—and an impending deadline—brought clarity. And, really, what was a measly five hundred thousand when compared to continuing to breathe without the help of a tube? Which was exactly what would happen to him if Eve didn't meet her end soon.

So, yes, he'd done the right thing, calling in the hit. And now all he had to do was sit and wait. Wait to give the big, sleazy assholes with their big, sleazy guns her whereabouts.

Glancing down at the glass of scotch in his hand, he watched the amber liquid catch the light from a nearby Tiffany lamp. It sparkled like agate, reminding him of the style of life he was used to living, of the style of life he *deserved.*

Raising the glass to his nose, he sucked in the peaty aroma of well-aged malted barley.

Yes, he assured himself. *I did the right thing.*

She was crying.

He could hear her through the door.

Damnit! The sound of her sobs, of her quiet sniffles, stabbed through him like shrapnel from a car bomb, tearing apart his insides. He was a sucker for women's tears, no doubt about it. Really, what decent, honorable man wasn't? But Eve's had always been particularly heartrending. She cried with her whole body. She shook from head to toe, her tears seeming to come up from the depths of her soul.

His steely cloak of determination slipped, and he pressed his forehead against the cool metal door, fighting the urge to just turn away. From her sorrow. From his own. Then he reminded himself of Ace's words and metaphorically reached back to adjust his mantle.

Flyboy was right. It was time for him to, if not forget, then at least *begin* to forgive. To heal his hurt as well as hers. And, yes, as much as it might grieve him to admit it, ever since their reunion he'd been doing his best to hurt her, to give her a taste of his suffering.

Of course, healing their hurts meant he had to start by marching into the room and asking her to answer the question that'd eaten at his brain like a tumor since the day he'd received that wedding invitation in the mail…

He needed to ask her *why*?

Why had she done things the way she'd done them? Why hadn't she treated him with a little more respect, a little more compassion? Hadn't he deserved that?

And maybe after he'd asked those questions, depending on her answers—or perhaps her answers didn't really matter so much as the act of *finally* confronting the issue—he could begin to move forward. Move on.

Okay, Billy boy. Let's man up and do this.

"Eve?" he knocked softly. "I…" He had to swallow the ton of sand that'd inexplicably taken up residence in his throat like the place was a friggin' Saudi desert or something. "I'm coming in, okay?"

He didn't wait for a reply, simply turned the knob and pushed into the room.

And there she was, sitting on the edge of the rumpled bed, Peanut curled up next to her, a loud purr rumbling from the big tomcat until he sounded like a furry, V-twin engine. Yes, there she was. The first woman to touch his heart. The only woman who'd ever broken it…

Her usually sleek, raven-black hair was a bird's nest, the end of her perfect nose pink and shiny. And her eyes? Well, they were so puffy and red he was hard-pressed to make out the blue of her irises. And yet she was still, hands down, the most beautiful woman he'd ever seen. *Shit.*

"I want to be alone, B-Billy," she hiccupped, wiping the backs of her hands over her wet cheeks.

"That's not what you told Ace," he reminded her as he edged closer and closer to the bed even as the urge to flee in the friggin' opposite direction grew stronger and stronger. Now that he was here, doing it, he wasn't sure he was ready. It suddenly felt as if he was poised to pull the pin on something, and the explosion was going to be far larger than he anticipated.

"That's because Ace isn't..." She shook her head helplessly, looking up at him when he came to stand beside her, her eyes begging him for mercy. No doubt she expected more disdain and vitriol from him. Why shouldn't she? That's all he'd given her for nearly a year...

Double shit.

Once again, that soft spot inside, the one he'd thought forever hardened, took one long look at her there, expression meek and pleading, and immediately turned to goo.

"Ace isn't what?" he asked, shoving Peanut back into the middle of the mattress, receiving a loud, disgruntled *mrrreow* for his trouble. He ignored the cat's furiously twitching tail and narrowed, yellow eyes as he gently lowered himself to the bed beside Eve.

"He's not *you*," she said, stiffening up like her whole body had been doused in Super Glue when he threw an arm around her shoulders, ignoring the little voice inside his head that yelled, *Danger! Danger, Will Robinson!* "Wh-what are you d-doing?"

"Comforting you," he said, his breath sawing from his lungs at the feel of her in his arms again. So delicate and fragile. Like a very fine, very rare crystal vase that had to be protected at all costs.

"B-but why?" she stuttered. One big, sparkling tear leaked from the corner of her eye to trail down her perfect, pale cheek. He reached up to thumb it away, and her breath hitched in her throat.

So soft. That's what he remembered about her. How soft her skin was. How good it smelled. Like handmade soap, designer lotion, and warm lace. He dragged in a deep breath. That lavish aroma would always make his dick hard enough to hammer nails.

Now being no exception…

He shifted, subtly adjusting himself into a more comfortable position. "Let's just say I'm putting a little change in the karma bank," he told her. "Besides, I think it's time to let bygones be bygones."

"Do you…" She licked her pale, peachy lips, and his eyes followed the dart of her pink tongue. The sexual beast inside him, the one he'd kept reined in around her since their reunion, began chomping at the bit. *Damnit all to hell*! She made him feel completely uncivilized, straight up animalistic, in fact. And the way he wanted her, hard, fast, and totally dirty was straight out of the jungle. Anytime he touched her, he was all about the *me Tarzan, you Jane*. And it was so very annoying that his libido had never gotten the note that she was persona non grata in the whole horizontal mambo department. "Do you mean that?" she finally managed.

Did he? If he was honest with himself, he wasn't sure.

What he *was* sure of was that, despite everything, despite the fact that their convoluted history meant there was no chance of a future between them, he wanted to kiss her. To taste those full, perfectly formed lips, to breathe in that sweet, soft breath, to feel her warm, lithe form pressed against the length of him once again.

Smudging her cookies indeed…

God, he remembered how she'd been all those years ago. So young and fresh. So eager to learn the ways of his body. So delighted as he learned the ways of hers.

Oh, great. And now his dick wasn't only hard enough to hammer nails, the damn thing was actually sucking all the blood away from his brain, causing him to, for a split second, consider doing something very, *very* stupid.

She must've sensed the change in him because a subtle trembling shook her shoulders. Her pupils dilated until they almost eclipsed the blue of her irises. And staring at her lovely face, he couldn't read her expression. Which was odd. Because open book or wide-open book, remember?

So call it Fate or bad luck or simply bad timing, but, in that moment, he couldn't tell if she was inviting him to lay her back on that bed or sizing him up for a coffin—payback for all the hell he'd put her through recently. And the not knowing meant he had to rely on instinct. So before he realized he even moved, he was palming the back of her neck and dragging her forward for a kiss, the little head in his pants instinctively taking over for the big head on his shoulders.

And the instant their lips touched? Well…let's just say he knew it for the mistake it was.

Suddenly, his big head was back online and shouting at him to *get the hell out!* Because the feel of her, the *taste* of her, made him want to forget everything, forget that she was a cruel, untrustworthy woman. And he absolutely *could not* forget that. If he did, there'd be nothing stopping him from throwing caution to the wind and giving her another chance, from allowing her the opportunity to crush him again.

Which could not, *would* not happen. He'd barely survived the heartbreak the first time. He *wouldn't* survive it a second...

But he couldn't make himself release her either. In fact, against all reason and good judgment, he did just the opposite. He slid his free hand down her arm, stopping to intertwine their fingers. Then he snaked their joined hands behind her back and pressed her forward until she was forced to scoot closer to him. She was trembling in his arms just as she had at eighteen, trembling with desire mixed with nerves. And just as he'd done all those years ago, he gentled his assault, kissing his way across her brow and then her closed lids, letting her lush lashes tickle his lips, sipping at the salty wetness that still clung there. Sliding his nose down the side of hers until their foreheads touched, he was surprised when she released his hand, grabbed his face, and angled his head, slamming her mouth over the top of his only to proceed to try to catalog his teeth with her tongue.

Sonofa—

And just like that, all his gentleness vanished. Okay, and Ace was right. He not only wanted to smudge her cookies, he wanted to flick her bean and eat her cake, too. But first he wanted to kiss her. Kiss her like he hadn't kissed a woman since her, with everything he had, with his whole body, with his whole...*heart.*

He slipped his hand under her blouse, and the warm skin of her back was soft yet firm, covering supple feminine muscles. Eve might look fragile, but she did not feel it. What she *did* feel like was his. She'd *always* felt like his and—

Shit on a stick!

How had everything gotten out of hand so quickly?

Once again, his body acted before his brain. With absolutely no finesse, he jumped from the bed like the thing had turned into a gaping mouth threatening to swallow him whole. The sudden move nearly had Eve face-planting into the colorful rug, and he steadied her by placing a hand on her shoulder.

"I, uh—" He stopped short, trying and failing to catch his breath. She was looking up at him with big, wary eyes, two graceful fingers touching her kiss-wet lips, her other hand wrapped around the pearl pendant at her throat. *Holy hell, you've got to get out of here, boy-o.*

"I didn't mean for that to—" He stopped again, shaking his head. "Goodnight, Eve."

He turned on his heel, gritting his teeth against the pain caused by the humungous bite his ulcer took out of his stomach when her softly whispered "G-goodnight, Billy" followed him out the door.

Chapter Nine

Black Knight Inc.'s Onsite Gym
Sunday, 6:36 a.m.

What did it mean? What did it mean? What did it mean?

The phrase circling around in Eve's head kept time with the pounding of her sneakers on the treadmill's conveyer belt.

He'd said he wanted to let bygones be bygones, and then he'd kissed her…

Holy moly, did he ever! Her lips were still tender, the skin on her chin still slightly pink from the rasp of his ever-present beard stubble. And, *oh*, she'd forgotten what it felt like to be good and truly kissed. To be swept away by the sensation of lips and teeth and tongues and sweet-tasting breath.

Nobody, and she meant *nobody*, kissed like William Wesley Reichert. The man was a veritable prodigy, especially when he did that thing where he put both palms on either side of her face and gently sucked her tongue into his mouth…or when he caught her lower lip between both of his and softly stroked the sensitive pad with his tongue…or when he was in the conquering mood and plunged inside her mouth like Genghis Khan, just flippin' *ravaging* her—which was what he'd done toward the end last night.

And, yes, she totally blamed him—and her early immersion in the wonder that *was* him—for the fact that the guys she'd dated and kissed since him hadn't measured up to her expectations. I mean, once a girl got a taste of triple-chocolate truffles, plain ol' graham crackers simply lost their appeal.

But what did it *mean*? Did it mean she'd been wrong about that look out in the Hummer? Did it mean he'd forgiven her and wanted to give it another try? Or was it, in fact, some sort of good-bye kiss, a way to mark the end of their tumultuous relationship, to bookend their time together, if you will?

Her phone sprang to life, dragging her from her restless thoughts, and she frowned down at the name on the screen. Her father wasn't very good at taking a hint. But she wasn't prepared to speak to him. Not yet, at least. Punching a button, she sent the call directly to voice mail just as a deep voice, spoken from directly behind her, had her hitting the emergency stop key on the treadmill.

"You still run like the wind."

She glanced over her shoulder, grabbing the towel draped over one of the handrails in order to wipe away the drops of sweat on her brow and throat.

"You're up early," she wheezed as she stepped off the machine, wondering if her breathlessness came from exertion or the fact that Billy looked so dang good that her lungs had seized up.

Erm...probably the second. Because she ran seven miles a day, five days a week, and she couldn't remember the last time she'd lost her breath while doing it.

Chastising herself for being a *complete* man-hungry ninny when it came to Billy and his miles of tan, tattooed muscles, she wiped the towel over her face and forced herself to drag in a steadying breath. The smell of the bleach the towel had been washed in combined with the aromas of the gym's astringent cleaning products and good, healthy, male sweat to ground her. Sort of. That is until her gaze once more landed on Billy.

Oh, good gracious. Today he was wearing baggy sweat pants slung low around his ultra-trim waist and a tight white tank top that emphasized the hulking muscles in his shoulders and just *happened* to showcase the colorful star tattoos cascading down his sculpted arms.

Her eyes were drawn to the red and blue ink, to the fierce points of each wickedly perfect beacon of patriotism. She wondered idly if the individual stars represented something. But the thought was fleeting, because she was distracted by the sea of testosterone surrounding Billy. The sea of testosterone that made her want to do something incredibly foolish like, oh, say, don snorkel gear and dive right in. Then again, before she could do that, she needed to figure out exactly what last night's kiss meant. If she could just drum up the courage, that is.

Come on, Eve. Stop being a wuss. Oh God, her heart was pounding a mile a minute.

"I like to get in a workout before the chaos of the day begins," Billy said in answer to her incredibly lame—insert eye roll here—*you're up early*. Geez, whoever it was who'd recently complimented her for being articulate should obviously go in for a CT scan. Because when it came to Billy, her vocabulary shrank to double and most times single syllable words.

Like, for instance, right now? Well, right now, as she watched him push away from the doorjamb, the only word she could seem to come up with was *yum*.

Her eyes devoured him as he sauntered over to a weight bench. Lowering himself, he bent to tighten the laces on his worn sneakers. Which is when she realized not only was her stomach quivering from the mere sight of him, but her hands were also shaking with fear. And *dangit,* a large part of her wanted to turn tail and run. Just skedaddle right on out of the outbuilding that served as BKI's home gymnasium and avoid any morning-after conversations. Because what if he told her that kiss meant nothing? Or worse, that it meant the end of everything…

But, no. That was the old Eve, the timid, little rabbit Eve. The new Eve? Well, the new Eve gnawed on her lip for a good two-second count before blurting, "You kissed me last night."

Okay, and that came out sounding more like an accusation than a question. *Curses.*

Billy planted his forearms on his thighs, letting his head hang between his shoulders and his big, lovely hands dangle between his legs. He was silent for a seemingly interminable moment during which time she was afraid her pounding heart might just leap right out of her chest. Then, he lifted those lovely eyes of his to her face, and his expression was…what?

Embarrassed? Wry? Self-deprecating?

She couldn't tell. Oh, *why* couldn't she tell?

"Guess there's no way to un-ring that bell, huh?" he muttered, lips twisting, and all the hope that'd been expanding in her chest burst. She was surprised a loud *pop* didn't echo around the room.

The urge to run was more powerful than ever. But she held her ground, lifting her chin. "Would you..." She licked her lips and swallowed...her pride, perhaps? "Would you *want* to un-ring it?"

He made a face. "Maybe," he said. Then, "Probably."

Well, a girl couldn't fault the guy for being honest.

"Oh," she murmured, trying very hard to keep her shoulders from drooping and her lower lip from quivering.

"I went up to your room last night to attempt to give you a little comfort after your hellacious last couple of months and to tell you that I'm done holding grudges about the past. But the urge to kiss you overcame me, probably something to do with old habits or bad instincts, and I wrongly acted on it. I'm sorry about that. It won't happen again."

But what if she *wanted* it to happen again? She opened her mouth to admit as much—talk about swallowing her pride—when his expression stopped her cold. She knew a wall when she ran into it, face-first.

He might be ready to try to forgive her for the past. But from the look of things, he wasn't ready, he'd *never* be ready, to start something new. There was just too much history there. Too many grievances and too much distrust...

She wanted to sit down and scream. Scream at herself

for having been so disloyal and cowardly. Scream at her father for pushing her away from a *good* man and into the arms of a manipulative one. Just scream, scream, *scream!* But, the time for self-pity and blame was gone. Now she needed to do the right thing, the *brave* thing and offer Bill the apology that'd been a long time coming. Too long…

"Since we're…uh…since we're baring our souls here," she began hesitantly, "I-I want to tell you I'm sorry for the way I behaved all those years ago."

"You were young," he said. And considering all the times she'd hoped to see a little compassion shining out at her from the depths of his warm, brown eyes, the fact that she was seeing it now should've brought her more comfort. Instead, it only made her grief and regret burn brighter, hotter. Tears scorched at the back of her throat.

"That's no excuse," she admitted, staring down at her Asics.

"We were both young. And it takes two to make an accident," he quoted quietly, and her gaze shot up to his face.

"*The Great Gatsby*?" she asked, lower lip trembling—*dang the thing!* "That's…that's one of my favorites."

"I remember." His voice was gruff. And it was then, because of the unspoken look in his eyes, that she wondered if maybe he'd taken to reading books, the classics in particular, to please her. Because when they'd dated that summer, reading the classics had been her thing.

Oh, God! Why had she agreed to go out with Blake Parish? Why hadn't she told her father to go jump in a lake when he kept harping on her to forget about Billy and give Blake a chance? And why hadn't she been brave enough to hop on a plane to go see Billy after the misleading photos and articles had been printed in the papers? Why had she relied on those stupid, impersonal letters that probably hadn't accurately portrayed her regret or remorse? Why hadn't she been courageous enough to explain everything to him face-to-face? Perhaps if she had, he would've forgiven her then and everything would be different now…

But hindsight, as they say, is 20/20. And there was no going back. Now all she could do was move forward, no matter how painful it might prove to be.

"I *am* sorry," she said again, her heart a clenched fist in her chest.

"I know you are." He nodded, his smile gentle.

God, that smile killed her. "I'd like to explain what happened. I think you deserve…I don't know…more than what I gave you. I think you deserve to hear—"

"And I *would* like to hear what you've got to say," he said, cutting her off. "But not now." She couldn't help it, the muscles in her shoulders loosened, and she dragged in a tired sigh. "First, let's figure out who's behind these attacks on you. Let's get you safe and secure before we sit down for a heart-to-heart, okay? That way there'll be no distractions."

She held his gaze for long seconds, feeling as if, regardless of the words coming out of his mouth, the book on that part of her life had inexplicably slammed shut. Just as she'd suspected, last night's kiss had been an ending.

"Do you think it's possible for us to maybe…to maybe be friends someday?" She didn't care that there was an obvious note of hope in her voice.

A muscled ticked in his jaw, and she rolled in her lips, waiting. Finally, he gave her a shrug, "Maybe… Someday…"

"Good." She blew out a shaky breath, having no choice but to accept what he was offering. "Thank you, Billy."

"You're welcome, Eve," he said in that deep voice of his that'd always reminded her of thunder rolling in over Lake Michigan. She took that as her cue.

Turning on her heel, she exited the outbuilding, carefully closing the door behind her, and stepping onto the slate flagstones of BKI's back courtyard. She lifted her face to the warm sun peeking over the eastern perimeter wall and closed her eyes, bathing in its warmth.

"It's enough," she murmured to herself. "If I can have his friendship, it'll be enough."

But the words fell flat on her ears, because what she wanted from him, what she'd *always* wanted from him, was so, *so* much more…

Belmont Avenue
4:15 p.m.

Mac was beat. We're talking dead-dog-roadkill tired. Or as he father used to say, *too pooped to pop*—whatever that was supposed to mean. Because not only had he spent the entire day with Bill and Eve and the shit-storm of angst that seemed to swirl around those two in a dizzying funnel cloud—something had happened between them last night that'd turned all their overt animosity and ill-disguised insults into covert glances and tense silences—but he'd also just blown the last hour trying to wheedle a yacht club members list from a guy with salon-quality hair and handmade Italian loafers.

The dude had had *silver spoon* stamped on his forehead and giant, unremitting *asshole* scrawled on top of that. And Mac had suffered so much of the guy's sneering, condescending looks that he'd been two seconds away from strangling the cocksucker, when Eve stepped in, cool and unflappable, finally getting the information they needed.

He had to give the woman some serious props. She was the picture of poise and grace, of geniality and charm...well, except when she was around Wild Bill. And now he was back to the first of his day's headaches. He glanced over at Bill only to find the man surreptitiously watching Eve in the rearview mirror. Eve, for her part, was staring out the rear passenger side window and gnawing her lower lip like the thing was tastier than apple pie.

What happened between those two last night to wind them tighter than fiddle strings? he wondered for the zillionth time. Then, quickly following that, he thought, *ah to hell with it.* Because he was done trying to figure them out. It was making his headache worse. Plus, he'd learned long ago it was best to leave all that ooey-gooey stuff to Ace.

Tilting his head from side to side, he was in the middle of working out the kinks in his neck when his iPhone blared the opening bars of "Amarillo Sky."

Damn. Sometimes he missed Texas.

"What's up, Ace?" he asked, holding the phone to his ear.

"Bad news." Ace sounded annoyed. "The motor on the door to the Bat Cave on this end has broken. *Again.* And I can't get the sorry sucker open."

"Shit," Mac muttered, rubbing a thumb against his pounding temple.

"That about sums it up," Ace concurred.

To avoid the reporters hanging out in front of BKI—Samantha Tate had been true to her word, it seemed—they'd exited the Knights' compound that morning via the top-secret underground tunnel that originated behind a heavy, twelve-foot-wide, brick and iron door in the motorcycle shop and terminated in a parking garage across the Chicago River. So, unfortunately, with their only other way back into BKI officially closed for business, they were left with the options of either driving in through the front gate—which couldn't happen because then the reporters would know that Black Knights Inc. came equipped with a very fancy, very illicit backdoor, and wouldn't *that* be just enough to pique their interest?—or he and Bill could stash Eve somewhere safe before frog-manning their way across the Chicago River, scaling the ten-foot-high, razor-wire topped fence commando-style, and helping Ace repair the motor. Fixing that rusting, old behemoth was always a two-, sometimes three-man job.

"Shit," he said again, realizing that instead of a couple of ibuprofen and a quick nap in his future, he was doomed to engage in full-on *Mission Impossible*-style maneuvers. "Hold tight, Ace," he muttered. "I'll call you back in a sec."

When he clicked off the phone, he turned to find Bill watching him with an expression like a biohazardous waste sign. "Let me guess," Bill said. "The motor is broken on the Bat Cave door. *Again.*"

Mac just smiled and nodded, taking a page from Ace's book and batting his lashes.

"Shit," Bill cursed, yanking the steering wheel on the Hummer, maneuvering the beast into a cramped parking space on the side of the street. Slamming the giant SUV out of gear and switching off the engine, he ran a hand through his hair and muttered again, "Shit."

"I'm sensing a theme here," Eve piped up from the back seat, and Mac turned to explain what the problem was and, as a result, what all the only possible solution entailed.

"Well," she shrugged, "I guess you can drop me back at my cousin's condo, or..." She wrinkled her nose. "I suppose I could go to my dad's house. At least that'd stop him from calling me every five seconds."

Bill shot Mac a sharp look.

"Yeah, well, here's the thing," he said, wracking his brain for a way to serve her this bitter pill of truth so that it went down smoothly. Then he realized this was a situation where it was probably best to avoid the *truth*—at least the *whole* truth—altogether. "We'd feel a lot better if we stashed you with someone we know and trust."

"Why?" Her brows formed a perfect V.

Good Lord, the woman was determined to make him perjure himself. He shrugged. "It's just better if you stay away from your usual spots."

"Oh." She nodded, her face clearing. "That makes sense." And he was going straight to hell for being a liar-liar-pants-on-fire. "Okay, so where to?"

Mac glanced at Bill, proposing, "Shell and Snake's house? There's a key to their place in the glove box and—"

"Boss would skin us, fillet us, cook us, eat us, and then use our bones as toothpicks if we involved his sister and his nephew in anything even remotely dangerous," Bill stated. "And that'd be a cakewalk compared to what Snake would do to us once he comes back from Mali."

Mac knew the guy wasn't just being dramatic. Boss, like any good big brother, was extremely overprotective of his sister and her son. And Snake? Well, let's just say that when it came to his wife and child and their safety, the man lived up to his code name. Deadly.

"Okay, so that leaves us with..." He made a rolling motion with his hand, encouraging Bill to offer another option since none of the rest of the Knights had family—or even close friends—living nearby.

"Red Delilah's," Bill said, and Mac's hand stopped turning as every cell in his body started running around like a blind dog in a meat factory. Delilah Fairchild, the owner of the biker bar Bill had just named, was everything Mac'd spent his whole life avoiding.

First, she was beautiful. Okay, that wasn't really

true. She was *beyond* beautiful. From her deep auburn hair and her green eyes that tilted up at the corners, giving her the look of a guileful feline and making it appear as if she were privy to the world's secrets, to her slow, sultry smile that informed everyone around her she wouldn't be sharing with any of them, she was, bar none, the *sexiest* woman he'd ever seen. And that was before you got to her body. Because, *damn*, Mother Nature had given her a set of curves guaranteed to lower any male IQ from within a hundred yards.

Next, she was used to getting any man she wanted. *Any* man. And that kind of power warped a person's psyche. He knew that from experience.

And last, but certainly not least, in any situation he'd seen her involved in, she'd come out on top. Whether it was bar brawls, raucous drunks, or bums who couldn't pay, she was somehow able to manipulate all sides into the middle and get what she wanted from anybody just by being herself. And that crazy ability made every instinct in him yell loud and clear to stay far, *far* away from her.

Unfortunately, she seemed *determined* he should do just the opposite. She was a big ol' scoop of sweet, melting, strawberry ice cream, and she was constantly daring him, *daring* him, to take a bite. She flirted with everyone, that was her nature, but she flat-out *propositioned* him every chance she got. And he was terrified he might one day, in a moment of weakness and unbearable horniness, take her up on one of those offers.

Which would be bad. For *many* reasons…

"I'm not sure Eve will be comfortable hanging out in—" he began but was cut off when Eve said, "Oh, no. That'll be good. I've met Delilah a couple of times. I like her."

Yeah, who doesn't?

"Perfect," Bill restarted the engine. "It's all set, then. We'll drop her at Delilah's then go get wet."

Oh, goody. This day just keeps getting better and better...

Chapter Ten

Red Delilah's Biker Bar
4:38 p.m.

DELILAH FAIRCHILD LIKED FOUR THINGS: HER motorcycle, her bar, her double-barreled shotgun—those folks who treated her right only saw the business ends of her motorcycle and bar—and Sunday nights.

Because Sunday nights were calm, at least when compared to the usual biker bar bullshit and chaos, and they allowed her a much-needed break. Tonight would be filled with the "usuals." The usual customers; those barflies who preferred to spend the last night of the weekend bellied up to a length of nicely polished mahogany. The usual drinks; whiskey and beer, both cheap and straight up. And the usual music on the jukebox; eighties hair bands and hard-driving rockabilly.

For her, this was a little slice of heaven.

And yup, she didn't know if that was poetic or just plain sad...

Running a dishtowel over the ring of condensation left behind by the empty Budweiser bottle she tossed into the thirty-gallon recycling can—the loud *clink* let her know she was about a twelve-pack away from needing to empty the sucker—she asked Buzzard, her most loyal and loveable patron, "Another round?"

"Keep 'em comin', doll face," Buzzard gave her his standard reply, flashing his gold tooth at her as he wiped a couple of stray droplets of beer from the scraggly gray hairs of his beard.

She'd just popped the top on another bottle of the King of Beers when the front door banged open. Late afternoon sunlight spilled into the place, highlighting the red vinyl booths, the buckets of unshelled peanuts sitting beside the tables, and the rough wooden slats of the flooring.

She set the fresh beer in front of Buzzard and moved toward the end of the bar and the empty seats that were the likely landing points of the new arrivals. But she'd gone no more than three steps when the *fifth* thing she liked—she'd totally forgotten to include him on her earlier list; where *had* her head been?—stepped out of the ray of sunlight and waltzed into view.

Okay, maybe not waltzed. Bryan "Mac" McMillan didn't waltz. He swaggered, or maybe *stalked* was a better word, walking with an efficiency that spoke of his previous career as an FBI agent as opposed to his current career as a motorcycle mechanic.

And, yup, there had to be a story there. Just like she knew there had to be a story behind *all* the men at the custom motorcycle shop known as Black Knights Inc. But she found herself only interested in Mac's tale... or was that tail?

She snorted, smiling at her own wit right before her lips curved into a frown.

No matter how much *she* liked Mac, no matter how much his sense of humor, his solid build, and his dauntless loyalty to his friends appealed to her, Mac always treated *her* like she was covered in poison ivy. And, for the life of her, she couldn't fathom why that should be. As far as she knew, she'd never done anything to garner his scorn. From day one, she'd been nothing but smiles and come-ons, so what was his deal?

She narrowed her eyes as she watched his approach, racking her brain and trying to figure it all out. As usual, all she came up with was, *damned if I know...*

Although, one thing she *did* know was that his surliness made the devil in her come out to play. Time and again, she couldn't help but push the buttons that seemed to stand out all over him like porcupine quills. So, pasting on a wide smile, she placed a hand on one cocked hip and used the other to toss her heavy hair over her shoulder. "Whoa," she called out. "Somebody slide me a glass, will ya? Because I just spied me a tall drink of water!"

Buzzard—never one to pass up being part of joke—leaned over the bar, snagged a whiskey tumbler, and slid it in her direction. The rest of the patrons dutifully lifted their drinks, allowing the glass to zip down the wide plank of lacquered mahogany unencumbered until she stopped it with a slap of her palm. Turning, she gave Buzzard a saucy wink.

Her gesture was returned with gusto.

"Gimme a break, will ya, Delilah?" Mac groused, stalking farther into the bar. His voice was low and rough, and with that slow Texas drawl, she figured he could give Sam Elliot a run for his money in that whole smoky, sexy cowboy thing.

"I'd like to give you something," she quipped right back as the front door slammed shut. She instantly recognized the other two people with Mac. Bill Reichert was the quiet, dark-eyed brother of Becky Reichert, the tiny spit-fire of a woman who designed the motorcycles over at Black Knights Inc. And Eve Edens was Chicago's own socialite *du jour* and Becky's best gal pal. And if that wasn't the strangest matchup on Earth, Delilah didn't know what was. One woman wore Chanel; the other wore bearing grease.

"Where's the rest of the crew?" she asked, strolling the last few feet to the empty bar stools. She cocked her head when Eve was the only one to take a seat.

"Busy," Mac said. One word.

"Geez, Mac." She frowned at him. "Let a girl get a word in edgewise, why don't ya?"

Mac growled. Actually growled. And a delighted *zing* of excitement shot up Delilah's spine. She grinned in response.

Bill glanced back and forth between them. "What *is* it with you two anyway? Why are you always sniping at each other?"

Sticking out her bottom lip in a pout, she said the one thing guaranteed to ruffle Mac's already wildly ruffled feathers, "Because Mac won't give me a ride on his pony."

"For Christ's sake, woman!" Mac glared out at her from under his thick eyebrows. *And bingo!* That was the look she'd been waiting on. The one that told her she'd succeeded in *really* nudging him over the edge. "You've got more nerve than my uncle's got liver pills."

Smiling into his flashing eyes, she gave herself a moment to study the face that'd haunted her dreams for the last few years. And, just like always, she was hard pressed to find anything she didn't like. Because Mac had one of those big, square faces typical of his Irish heritage. Only, instead of the red hair and freckles, he sported the coloring of the black Irish: dark brown locks and striking blue eyes.

No one would call him handsome. Not with that sizeable jaw and that nose that listed slightly to the left—no doubt from some long-ago brawl or youthful indiscretion. But Delilah had always been a sucker for his kind of face. The kind that looked like it'd been forged from raw steel, all hard angles and brutal expanses. And that was before she got to his smile. Because his smile? Oh, man, it lit him up like a glow stick. And it tempted a woman to do seriously stupid things to try to keep the expression in place.

Unfortunately—or fortunately, depending on your point of view—right now, he wasn't even close to smiling as he continued to gripe at her, "Has it ever occurred to you to try a little subtlety?"

She made a face before slowly glancing down at her body. In the vernacular of the former generation, she was a brick house. And she didn't say that with any sort of vanity or pride. It was just the way of things, the way she'd been put together since the age of fourteen. It had its pros, it had its cons, but one thing it didn't have was subtlety.

"Are you serious?" she gaped, shaking her head. "What about me leads you to think *subtlety* is an option?"

"I have the feeling," Bill said, "that if I don't cut you two off right now, we'll be here all night. And Mac and I don't have time for that. Delilah," he reached across the bar and patted her shoulder, "we're going to leave Eve in your care for a couple of hours."

"Leave her in my care?" she asked, one brow raised as she glanced at the woman in question. Eve just rolled her eyes. "Why do you need to leave her in my care?"

"It's a long story for another time," Bill assured her, and it occurred to her then that *all* the Black Knights tended to be evasive. None so much as Mac though.

She slid her gaze over to the man, not surprised to find his expression churlish. "Fine," she said. "Good. Whatever." She made a shooing motion with her hands. "Off you go, boys. Leave us girls here alone so we can gossip about you."

She didn't pretend to fight the smile that tilted her lips when she saw Mac's back teeth set. Still, the guy held his tongue as Bill slapped him on the shoulder and motioned with his head toward the front door.

Delilah watched them go, idly wondering what they were up to—excitement generally followed that group of ruffians for one reason or another. And not for the first time, she speculated on whether or not they were running more than motorcycles out of that shop on Goose Island. They weren't a chartered MC—motorcycle club—but that didn't mean they weren't living the whole outlaw lifestyle all the same. And there had to be *some* reason, regardless of their past government and military careers, as to why the BKI boys always wore an air of constantly being on edge, of looking over their shoulders.

Drugs?

Nah, she couldn't see that.

Guns maybe?

But that was just too stereotypical.

Well, whatever it is, as long as they keep it out of my bar, we're golden.

After the front door slammed shut, she turned her attention to Eve. Only Eve wasn't staring back at her. Instead, the woman was gazing wistfully after the departed men.

"Which one?" Delilah asked, a sharp stab of jealously slicing through her. Eve was a gorgeous woman, and even though Delilah hadn't seen Mac on Eve's arm in any of those pictures that ran in the society papers, she could totally envision a guy like him going for a woman like Eve. *Eve* was subtle.

"Which one what?" Eve asked, turning to her.

"Which one of those handsome motorcycle hunks do you wish was your boyfriend?" *Please, don't say Mac. Please, don't say Mac. Please, don't say—*

"I don't wish *anyone* was my boyfriend," Eve stated with forced conviction, wrinkling her nose.

Huh. Delilah reached up to scratch her head, studying the well-coifed woman across the bar. Finally she shook her head and blurted, "Well, you just said that like it's a good thing when, in fact, I'd say it's probably an example of where you've gone wrong in life. Either one of those guys could guarantee a girl a good time and—"

"Billy," Eve blurted, gnawing on her bottom lip.

For someone as pretty, smart, and *rich* as Eve was, it was kind of amazing that she still managed to come off as self-conscious and shy. For the life of her, Delilah couldn't understand it. But perhaps that's because there wasn't an ounce of self-consciousness or shyness in her own makeup, meaning she had little to draw on for empathy.

To each his own, she thought, refusing to look too closely at the wave of relief that washed through her upon Eve's confession. Reaching across the bar to give the woman's hand a sisterly pat, she cocked her head and pursed her lips in consideration. "Bill, huh? Sure, I can see that. He's got that whole ruggedly handsome, Josh Brolin thing going." A little too pretty for her tastes, but again, to each his own. "So, then, why haven't you bought a ticket on that bus?"

Eve frowned and started chewing on the side of her thumb. "Well, probably because of the conversation he and I had this morning, where he made it clear the only stops that…uh…*bus* makes are in Buddyville and Friendtown."

"Ouch," Delilah winced. The Friend Card: the worst one in the deck when it was played by the man a girl dreamed of being so much more. She could relate. Although, come to think of it, Mac hadn't even offered her *that* option. Hell, no. He was firmly holding *all* his cards close to his vest, the exasperating jerk. And when she added, "That sucks," she wasn't sure if she was referring to Eve's situation or her own. Perhaps both?

"Yes," Eve grimaced. "It certainly does."

Shaking away her own troubling thoughts, Delilah pulled on her bartender hat and tapped a ruby-red fingernail on the bar. "But you know what's a guaranteed cure?"

"What?"

"One of my world-class strawberry daiquiris."

Eve smiled wanly before shrugging. "Well, then serve me up. Because I need all the help I can get."

And now they were *really* talking turkey, which was Delilah's forte…every good bartender's forte as a matter of fact. She was a pro at hashing out troubles and patching up heartbreak with Band-Aids in the form of alcoholic beverages.

"Still," she propped a hip against the bar, narrowing her eyes at Eve, "I'm sensing there's more here than a simple rejection. I'm sensing you've been…what? Having a bit of a dry spell, maybe?"

"Dry spell?"

"You know," she waved her hand through the air. "No sex, or *bad* sex, which is sometimes *worse* than no sex."

Eve's blush stretched from the roots of her hair into the collar of her delicate-looking blouse. Delilah lifted a brow. She'd never seen someone actually *do* that, and *she* was a natural redhead…

Glancing down at the bar, Eve cleared her throat softly, and whispered, "Between you and me, I haven't had sex, good, bad, or anything in between, for years. I have enough pent-up sexual energy to power all of Chicago for a month."

Delilah chuckled. "I hear ya, sister."

Eve flashed her a look of disbelief.

"Hey," she motioned toward her boobs, held up by an industrial-strength underwire bra and tight T-shirt, "don't let these things fool you. I'm incredibly choosy when it comes to men."

Eve bit her lip, smiling, more comfortable now that they'd both shared confidences. It was another hallmark of any good bartender. "And you'd choose Mac if he let you?"

"In a heartbeat," she admitted. "But, alas, he wants no part of me." She shook her head, frowning, thinking back on all his rejections and trying and failing not to feel the sharp sting of them. *What does he have against me?* Again, she racked her brain and came up with a big ol' handful of…nothing. "I think I'll join you in that strawberry daiquiri," she told Eve who laughed delightedly.

"I'd love that."

Nodding, Delilah turned toward the freezer. Pulling out a bag of frozen strawberries and some ice, she mulled over Mac's decree that she could use a little subtlety—Subtlety? Her? *Pfft, as if*—as she dumped the load in the blender before adding sugar, lime juice, lemon juice, and top shelf rum. From the corner of her eye, she saw Eve fiddling with her phone, playing a game or texting or something. Then the device jingled out the opening bars to a Styx song and, with half an ear, she caught the woman's exasperated-sounding, "Enough with the phone calls, Dad. I'm fine." That was followed up by, "No, I'm not going to come back home. And, *no*, I'm not going to make it to our weekly dinner tonight. Didn't you read the email I sent you this morning?" Delilah hit the button on the machine, drowning out the rest of the conversation, and allowed herself to focus all her efforts on forgetting about one infuriating ex-FBI agent turned motorcycle mechanic.

~

Somewhere on Lake Shore Drive
5:13 p.m.

He ran a hand over his mouth once he thumbed off the cell phone, staring at the device as his heart thundered out a terrible rhythm. The time was now. It was do or die. Meaning, he'd better *do* what he'd promised or he was likely going to *die*.

It was awful, really, what it'd all come down to. But self-preservation won out every day of the week. And, yes, he fully realized there'd be many who'd disagree with him. Many who'd think he was the scum of the Earth for choosing himself over her. Hell, even *he* would've shouted from the rooftops a couple of years ago that no way, no how would he sacrifice her to save himself. But that's only because he hadn't been faced with the actual choice back then. When a person was faced with the actual choice of their life in exchange for the life of someone they loved, convictions often crumbled.

His certainly had...

It's time. Time to finally end it.

Taking a deep breath, he punched in a number that made his upper lip curl with distaste.

"Yo," a man whose accent was pure Southside Chicago gangster answered. "You got a location for us or what?"

"I do," he said. "She's at Red Delilah's biker bar for the next hour or so. Hurry."

"Don't you worry. We'll finish the job you were too chicken-shit to do on your own."

Wishing he could reach through the phone and shove his thumb in the fucker's eye, he satisfied himself instead by jamming a finger down on the phone's keypad, instantly ending the call.

"Goddamn sonsofbitches," he growled into the empty room, reaching for the decanter of scotch, disgusted to find his hands were shaking.

I'm sorry, my dear, sweet Eve, he thought as he raked in a steadying breath. *I wish there could've been another way...*

Chapter Eleven

Red Delilah's Biker Bar
6:01 p.m.

FIGHTING WITH THE COLORFULLY LIT JUKEBOX, trying to get the darned thing to accept her five-dollar bill, Eve felt woozy. And sad.

The wooziness was a direct result of having gulped down two of Delilah's world-class strawberry daiquiris in record time. The sadness was a direct result of the way her life was going.

Oh, let me count the ways...

For starters, her PhD—the goal she'd been striving toward for three, long years—was on indefinite hold because not only had her laptop burned up in her condo fire, but now all her dissertation materials were sitting at the bottom of Lake Michigan. Also, someone, possibly someone she *knew*, was out there right now with a mind to kill her. And as if those two things weren't bad enough, it now appeared that her love life—never a thing of beauty except for a brief, three-month period twelve years ago—was floating in the toilet while the Fates fiddled with the lever.

Yep. It's official. You're a real piece of work, Eve Edens.

She was just about to give up on the jukebox when the fickle machine suddenly decided that, yes, in fact it *was* hungry. It sucked in her money in one greedy gulp.

Victory!

It was a small win, sure, but at this point she was taking what she could get.

Scrolling through the options, she choked on a strangled sob when one particular number met her bleary gaze. Punching in the request for the tune, she used the rest of her money to jump the other songs currently waiting in the musical queue and turned just as the first driving drumbeat sounded.

This song reminded her of that magical summer with Billy and—

"Boo!" one of the patrons shouted. "No contemporary country music allowed on Sundays!"

"Can it, Buzzard!" Delilah yelled from behind the bar, throwing an olive at a bearded man Eve recognized from the two previous times she'd been in Red Delilah's. Idly, she wondered if the old, pot-bellied biker actually *lived* there. Maybe he had a sleeping bag somewhere in the back? But then Eric Church started singing about young love and loss, and she closed her eyes, letting the familiar lyrics of "Springsteen" wash over her, wallowing—yes, *wallowing;* a girl was allowed to do that on occasion—in her own regret.

A memory of Billy lying with his head in her lap on a patchwork quilt under a tree in Grant Park, listening as she read from *Breakfast at Tiffany's*, stumbled through her slightly sluggish, strawberry daiquiri-addled brain. He'd been idly twirling a yellow flower—A dandelion? She couldn't recall precisely—between his thumb and forefinger. And when she glanced down at him, down into his handsome face dappled with the sunlight spilling in through the leaves, she expected to find his warm, laughing eyes closed. But his gaze hadn't been shuttered by his lids and long, dark lashes. Just the opposite, in fact. He'd been looking right at her, and the expression on his face? Oh, sweet Lord, it'd made her heart jump in her chest. Okay, not jump. *Leap!* Because it was the first time she'd ever seen *love* in a man's eyes. And not those pale-by-comparison kinds of loves like *puppy* or *platonic*. Heck no. It was *romantic* love. And oh, it'd frightened her almost as much as it'd delighted her...

Wistfully swaying beside the jukebox, lost in the bittersweet memory, she was completely caught off-guard and more than a little stunned—her eyes snapping wide—when the front door flew open with a *bang*. Of course, even more shocking than the unexpected interruption was the man in baggy jeans, gold chains, and a ski mask who immediately charged inside.

"Hands in the air!" he yelled, holding a nickel-plated pistol out in front of him gangster-style, on its side, just as a second, similarly attired gunman stepped over the threshold.

Of course, there's another gunman, she thought with distaste, her mind working a little slowly due to either the shock or the second daiquiri or, more likely, both. *Like nuns, guys like these always travel in pairs.*

Only this duo was far from anything holy...

The second thought to stumble through her

sluggish brain was, *geez, I just can't catch a break, can I?* The third thought was *he's holding that gun all wrong.* And the fourth thought, the most *appropriate* thought—Hello! Finally, the right synapses were firing—was *oh, crap!* But before she could form a fifth thought, the unmistakable *chick-schnick* of a shotgun being wracked assaulted her ears.

"You picked the wrong place to rob, my friends," Delilah growled, and Eve's eyes flashed toward the bar. The redheaded proprietress was standing there looking, for all intents and purposes, like a playboy model—except for the teensy, tiny fact that she had a sawed-off shotgun pressed tightly against her shoulder, and a deadly challenge gleaming in her green eyes. "And in case you're too stupid to understand ballistics, let me give you a lesson." Her voice was tough and strident, not belying an ounce of the fear Eve knew she *had* to be feeling. "The chances of me tearing you to shreds with this here scatter-gun are much higher than you hitting me with one of those nine millimeter slugs."

The masked men seemed to hesitate, then the one closest to the open door turned to look directly at Eve.

"There she is," he said. And before she could *begin* to contemplate what on God's green Earth he could possibly mean by that, he raised a gun toward her head.

Yep. Gun. Raised. Toward. Her. Head...

Everything that happened next was a blur, because her self-defense training kicked in and she instinctively dove for the man's ankles. Knocking him off balance, he crashed onto her back, crushing her and forcing all the air from her lungs like she'd been punched in the sternum.

"Uhhhhh," she gasped, raking in much-needed air and the not-so-much-needed aromas of heavy cologne and weed. Fear sizzled along each of her nerve-endings until she was the human version of a live wire, and it combined with the hot burst of adrenaline to give her more strength than she would have under normal circumstances. When she pushed up from the floor, she was able to partially dislodge her assailant. And then the fight was on!

"Bitch!" he yelled as they became a tangled mess of grappling arms and kicking legs, each wrestling for control of the weapon with a killing intensity. It seemed like hours passed as they strained and struggled, heaved and bucked. But in reality, it was probably only seconds. Then, Eve misjudged which way the gunman was moving, and he was able to use her lapse along with his superior strength to pin her to the floor. His black eyes bored into her from the holes in his ski mask, promising death.

If you think I'm done, her burning eyes screamed up at him, *then you're dead wrong! I'm not going down without a fight, by God!*

She wrapped both fists around the wrist of his gun hand, grunting and snarling while simultaneously kicking and flailing to try to heave him off her. But to her utter horror, with both of her hands occupied with the task of preventing the masked man from pointing that Smith and Wesson at her head, there was nothing to stop him from reaching over with his free hand to enclose her throat in a meaty grip. Which was exactly what he did.

Instantly her brain buzzed from lack of oxygen, and darkness edged into her vision.

Oh, no! Help me, Lord, I'm losing it!

Her vision tunneled, and she couldn't seem to form a whole thought. As her world dimmed, she vaguely registered the *boom* of a shotgun and the wall next to the front door exploding in a shower of splinters.

Bam! The first gunman returned fire, and in a tiny corner of Eve's mind she recognized the sound of bottles breaking.

Miraculously, the gunplay was enough to distract her attacker, and with only the most instinctual portion of her brain working, she saw an opportunity. *Now!* Twisting the gun from her opponent's hand, she wanted to yell in triumph when the warm metal settled into her fist. But the sweat on her palms, and the fact that there was a two-hundred-pound man strangling her, precluded any whoop of victory and had the weapon slipping from her grip.

It fell to the wooden slats of the floor with a loud *thump*. The masked man released her throat to make a grab for it, and she barely had enough time to drag in a wheezing breath that instantly snapped the world into focus before she was wholly occupied in the mad scuffle and scramble to retrieve the dropped pistol. She twisted out from under her attacker, latching onto his wrists. But in the process she inadvertently kicked the gun beneath the happily playing jukebox.

Damnit!

Boom! Another blast of the shotgun, this time aimed directly above her assailant's head. The top of the jukebox shattered, the music coming to a record-scratching halt, and a shower of colorful glass rained down on them like sharp, stinging confetti. In the ear-ringing silence that followed, her attacker, now relieved of his weapon, must've figured Delilah was right about that lesson in ballistics. Because he scrambled to his feet and dove for the open door.

Eve flipped onto her stomach in time to see his Nikes disappear over the threshold.

Delilah had just saved her life…

But for how long?

Her head weighed a hundred pounds, but she still managed to lift it, fully expecting that when she did she'd be staring down the barrel of the first gunman's weapon, but—

Boom! A third blast from the shotgun.

This time, Delilah caught a piece of the first masked man's leg, shredding his jeans and the flesh beneath. He howled in agony, grabbing at the wound with one hand and squeezing the trigger of his pistol with the other. Bullets exploded from the gun in quick, ear-shattering succession as the gangster wildly laid down covering fire, his limping retreat toward the door leaving a shower of blood droplets in his wake. A light fixture burst with a crash. The red vinyl cushion on an empty booth belched up a cloud of cotton stuffing after absorbing a round.

Eve once more covered her head, her blood rushing through her veins so hard and fast it sounded like a waterfall roaring between her ears. When she breathed, the acrid smell of cordite and the iron-like aroma of hemoglobin filled her nose, making her fight the urge to gag. A vehicle roared to life followed by the sound of tires squealing. Through the swinging front door, she caught a glimpse of what appeared to be a white van hauling butt away from the place.

Then, silence reigned…

For one heartbeat, maybe two, the world stopped spinning, and Eve glanced up to find the bar set in a motionless tableau. Patrons littered the floor, hands over their heads, completely and totally frozen in fear. Then, an ear-piercing scream splintered the silence, and Eve turned to see Delilah scrambling over the bar, the bartender's pretty face twisted with horror.

What…?

But then she saw it. The potbellied biker—Buzzard?—was slumped on his stool, a ghastly river of red dripping down his stomach and pants, pooling beneath his dangling black biker boots in a slick, gruesome puddle.

"No!" Delilah screamed, pressing a hand to the gushing wound in the center of Buzzard's chest. "No, Buzzard! No!"

Eve was the first to jump to her feet, hurdling prone patrons as she raced toward her purse still sitting on the bar, digging frantically for her cell phone.

Where are you? Where the heck are—

When she finally found it, she punched in 9-1-1 with shaky fingers and looked over at Buzzard—Delilah was sobbing hysterically and continuing to try to apply pressure to that gruesome wound. To her utter horror, she discovered the man's eyes were open and vacant, staring at nothing but death.

Oh, sweet Lord, no...

"Nine, one, one. What's your emergency?" a nasally voice sounded over the phone.

"I-I need an ambulance at..." she had to swallow the bile and tears burning up the back of her throat. "At Red Delilah's biker bar." She gave the address. "A man has been sh-shot."

The emergency operator asked her a question, but she didn't hear it as the phone slipped from her nerveless fingers.

There she is. That's what the second gunman said before raising his weapon. Which meant they'd come here for her. To kill *her*. But instead...Buzzard was dead.

And *that* meant this was all her fault...

No God, no! She choked on a sob, her knees threatening to buckle beneath her, but she refused to give in to the grief and hysteria bubbling just beneath her surface. It might be too late to help Buzzard, but perhaps she could still help poor Delilah...

The Corner of Western and North Avenues
6:32 p.m.

"What in the world?" Bill heard Mac yell over the grumbling sound of dual V-twin engines. He gripped Phoenix's handlebars tighter as he squinted up the block to where the red-blue-red flash of emergency vehicle lights bounced menacingly against the surrounding buildings.

They'd kinda, sorta, pseudo-fixed the Bat Cave door. But the thing was still acting sketchy as fuck, sometimes opening and closing of its own volition, so they'd decided to ditch the Hummer in exchange for the bikes. Especially considering that the tunnel was such a tight fit for the giant SUV that opening the doors of the vehicle once *inside* the sucker was nearly impossible.

Yeah, to say neither one of them had fancied the idea of getting stuck inside the Hummer down in the tunnel and having to pull the Holy Grail of all reverse maneuvers back out to the exit in the parking garage was putting it mildly. Bill just hoped Eve was okay with riding—

"I think that's Delilah's!" Mac's voice sliced into his thoughts.

He realized in that moment, as he twisted his wrist and blazed through the red light and cross traffic—heedless of the sound of squealing tires on either side of him and the fact that the silver bumper on a Chevy half-ton pickup truck came within an inch of his biker boot—what it meant when people said their hearts froze. Because his stopped beating, turned to a hard fist of dry ice in his chest, and proceeded to burn a hole straight through his soul.

Eve...

He wasn't thinking when he blasted into the little parking lot in front of Red Delilah's, Phoenix's fat rear tire bouncing over the curb until his teeth clacked together with brain-jostling force. He wasn't thinking when he toed out the kickstand and jumped from the bike, switching off the growling engine. He wasn't thinking when he ran toward the waiting ambulance and the body-bag-laden stretcher being loaded inside.

"Eve!" He frantically tossed off the restraining hands of the police officers who leapt toward him, instinctively shoving an elbow into someone's nose. "Eve! Eve!" His wailing, breathless cries howled from him like the wind blowing over the dunes in the desert. His lungs worked like bellows, but no oxygen got to his brain.

"Stand down, asshole!" one of the officers shouted in his ear, snaking an arm around his throat as two, then three more uniformed CPD boys tried to wrestle him to the ground. He fought them like he was fighting for his life, hissing and biting, punching and kicking. He was a mindless beast, bent on only one thing: getting inside that ambulance and—

"Billy!"

When he heard his name, when he heard her sweet voice, all the fight seeped out of him like air from a torn balloon. He choked on a hard, wet sob that lodged in the center of his chest. Then, the next thing he knew, he was kissing concrete, there were an unknown number of very pointy knees digging into his back, and his wrists were being secured by a cold, hard set of handcuffs.

He didn't care. Because she was alive! The CPD could take out their billy clubs and pound the living shit out of him for the rest of the evening if they wanted to, and he'd still be smiling.

"Get off him! Get off him!" From the corner of his eye—the one not being ground into the parking lot's hot pavement—he could see Eve pushing officers aside. "He's with me!"

Slowly, the restraining hands disappeared, as did the pointy knees. And after a ringing command from Eve that someone should help him up, two policemen grabbed his elbows and hauled him to his feet. The very next instant, Eve was pressed against him. Her arms were around his neck, her head was on his shoulder—the smell of her fruity shampoo obscured the more pungent aroma of car exhaust—and she was sobbing and squeezing him so tightly he could barely breathe.

Who cares? Oxygen is overrated anyway.

"Jesus, Eve..." Her name was a benediction and a prayer all rolled into one. He wasn't a religious man, but he whispered a quick thanks skyward to anyone who might be listening and went to wrap his arms around her, to hold her close to his pounding heart. But the handcuffs stopped him with the bite of unyielding steel.

"Get these fucking things off me," he growled at the officer closest to him.

The man wiped a hand under his bleeding nose—apparently this was the one Bill'd clocked with his elbow—and glowered. Then the policeman took a deep breath, obviously deciding he might've done the same thing had he thought the body of someone he cared about was being loaded into a waiting ambulance, and moved to oblige Bill's request.

Bill had just enough time to wonder uneasily at the direction of his thoughts—*Someone he cared about?*—when the handcuffs disappeared and his mind blanked because…*heaven.* She was safe in his arms, warm and alive and breathing his name into the space where his T-shirt ended and his chest began.

"What happened here, Eve?" He dipped his chin to whisper against her ear, the delicate shell felt baby-soft against his lips, and the subtle smell of her lotion elicited an ill-timed response from the imbecile housed behind his zipper.

For the love of God, nuclear bombs could be exploding around me and being this close to Eve would still have me springing a chubby.

She pulled back, and he recognized the look on her tear-soaked face. He'd seen it plenty of times in the killing fields of this war or that conflict. It was a combination of shock and horror…and guilt. And it was enough to take the edge off his unrepentant libido.

"Th-that was s-s-supposed to be me." She nodded toward the ambulance, her expression caving in on itself, her slender form quaking like a rickety telephone pole on the edge of an immense fault line. "They c-came here for m-me."

Supposed to be her? What?

"What do you mean?" he demanded, instinctively thumbing away a glistening tear from her smooth cheek, growling when he noticed the circle of angry bruises darkening up around her neck making the white of her pearl pendant stand out in harsh contrast. He'd seen that before, too. Some sorry sonofabitch had tried to strangle Eve. Some sorry, *dead* sonofabitch should Bill ever find him and get his hands on him…

"Th-the men who killed Buzzard," she choked.

Buzzard? He glanced toward the ambulance, then closed his eyes as a wedge of remorse briefly invaded his mounting rage. The rascally biker had been an annoying, charming, and licentious old fart by turns. But he'd been a decent fellow, all things considered. And he'd certainly deserved a shitload better than whatever violent end he'd obviously met. "He caught a stray bullet," she went on, and once again his heart stopped cold because…*bullet.* There'd been fucking bullets involved? *Jesus Christ.* "But it was a bullet meant for…for *me.*"

Her voice rose with each syllable, and he knew the sounds of hysteria and shock when he heard them. Soon, she was very likely to either completely lose it or go catatonic. He'd seen both, experienced both, and he wasn't sure which was better. One allowed the horror to spill out in a vile, endless stream. The other allowed it to slowly simmer until the terror coagulated and hardened into something awful that you carried around inside yourself for life.

Sweet Jesus, how he wished he could take it all away. Just pluck the experience from her psyche and take it into his own, lock it in the box where he kept all *his* unspeakable memories…

"H-he…he said," Eve stammered, and he could tell she was becoming more and more unstrung with each passing second. "He said, *there she is* and pointed his gun at me. I dove for him. We…we struggled. So…

so—" She couldn't go on, and he did the only thing he could think to do. He pulled her against him again, holding her as tight as he could.

So, whoever wanted to kill her had found her here at Delilah's? But how?

Confusion and rage warred inside him for supremacy. But he knew neither of those emotions was what Eve needed from him now. So tamping down his desire to ask more questions or just begin to arbitrarily kill everybody she knew for good measure, he cupped the back of her warm head in his palm and tried his best to hold her together because she felt like she was about to blow apart.

Then, she did something so shocking he could only stand there like a friggin' idiot.

She kissed him.

One second the woman's nose was buried in the crook of his shoulder, and the next second she grabbed his ears and slammed her mouth—her *open* mouth—over the top of his.

And unlike that girl he'd known years ago, this one didn't hesitate. There was no slow, tentative tasting, or gentle foray of her tongue into his mouth. Hell, no. This was the kiss equivalent of zero to sixty in less than a second, and all he could do was blink at her blurry face in cross-eyed confusion for a long moment during which time she kissed him so passionately he was surprised he didn't just melt into a puddle of lust around his biker boots.

Eventually, however, instinct and bone-deep hunger took over, and he reached up to palm her tear-wet cheeks, angling her head so he could join in on the two-tongued fun fair they had going.

And, it was confession time again. Because, he didn't give a rat's ass that this was undoubtedly one of those instances when a person had mistaken grief for lust. He didn't give a rat's ass that she'd likely regret this in about two seconds flat…that he'd likely regret it, too. Because for one blessedly passionate moment, the past was forgotten. For one brilliant instant, it was just the two of them, locked together, giving in to the flame of desire that'd burned in them since the moment they first locked eyes on each other.

She moved against him, her whole body sinuously sliding, and she was sultry and hot when he pushed his thigh between her legs. And then sanity returned. For her, not for him. He'd have probably laid her down right there in the parking lot if she hadn't suddenly pulled back, blinking up at him with over-bright eyes and an expression of…

What was that? Confusion? Regret? Horror?

He didn't have time to figure it out, or to contemplate the ramifications of what it meant to have lost his control around her *yet again*, because movement out of the corner of his eye snagged his attention. He looked over to find Delilah standing in the doorway of the bar, dried blood streaked down her T-shirt.

She looked like an extra in a slasher film. Scratch that, she looked that the *slasher* in a slasher film, because her expression was straight-up, undiluted I'm-shithouse-crazy-enough-to-kill-someone-right-now. Nostrils flaring, jaw grinding, fists clenching and unclenching, she stepped into the parking lot and started marching stiffly toward Mac.

Oh, damn.

Bill knew what was coming before the loud *smack* of Delilah's open palm meeting Mac's hard jaw echoed around the block. The former FBI agent's head snapped back and to the side, emphasizing the strength of the blow. But no sooner had he shaken off the harsh strike than Delilah was grabbing the collar of his light-weight motorcycle jacket and screaming into his face, "How *dare* you bring whatever bullshit you're involved in to my doorstep, you bastard!"

Chapter Twelve

EVE PUSHED AWAY FROM BILLY'S WARM, REASSURING, oh-so-deliciously-solid chest—she could not *believe* she'd just kissed him or, considering their talk this morning, that he'd actually kissed her back—when she heard Delilah's words explode into the noisy city air. All the blood that'd been sizzling through her veins because of Billy's scorching kiss instantly froze into solid red rivers of ice.

No. Oh, no! Delilah couldn't blame this on Mac. She just *couldn't*. This wasn't Mac's fault. It was *her* fault. All her fault…

Without a second thought, she turned and raced toward the tussling couple. Through her tears—was she crying?—she could see Mac dragging Delilah around the corner and into the alley where he wrapped her in a reverse bear hug, seizing her from behind by securing her wrists low across her waist as he bodily lifted her from the ground until all she could do was kick ineffectually as she screamed profanities hot enough to blister the ears off a sailor.

"Delilah," she breathed. Was that her voice? Why did it sound like that? Like it was being pushed through water. "It's n-not Mac's f-fault."

But her words were too hoarse and too quiet for Delilah to hear, and before she could swallow and try again, Billy stopped a group of police officers from moving in to investigate the commotion. "Gentlemen, my friend back there doesn't need any help. He's man enough to handle what she's dishing; don't you worry."

One of the officers eyed him skeptically, and Billy made a face. "She's hurt and grieving," he explained, and Eve knew all about that, didn't she? "And she needs to take it out on someone. She's decided to take it out on him." He pointed his chin toward the alley where Mac and Delilah had moved out of sight. "And like I said, he's man enough to handle it."

The policeman nodded once before motioning for the rest of the officers to follow him to the ambulance.

The ambulance…

Eve winced when the loud *thunk* of its door slamming shut ricocheted around the parking lot. Holy moly, if there was ever a sound of absolute finality, then that was definitely it. Instantly, her blood thawed, rushing through her system and pooling in her head until she was dizzy.

Don't look. Don't look.

But she couldn't help herself. Turning, she saw a medic hop into the passenger seat of the ambulance. A heartbeat later, the vehicle's lights began flashing accompanied by…silence. Deafening, head-splitting, soul-shattering silence. There was no blaring siren or honking horn, just the sad rumble of a big engine turning over and the quiet crackling of tires rolling over rock-strewn pavement.

Which, *dear God*, was so much worse.

It emphasized the fact that this was no emergency. That the life this ambulance had raced in to rescue was beyond salvation. That the life had been cut short because somehow, in some way, *she* had done something to someone that was so horrible they were determined to see her dead.

This is all my fault...

Again, the sentence circled through her overwrought brain, and the shaking she thought she'd finally gotten under control returned with brutal, teeth-clacking force. The urge to scream her frustration and regret and guilt overwhelmed her. It built in her chest, burning like a jellyfish sting as it seared its way up her throat, singeing the tissue in its path until she wondered if she'd ever speak or swallow correctly again. But just before she opened her mouth to let loose with all the dark emotions bubbling and seething inside her, Billy was there, wrapping a steadying arm around her shoulders and bending to whisper in her ear.

"This isn't your fault, sweetheart," he crooned in his deep, smooth baritone. "The men who did this are the ones to blame. No one but them, you understand me? No one killed Buzzard but *them*."

And more than his words, it was the feel of his warm breath against the side of her jaw, the smell of him, all buttery leather and strong soap, that gave her enough strength to swallow down the scream burning at the back of her throat.

Keep it together, Eve, she coached herself as she rolled in her lips, the world around her nothing but a hazy kaleidoscope of colors through her tears. She wanted to believe Billy. Oh, how she wanted to believe him. *Keep it together for Delilah's sake...*

And suddenly she remembered where she'd been heading before the police and the ambulance's departure distracted her. "We have to go help Mac," she said.

"Like I told the police, Mac can—"

"No," she shook her head vehemently. "Delilah thinks this is Mac's fault." And there was no way she could allow Mac to take the fall for something she'd done. Once upon a time she might have taken that coward's way out. But not anymore. And if she had any say in it, never again. Eve Edens was *done* being a coward.

Grabbing Billy's big hand, she stumbled across the lot and around the corner of the building to the shaded alley where a set of metal stairs led to a back door on the second story of the bar. The air smelled dank and musty, likely due to the four green trash bins pushed up against the building on the opposite side of the narrow space. Mac was standing in front of the nearest one, still holding Delilah in a reverse bear hug, and the poor bartender was still whipping around like a sea snake caught by the tail.

"And *you!*" she shrieked the instant she saw Billy. "You're as much to blame! Buzzard's dead because—"

Billy dropped Eve's hand in order to step up to Delilah. Gently, he placed a palm on each of her red, splotchy, tear-soaked cheeks.

"No," he told her quietly. Just that one word.

But it was that one word, spoken with absolute conviction, that had the fight abandoning Delilah. The kicking and the thrashing stopped, and she hung limp as a rag doll in Mac's big arms, quietly sobbing.

"Delilah, I'm so sorry," Eve whispered quietly, stepping up to the woman, nodding at Mac to lower the poor creature to the ground. And though the words were heartfelt, they sounded hollow, even to her own ears. Because nothing she could say would ever accurately convey the depth of her remorse.

A man was dead from a bullet intended for her. It was that simple. And that horrible. She knew she'd always carry the guilt of it with her.

When Mac lowered Delilah to the ground, the grief-stricken woman crumpled into Eve's arms, and Eve choked on the sobs she could no longer hold at bay. It didn't matter. They were women, so they clung to each other and cried together, taking strength and lending it in the way only the females of the species could do.

Then, after a time, their tears slowed, and Eve blubbered out the truth, "It's my fault. D-don't blame Mac and…and Billy. It has nothing to do with them. I brought this to your doorstep. Th-those men came to your bar to k-kill *me*."

Delilah pushed out of her embrace, rubbing a forearm under her runny nose to blink at her blearily. "I know they did," she nodded, wiping away her tears with a perfunctory swipe of her hand. "I h-heard what that one said when he saw you."

There she is… The words were etched on the back of Eve's brain with a carving knife.

"But after Bill told me he was leaving you in my care, I just…" Delilah shrugged miserably. "I just figured it must have something t-to do with whatever shady dealings they're involved in out on Goose Island and—"

"We're not involved in any shady dealings," Mac muttered, brow furrowed in a deep scowl.

Eve wiped away her own tears as she slid the man a look of utter disbelief. How could he say that with such conviction when their business was the *definition* of shady? Then again, he probably thought Delilah meant *shady* as in *illegal*, so maybe that's how he could pull off that whole hook-me-up-to-a-lie-detector-right-now-and-see-I'm-telling-God's-honest-truth expression.

Delilah narrowed her eyes, the very picture of skepticism. "You're involved in *something* out there," she maintained, and even through the riot of her emotions, Eve had to give it to the woman. Delilah's instincts were spot-on. Unlike hers. Because *she* hadn't believed Becky about the true nature of the men of Black Knights Inc. until the moment she saw Billy, dressed from head to toe in black, sneaking up behind a Somali pirate in order to point a rather terrifying machine gun at the man's head. *Then* she'd believed. Boy, oh boy, had she ever. Kind of hard not to when the truth was wearing black and green face paint and staring you smack-dab between the eyes. "It's in the way you carry yourselves, always on alert," Delilah continued, underscoring her astuteness. "So, what is it? Drugs? Guns? Forgeries? Money laundering?"

Holy smokes, honey, you're way *off.*

"We carry ourselves like a group of guys who've

seen the darkest side of life and who've learned not to trust their fellow man," Mac insisted.

Delilah didn't try to disguise her look of disbelief. "Fine," she spat. "So whatever *side* business you have going," Mac growled like a grizzly bear, but Delilah ignored him, "may not be a contributing factor to what happened in my bar tonight." And saying the words must've reminded the woman of the one she'd lost, because her chin trembled, and Eve's immediately threatened to follow suit—*the stupid sympathetic thing!* But Delilah kept it together, which helped Eve to do the same. And after dragging in a steadying breath, Delilah continued, "But the questions remain," now she turned to pin a pointed look on Eve, "*why* did they come here to kill you and *who* were they?"

"Those *are* the questions, now aren't they?"

Eve spun when she heard her cousin's voice. He was marching down the alley with his badge clipped to the waistband of his jeans and murder written all over his handsome face. She'd never been so happy to see him in her entire life. "Jeremy!" she choked, running to him.

He caught her in a fierce embrace. "Jesus Christ, Eve! I came the minute I heard it over the radio. Are you okay?"

"It w-was awful," she sobbed, pressing her nose into his light blue button-down shirt and dragging in the familiar smell of his cologne.

"Yeah," he nodded, gently pushing her back so he could run his eyes over her from head to toe. "I heard that, too." And if she thought he'd had murder written all over his face before, then *mass* murder was written all over his face now that he saw the bruises on her throat. He hooked a thumb under her chin to tilt her head back, but she batted his hand away.

"It's nothing," she assured him. "I'm fine." His lips twisted, his eyes calling her bluff. "O-okay," she admitted. "I'm not fine. But I'm alive. And that's more than I can say for s-some."

Dang it! Her lower lip started to wobble again, which caused Jeremy's jaw to saw from side to side.

"This isn't your fault, Cuz," he assured her. And, yep, everybody kept telling her that, but somehow she just couldn't bring herself to believe it. "Nod your head so I know you heard me," he commanded. She nodded just so he'd hush up about it. Her guilt and culpability weren't anything she wanted to talk about. At least not right now. "Good." He threw an arm around her shoulders, leading her back to the group where his attention immediately turned to Bill and Mac. "So, the CPD knows *why* they came here. To off Eve." The way he said it had tears once more pricking behind her eyes. She must've shaken or something, because he squeezed her closer to his side, his fingers firm on her shoulder, offering her the comfort of his strength. "But the jury is still out as to *who* they were."

And now they'd come full circle, hadn't they? Because that was the question Delilah had posed before Jeremy arrived on the scene. She met Delilah's red-rimmed gaze head-on. "I swear to you, I have no idea."

Delilah searched for the truth in her face, and she

must've found it, because she nodded. And then her expression sharpened. "All those things I've been reading about you in the paper...Those weren't accidents, were they?"

Yep, and talk about astute. Maybe Delilah should join the gang at Black Knights Inc. The woman was certainly proving she had the instincts for it. Without hesitation, Eve laid it all on the line—she figured Delilah deserved that—and told her about the fire, the mugging, the cut brake lines, and the police closing the cases. "And when nobody would believe me," she finished, "I went to Black Knights Inc., hoping they could help me figure out who's doing this."

Delilah's green eyes narrowed, and she blinked rapidly as if she were physically trying to take it all in—and having trouble in the endeavor. Eve had to admit, it was quite a tale. "Because Mac is a former FBI agent," Delilah finally murmured, "you thought he'd be able to succeed where the CPD failed?"

"Yes," she said, hoping Jeremy didn't feel her stiffen at the question. "Th-that's what I figured."

Delilah fell into a long silence as she glanced off into the distance. The thousand-yard stare...Eve remembered Becky referring to such a thing, but until this moment she wasn't sure she'd actually ever seen it. Then again, she'd never taken part in an all-out gun battle either, so, *yippee! Lots of firsts today!*

Mac was the one to finally break into the quiet pall that'd momentarily fallen over the group. He lifted a hand toward Jeremy. "Mac McMillan." His deep Texas twang was softer than usual. "Sorry to be meetin' you for the first time under these circumstances."

"Likewise." Jeremy shook his hand.

"They were hired guns," Billy blurted, and everyone in the group turned to stare at him.

"What?" Jeremy was the first to recover. "How do you figure that?" Eve seconded that question.

"Two reasons," Billy said, and something in Eve told her she wasn't going to like where he was going with this. "The first one being that the nature of the other attempts on her life led us to believe whoever is behind this thing is someone she knows."

Sweet Jesus help her, she couldn't begin to fathom who that could be...And the fact that Jeremy instinctively hugged her closer, a slight tremor running down the length of his big body? Well, that just made it all the more terrifying. Because he was Jeremy, the guy who'd punched out Todd Stockwell for pinching her butt from beneath the bleachers. Jeremy, the guy who'd raced to her rescue the night she found out her marriage was a sham. Jeremy, the guy who put seriously bad men behind bars on a daily basis. He wasn't supposed to get scared. But she could tell he was. He was scared. Scared for her.

"And considering how the witnesses described these two men," Billy continued, "they don't exactly sound like the types to find themselves on the inside of Eve's social circle."

Erm...yes, so *that* was putting it mildly. The only guy she knew who even came *close* to wearing gold chains was Preston Ferrell who sometimes, for a laugh, donned the gold medal he'd won in the 1998 winter Olympics.

"Okay." Delilah cocked her head, looking far steadier, suddenly, than Eve was feeling. *This is bad*, a little voice whispered through her head, followed immediately by, *this is really bad.* She wanted to tell the little bugger to shove off, because she *knew* things were bad. They had been for months and—"So," Delilah continued, "what's the second reason?"

"Well," Billy said, and the look on his face when he slid her a quick glance? Holy cow, it was enough to give her nightmares.

Don't say it! she wanted to scream at him. *Don't say what I don't want to hear! Don't say what I'll* never *be ready to hear!*

"The second reason is that, since we knew someone was out to get her, we were very careful on the drive here to ensure nobody followed us." Which would explain their convoluted route to the bar. "And *that* means those two gunman," oh, God, and suddenly she knew *exactly* where Billy was going, "had to have received notification of her whereabouts. Which begs the question..." Now, he turned toward her, and before he even opened his mouth, her world dimmed. Everything around her faded to black, and her vision tunneled down to a single point of reference: Billy's hard, uncompromising face. "Who did you call, Eve? Who knew you were here?"

Chapter Thirteen

Bill watched as Eve's lovely, tear-laden eyes blinked rapidly, and he cursed himself and the bastard behind all this for making her go through it. But there was no other way. And he *needed* to know who she'd called...

Of course, he could tell from the way her face drained of blood, from the way her nostrils flared unnaturally wide, that she was having trouble grasping the reality of the situation.

The truth hurts? Yeah, whoever came up with *that* little nugget should be crowned High King of the Understaters, because from the look on her face, the truth not only hurt, but it tore apart her whole friggin' existence, her whole sense of self and what she knew to be real.

"No," she shook her head, her chest rising and falling with each panting breath—he called himself ten kinds of asshole for noticing how it made her breasts press against her thin blouse. She looked around as if the world had suddenly changed shape. As if up was down, and black was white. "No," she choked again, wrenching away from her cousin's embrace. "It can't be."

"*Who*?" he demanded. But it didn't do any good. She was lost in her own denial, shaking her head and whispering, "No, it can't be," over and over again.

"Her father," Delilah piped up.

Eve swung on the woman, screaming, "No!"

"I heard her talking to him and—"

"No!" Eve yelled again, reaching up to fist double handfuls of her own hair.

Bill went with his gut and dragged her into his arms, ignoring the fact that Buchanan narrowed his eyes at the move. Eve fought initially, writhing in his embrace, beating his chest, but she had no more strength than a kitten. And in seconds, her struggling stopped and she collapsed against him in a sad, sobbing heap—which was so, *so* much worse than her pitiful fighting had been.

His hardened warrior's heart *bled* for her. And once again, their sad history was forgotten, all the hurts and disappointments trivialized when compared to a father's ultimate betrayal. He silently promised to kill Patrick Edens…*slowly*. But aloud he crooned, "Shh, Eve. It's gonna be okay. We'll figure this out. We'll—"

"No, Billy!" she wailed, hiccupping on her tears. "It-it can't be him! He's my *f-father*. He-he loves me! He wouldn't do this to me!"

"Eve—"

"Why?" she demanded, pushing away from him, her expression telegraphing the fact that her denial was quickly morphing into anger. "What *reason* would he have? None!" She sliced a hand through the air karate-chop style. "Tell him, Jeremy!" She swung on her cousin. "Tell him Dad wouldn't do this!"

"Eve, I—" Buchanan shook his head, his eyes full

of pity. "I don't—" He stopped, his Adam's apple bobbing in his throat.

"Not you, too!" she wailed. "Just because he didn't believe you when you said someone was trying to kill me, now you think *he's* the one? No!"

"I'm not saying—" Jeremy began, but he was stopped by the buzzing of his cell phone. He slapped a hand over his hip pocket, cursing. "I've got to take this," he said. His expression was tortured when his gaze landed on Eve. "I'm still on the clock, and that might be my partner calling, and—"

"Just do it." Eve's face was streaked with tears and red as a ripe cherry.

Buchanan hesitated a second more, and Bill felt himself softening toward the guy again. Just a little bit. Because Buchanan had done everything he'd known to do to protect Eve. But who would think to protect her against her own father. *Christ!* When the guy's phone continued to buzz imperiously Buchanan was forced to spin away, quickly moving down the alley and disappearing around the corner as he answered the call.

"You're wrong, Billy," Eve hissed, swinging back to him. "You're so dead wrong and—"

"Okay." Delilah stepped into the brink. Literally. She jumped between him and Eve, and it was probably a good thing she did. Because Eve's hands were curled into fists, and Bill figured he was about two seconds away from experiencing one or two of those self-defense moves she'd been practicing for the past year. And, yeah, he knew that *she* knew none of this was really his fault. But that didn't change the fact that she needed an outlet for all her rage and denial. And since he was quite handily standing right in front of her—presto changeo—he could play the part of scapegoat.

"I have to agree with Eve that this all seems a little farfetched. I mean," Delilah slid a placating look toward Eve, but Eve missed it since she was busy staring ice-tipped daggers at him, "what kind of father would pay a couple of Southside gangbangers to barge into a biker bar and shoot his only daughter in cold blood?"

The kind of father who'd kept his only daughter caged away in an ivory tower, never allowing her to develop any sort of social confidence. The kind of father who'd fostered his only daughter's natural shyness and timidity so he could control her life.

Basically, a father exactly like Patrick Edens.

Of course, Bill kept all this to himself as Delilah continued, "I mean, isn't it possible that Eve is bugged or something? Couldn't she have been followed or located another way?"

"Yes!" Eve stopped her frantic pacing, her expression suddenly filled with so much hope it caused a jagged crack to open in Bill's already ragged heart. "That's it! I have to be bugged. I have—"

"No," Mac cut her off, and Bill was glad he wasn't the one who'd been forced to do it, forced to dash all her misplaced faith.

"What do you mean *no*?" she demanded, planting her hands on her hips and glaring at the poor guy. Bill could tell by the former FBI agent's face that he didn't want to be the one to crush her sudden optimism, but he cowboyed-up and did it all the same.

"There's no way you're bugged, Eve," Mac said, and Bill held his breath and slid a glance toward Delilah who was listening intently...Intently? Pshht. More like she was monitoring the conversation with the dedication of a submarine sonar specialist.

Shit. This could get sticky. Er...*stickier.* The situation was already as sticky as the birdlime they used in anti-tank bombs.

"How can you possibly know that?" Eve asked, her eyes daring Mac to come up with something she would believe.

"Uh," Mac made a face and scratched the back of his head, peeking over at Delilah, "because you've been to the shop today, and we have wall-mounted... um...call it bug-detection equipment. So, if someone had a tracking device on you, believe me, we'd know about it. The entire shop would've flashed and wailed like a Lady Gaga concert."

"Aha!" Delilah pointed a blood-red fingernail straight at Mac's face. "I *knew* it! I knew—"

"Excuse me." A man in a rumpled gray suit walked up to them. He was on the downhill side of fifty and couldn't care less, evidenced by the fact that he didn't try to hide his receding hairline or the ketchup stain on the shirt stretched tight over his beer gut. "Hello again, Ms. Edens." The guy nodded once to Eve before addressing the group. "I'm Detective Normandy, and I need you folks to come with me down to the station where I can ask you some questions regarding tonight's events."

"Oh, *now* you're ready to take me down to the station to ask me some questions?" Eve was already shaking her head before Normandy finished his little speech. Bill got the distinct impression she'd found a new outlet for all her frustration and denial. And call him a lily-livered coward, but he couldn't say he was sorry all that vitriol was no longer directed at him. "*Now* you're ready*?* So the fire and the mugging and the cut brakes lines weren't enough to warrant an interview, but masked men barging into a bar to point guns at my head, not to mention strangling me," she pointed at the bruises on her neck, and once again, Bill's rage began to boil, "*are*? Sheesh!" She threw her hands in the air sarcastically. "Why didn't you just say that before, Detective?"

"Ms. Edens," Normandy placated, "if you'll just calm down—"

"Oh, you did *not* just tell me to calm down!" she shrieked, blue fire shooting from her eyes. It was a good thing Normandy was mostly bald or his hair might've burst into flames. "And let's get something straight right now, I'm not going anywhere with you until I get a chance to speak with my father!"

And Bill could admit he, *too*, would like a chance to confront Patrick Edens before the CPD carted the sonofabitch off to a nice, tidy jail cell. If only to look into the man's eyes when he admitted what low-down, dirty, scum-of-the-earth he really was.

Then again, a confession was probably a little too

much to hope for, but Bill still wanted to see the man's face when his daughter finally stood up to him. The part of him that remembered being looked down upon and openly sneered at had waited a very *long* time to see the lion bearded in his own den.

And in the name of avoiding an immediate police-cruiser ride down to the station and missing his chance to witness said bearding, he stepped away from the group, pulled his cell phone from his pocket, and punched in Chief Washington's number. As he listened to it ring on the other end, he watched Normandy produce a notepad from the inside pocket of his wrinkled suit coat.

"Why would you need to speak with your father?" he heard Normandy ask, but he didn't catch Eve's response, because right at that moment Washington answered with a gruff, "What the hell do you want, Reichert?"

Taking a few more steps away from the group, Bill explained the situation to the CPD police chief.

"Hell, no!" was Washington's immediate response to his request that he keep Normandy off their backs for a couple of hours. "If Patrick Edens is really behind Ms. Edens's recent mishaps and tonight's attempted murder, then you need to let Detective Normandy do his goddamned job. Let him question the man and—"

"You know as well as I do," Bill interrupted, "if the police approach Patrick Edens first, he'll lawyer-up quicker than I'll be able to say *I told you so*, and we'll miss any opportunity we had at surprising him into a confession."

"Yeah, right. You're crazier than I thought, and

I already thought you were bat-shit crazy, if you're under the impression a man like Patrick Edens will cop to trying to kill his own daughter," Washington snorted. "Besides, anything he admits to you won't stand up in court. It'll be nothing but hearsay. Unless... this isn't about a confession at all, but revenge? That's it, isn't it?" Washington's bass boomed through the connection. "Don't you even *think* about going all vigilante on his ass, Reichert! You may be some hot-shot, super-secret agent, but you're a Chicago citizen, too. Which means you fall under the purview of a little thing known as Illinois law and—"

"Cool your jets, Chief," Bill cut in. "I'm not going to kill the guy. I just want to give Eve the opportunity to look the man in the eye and tell him she knows what he's been up to."

"It's too dangerous," Washington insisted. "If he *is* the man behind these attacks, then what's to keep him from plugging her then and there?"

"You mean with two witnesses watching? Me and Mac? Come on, Chief. Give me—"

"Hand me the phone." Bill turned to see Buchanan standing behind him, the man's hand extended in his direction.

His first instinct was to tell Eve's cousin to fuck off, but he reminded himself of how hard Buchanan had been working—begrudgingly albeit—to help them. So, instead he tempered his response to, "Excuse me?"

"I couldn't help but overhear," Buchanan said. "I know you're talking to my police chief, and I think

I have a way to convince him to let you have what you want."

Bill lifted his brows, making his skepticism known, and then handed the phone over. He listened as Buchanan said something about a wire being inadmissible in court but going a long way in securing a search warrant before the man fell silent, no doubt intent on Washington's response on the other end.

Then he gave Bill a thumbs-up and handed back the phone.

"What's up, Chief?" Bill asked.

"Two hours," Washington muttered, and Bill shot a mental fist in the air. "I'll give you two hours to do your confronting. Jeremy's gonna give you a wire for Eve, and I want you to make damned sure she wears it!"

"You got it."

"And then when those two hours are up, I want all your asses down at the goddamned station answering any goddamned questions Normandy thinks to throw your goddamned way!"

Three *goddamns* in the same sentence? Washington meant business. "You have my word," he was quick to assure the man.

"And in the meantime, just in case Edens thinks to vamoose himself from the city, I'm sending unmarked units to keep an eye on him. You hear what I'm saying to you, Reichert? You catch my meaning?"

Bill rolled his eyes. He may be crazier than Washington thought he was, but he wasn't stupider. "You're telling me I shouldn't do anything hinky, because, if I do, your watchdogs will see it and then they'll be forced to cuff me and throw me in the nearest eight by ten."

"Bingo," Washington said. "You're not as dumb as you look, white boy." *Ha! Well, you can take the man out of the Marines, but you can't take the Marine out of the man.* The drill sergeant in Washington tended to pop up when least expected. "And tell Normandy to call me immediately!" he yelled before the line went dead.

Bill thumbed off his cell phone and turned to walk back toward the group. Buchanan, striding beside him, asked, "How the hell do you know my police chief?"

Well shit on a stick...

"Uh...a former military connection," Bill lied. "We go way back. But I don't think all the semper-fi love on the planet would've changed his mind about this plan before you stepped in. So, thank you. I really think Eve needs this."

Jeremy snorted. "Yeah, well, don't thank me too quickly. If this blows up, my name will be Mud with the CPD, and I might need to come to you for a job. I'll be honest and tell you right now that I'm total shit in the mechanic category, but I'm a quick learner."

Bill slid the man a sidelong glance. Buchanan as a Black Knight? Two days ago he would've laughed at the idea. Now? Not so much...

"I'll run and get the wire from my duty vehicle," Buchanan said.

"You're not going with us?"

"I wish. I'd like nothing more than to see Eve finally stand up to her father." And that made two of them. "But that was my partner who called a minute ago, and I'm still on the clock."

Bill nodded and watched Buchanan spin on his heel and jog down the alley. Turning back, he closed the distance to the group and handed his cell phone to the detective who was still attempting to question an uncooperative Eve.

"What's this?" Normandy asked, one bushy gray eyebrow sliding up his age-spotted forehead.

"It'll be your police chief on the other end once you hit redial," Bill said, trying not to sound overly pleased with himself.

The look on Normandy's face before he turned away to do as Bill suggested told him he'd failed in that endeavor. He couldn't bring himself to care overly much, especially when, after a quick conversation, the detective turned back to him, gaze speculative. "You've got two hours," the man said, echoing Washington's decree. "Then I expect to see you at the station."

"You got it," Bill repeated the assurance he'd given to Washington before glancing over at Eve. "Now, let's go question your father, shall we?"

"Yes," she declared, eyes flashing, nose lifted so high in the air he was surprised she couldn't smell the aviation fuel from the jetliners flying into O'Hare. But he much preferred cocky, pissed-off Eve, to terrified, guilt-ridden Eve. Pissed-off Eve allowed him to keep his defenses up in a way terrified Eve did not. "And then you'll see you're wrong about him, Billy. Dad will explain everything."

"I hope you're right, sweetheart," he told her. Sweetheart? Damn, he just couldn't get away from that, could he? And then he quietly added, "For your sake."

Her lower lip quivered, and for a moment he thought he'd gone and ruined it all, smashed all her hard-won temerity and bravado. *Way to go, Reichert.* But then she firmed her shoulders, and he breathed a quick sigh of relief.

"I am right," she declared, although the doubt in her voice was as loud and bright as a flashbang.

"I'm coming, too," Delilah announced, and Bill turned to her with a frown. He opened his mouth to tell her she wasn't involved when Mac beat him to it.

"If this man played a part in Buzzard's death," Delilah ignored Mac's words as she slid a look toward Eve, wincing and laying a hand on Eve's forearm, "I'm not saying he did, honey, but *if* he did, I want to be there when he's confronted."

And Bill could totally understand that. After all, it was his own desire to stare into Patrick Edens's face when Eve questioned him that'd led him to make that call to Washington in the first place. And as much as Buzzard had exemplified his nickname—the dude had been a wizened old bird who'd hung around the bar waiting to feed, in the form of a quick bathroom hump, on the carcasses of the drunk and over fifty crowd—Bill knew the man had also been one of Delilah's friends.

"What do you think, sweetheart?" he asked, turning to her and barely managing to keep from wincing. *Damnit. Again with the sweetheart?* "Everything that happens from here on out is your show."

"She can come," Eve declared, still standing tall and refusing to believe the evidence that was staring them all in the face. "If only to bear witness to my father's innocence."

You keep telling yourself that. You just keep telling yourself that until you're ready to face the truth.

And, Lord help him, but when she *was* ready to face the truth and the inevitable psychological fallout it would unquestionably cause, he was probably going to have to be the one to help her pick up the pieces and put herself back together again. And how the hell was he going to do that and still keep his hands to himself? For shit's sake, he hadn't even been able to sit on her bed offering her comfort for two minutes before he'd slammed his mouth over hers. And ten minutes ago, he'd nearly screwed her cross-eyed in the middle of Delilah's parking lot despite the fact that she'd very recently wrestled with a gunman for her life right before witnessing the gruesome death of an old man.

Christ, he was going to be in trouble. But he supposed he'd have to cross that bridge when he got there. For now, their two hours were quickly ticking away.

"Okay, so you're coming," he told Delilah, shrugging when Mac turned to him with a look that screamed *what the hell, man?* "If it's okay with Eve," he told the former FBI agent, "then I don't see how we can stop her."

Mac spun to Delilah, his mouth open with what was undoubtedly a very reasonable and logical argument as to why she should stay here or else go with Normandy down to the police station. But before he could spit out one single syllable, Delilah raised a finger, shaking her head. "Uh-uh. You may as well check whatever you're about to say at the back of your teeth, because I've done all I can here. I've made sure my patrons are okay and giving statements. The police tell me they're closing the bar for the foreseeable future while they investigate the shooting. My uncle is down South somewhere and not answering his cell phone." It was Bill's understanding that Delilah's uncle had been the one to raise her. "And I can't stay here a second longer because I keep seeing Buzzard s-slumped and…" her voice faltered before she dragged in a deep breath, squaring her shoulders and continuing, "and bleeding on that barstool. And if you must know it's making me absolutely crazy. So, I'm going. End of story."

Mac was a smart man. He knew when to raise the white flag. "Fine," he mumbled, sliding her a look that was both resigned and, if Bill wasn't mistaken, verging on protective, "can you ride?"

"Uh…" Delilah hesitated, twisting her hands together and making a face. "I'd like to say *yes*, but in all honesty I'd probably lay my bike over. Can I just ride with you?"

If the situation were any less dire, Bill might've laughed out loud at the unfettered horror that passed over Mac's face.

Obviously Delilah didn't see the humor in it because she planted her hands on her hips and scowled. "Oh, for heaven's sake! You can wipe off that expression this instant, Bryan McMillan!" She motioned to the dried blood staining her shirt. "Do you really think after all I've been through today, after having l-lost," her voice faltered again, and Bill wished like hell he could go back and erase the last two hours, for her sake and for Eve's, "Buzzard, that I'm in the mood to work my feminine wiles on you?"

"Um..." Mac didn't get the chance to say any more than that, because Delilah turned on her heel and marched down the alley toward their waiting motorcycles. Which reminded Bill...

"We, uh, we had to ditch the Hummer," he explained to Eve, closely watching her expression. As if the poor woman needed *another* frightening ordeal to have to contend with today.

"No problem," she said, traipsing over to Phoenix and hopping into position on the recently installed king and queen seat.

With a surprised lift of his brow, he followed her, hesitating only a second to study her determined, tear-stained face before swinging astride the bike. And points for him, he stiffened only *slightly*, just ever so slightly, when she wrapped her arms around his waist.

Buchanan jogged over to them, wire and small recording device in hand. "Lift your shirt, Cuz," he said.

"Wh-why?" Eve sputtered.

"Because the only way I could convince my chief to let you go talk to your father was if you're wearing a wire."

Bill was almost afraid to glance over his shoulder at Eve's face. But he did. And he was surprised to find only confidence in her expression. "Good. Then everyone will be able to hear Dad explain everything."

Oh, sweetheart...

He felt so goddamned sorry for her, and he faced forward once again while Buchanan made quick work with the wire.

"The investigators are going to need your phone, too," Buchanan said, his tone apologetic. "It's evidence of the call between you and your dad." He held out his hand.

"It's still in the bar," Eve said. "Help yourself."

When Buchanan glanced at Bill, his expression was tortured. "Don't worry," Bill assured the man. "I'll keep her safe."

A muscle twitched in Buchanan's cheek, and Bill could tell the guy was having a difficult time letting someone else take the lead on this, take the lead on protecting Eve. But then Buchanan blew out a deep breath and nodded, stepping back.

Bill cranked over Phoenix's big engine, and the bike came to life with a guttural roar. He stiffened wondering how Eve would react to the vibrating, snarling steel beast beneath her butt. But she didn't wince. She simply leaned forward, pressing herself against his back.

"I thought you didn't like motorcycles," he yelled above the growling engine.

Her words, spoken directly in his ear, had goose bumps erupting across the back of his neck. "That was a long time ago, Billy," she said, her tone low and sure. "And I'm not the same person you used to know."

And as much as it might scare the living crap out of him to admit it, she was right. She *wasn't* that same timid, wide-eyed girl anymore. Now, she was a fully grown, fully actualized woman, with all the mysteries and complexities inherent therein.

Unfortunately—and talk about scaring the living crap out of a guy—he realized there was a part of him, a *foolish* part obviously, that desperately wanted to get to know this new Eve…

Chapter Fourteen

Patrick Edens's Condo Building
7:14 p.m.

DELILAH TUGGED OFF THE HELMET MAC HAD loaned her. At any other time, she'd probably be turned on from snuggling up against his very broad, very warm back—especially with a badass bike rumbling between her legs—but she hadn't been shitting him back there in the parking lot when she told him she was in no mood to work her feminine wiles. Because poor Buzzard...

The image of him sitting on that barstool, dead eyes open and glassy, blood pouring out of him in a gruesome flood, would forever be imprinted on the backs of her lids like a monstrous tattoo. And, yes, he'd been a patron. Someone who paid her to pop the tops on his beers and keep his pretzel dish full. But he'd also been a friend. When the guy spent most of his evenings warming a stool in front of the bar she manned, it was kind of hard for him to be anything less.

She knew about his three failed marriages, his shady insurance scams, and his unrequited love for one of her waitresses. And she knew he'd fought in Vietnam and had shrapnel in his hip that pained him on rainy days.

A knot of sorrow lodged in the back of her throat,

and to help swallow it down—she *so* couldn't fall apart after they'd agreed to let her come along—she glanced up, *way* up, at the sparkling glass and steel structure of the downtown high-rise.

Instantly, her sorrow was replaced by red-hot rage.

"So this is how rich murderers live," she snarled, swinging from the motorcycle with the ease of a frequent rider.

"We don't know that for sure," Mac warned, hooking the helmet she handed him over the handlebars of his tricked-out ride. And speaking of tricked-out rides…

"Says the ex-FBI-agent-turned-motorcycle-mechanic slash…" she let the sentence dangle, frowning when he refused to fill in the blank. "Oh, come on!" she wailed over the loud, gut-rumbling roar of Bill and Eve pulling up behind them. All her sorrow and anger needed an outlet, and right now Mac and his goddamned reticence were awfully handy. "You have bug-detection equipment in your shop and a direct line to the Chicago police chief. So do you really expect me to continue to believe that incredibly sucktastic we're-just-a-bunch-of-grease-monkeys line? Seriously, dude, I could eat a bowl of Alpha-Bits cereal and crap out a better story than that!"

When one corner of his mouth twitched, she narrowed her eyes and pointed a finger at his rugged face. "It's not funny! Nothing about this day has been funny!"

And, just like that, the picture of Buzzard's last moments burned in front of her eyes, immediately causing tears to scald the back of her nose.

Why didn't you hit the floor like everybody else, Buzzard? Why didn't you—

And she realized she was shaking when Mac cursed beneath his breath before swinging from the bike. He wrapped a heavy arm around her shoulders just as Bill killed his cycle's engine. The sudden, ringing silence made her feel unmoored. She imagined it was only the weight of Mac's arm that kept her from floating up into the balmy evening air. Sucking in a calming breath, she turned to watch Bill and Eve's approach.

Eve…

Now *there* was something to take her mind off her own troubles. She cocked her head at the woman, lifting a brow at the sure steps, the steady expression, the eyes that were clear and determined.

Damn. Considering they were going upstairs to accuse Eve's father of attempting to murder her, Delilah was shocked and impressed to discover Eve was doing one hell of a job of keeping her shit together. Then again, delusion combined with denial had been known to be a wonderful cocktail when it came to pumping up a person's courage.

Her own father. Holy shit…

Delilah couldn't fathom it. Then again, in her experience, the ultra-wealthy sometimes had very skewed priorities, and often had very questionable loyalties. Scrooge McDuck-style piles of cash did strange things to folks…

"Are you guys ready?" Bill asked, and Delilah wondered if he realized he reached for Eve's hand, or if the gesture was subconscious.

"I, uh…" Mac gingerly removed his arm—she immediately missed his warmth and the grounding effect it had on her—and ducked his chin to peer into her face. "Are we?"

Seriously? *She* was the weak link in this not-so-happy little chain?

Nuh-uh. Oh, hell no. Because she was supposed to be the ass-kicking, Harley-riding, shotgun-toting, beer-slinger-from-hell!

Okay, so maybe not all of *that*. But she was definitely determined to hold her own.

"Of course I'm ready." She lifted her chin while simultaneously girding her loins.

Although, she had to admit, when they walked into the building's posh, air-conditioned lobby and the stuffy, balding, Armani-clad doorman took one look at her before curling his lip in disdain, some of her bravado abandoned her. Then the man's eyes came to a full stop on her boobs and remained glued there for a ridiculous length of time, and all her spit and vinegar returned in full measure. She found herself battling the distinct urge to punch the douchebag in the plums.

Instead, she smiled acidly and chirped, "Mesmerizing, aren't they?"

"Oh, uh…" The doorman had the wherewithal to look appropriately chagrined. "Ms. Edens," he said, turning toward Eve and frowning when he took in her disheveled appearance. "Shall I call your father and tell him you've—"

"No need, Arthur." Eve waved him off, sailing toward the bank of elevators, ignoring the curious and pointed looks of the well-coifed couple signing the ledger at the front desk.

"But, madam, I've been instructed to—"

"I said there's no need, Arthur," Eve tossed over her shoulder, and *damn!* The woman could do haughty and entitled like no other. Which was kind of amazing since Delilah knew Eve was, at her core, as shy and retiring as a field mouse.

Then again, she *had* come out on top in the fight with that masked gunman, so obviously the woman had hidden depths.

Good for you, girlfriend, she thought. *You're going to have to plumb those depths during the ordeal to come...*

The four of them loaded into a waiting elevator—Sir Arthur Stares-A-Lot still making noises about needing to call up to Eve's father—and when the silver doors slid shut with a dainty *ding*, Delilah was confronted with her hazy reflection.

Jesus, Mary, and Joseph, she was a horror show...

Her hair was an absolute rat's nest. Mascara was smudged under her bloodshot eyes, giving her the look of a drunken raccoon. And her lipstick red T-shirt was stained brown with dried blood. *Buzzard's* blood...

And before she knew it, her chin was wobbling again.

"Delilah," Mac began, turning toward her, concern twisting his face. "You don't have to do this. You could—"

But that's as far as he got before the express elevator *bing-bonged* their arrival on the penthouse floor.

"I got this," she told him, never so happy to see a set of doors slide open in her life.

He narrowed his keen blue eyes. In return, she gave him a look that said, *Dude, I told you, I got this!*

He either believed her or figured this was no time to argue, because he didn't try to stop her as she followed Bill and Eve from the elevator into the marble foyer of the penthouse. Immediately she felt the urge to whistle through her teeth. With the grand archways, mahogany pillars, and soaring twenty-foot ceilings—not to mention the frou-frou smell of expensive furniture polish hanging in the air—the place belonged on an episode of *Lifestyles of the Rich and Famous*.

Talk about champagne wishes and caviar dreams. *Holy shit!*

"Dad!" Eve yelled, and the word bounced around the cavernous space, shrill and incongruous against all the opulence.

"Dad!" Eve yelled again, angrily shaking off the restraining hand Bill placed on her shoulder. "Stop it, Billy. I don't need you to coddle me."

"I wasn't cod—" But that was as far as Bill got, because Patrick Edens appeared at the top of the grand, sweeping staircase. Delilah recognized him from the covers of a few local magazines.

"Eve?" he murmured, lifting one brow. The man was wearing precisely pressed silk slacks and a navy and maroon velvet smoking jacket which, seriously? A velvet smoking jacket? Delilah always assumed those were used strictly for gag gifts and bad Halloween costumes. But, apparently not. Because Patrick Edens didn't seem the least bit whimsical as he descended the stairs like a king coming to court. She wouldn't have been all that surprised had the brass band notes of "Hail to the Chief" begun blasting through hidden speakers in the walls.

"Darling?" Patrick Edens cooed once he'd stepped from the last tread, his expensive, calf-skin loafers shushing on the polished tile. The endearment, spoken in that precisely cultured voice, went through Delilah like the stomach flu, making her want to puke her guts up. "This is a pleasant surprise. I thought you weren't making it to dinner tonight." Then, "Oh! Sweet Lord! What happened to you?"

Like you don't know. Delilah seethed, barely resisting the urge to clap and yell *bravo* in response to that lovely performance. How could the man stand there, talking to his daughter as if he hadn't just hired two thugs to shoot her down?

"I was attacked by masked gunmen inside Delilah's biker bar a little over an hour ago," Eve said, lifting her chin and refusing the concerned hand her father extended in her direction.

Patrick Edens frowned at her rebuff, and Delilah figured he'd chosen the wrong profession. With his perfectly coiffed salt-and-pepper hair, aristocratically handsome face, and Oscar-worthy acting ability, he should've gone out West in order to grace the silver screen.

"Christ! Are you okay?" Edens asked, taking the opportunity to glance around the group. If Delilah wasn't mistaken, that was one-hundred-percent pure hatred gleaming from his dark blue eyes when his gaze landed on Bill.

Huh, so there's a story there. Although, she was learning that when it came to the Black Knights, there was a story *everywhere*.

"I'll be f-fine once you tell me you had nothing to do with it," Eve said, her lips quivering, belying the fact that the brave face she was putting on was just that, a face…

Hang tough. You can do this.

"M-me?" Edens sputtered. "What in the world would lead you to think I—"

"You're the only one who knew where I *was!*" Eve shouted, her decorous mask slipping another inch. Delilah saw the red splotches standing like flags on the poor woman's neck and chest.

"Darling." Edens stepped forward again, this time not allowing Eve to shake off the hand he laid on her arm. Delilah bit her tongue to keep from screaming, *Don't touch her, you murdering bastard!* "Just listen to yourself. You're losing it, jumping at shadows again because your cousin was silly enough to encourage your paranoia. No one is out to kill you. Who would dare?"

Uh, I don't know…maybe you?

"And as for these masked gunmen in the biker bar," he went on, "what do you expect when you hang out in those types of seedy, lowbrow establishments?"

Oh no he didn't. If Mac hadn't placed a restraining hand on her arm, Delilah would have stepped forward to clock the pompous bastard. As it stood, she remained rooted to the spot, wondering if it was possible for steam to actually pour from her ears or if that only happened on Saturday morning cartoons.

"And," it appeared Patrick Edens wasn't done, "when you align yourself with seedy, lowbrow people?"

That was it. Delilah was going to slug him. Unfortunately, Bill beat her to the mark. From the corner of her eye, she saw him blow up like a rooster in a chicken coop when a rival struts in. All ruffled feathers and pomp. Only Bill's ruffled feathers were really big, really impressive muscles, and his pomp was the two vigorous steps he took in Patrick Edens's direction. "You better step up, or step off, asshole," he growled, and Delilah figured her teeth were going to leave permanent marks on her tongue. Now she was biting it to keep from shouting, *you tell him, Bill!* "Because you keep looking at me and my friends that way, you keep referring to us in that snide tone, and I'm liable to take a swipe at you." Bill lifted his chin, staring Eve's father down. "And you know for goddamned sure you're not ready for that."

"He's really good at that, isn't he?" Mac bent to whisper in her ear.

"At what?" she whispered right back, mesmerized by the staring contest happening eight feet in front of her. Men! They stomped around each other, taking bites, when the truth was they should just whip 'em out and measure, solve everything just like that.

And, if she was a betting woman—which she so totally was—Bill would win that little competition hands down. *Hands* being the operative word. Because

Bill's were big and square and strong-looking, while Patrick Edens's were long and thin and almost feminine. And in her experience that old wives' tale about the size of a man's hands compared to the size of his… erm…*bits* was right far more times than it was wrong.

"At making little speeches that encourage a man to fill his drawers," Mac breathed against her cheek, his breath warm and distracting. She started to turn to him, but Patrick Edens took a small step back, riveting her attention to the scene playing out in front of her.

You won that one, Bill! Way to go!

And, yes, it appeared she'd become the silent cheering section, but she just couldn't help herself. For Buzzard's sake, she hoped Eve and Bill ripped the bastard a new asshole, except…when she thought about it, even *that* wasn't good enough. Okay, so revised wish: she hoped Eve and Bill ripped the bastard's whole freakin' head off…

"Y-you're proving my point, are you not, Mr. R-Reichert?" Edens asked, but the fact that he stumbled over his words ruined any hope he had of maintaining his superior air. It didn't however, stop his smile. It was thin and sharp as a knife's edge and made Delilah's skin crawl. "And if you're not careful, you're going to make me mad. Believe me," his smile transformed into an ugly sneer, "you won't like me when I'm mad."

Bill laughed, actually *laughed*, and Delilah had to give him points for being able to find any humor in this god-awful situation. "For the record, *Patrick*," he taunted, and Delilah had never seen Bill look anything but composed. But right now? Well, right now he looked like he was moments away from shoving Patrick Edens's teeth down his throat. "I don't like you, period, angry or not. But come on. Give me your best Hulk impression. I dare you."

"Wh-hat are you talking about?" Patrick Eden's blustered. "I'm not familiar with your ghetto, street lingo and—"

"Oh, cut the crap!" Delilah couldn't stand it anymore. "Did you send those gangbangers to kill your daughter or not?"

"Of *course* not!" Patrick Edens shouted right back, proving he wasn't such a hoity-toity, keep-my-cool-under-any-pressure kind of guy after all. "Why would I *do* that?"

Before Delilah could utter another word, the elevator doors opened behind them with that melodic *ding-dong*, and a man who belonged in the centerfold of a women's magazine strolled into the opulent foyer. He was over six feet of blond-haired, blue-eyed, well-dressed, homina-homina-handsome, but something about the way he carried himself made Delilah's hackles twang to life.

"Uh-oh," Mac muttered.

"What?" she asked, turning to frown up at him.

"This just turned into a traditional backwoods goatfuck."

"Huh?" She lifted a brow, watching as the new arrival hesitated before advancing farther into the room. "What do you mean?"

"I mean," Mac murmured so far beneath his breath

it was hard to hear, "that if I'm not mistaken, that's Eve's ex-husband."

"Um, hello, everyone," Mr. Universe/Eve's ex-husband addressed the group before focusing on Eve. "Jesus, Eve, what in the world happened to you?" His demeanor actually appeared concerned, and that was the first time Delilah had seen that particular expression on an ex-husband's face in regard to an ex-wife.

"I was attacked at a bar," Eve said, *her* expression loudly broadcasting her dislike of the man.

Ah, now that's *more like it.*

"How awful for you!" Mr. Universe cried, stepping toward her.

"Don't you lay on hand on me, Blake," Eve warned, glowering.

"Why, Eve," the man looked genuinely shocked, "what's gotten into you?"

Before Eve could answer, Patrick Edens spoke up. "Sorry, I didn't call you back and cancel, Blake," he said. "This," he waved a dismissive hand at the group, "just showed up on my doorstep."

"That's quite all right," Mr. Universe…er…*Blake* said. "I actually postponed other plans when you initially called to tell me Eve'd bailed on you. It'll be a snap to reinstate them and—"

"What the hell are you two doing together?" Eve interrupted, staring daggers first at one man, then the other, her color so high Delilah worried the poor woman might just stroke out.

"We went in on a mutual business endeavor a few years back," Edens answered. "There've been some recent developments we need to discuss. And when you canceled on me, I thought it was as good a time as any to call Blake over for a meeting."

"A mutual business endeavor, huh?" Eve rolled in her lips, nodding her head. But it was obvious even before she said, "Between my father and my ex-husband; why am I not surprised?" that the association between the two men bothered her.

"This, uh, this appears to be a family affair." Blake raised his hands. "And since I'm no longer officially part of the family, I…I think I'll just show myself out." He turned to leave but hesitated, glancing over his shoulder once more. "I really am sorry to hear about what happened to you, Eve" he murmured, then added, "but what can you expect from hanging out in biker bars?"

And what was that? The party line for snobby rich folks or something? And just when Delilah was about to bust out, this time for real, with *oh no you didn't*, a thought occurred to her. "Wait a damn minute," she declared. "How did you know she was attacked in a *biker* bar? She never said it was a *biker* bar."

"Because Patrick told me where she'd decided to spend her evening when he called to invite me over," the man said.

Oh, hell. Mac was right. This *was* a traditional backwoods goatfuck…

Chapter Fifteen

"You!" Eve screamed, jumping toward Blake with her hands curled into fists, her mind burning with so much rage she could barely see beyond the red haze clouding her vision. Of course, that red haze didn't affect her ears, so she had no trouble hearing Blake's surprised squawk of pain when her well-practiced right jab landed on the bridge of his nose.

Crunch! Cartilage cracked beneath her knuckles, and a bright burst of white-hot agony reverberated up her arm to explode in her shoulder. She paid it no mind as she reached back with her left fist to follow that first punch up with a second aimed straight at Blake's soft belly. He wheezed a cartoonish, "oof," as he bent in half, one hand holding his stomach, the other coming up to cup the blood draining from his nose.

Okay, so…she'd lost it. She'd absolutely, positively lost her flippin' mind. And even though a part of her was standing outside herself, watching as she hurled punches like a bantam-weight boxer, she couldn't seem to make herself stop. Not when her brain was screaming, *after everything he put me through! After tricking me all those years ago! After ruining any chance I had at happiness, now he has the audacity to try to…to try to* kill *me?*

She wanted to scratch his eyes out, rip his heart out! She wanted to scream and scream and—

Two strong arms wrapped around her from behind, bodily lifting her away from Blake's folded form. She struggled against the embrace, her blood boiling through her veins like molten lava, her reasoning and restraint burned down to ashes from the roiling inferno of her heartache and fury.

"How *could* you?" she wailed at Blake even as she tried to wrestle out of the human vice clamping her arms against her sides. "After everything! How *could* you?"

"Stop this, Eve!" she heard her father command. And there was a time she'd have followed his order without a second thought. A time she'd have wilted like a lily to be yelled at in such a way. But, boy, oh boy, was that time ever gone.

Briefly she registered the shift in paradigm, but she barely paid it a fleeting thought. Because, suddenly, all the years of manipulation, all the times her father had disregarded her wants and needs in order to forward his own desires, all the pushing and prodding and wheedling flashed through her overheated head like a slideshow projector set on overdrive, and she turned on him with a snarl. By the way he stumbled back, his hand jumping to his throat, she knew the bitterness she felt in her heart blazed clear and bright in her eyes despite the fact that her hair hung in front of her face.

"Shut up!" she shrieked at him, blowing like the time she'd run the Chicago marathon in just over four hours. "This is your fault, too! You *pushed* me at him!" She jerked her chin toward Blake who was staggering back against the wall, still cupping his ruined nose in his hand as dark red blood seeped between his fingers. "You wouldn't stop badgering me until I agreed to go out with him!"

"You've gone f-fucking cr-crazy!" Blake wailed, blinking against the tears pouring from his eyes.

Something inside Eve, something she'd never known existed, something feral and bloodthirsty smiled at the carnage she'd created. She opened her mouth to scream at him that the jig was up. That no amount of blustering or deflection was going to save him now. But then she heard Billy growl behind her, and she realized he was the one who'd yanked her away from Blake. He was the one who'd kept her from beating her ex-husband to a bloody pulp…er…*bloodier* pulp. And she didn't know whether she should thank him for the effort or give him a taste of what she'd just given Blake.

But when he snarled, "You better watch your mouth, asshole. Because in case you can't see through all your tears, Eve really wants off the leash here. And, rest assured, the only thing standing between you and a ripped out throat is the fact that I'm holding that leash," she realized she didn't want to thank him or feed him a fist sandwich at all. What she wanted was to turn around and kiss him. Kiss him for the strength in the hard grip he had on her, kiss him for the strength in the words he'd just spoken. Because that was something she'd never had before. A man's strength to *add* to her own. A man to have her back.

In this case, literally.

And it was that strength, the knowledge that even after everything he still had her back, that allowed all the savagery and hysteria, all the mindless fight that'd overtaken her reason, to drain from her body like a river drains into the sea. One minute, she was completely out of control. The next, she was as calm as calm can be. Well, as calm as anyone could be when coming face-to-face with an ex-husband who'd attempted to murder her in cold blood not once, but *four* times ...

Billy must've felt the sudden change in her, because he slowly loosened his grip.

No, she wanted to say. *Don't let go of me. I need you to—*

And maybe he could read minds, or maybe he could just read *her*, because in the next instant he stepped up beside her, lacing their fingers together so they could confront Blake as a unit.

Sweet Lord in heaven. Okay, and she was officially on the emotional roller coaster from hell, because now she felt like crying. Her lip quivered in warning.

"You got this, sweetheart." Billy squeezed her hand, his big palm so warm and reassuring against hers. "Go ahead." He jerked his chin toward Blake. "Let him have it."

Eve glanced up at him, into his wonderful face—the best face on the whole planet; her *favorite* face—and what she saw was one-hundred-percent, no-holds-barred, *Whatever happens, I'm right here with you* shining in his dark, diamond-bright eyes.

Yes, I've got this, she thought, her stomach quivering with gratitude. *With you by my side, I've got everything.*

Pushing her hair out of her face, she turned to throw

down the gauntlet in front of the man who'd been the one to orchestrate so much of the sorrow she'd suffered over last dozen years. The man who, for some reason she couldn't *begin* to fathom, was trying to kill her...

Dragging in a deep, fortifying breath, she glanced around the foyer and noted Mac and Delilah were standing quietly off to the side. Mac was watching the proceedings with his usual stoicism, face blank, arms crossed, gaze narrowed ever-so-slightly. Delilah, on the other hand, wasn't so good at hiding her feelings. If Eve wasn't mistaken, that was unfettered glee she saw in the woman's eyes as she watched Blake use the hem of his shirt in an attempt to stymie the river of red that continued to sluggishly leak from his broken nose.

And, yes, she should probably be embarrassed that they'd witnessed her losing her...erm...*S-H-I-T.* as Billy would say—although he'd never spell it out, silently or otherwise. But instead, she was bolstered by the knowledge that she could put two more check marks on her mental scoreboard under the heading: Folks Who are on My Side.

On the other hand, there was her father...

When she turned her gaze to him, the look on his face had her lungs seizing in her chest and her heart skipping one horrid beat. No support there. Huh-uh. In fact, it was just the opposite. In a word, her father's expression was one of...*disgust.*

Billy squeezed her hand again, and she shook her head, blowing out a resigned breath, because *that was it. That was the straw that broke the camel's back.* She'd tried for so long to gain her father's approval. And to have him look at her like he was looking at her right now was just too much. She was done. Done caring.

Your loss, Dad, she thought savagely before turning away from him, from his frown of displeasure, and from any hope that they'd ever share the kind of love and understanding she'd always craved. Sucking in another deep breath, taking comfort in the smell of soap and soft leather that clung to Billy in a soothing cloud, she focused her mind and her gaze on Blake.

It was time to face the music. For both of them…

"Why did you try to have me killed?" she asked, surprised and gratified when her voice came out as steady as the Rock of Gibraltar. Not one ounce of the betrayal she was feeling was evident in her tone. And perhaps it was the feel of Billy standing so tall and strong beside her—a real-life knight in shining biker books—or maybe she'd *finally* grown that set of brass ladyballs, but in that instant she knew there was nothing Blake could say to hurt her, nothing he could do to make her back away from the truth, however unsavory that truth might be.

"I don't know what you're talking about," he insisted, his words garbled and nasally as he pinched the end of his nose, tilting his head back.

Had she been expecting anything more? No, not really. But still she pressed, "Don't play games, Blake. The only two people who knew where I was tonight were you and Dad."

"Eve," her father cut in, "stop this nonsense. Blake wouldn't—"

"Shut up," she commanded, turning to glare at him and his startled expression. *Yep, you're starting to get it, aren't you? I'm not a scared little girl you can push around anymore.* "You've done quite enough already."

"Wh-what?" he sputtered, nostril's flaring before he realized his veneer of elegance was slipping. Sniffing, he said, "I can't imagine what you mean, I—"

"Save it, Dad," she told him. "The fact remains you knew I was afraid. You knew Jeremy and I both believed there was something insidious behind all my *accidents*," she made the quote marks with the fingers of one hand. "But you chose to ignore us, ignore my fear. And for that and for the fact that you're still associating with my ex-husband when you know I've been trying for over a decade to distance myself from him, not to mention the way you pushed me at him twelve years ago, I'll never forgive you."

"Eve," he placated, reaching toward her. "You don't mean that."

"I do," she promised, nodding her head, meeting his gaze head-on. *Read the truth in my eyes, Dad.* "I mean every single word of it."

He dropped his hand, his face draining of blood until his cheeks looked sallow. And she'd be lying if she said she didn't feel a pinch of regret at the harshness of her words. But she'd come too far to back down now. Sparing him one last pitying glance, she turned back to Blake.

"Tell me, Blake," she demanded, "what possible motive could you have for paying two thugs to come into Delilah's bar to gun me down. Tell me," a sharp note edged into her tone, but she couldn't help it, "one good reason why you'd set fire to my condo, or cut my brake lines, or have someone try to shoot me outside the aquarium. I'd really, *really* like to know."

And that was an understatement. Because, even though they weren't on *great* terms, neither had she thought they were mortal enemies. And, yes, if she wanted to keep riding the Honesty Train, she had to admit that it *hurt* to think of him hating her so much that he'd pay to see her dead. *Dear God, haven't I always tried to be nice to him? Even after I found out what he did? Haven't I always treated him with kindness?*

"Is it because I refused to come back to you?" she asked, shaking her head, her voice thick with confusion. "Is it because you—"

"I don't know what you're *talking* about!" he yelled, spitting blood onto the marble tiles.

She snorted a laugh, but there was no humor in it, just bone-deep sadness and the type of weariness that reached right down to the soul. "And I guess I'm just supposed to believe you after what happened? I guess I'm just supposed to believe—"

"What happened all those years ago is as much *his* fault as it is mine," Blake snarled. He thrust his bloody chin toward her father.

"Not another word, Blake," her dad warned, his eyes boring into her ex-husband's until she was surprised the back of Blake's head didn't blow out.

She glanced back and forth between the men, frowning. She knew it was her father who'd pressured her unrelentingly until she finally, *sullenly* agreed to go out with Blake, but...but there was something more going on here...

A deep sense of foreboding scratched at the back of her brain with sharp, broken nails, causing her to narrow her eyes. "What are you talking about?" she breathed, her heart crashing against her breastbone like hurricane-force waves against a rocky shore.

"All these years," Blake shook his head, his lips pulling into the kind of smile that was really more of a grimace. With the blood staining his teeth, the gesture was particularly macabre, "you thought it was *my* idea to call the press and have them waiting to snap pictures of the two of us that night."

Oh, yes. The infamous pictures...the ones that showed her laughing at Blake over a bottle of Chianti. The ones that showed her and Blake dancing in the moonlight, smiling up at each other, looking, for all the world, like two people madly in love. The ones that showed Blake kissing her passionately outside the front door of her dorm. The ones that had run with headlines like: *A Love Affair Made in Real Estate Mogul Heaven.* The ones that'd pushed Billy away and forced her to admit that her dreams were dead and buried after the letters she sent to him, begging him for forgiveness, went unanswered.

Of course, what those pictures *hadn't* shown was her checking her watch every five minutes, counting down the seconds until the date was over. What they *hadn't* shown was her angrily pushing Blake away after he grabbed her and slammed his mouth down over hers. What they *hadn't* shown was...the truth. Not that it mattered anyway, considering she'd betrayed Billy the second she agreed to that awful date, but still...

"You divorced me six measly months after we said our vows because you thought it was *me*," Blake shoved his thumb into his chest, "who called in the tip to the press."

"It *was* you," she insisted, her foreboding morphing into the kind of dread that had her scalp tingling. But there was no reason for it. Because she knew for *fact* it'd been Blake. After they'd been married only a few weeks and her head had had time to clear from the heartache of losing Billy and the whirlwind of the rushed wedding, she'd started having misgivings. Misgivings about the way Blake had been a little *too* outspoken in his anger with the press. Misgivings about the fact that he'd been a little *too* willing to hold her close and dry her tears while she cried over another man. Misgivings about how he'd been just a little *too* quick to propose marriage after it became apparent Billy was out of the picture. She'd started to feel instinctively that something wasn't right, that it all felt...*planned* somehow.

It'd taken her a couple of months to work up the courage to hire a private investigator, but she finally did it. And what'd turned up after some digging? Well, the not-so-insignificant fact that the phone call to the local media had come directly from Blake's cell phone that night. "You'd been hounding me to go out with you for months, just as much as my father had," she insisted. "And when I finally agreed, you found a way to make sure I stayed with you. You found a way to ruin my only other option. The phone records don't lie, Blake."

He shook his head, his expression derisive. "It's true I wanted you since the first moment I saw you on campus. I *still* want you." Ah, and now the *real* truth was coming out. *Want.* He *wanted* her. Which was a *completely* different song than the one he'd been singing for the last decade or so. The song of love. Like most spoiled rich boys, the one thing Blake Parish coveted more than anything was the one thing he couldn't have. And, deep down, even while they'd been married, he must've known he couldn't have *her*. Not in any way that mattered. "We're perfect together."

She barely resisted snorting and rolling her eyes. *Perfect together? In what world?* Certainly not hers.

"And I would've gotten you eventually, fair and square," he continued. Again, in *what* world? "had he," he tilted his chin toward her father, "not gotten impatient and decided to…*help* things along."

Wait, what? The room did a slow tilt to the left, and she found herself eternally grateful Billy was beside her to steady her when she wobbled. What was Blake saying? That it was her…her *father's* idea to call the press that night?

She slowly turned to the man accused. And from the way the muscle ticked in his jaw, from the way he couldn't quite hold her gaze, he didn't need to affirm or deny Blake's allegation.

No…

But the truth was written all over her father's face, flashing at her as brightly as a neon sign. Good God, had she really thought there was nothing Blake could say that would hurt her? Had she really thought there was nothing he could tell her to make her want to back away from the truth?

"How could you *do* that?" She meant to scream the words at her father, but they croaked out of her in a hoarse whisper.

"Eve," he began, lifting his chin at a defensive angle, even now refusing to give so much as an inch. "I did what I thought was best for you and for your future. I did what—"

"And more than that," Blake cut him off. "He *paid* the newspapers and tabloids to run those articles, to make sure they were publicized both far and wide. It was *his* idea for—"

"Shut up, Blake!" her father yelled.

"Fuck you, Patrick!" Blake shot back. "I'm done being your puppet! I could've won Eve all on my own if you'd just given me more time! If you'd kept your nose out of—"

She stopped listening because suddenly it was all too much. Her entire world, everything she'd ever known to be true, every*one* she'd ever known to be true was just one big, stinking lie.

"G-get me out of h-here, Billy," she whispered. "I can't breathe in here."

"Done," he said. Then to Mac and Delilah he called, "Come on. We're getting the hell out of this snake pit."

Snake pit? *Yep, that's about right*. And she'd been the field mouse, timidly waiting to be eaten alive by two vipers.

Well, not anymore! She was finished with them. Finished with—

She didn't get to finish the thought because Billy started half carrying/half dragging her in a beeline toward the elevator. *What the heck is wrong with my legs?* It appeared they were only partially working. Well, she supposed that's what happened when one found herself stabbed in the back by her own father. But she didn't have time to worry about that now. Because Delilah, God bless her, had already punched the button for the elevator, and Eve could hear the car cables creaking behind the closed silver door.

"Wait, Eve, I—" her father jogged over to them and reached for her. On instinct she pressed closer to Billy.

"Retract that hand before I rip it off, fuckwad," Billy snarled lowly, sounding more like a beast than a man.

Her father snatched his fingers back like the air between them had turned into a gaping shark's mouth. His eyes, his lying, double-crossing eyes pleaded with her when he said, "Please, Eve, I—"

Bing-bong. No sound had ever been sweeter than that of the elevator arriving on the penthouse floor. Billy hustled her inside the car, and Mac and Delilah stepped in behind them, immediately turning around to create a wall of flesh and blood between her and her father. And when he tried to get into the elevator car with them, Mac stopped him with a straight-armed palm centered in the middle of his chest. "I'm not sure I understand exactly what just went down," Mac drawled, shaking his head. "But if I were you, I believe I'd wait for the next car. I reckon you're not very welcome in this one."

"But I haven't finished speaking with my daughter,"

her father announced, still trying to play the I'm-rich-and-entitled-and-you-don't-scare-me card even though everyone in the elevator knew it was all just a show. Because even Eve, naïve, sheltered Eve could see the fear in her father's face.

"I believe you've said just about everything that needs sayin'," Mac informed him. "Now, please be so kind as to step back."

The words might've been phrased as a request, but Mac's tone was more in the line of do-as-I-say-or-find-yourself-eating-my-fist.

Her father obeyed. But before the silver doors slid shut completely, Blake got in one final, parting shot.

"And if someone's trying to kill you," he yelled, "start looking at your father! That business deal he got us involved in? Well, it's sunk! We're all bankrupt! And your inheritance and life-insurance policy are probably looking pretty sweet right now!"

Okay, she couldn't hold it in any longer. She tossed her head back and cried out with her all her fury and betrayal, all her grief and hurt. Billy raked her into his arms, pressing her face against his chest, whispering in her ear, "Shh, sweetheart. I've got you. I've got you, and nobody's gonna hurt you again."

Oh, if only she could believe him…

Chapter Sixteen

Chicago Police Station, District 2, Second Floor, Homicide Division
10:45 p.m.

Bill stared down into his Styrofoam coffee cup. Its contents reflected his mood. Black. And bitter...

"They still back there?" Mac asked after returning from the vending machine. He ripped open a box of raisins, dumped a handful into his palm and tossed the lot to the back of his mouth before slumping onto the bench beside Bill. *Bench? Ha!* That was a nice name for the mesh and metal ass-cheek-torture device that was pushed up against the drab, taupe-colored wall.

Taking a quick swig from his cup, Bill winced at the acrid taste—as far as he could figure, the only people who liked their bean juice stronger than covert operators were cops—before glancing across the sea of messy desks that made up the bullpen of Chicago's overworked homicide department. The place looked like an office supply store had thrown up. Post-its were stuck everywhere, white boards were covered with pictures and notes and magnets, and inboxes were overflowing with thick manila file folders. The air smelled like years of desperation, frustration, and sweat...and stale doughnuts.

Yeah, doughnuts. Stereotypes were stereotypes because they were usually true.

The late hour meant the floor was nearly deserted, though one detective still sat over in the corner wearing a half-undone tie and wilted suit jacket—apparently that was the standard uniform for Chicago's murder-cop force—and henpecking his keyboard with the index fingers on each hand. The sharp, intermittent *click-clack* was setting Bill's teeth on edge.

Or maybe it was the fact that, for the last hour, Eve and Delilah had been MIA, sequestered in separate interrogation rooms, getting grilled over the details of the stick-up and murder at Delilah's and that nasty scene up in her father's condo. And his not being able to check on Eve to make sure she wasn't having a nervous breakdown was making him…well…teeter on the edge of having a nervous breakdown.

"Yeah." He reached into his hip pocket to pull out his trusty bottle of Pepto. If anything deserved an antacid chaser it was that coffee. "They're still being questioned."

And damn, but the thought of Eve having to relive this awful day was enough to have his ulcer doing hat tricks that had nothing to do with the strength and acidity of the police station java. Unscrewing the cap on the bottle of pink medicine, he tossed back a mouthful. The chalky liquid was a welcome relief to his burning stomach. Too bad there wasn't a similar cure for his blistering thoughts or the hot ache in his heart.

Poor Eve…

She'd been through so much in less than twelve

hours. *Hell*, more than that. She'd been through so much over the past three *months*. Wait, back up and rewind again. Because after that little exposé in her father's penthouse, he realized she'd been the victim of years upon years of schemes and plots. And, to his utter shock and perhaps horror, he realized she *hadn't* really thrown him over for Blake Parish as he'd always thought. At least not in the traditional sense. It'd been her *father* who pushed her at the man.

Then again...she *had* ended up marrying Blake...

So, yeah. There was still that.

Why, Eve? Why? Even after today's revelations it seemed it was the same ol' question spinning through his cerebral cortex.

Mac interrupted his dismayed musings. "Did you see those photos they were talkin' about?"

"Yeah." He blew out a breath. It ruffled the hair that'd fallen over his forehead. "But not until months after they'd been published." One of his teammates who'd been sick and tired of his hangdog face had shoved one of the articles under his nose in an attempt to snap him out of his funk. Unfortunately, it'd had the opposite effect. Because even though at the time he'd already known he'd lost Eve forever—she'd been married for two weeks by then—seeing her in another man's arms, seeing her laughing and smiling had ground Bill's already broken heart into a fine powder. "Apparently during the time those stories were running in the papers, I was cut off from the world."

Mac lifted a brow.

"I was drowning—sometimes literally—in the

third phase of SEAL training," he explained. "And by the time I was able to come up for air, I discovered Eve's phone had been disconnected, and her letters had stopped." Of course, now Bill understood it was because she'd been caught red-handed out with another man, and she undoubtedly didn't want to have to come face-to-face with his anger and betrayal. She'd likely thought it was easier just to cut off communication altogether. Make a clean break as opposed to dealing with the drama.

Damnit, Eve! Why didn't you at least try *to talk to me? Why didn't you give me a chance to listen to an explanation? Didn't I deserve that?*

Of course, coulda, woulda, shoulda. It was all water under the bridge now. Or was it? Did this change things? Change the way he thought about her? Felt about her? He looked inside himself, at all the years of hurt, at all the years of wondering, *why, goddamnit, why?* And realized he didn't know. The truth of the matter was she betrayed him and the vows they made to each other the moment she agreed to go out on that date…

Shit on a stick. Why the hell does life, and matters of the heart in particular, have to be so craptastically complicated? Seriously. That wasn't a rhetorical question. He was really throwing that silent inquiry out into the ether, waiting for the universe to answer him.

A couple of seconds ticked by, but he heard nothing but radio silence. *Go figure.* In his experience, the universe was, more times than not, a total wad when it came to replying to the big questions.

"And then two days before I was due to *finally* get leave—I'd planned to fly to her university to figure out just what the hell was going on—I received an invitation to her wedding," he finished the story in one long, weary breath. Once again, he glanced across the expanse of desks to the gray metal door leading to the interrogation rooms.

"Harsh," Mac muttered, and Bill snorted.

"Yeah. You might call it that." Or you might call it friggin' *heartbreaking*. Lord knows his ticker had damn near exploded inside his chest cavity when he opened that envelope. To this day, he could still see that red and white invitation, still quote it word for word: *With a joyful heart, Patrick Alastair Edens requests the honor of your presence at the marriage of his daughter Evelyn Rose Edens to Jonathon Blake Parish. The ceremony will take place at half past two o'clock on the afternoon of blah, blah, blah...*

Christ.

Why had she sent him that awful invitation? He'd never taken her to be spiteful. Not the Eve he'd known then, and not the Eve he knew now. Unless...perhaps she'd thought it would be a signal for him to come crash the party? Perhaps she'd thought—

"Then again," Mac mused, his lips pursed in consideration, "sounds to me like she might have been manipulated into the marriage. After those articles ran in the papers, perhaps she felt there were expectations placed on her. You know, from friends and family. Maybe she thought she didn't have another choice."

Bill wanted to tell Mac he was *wrong*. That she'd

had another choice, goddamnit, because she'd had *him*. But the wide set of double doors connecting the elevator bank to the bullpen burst open, revealing the deep frown of none other than Chief Washington himself. Directly on his heels were Blake Parish and Patrick Edens.

At some point, Blake had changed his blood-soaked shirt for a fresh button-down and a linen sport coat. But the getup looked a bit ridiculous considering the man's nose was three times its normal size and both of his eyes were swollen and turning a painful-looking purple. Bill didn't even try to hide his gleeful smile. And it only spread wider when he discovered Patrick Edens, freshly attired in a light summer sweater, was trying to stare holes through him.

"You better redirect that gaze, cocksucker," he called to Edens. "Or else I might just decide to jump up and put a limp in that Jimmy Stewart swagger of yours."

"Can it, Reichert," Washington barked, just as the doors belched open again, admitting two gentlemen wearing pinstripe suits, shiny handmade loafers, and carrying briefcases.

Ah, yes. The ambulance-chasers. Although, Bill would bet a dollar to anyone's dime that these two overdressed, and no doubt overpaid lawyers had never chased an ambulance, or anything else for that matter, in their entire lives.

"Thank God you're here," Edens said to the men, studiously avoiding Bill's gaze as Washington led the group on a circuitous route through the desks in an attempt to bypass Bill and Mac's position by the wall.

Probably a good idea, Chief, Bill inwardly admitted. Because the reality was it wouldn't take much, maybe just a whiff of Edens's overpowering cologne, for him to follow through on that threat he'd just made.

Of course, he was careful to make sure none of this showed on his face when Washington glanced at him over his shoulder. Instead, he lifted a brow, letting his eyes drift to the lawyers before returning his gaze to Washington and calling, "What was that I mentioned earlier about me being able to say *I told you so*?"

Washington thrust out his lower lip all pugnacious-like and glared with those black eyes that seemed to see straight into a man's soul. Bill had always kind of figured the role of Sergeant Foley played by Louis Gossett Jr. in *An Officer and a Gentleman* was modeled after Washington.

"What did I just say, Reichert?" Washington bellowed.

He grinned cheekily. "About what, Chief?"

"About canning it," Washington barked.

"Um," Bill twisted up his face like the IQ fairy had passed him by on Extra Points Day. "That I should do so?"

"Exactly," Washington said, holding the gray door leading to the interrogation wing wide so his train of murderers, manipulators, and, worse, *lawyers,* could precede him. "But don't you leave," the police chief added before following the group. "After I see these, uh, gentlemen in for questioning, I'm gonna want to have a word with you."

"I'll be right here, Chief," he promised.

The detective pecking at his keyboard spared the group a brief glance before they disappeared behind the door. Then he went back to glaring at his computer screen. And when Bill turned to Mac, he found the man's expression was as amused as Washington's had been irritated.

"I dealt with a lot of police chiefs during my time as a fed," Mac drawled. "But I never came across one with quite the…eh…what *is* that particular aura that hangs around our intrepid Chief Washington? I can't quite put my finger on it?"

"It's one part *don't fuck with me*," Bill supplied helpfully.

"And the other part?" Mac queried.

"Don't fuck with me."

Mac chuckled. "Yeah, I think you nailed it."

For a couple of minutes, the police station was silent save for the monotonous *tick, tick, tick* of the clock on the wall above their heads, and the intermittent *clickety-clack* of the detective's keyboard. Then Washington burst back onto the scene with the force and vigor of hurricane.

Bill and Mac both jumped to their feet. "How much longer will Eve be in there?" Bill asked before Washington finished crossing the room.

The chief didn't deign to answer, *the confounding sonofagun*, until after he'd sidled up beside them, all the while eyeing Bill in that deeply disturbing and blatantly considering way he had. He took his time loosening his red and blue tie, shrugging out of his suit jacket, and unbuttoning and rolling up the sleeves on his white dress shirt. And Bill knew the chief was being purposefully annoying, proving to everyone that in *this* place *he* was the big, swinging dick. But finally Washington relented, throwing his jacket on the bench and saying, "I suspect she'll be out soon. Normandy was wrapping things up when I looked in on them just a minute ago."

Bill was able to drag in a deep breath for the first time since she'd disappeared through that door. "Good," he said. "That's good." Because Lord knew he was completely wiped out from the day's events, which meant Eve had to be dead on her feet. And, yes, the truth was he was worried about her.

There. He admitted it.

He shook his head. At himself. At Fate. At the goddamned, never-ending, roller coaster ride that happened to be his feelings for Eve Edens.

"And once Normandy's finished with her, he'll move on to questioning her father and her ex-husband," Washington added.

"That's good." Bill hoped they were questioned until they squirmed holes right through their designer pants. Questioned until they sweated blood...

"And we're in the process of pulling records to determine the locations of both men on the dates of Ms. Edens's previous...uh...mishaps."

"Good." Bill nodded. "That's good." He realized he'd gotten himself stuck in a loop when Washington's dark face pulled down a fierce frown.

"What the hell's the matter with you?" the chief thundered. "You swallow a parrot or something?"

"Sorry." Bill shook his head, trying to wrangle his wayward thoughts. "My mind is all over the place tonight."

"Yeah." Washington's big lips twisted into what Bill suspected was supposed to be a grin but looked more like the man had a serious case of gas. "And if I had to guess, right now it's back in that interrogation room where a certain socialite is being interviewed. You got a hard-on for Evelyn Edens, Reichert? Is that why you're all rolled up into this mess? I just thought you were helping her out because she's your kid sister's friend."

A hard-on for Eve Edens? Yeah, that was *one* way of putting it. But he sure as hell wasn't going to tell Washington as much. "Let's just say we're old acquaintances and leave it at that, huh?"

"If you insist," Washington said, still eyeing Bill with blatant curiosity.

"I insist." Bill mirrored the police chief's stance by crossing his arms over his chest. And then, to redirect Washington's line of questioning, he posed a question himself. "Did the…uh…did the wire help any?"

"It gave us enough reason to sequester Edens's and Parish's phone records." Washington said. "We've got a request in to a judge right now. Currently he's at a fund-raiser, but as soon as he's done, he'll sign the writ. Then we'll send it to the respective phone companies, which probably won't have anybody on staff until work hours tomorrow morning. So that means we'll *likely* have the logs in our hands by noon at the latest."

Noon? "Jesus Christ!" Bill gaped at the chief then

glanced around, blinking. "Was I transported through a wormhole back to 1989? Isn't everything electronic now? Don't you just need the right geek to push the right button and *voila!* The information is yours for the taking?"

Where was Ozzie, BKI's resident techno-geek extraordinaire, when Bill needed him? *Oh, yeah.* The guy was doing a four-month stint down in South America, trying to, you know, save the world or some shit. *Goddamnit.*

"I work in the real word, Reichert. Not some..." Washington glanced over his shoulder at the detective still working, then turned back and lowered his voice. "Not some dick-shriveled, government blow-job factory." Despite himself, despite the horridness of this god-awful day, Bill felt a grin pull at his lips. "So if you think you can do a better job of getting that info ASAP, be my guest."

Chewing on the inside of his cheek, Bill said, "What you said was *be my guest.* So why did I just hear *go fuck yourself?*"

"Maybe because you've got good ears," Washington replied.

Bill chuckled. But the sound died in his throat when Washington continued, "Although, if you ask me, chances are slim-to-none the phone records will reveal anything. These guys might look like a couple of dandies, but I'm sure whichever one of them is behind this was smart enough to have covered his ass before calling in a hit."

"You think he used a burner?" Bill asked, referring

to the cheap, prepaid cell phones available in gas stations for a song.

"Yeah." Washington nodded. "Which means, short of a confession, I suspect it's gonna take some old-fashioned police work to get to the bottom of this thing."

"You and I both know a confession is out of the question." Bill would like nothing better than that, but in order for a person to confess, they usually had to feel guilty about whatever it was they were confessing to. And in order to feel guilty, a person needed a conscience. As far as he could figure, Parish and Edens were each missing that essential ingredient.

"Maybe." Washington shrugged. "Stranger things have happened."

Bill opened his mouth to respond but snapped it closed again, his lungs seizing, when the gray door swung open and Eve and Delilah pushed into the room. *Sweet Mother Mary*, if there were ever two women who looked like death warmed over, it was those two. And one glance at Eve's ravaged, splotchy face, at the hard line between her brows and the heavy bags beneath her brilliant blue eyes, and his foolish, sympathetic, *insane* heart turned a somersault in his chest.

Wee!

Yessir, and that would be the sound of his feelings for Eve, going for yet another roller coaster ride.

Well, for shit's sake...

Chapter Seventeen

Watching the women make their way through the messy desks of the Chicago police station's Homicide Department made Mac's stomach ache with so much sympathy he felt nauseous. Like someone had sucker punched his happy sack. And, *sonofabitch,* but he wished he could fall into that wormhole Bill'd spoken of and go back to this morning.

If any day deserved a do-over, it was this day. *Holy crow...*

But if I had a do-over, I'd never have taken that ride with Delilah.

Okay, so there was *that.* Because despite everything she'd been through, despite the fact that she'd survived a gun battle where she'd witnessed one of her friends cut down in cold blood, the truth was that having Delilah Fairchild snuggled up against his back on the ride over to Patrick Edens's condo had made it onto Mac's personal highlight reel. Which probably just proved how much of a degenerate he really was, but *hot damn!*

To his utter chagrin, he'd always been a sucker for that whole pin-up girl, Sophia Loren type, and Delilah pretty much personified the category. Hell, if the woman was a mathematics discipline, she'd be Trigonometry as opposed to Algebra, because she was all curves: not a straight line on her. And even now, makeup washed away, T-shirt stained with blood, and auburn hair sticking out like she'd shoved her finger in an electrical socket, she was still in the running for the top slot in the Sexiest Woman on the Planet Contest, which...*damnit*...was *exactly* what he *didn't* need in his life right now. Or *ever*, come to think of it.

What was that thing Ozzie liked to say? You better check yourself before you wreck yourself? Well, in the case of Mac's prodigious attraction to, nah, *lust for* Delilah, that was damn good advice.

Ripping his eyeballs away from her rolling gait took considerable effort, but he finally managed it. And when he let his gaze fall on Eve, his nausea returned with a vengeance.

Good thing Bill's taken to carrying around that bottle of Pepto again, because I might just have to borrow it...

For pity's sake, poor Eve looked like she'd been put through the wringer, taken out, dried off, then put through again...only inside-out. And in his not-so-humble opinion, she deserved a gold medal for the way she'd handled herself today. Scratch that, she deserved a parade and a whole freakin' statue erected in her honor.

Had Bill really likened her to a china doll? Had *he* really agreed with that comparison? It was hard to believe either of them could've been so far off the mark, like, not even on the same freakin' playing field. Because Eve Edens was proving to be one of the toughest, most courageous women Mac had ever met. And ol' Billy-boy didn't know it yet—or maybe the guy just didn't want to admit it to himself—but he was a complete goner where she was concerned. At the moment, the dude was literally vibrating beside him while watching Eve approach, strung tighter than a piano wire. And his expression? Well, if *possessiveness* had a particular look, then it was the one wallpapered all over Wild Bill's face.

Mac wondered if the man realized he instinctively reached for Eve when she stopped in front of him. Pulling her under his arm and tucking her in close, he asked, "Are you okay?" while bending to press his nose into her hair, inhaling the fragrance of her shampoo like nicotine addicts inhale secondary smoke.

G-O-N-E-R. What does that spell? Bill Reichert…

Eve pulled back to look up at him, and from the expression on her face, Bill wasn't the only one running for mayor of Lovey Dovey Land. In fact, if Mac listened real close, he imagined he could hear Eve making those sad, whimpering puppy dog noises. Of course, Bill *was* the big, handsome guy who'd been trying to help her and protect her for the last couple of days, so Mac could totally get why Eve was pulling the whole hearts and flowers and soft sighs routine. As far as he could figure, she'd placed Bill in the role of real life superhero, which, honestly, Mac could sort of agree with. Unlike Dale Pennyworth, Wild Bill didn't need a weird bodysuit to make him heroic. His personal attributes did that for him: courage, honor, loyalty…

Although if Bill's the superhero, that makes you the trusty sidekick, a voice whispered.

Okay, so he didn't particularly like the sound of *that*. After all, everyone wanted to be the hero of his own script. And he was *totally* going to chalk up wanting to be the hero of his own script as the reason why he didn't pull away when Delilah sidled next to him, tentatively reaching for his hand. He laced his fingers with hers, giving them a squeeze as he tried to convey his support and perhaps lend a little bit of comfort. Then again, with one of her luscious boobs pressed against the back of his arm, it was kind of hard to think comforting and supportive thoughts and—

For the love of Christ. Pull your head out of the gutter, McMillan, he mentally groused at himself, *and stop being such a cockstain.*

Delilah pressed closer.

All right, so cockstain it was, because he couldn't seem to concentrate on anything other than the fact that he thought maybe, just maybe, he could feel her nipple rubbing against his triceps.

And so much for being the superhero of his own script. Unless, of course, he was dressed as Batman in the porno movie playing in his head. *Shit.*

"Is there anything I or the Chicago Police Department can do for you, ladies?" Chief Washington asked, and right, so that did it. That was enough to distract Mac from the feel of Delilah's warm hand laced with his, to take his mind—kinda, sorta, maybe—off the sensation of her breast pressing against his arm. Because if he hadn't seen it with his own two eyes, he wouldn't have believed the man standing beside him, dark face as smooth and serene as an angel's, was the same guy who'd just accused them of working for a government blow-job factory.

"You can find the thugs who shot up my bar and killed Buzzard," Delilah said, her usually breathy, sex-star voice sounded hoarse, belying the fact that she'd been crying, freakin' *crying her pretty green eyes out*, while she'd been giving her statement.

Right. And he'd been thinking about her boobs. He really was a degenerate. Worse than that. A shit-heel. A bona fide, grade-A shit-heel…

"We're doing everything we can," Washington assured her. "We've got alerts in to all the local hospitals and clinics. If a man comes in with shot pellets in his leg, we'll be the first to know. And we've sent a sample of his blood for DNA testing. If he's in the system, we'll have his identity in seven to ten days."

Okay, and shit-heel or not, Mac knew seven to ten days was probably optimistic. Because, unlike Bill, he was well-schooled on how slowly things worked outside the high-tech realm of top-tier government intelligence. So, despite the police chief's assurance, if the CPD had the results of the DNA test by the end of two weeks, Mac would be shocked.

"And my father and ex-husband?" Eve asked, staring up at Washington with those wide blue eyes of hers. They were bruised and, at the same time, so innocent looking. Eyes like that, *women* like that, were the reasons men went to war. And, yessiree. No two ways about it. Wild Bill was toast. Just cover him in butter and jelly and slap him on a plate. "What are you going to do with them?" she asked.

"We're going to question them and figure out which one of them is behind the attacks," Washington assured her. "It appears they both have a motive to—"

"Wait," Eve interrupted, shaking her head and looking as if the only thing holding her up was the fact that Bill had his arm around her. She lifted her hand to start gnawing on the side of her thumb. "What motive does Blake have again?"

Washington opened his mouth, but Mac beat him to the punch. "If what he said was true," he explained, "then it's possible your father could use your life insurance and inheritance to save their bad business deal, thereby savin' Parish's ass in the process."

"But then why would he come out and admit the business deal was a bust?" Her brows formed a perfect V. "Why wouldn't he try to keep his motive a secret?"

"Maybe to throw us off the scent," Washington said. "Maybe he thought if he pointed the finger at your father, we wouldn't look as closely at *him*."

"I hate to add more fuel to the fire," Delilah murmured as she released Mac's hand and took a small step away. No shit, the muscle in the back of his arm actually twitched with displeasure, and his deserted fingers instinctively curled into a fist. And *that* was why he'd always gone out of his way to avoid touching Delilah. Because the feel of her, the feel of all that pale skin was like crack. And one hit was enough to have him hooked for life. "But isn't it possible they're actually working *together*? By each of them saying it's the other, it muddies the waters all around. And this business deal, whatever it is, could—"

"Keystone Property Development," Washington interrupted.

"Which is what?" Eve asked, not batting a lash at the idea that her father and ex-husband might have teamed up to have her murdered. Either she'd already considered the possibility herself, or nothing more could surprise her today. If Mac was the betting kind, he'd lay ten-to-one odds that it was probably both. "I'm sorry, Chief Washington, but I didn't know Blake and my father were doing business together, so I'm at a loss here. Would you mind filling me in on what you know?"

"Well, right now I don't know much," Washington admitted. "Between the time Bill initially called me with suspicions about your father and the time he and your ex-husband turned themselves in, I had one of the detectives on the corporate investigations task force pull some quick public records. The most he was able to discover was that a few years ago, after Blake took over Parish Properties following his father's death, he and *your* father teamed up on a joint venture. Parish Properties and Edens Enterprises are now one large corporation operating under the name Keystone Property Development. Apparently, they went gang-busters for a while, buying up vacant lots and old buildings all over the city. I think they were riding the wave of the building boom. Then the housing bubble burst, and they were left with squat. Contracts dried up. Demand for new construction fell through the floor. And they've been hemorrhaging money ever since."

"And my life-insurance policy and inheritance

would be enough to cover their losses?" Eve asked, her brow furrowed.

"We'll find out more once we dig a little deeper," Washington assured her. "And we *will* dig deeper this time. I promise you that."

Yeah, and Mac knew these types of cases could drag on for months, sometimes years. Apparently Washington knew it too, because he added, "And who knows. Maybe the guy Miss Fairchild shot *will* be in the system, and we'll be able to cut him a deal if he agrees to tell us who hired him." Which would be the better and certainly quicker solution all around. "But in the meantime, I'm gonna assign you around-the-clock surveillance."

Eve's eyes widened, her jaw falling open like it was attached to her head by loose hinges. "Surveillance? Do you really think that's necessary?"

"Whoever tried to shoot you is still out there. They might make another attempt on your life, or maybe whoever hired them will task someone else with the job. It's time we, the CPD, were vigilant about your safety. Jesus knows we dropped the ball the first three times." Washington's lips turned down.

"But Billy would—"

"We have no idea how long this will drag on," the chief interrupted. "And Reichert has other responsibilities. You can't expect him to drop everything to be your bullet catcher for—"

"But I will," Bill cut in. "I'll stick to her like honey on—"

"No, Billy," Eve touched his arm. "Chief

Washington is right. It's just that after everything that's happened today, I was sort of hoping to get away from the city for a while. Just..." She shook her head, and her expression was so bleak that Mac could almost feel her pain and frustration and weariness—and guilt. That was definitely in there, too. But, really, how could it not be? She'd just spent over an hour going through the details of a man's death...a man's death that was meant to be her own. She'd likely suffer from the guilt of that for the rest of her life. Which was so goddamned sad he almost felt like crying himself.

What a goatscrew.

"Just disappear for a while," she finished slowly.

Washington cocked his head. "And where would you disappear to, may I ask?"

"I—" She shrugged, gnawing on her lower lip and gazing out the tall windows on the western wall. The city was a mass of darkness and twinkling lights beyond. "I don't really know. I suppose I could go down to my vacation house in Costa Rica and—"

"Out of the question," Washington interrupted. "We need you to stay in the states. Close by, if possible, in case something comes up or in case we need to question you further."

"Yes." Eve bit her lip, nodding. "I kind of figured that. So maybe...I don't know. Maybe...do you think it's possible I could go out on my sailboat? Just drift away for a couple of days? Perhaps head over to Michigan? I could lose myself in a little coastal town there. Go where no one knows me, where no one's trying to kill me."

Bill frowned. "Perhaps it *would* be better for her to get out of Chicago for a while. In case you're right about someone trying to make another attempt on her life."

"Mmph," Washington grunted, scowling at the floor with his lower lip thrust out. "I suppose." He glanced up at Bill. "But I wouldn't want her going alone. I could put a couple of my men—"

"No need." Bill lifted his hand, shaking his head. "I've got it covered."

Yeah, Mac thought. *I'm sure you do.*

"I've got a cabin over on the west side of Michigan, up near Ludington," Bill continued, looking at Eve to see if she was okay with the plan so far. If the hero worship…no, not hero worship…*super*hero worship shining in her eyes was anything to go by, she wasn't just on board with the plan, she'd packed her bags, waved her good-byes, and was already sitting on the deck drinking a Mai Tai. "I think we could hole up there for a while. It'd give Eve the chance to get away but keep her close enough so she could drive back to the city in three or four hours if she needed to."

Washington's eyes narrowed as he opened his mouth. But before he could agree or disagree with Bill's plan, the double doors leading to the exterior elevator bank burst open and Jeremy Buchanan strolled into the room.

"Jeremy!" Eve sobbed, ducking out from under Bill's arm to run to the man. Buchanan caught her up in a hug that lifted her feet from the station's tiled floor.

"I came as soon as my shift ended," he said, slowly

lowering her to the ground so he could pull back and look at her. "How did it go?"

"It was awful," Eve admitted. "But now it's done."

"Did you..." His expression and tone illustrated both his reluctance and his curiosity. "Did you find out anything when you met with your father?"

She shook her head. "Not really."

"Damn," he cursed, his jaw sawing back and forth. "Well, it doesn't matter. Because I swear to you, we're going to find out who did this."

"You mean Detective Normandy is gonna find out who did this. Right, Lieutenant?" Washington said. "From what I hear, you've got your hands full over in vice."

"Sure. I'll let the murder boys handle it." Jeremy laced his fingers with Eve's, and Mac was pretty sure that grinding noise he was hearing was Bill's back teeth again. Too bad they weren't sitting down at a conference table somewhere so he could kick the man in the shins. "Now that you guys actually believe what I've been saying to you for the last three months," he added as he joined the group.

"Don't push it, Lieutenant," Washington harrumphed. "No one likes to hear *I told you so*."

"Not gloating," Jeremy was quick to explain. "Just happy to know something's *finally* being done."

"Mmph." Washington waved him off, turning back to Bill. "Now about this little sailing trip up to Ludington. I don't suppose it'd be a problem as long as—"

The gray door at the back of the room swung open, and Edens, Parish, and their lawyers stood on the threshold. Mac fleetingly wondered how much they'd heard of the conversation. Then he figured, not much. That was a steel door leading to the hall where Chicago's finest interrogated Chicago's scum. And speaking of Chicago's finest, Detective Normandy appeared behind the group. If Mac wasn't mistaken, there was a new coffee stain on the man's shirt that hadn't been there before.

Holy crow, I hope he's better at catching crooks than he is at personal hygiene. Damn.

"Normandy?" the chief asked. "What's going on?"

"These assho—" Normandy stopped, scratched his balding head, and rephrased. "Their lawyers have requested they be allowed to consult with their clients in a room *other* than an interrogation room. You know, the cameras, the two-way glass...So, I'm taking them to conference room number two. And after they've had a little consult," he sneered the word, "we'll continue the questioning. In an *interrogation* room."

"Fine," Washington said, his expression that of a man who'd just stepped in something sticky and smelly.

Normandy nodded, ushering the group toward an adjacent hallway. Then his gaze snagged on Eve's cousin. "Oh, and I'm glad you're here, Lieutenant Buchanan. I've got a couple of questions to ask you about your uncle and Blake Parish."

"Sure thing." Buchanan nodded, though his expression betrayed his distaste. Mac wondered how close the guy was to his uncle, and what *his* take on Edens was. The FBI investigator in Mac would *love* to poke around inside Buchanan's brain for a minute or two.

"I'll be there in a sec," Buchanan added, then turned back to Eve. "I think it's good you're getting out of town," he told her.

Eve's lips trembled as she glanced up at her cousin. "You don't think I'm running away? You don't think I'm being a coward?"

"Hell no." Buchanan pulled her in for another hug. Mac lifted a brow when Bill's jaw started to twitch. "I absolutely do not think either of those things. I think you're strong and tough and—"

"Lieutenant," Normandy cut in after re-entering the bullpen. "Let's get going on those questions, huh? I'm working on a short clock here."

"Yeah, sure." Buchanan gestured him on before releasing Eve. Mac fought not to roll his eyes when Bill immediately snagged her by the shoulder and dragged her back, tucking her under his arm. "You better take care of her, Reichert," Buchanan warned. "Or you'll have me to answer to."

"I'll protect her with my life," Bill vowed, lifting his chin.

Buchanan must've heard the crystal clear ring of truth in that statement—hard not to—because a look of relief…or maybe contentment was the better word, passed over his face. He jerked his head in a quick nod, then turned to zigzag his way through the desks and over to Normandy.

"Protect her with your life, huh?" Washington muttered, his dark brow furrowed. "Let's hope it doesn't come to that."

And for no reason Mac could explain, the phrase

famous last words skittered through his mind like rancid, diseased leaves on a hot breeze. He shuddered…

Chapter Eighteen

Chicago Police Station, District 2, Second Floor,
Interrogation Room #6
11:42 p.m...

They don't know. I played my cards just right. They may have their suspicions, but they don't know. *I was able to keep up the act around them, around her...*

Her...the damned woman who was turning out to be impossible to kill. The damned woman who seemed to have nine lives. Who would've ever thought it? Certainly not him.

As he sat on the cold metal chair, staring at his reflection in the two-way glass on the opposite wall, he was careful to keep his expression shuttered. Careful to keep his face completely impassive as he mentally cursed those useless, moronic gangbangers straight to hell for botching what should've been an easy job.

And okay, fine. He realized *he'd* botched the first three attempts on her life, but that's only because his heart hadn't really been in it. He still *loved* her, dam-nit! Which made his failures understandable, perhaps even reasonable. But Christ! How hard was it for a couple of dickheads who—for shits and giggles—spent their weekends doing drive-bys to walk into a bar full of slow, fat bikers and put a bullet in the brain of one unarmed woman? Really? How hard was *that*?

Apparently too hard. And now not only did he have to deal with the fact that he was *still* at square one when it came to getting his hands on the money he needed, but there was also physical evidence left behind at the scene in the form of a blood sample—a blood sample that, when he stopped for a moment to think about it, was probably teeming with all manner of STDs; he knew the guy in question liked his crack as much as he liked his whores—that could eventually lead back to him…

No, no, no. I've been too smart. There's no way this will come back to bite me. I used a burner. I have alibis. And, besides, Devon Price won't let his man talk…

Devon Price. Just *thinking* the name of the leader of Chicago's biggest Southside gang, known as the Black Apostles, was enough to have the scotch he'd sipped earlier turning to bitter, burning acid in his stomach. And when he quietly and slowly blew out a breath, he could smell the anxiety and…*fear*—let's just call it what it was—coming up from deep inside him, from the pit of his somersaulting stomach.

He owed the man so much money. *Too* much money. Then again, the nice thing about being indebted to that snake-mean sonofabitch was that Devon needed him alive and out of jail in order to be able to cash in on the fat check he hoped to receive upon Eve's death. Which meant Devon would do what needed to be done to make sure the police didn't get anything on him.

For instance, he knew there'd be no hospital report of a man with buckshot in the leg, because the man with buckshot in his leg wouldn't be *going* to any hospital. In fact, the man with buckshot in his leg was currently being tended to by a veterinarian who made his bank by sewing up the bodies of Devon's gangland crew.

Bleh. He shivered just thinking of lying on a cold, metal slab where a whole slew of filthy, furry critters had lain before him, having his open wounds poked and prodded at with instruments that were likely seeing their second, third, or *fourth* use. But whatever. The bumbling idiot's medical care, or lack thereof, wasn't his problem. *His* problem was whether or not the gangbanger's DNA profile was in the system.

But if it is, it won't matter. It's not like Devon will let the man cut a deal even if he's inclined to, which, considering where the guy comes from, he's probably not.

One of the nice things about dealing with society's bottom-feeders was that, though they tended to have very few scruples, the one tenet they clung to more stubbornly than a cocklebur in a wool sock was the fact that they didn't rat. They didn't squeal. They kept their goddamned mouths shut at any and all costs, no matter what they were accused of or what sort of sentence was coming down on their heads. Because they knew that to do otherwise would compromise the integrity of the gang and ensure one thing and one thing only for themselves: a good ol' fashioned shanking in the shower after being ass-raped and beaten.

Okay. He blew out another sly, guarded breath. So, he was fine. He was covered. There was nothing to worry about on that front.

Which means now all I have to contend with is motive...

Shit.

And there was *that.* Then again, he could rest easy knowing he wasn't the only one with cause to want Eve dead...

So, I just need to continue to play it cool. Continue to cast doubt and continue to manipulate all the players around the board.

A smile threatened to curve his lips as he thought, *it's a good thing I've always been so good at chess.* But he knew any show of emotion other than concern would be viewed as suspect, so he folded his hands in his lap and looked up expectantly when the CPD detective threw open the door and schlepped his rumpled, hygiene-deficient self into the room...

Outside Red Delilah's Biker Bar
Monday, 12:56 a.m.

Delilah glanced at the yellow and black police tape crisscrossed over her front door and shuddered as she swung from the back of Mac's big, gnarly bike. Reaching up to tug the helmet from her head, her arms felt like they weighed two hundred pounds. And she realized someone, at some point, had thrown a handful of grit in her eyes, because the suckers burned like fire as she watched Mac toe out the kickstand and switch off the loudly growling engine.

Crime scene...

Her beloved bar was a crime scene. The scene where her staunchest patron had been shot down in cold blood.

Cold blood...

Why did people use that phrase? Blood wasn't cold. It was hot. Hot and slick and smelling of the iron-richness of life, and—

God, I'm exhausted. Exhausted and sad and—

She glanced at the taped-up doorway again, and her stomach did a series of flips like it was competing for a slot on the Olympic gymnastics team or something. She had to toss Mac the helmet so she could put her hands on her hips and bend at the waist, taking deep, gulping breaths of the dense city air lest she loose her cookies on the spot.

"Hey," Mac reached forward to lay one of his big, broad hands on her shoulder. "Are you okay?"

Okay? "No, I don't think I am, I—"

She glanced up, and there it was again. All that glaring, yellow tape. A reminder that she'd *watched* as the last of Buzzard's life-giving blood seeped from his chest and puddled onto the floor and—

Holy shit, she didn't think she could stay here. Not tonight. Not when the memory of...*everything* was still so fresh. Too fresh. Too goddamned fresh to stay here and face it all...

Tomorrow, she promised herself. *Tomorrow, if the police will let me, I'll start putting my business back together. Tomorrow, I'll look into contacting Buzzard's estranged sister to tell her he's dead.* Sweet Mary and Joseph, *dead.* She still couldn't quite believe it, except that the tears burning the back of her nose and the bile scalding the back of her throat told her it was true. *Tomorrow, I'll suck-it-up-buttercup and deal with what has to be dealt with.*

But not tonight...

Tonight she just needed to be...*away*. And despite everything that Eve had suffered, despite what the woman was *still* dealing with, Delilah discovered she was green with envy. Because Eve was...*away*.

After they'd left the police station, she and Mac had waited at a nearby coffeehouse while Bill and Eve went to the BKI chopper shop on Goose Island to pack a couple of bags—and, yes, Delilah totally suspected they'd done it that way because neither Mac nor Bill wanted her going inside the place. Although, when she'd said as much to Mac while trying to choke down a cappuccino, he'd simply pointed a finger at his slightly crooked nose and sing-songed, "You see this? You can't read my p-p-p-poker face."

Which truthfully, and despite a day that'd gone from perfect to puke, and despite the fact that she couldn't close her eyes without seeing Buzzard's last moments emblazoned on the backs of her lids, it'd made her laugh. To hear a big, burly guy like Mac quoting Lady Gaga in a slow, Texas twang was nothing short of hilarious. She figured he'd offered up the levity on purpose—God love him—in an attempt to lighten the tense atmosphere and brighten her black-on-black mood. And it'd worked. For all of about half a second. Then her laughter had died a quick death when he'd added, "Besides, you're completely wrong. We're waiting here because I thought you could use this time to gather your thoughts."

Gather her thoughts? *Gather her thoughts?* Really? He thought she needed to *gather her thoughts*? That was the *last* thing she needed! In fact, what she needed then, what she needed now, was to *stop* thinking altogether. Just stop the sickening cascade of memories… And for a moment, after Bill and Eve had returned, and while she and Mac had followed them out to Belmont Harbor, and especially when Mac had…wait for it… helped Bill check the boat for bugs—and not the creepy/crawly kind, either; the black wands the men had waved over the entire vessel had been searching for the transmit-y/receive-y kind—she'd gotten her wish. For those few, *too* few blessed minutes, she'd completely forgotten about her own troubles. She'd been too busy watching the men flit around the boat like drain flies while simultaneously trying to swallow down the giant serving of bullshit, a.k.a. *we're nothing more than motorcycle mechanics who've seen the darker side of life*, that Mac'd served her earlier.

Sheesh. The man was obviously under the impression she'd fallen off the turnip truck only yesterday. Or else, he simply didn't care *what* she thought.

Then again, none of that mattered now because the point was she didn't *want* to be alone with her thoughts, she didn't *want* to stay here tonight, and she'd watched with an envious heart as Bill and

Eve fired up the inboard engine on the sailboat. She barely resisted calling out "Take me with you!" as she stood on the softly rocking dock, the stars glinting overhead while the vessel motored out into the vast midnight blue of Lake Michigan. So, yup. She was jealous of Eve. Because she, too, wanted…no, *needed* to get away.

And then an idea washed over her so brightly, she actually tilted her head back to see if there was a light bulb shining above her. Nope. No light bulb. But an epiphany nonetheless.

"Let me stay with you tonight, Mac," she blurted. When he blanched like she'd kicked his dog, she tried really hard, really, really, *really* hard not to let the expression get to her. And before he could open his mouth to reject her, *again*, she pushed ahead. "The cringe-factor here is just way too high. I could seriously use a few hours away." And when he hesitated once more, she swallowed her pride and begged. Well, as much begging as her ego—her very well-adjusted and perfectly proportioned ego, thank you very much—would allow her. "Please," she added.

He twisted up his lips, narrowing his eyes at her. And when he said, "Is there a mathematical way to calculate a cringe-factor that *isn't* too high?" she realized she was holding her breath.

Blowing it out in one exasperated puff, she said, "I'm serious, Mac. I don't want to stay here. And I don't care what you're trying to hide at the chopper shop. Really, I don't. My motto has always been *don't get other people's shit on my shoes*. So, my lips are sealed, whatever it is. I can promise you. My. Lips. Are. Sealed. I just want a warm bed somewhere *other* than the place one of my friends died. And I don't think I can stand to be alone in some hotel. Is that too much to ask?"

He had that stop-and-stare thing down pat. And as he sat there straddling his big, mean-looking motorcycle, regarding her so intently, she realized why it was she was so attracted to him. Forget about the muscles and the thick, dark hair, forget about the piercing blue eyes and the air of mystery. Because, to put it simply, all that stoicism, all that quiet, macho-man reticence was like a hit of cocaine for a woman like her. A hit of cocaine for a woman who knew that still waters ran deep.

Of course, he went and ruined it all, ruined all her softer feelings toward him, when he cocked his head and said, "Are you tryin' to pull my heart strings? Because I have to tell you, they're not really attached to anything. And I'm not gonna let you use the excuse of what you've been through today to try to finagle me into climbin' in bed with you."

And, yes. That would be her jaw hanging down to her chest. She snapped it shut so hard her teeth clacked. Disappointment, then anger, had her lips thinning into a tight line, and all of her exhaustion disappeared in a flash. "That's *not* what I was doing," she ground out, horrified when tears of humiliation and rejection burned at the back of her throat.

"No?" He lifted one infuriating brow.

"No," she declared, her cheeks burning despite the soft puff of cool evening air that tried, without much success, to ruffle her tangled, matted hair. "I just wanted a friend. Do you know what that is, Mac? A friend?" Her upper lip curled. "As in, a person who's there for me when someone I care about dies?" And then, because she had the tendency to become petty and biting when she'd been intentionally and cruelly dissed—no, she wasn't proud of it, but neither could she seem to help it—she added, "Besides, I thought you were gay."

His dimpled chin jerked back, and for a moment she thought she could see his thoughts spinning almost visibly behind his bright blue eyes. Then he smiled. Yes, smiled. The bastard had the audacity to *smile* at her. And *damnit*, Mac's smile could melt the polar ice caps. But it wasn't going to melt her ire. No. N-O. Hell no. He'd just been a complete *ass* to her. And she wasn't about to let him get away with that just because he had a nice smile. A blindingly *wonderful* smile.

"Just what is it about me, besides the fact that I might be the only man on the planet who doesn't want to sleep with you, that would lead you to believe I'm gay?" he asked.

"Honey," she cocked a hip and batted her lashes sarcastically, "after *Brokeback Mountain* I don't take anything for granted. And the truth is, you're not wearing a ring, you're always surrounded by men, and I've never seen you take a woman home from my bar. So," she shrugged, making a nasty face, "ipso facto, you can't blame me for thinking you might be rockin' the rainbow."

"I'm not gay," he growled, his smile disappearing as quickly as it'd appeared.

"And I'm not trying to sleep with you, you miserable prick," she shot back, glaring at him so hard it was a wonder he wasn't catapulted off his bike. "Holy shit, why don't you get over yourself already?"

He licked his lips and, *damnit, damnit, damnit,* the dart of his tongue momentarily distracted her. But not so much as his next words…

"I'm sorry."

Uh-huh. Just like that. No defensiveness. No counterattack. Just an apology. Straight up and to the point. And what had she said about quiet, stoic, still-waters-running-deep men like him being cocaine to her?

Shit. She wanted to hold on to her anger. She really did. It made the grief and the remorse she was feeling less sharp, the memories less soul-crushingly painful. But despite herself, despite her desire to the contrary, all her fury seeped out of her like flat beer down the drain on the bar's sink.

"Seriously," he added. "I *am* sorry. I just thought," he motioned with a hand toward the taped-up front door, "you know, after all the flirtin' and propositioning, after you sayin' that thing about a warm bed, that you were tryin' to—"

"Okay, I get it," she cut him off. "Whatever. I just—"

"Delilah," he interrupted her. "I can't let you stay at the shop. I really wish I could, but I can't." He dipped his chin. "Do you get me? I *can't.*"

Can't. It wasn't a word that carried much weight with her. He could if he wanted to. He *could*. It wasn't like there was an invisible force field around the place that prohibited the entrance of outsiders. It wasn't like the compound was some sort of top secret military installation like Area 51, where he'd be forced to kill her after showing her around. He *wouldn't* take her back to the chopper shop. *Wouldn't.* For whatever reason. Not *couldn't.*

"Fine. Whatever. Listen, you're off the hook, okay? I'll be okay here tonight."

"Delilah, I—"

"And you know what?" An idea suddenly occurred to her. Another epiphany. She hoped this one worked out better than the last had. "I'll even do you one better."

Again that dark brow climbed up his forehead. It *was* an infuriating brow. "What's that?" he asked hesitantly. And instead of ignoring the note of skepticism in his voice, she allowed it to fuel her ire.

"I'm going to use my contacts at the McClovern and Brown law firm to determine just how much hot water this Keystone Property Development company is in. Maybe there's something in the company's records that'll help determine which one of those men, Blake Parish or Patrick Edens, has more incentive to see Eve dead."

And *that* would kill two birds with one stone. It'd allow her mind to focus on something other the horror of this god-awful, fantastically craptastic day, and it'd help her feel like she was doing her part to bring Buzzard's murderer to justice. *Booyah!* If she'd had a football in her hand, she'd have spiked it into the dusty pavement of the parking lot.

She didn't need to go home with Mac. She didn't need to hide behind the wide shoulders of some man.

Hell no! She was Delilah Fairchild! The ass-kicking, Harley-riding, shotgun-toting, beer-slinger-from-hell! ...And also, she was Delilah Fairchild, the certified forensic accountant who moonlighted—when she needed the extra cash—for one of Chicago's top firms.

For a good, long moment—during which time she offered Mac a smile like a cat might offer a canary—he just sat there blinking at her. He opened his mouth once. Closed it. Opened it again, and asked, "McClovern and Brown?"

With more than an ounce or two of pride—okay, so maybe her ego wasn't so well-adjusted or perfectly proportioned, after all—she told him about her advanced degrees and her second job. Then she finished with, "What? Did you think I'd worked in this bar my entire life?"

"Well, I—" He stopped. Shook his head. Stared at her for a little while longer, then said, "But if you're a CFA, what are you doing bartending?"

Well for one thing, she loved it. And for another thing, she loved it. And finally...well...she loved it. It was just that simple. Of course, what she said to him was, "Oh, I don't know, Mac. Maybe I'm doing the same thing you're doing. You *are* an FBI agent currently working as a motorcycle mechanic, are you not?" She tilted her head, batting her lashes. She didn't need to say, *gotcha!* She made sure the sentiment was plastered all over her face.

A vein pulsed in his forehead, and the little devil he always managed to bring out in her rejoiced that she'd gotten the best of him. Then he swallowed, his Adam's apple bobbing in the thick column of his throat, and crossed his powerful arms, stretching the leather of his summer weight motorcycle jacket as he leaned back on the seat. "You really think you can discover anything the police can't?" he finally asked, after another long sit-'n'-stare session.

She shrugged. "I won't know until I try." She didn't dare look back at the taped-up door—she didn't want to lose all the bravado she'd just acquired—as she motioned toward it. "It's not like there's much else I can do right now."

He nodded, still eyeing her in that too-discerning way he had. It made her skin itch, her scalp tingle. It made her wonder if she really *was* feeling better, if she really *was* able to toss aside all her earlier fear and angst and discomposure now that she had a purpose, or if she was just fooling herself. It made her wonder if the moment she walked through that door she was going to lose her shit again.

No, she assured herself. *I won't. I had a moment. But now I'm done. I'm done feeling sorry for myself, done acting like a ninny. Just done...Aren't I...?*

"I could drop you at a friend's house, or—"

She held up a hand, cutting him off. "No need." And to prove to herself that, *yes*, indeed she *was* done feeling sorry for herself, done being a ninny, she dragged in a deep breath—the city air smelled damp and heavy, electric, like a storm lay brewing on some distant horizon—and said, "I'm fine. I was having a bit of a personal crisis there, a momentary breakdown, but now it's over. It's..." She shook her head. "It's all over."

He swallowed again, his expression softening. *Shit.* "Delilah, I want you to know it's—"

Oh, no. She wasn't in any sort of emotional state to stomach an it's-not-you-it's-me speech. That might be just enough to push her over the edge. Again. "Save it," she told him. "I'm going inside now. I'll email the assistant at McClovern and Brown tonight, and maybe by tomorrow afternoon she'll have had time to gather some files and records on Keystone Property Development. If I find anything interesting, I'll let you know. Goodnight, Mac."

She considered offering him a handshake, but that would be too weird. And leaning forward to kiss his cheek would be weirder still, especially after their little conversation. So she simply turned and walked across the parking lot, studiously averting her eyes from all that tape on the front door, to the corner of the building. She'd use the alley stairs to reach her apartment on the second floor so she wouldn't have to go in through the bar. She might be done being a ninny, but she wasn't ready to see the broken bottles, or the busted jukebox…or the blood…

The urge to flee once more raced up her spine to scratch at the back of her head, but she beat it back. This was her *home*. It'd *always* been her home. Since the moment her parents died and her uncle Theo brought her here to raise her. And there were too many *good* memories in this place to let one bad one ruin everything. She wasn't going to run. She wasn't going to hide. Even for one night. This is where she belonged.

I can do this. I can do this. I can do this.

The mantra spun through her head, reminding her of *The Little Engine That Could* and all the bedtime stories her uncle had read to her before heading back down to tend to the bar. And see? *Good* memories...

She lifted her chin, squared her shoulders, and lengthened her stride. She'd just stepped onto the first metal tread of the stairs when she heard Mac fire up his Harley. The bike growled happily, all low and guttural, smooth and even. It was the sound of a well-tended machine. A sound she loved.

She was on the landing when she heard him pull up and stop in the alley below. "What is it?" she yelled, leaning over the iron rail.

When Mac threw his head back to stare up at her, the light from a nearby streetlamp caught on his face, highlighting the dimple in his stubborn chin and the hollows beneath his high, flat cheekbones. With the soft, yellow glow shining on him like that, she thought perhaps, just perhaps, he might be the most beautiful man she'd ever seen.

"If you need anything, anything at all…" He raised his voice over the sound of the contentedly rumbling engine, letting the sentence dangle.

She lifted a hand and nodded. And when he dipped his chin before pushing his helmet down over his head, torqueing his wrist, and motoring loudly down the alley, she realized, quite disgustedly, that she was a glutton for punishment. Because despite everything, despite *all* his rejections, she still had a thing for him. A silly, stupid, unrequited, unreturned, goddamned demoralizing *thing* for him.

And, *shit!*

But at least that gave her something to think about tonight other than the fact that one floor below her lay all the reminders of what'd happened that day. At least if she kept herself occupied and stewing over the idiotic fact that she was pining over a man who obviously didn't return her feelings, she wouldn't be thinking about Buzzard and agonizing over what she could have done differently. *If* she could have done something differently…

Chapter Nineteen

Lake Michigan
2:02 a.m.

Come on. Come on, Eve silently begged the small inboard engine as she leaned down into the cramped motor compartment, checking the plugs and the fuel lines even though she'd already checked them three times before, and they were working fine. Which mean they *weren't* the reason the engine had suddenly stalled out. And it wasn't the dreaded zebra mussels—those pesky little critters that'd been introduced to the Great Lakes by the bilge water from transoceanic vessels—that'd fouled the lines. Because there was no tell-tale sooty residue near the output port. Which meant…what?

What the heck was wrong with the stupid thing?

She wracked her brain, coming up with a big load of nada. Which wouldn't normally be a problem. Just like being engineless on a sailboat wouldn't normally a problem. Sailboat equals sails, after all. Sails catch wind and *voila!* The boat moves.

Except for tonight…

Because tonight there wasn't a breath of wind. Tonight Lake Michigan showcased a glassine surface, not even one tiny ripple marred its blue-black expanse.

Tonight it was an inky mirror, perfectly reflecting the glittering stars overhead and the minute glow of Chicago's city lights far, far in the distance.

Please tell me whatever is wrong with you is something simple. An easy fix, she begged the motor.

But in the general way of inanimate objects, the engine refused to answer her.

Thump. She pushed up and spun around in time to see Billy toss a big, yellow waterproof flashlight onto the turquoise cushion of the captain's chair. The softly glowing LED lights that ran the length of the sailboat's cabin and surrounded the small wheelhouse washed his dripping form in faint, bluish light. He tugged off his sopping T-shirt using that quintessential guy-move where he reached over his shoulder and grabbed the collar, dragging the entire garment off in one fell swoop. It landed on the teakwood deck with a splat. And if the sight of his mile-wide chest with its smattering of hair, and his tan, corrugated belly wasn't enough to make her heart skip a beat, then the stars tattooed just inside each of his hipbones, emphasizing the delineation of his abdomen muscles and accentuating the large veins that ran down into his groin certainly were.

Holy schnikes! Billy is ripped! Like seriously, brutally, cause-a-girl's-tongue-to-hang-out *ripped.* And, sweet Lord in heaven, those tattoos. He hadn't had them twelve years ago. And just looking at them now, looking at the perfection of his male body, watching the crystalline water droplets run down his chest and his stomach into the waistband of his swim trunks was enough to make the breath catch at the back of her throat, and caused most of her blood to pool hot and heavy between her legs.

Well, that's an improvement, I suppose. Because ever since she'd stood in the parking lot at Delilah's, contemplating the fact that her father might be the one behind the attempts on her life—and *certainly* after she'd discovered he and Blake had conspired against her with the press—her blood had been like ice.

"Jesus Christ!" Billy yanked off a set of diving goggles and tossed them onto the captain's chair to join the flashlight. Grabbing the white fluffy towel that was draped over the back of the seat, he used it to roughly scrub the water from his hair before moving to dry off his arms and chest. "That water is colder than a penguin's backside." He shivered once, then shook himself like a dog shaking off water before wrapping the towel around his shoulders.

Cold? Yep, she remembered just how cold it could be. Which was why she hadn't put up a fight over which one of them would jump overboard to see if whatever was wrong with the engine had something to do with the propeller.

And speaking of…

"Did you see anything?" she asked, unconsciously licking her lips when her gaze snagged on one lone droplet of water as it rolled lazily down the center of his torso until it dipped into his bellybutton, reemerged, and got caught in the thin line of hair that arrowed down the lower portion of his stomach.

Ripped. Jacked. Buff. A whole slurry of descriptors

tumbled through her head, but none seemed quite up to snuff when it came to encapsulating the wonder that was Billy and—

"We ran over some sort of rope, I think. The damn thing's wrapped six ways from Sunday around the prop," he said, bending to wring out what water he could from his loose swim trunks. "I'm going to need to go back down there with a knife and see if I can saw it loose."

Saw it loose…which meant he'd have to go back into that frigid, pitch-black water time and time again. Coming up for air, going back under. Rinse and repeat until he was a human popsicle. Although, it would certainly go much faster if she just went with him. She could hold the light while he worked on the rope.

She could hold the light…in all that endless, frigid, pitch-black water…

The memory of the scooter ride, of the weight of her backpack pulling her down, down, *down* into the abyss flashed through her head and refroze her blood in an instant.

"*Crap,*" she cursed, biting her lip and glancing out over the lake. "Crap, crap, *crap*!" She turned to slam the teakwood hatch down over the top of the engine compartment.

Blam!

The loud report echoed out over the water and gave her a tiny niggle of satisfaction. But not enough to mitigate the tsunami wave of self-pity and frustration and…*fear* that threatened to engulf her. And was it too much to ask that Fate throw her one, just one—she didn't need more than one, but she'd like just one—flippin' bone? Seriously? After everything, didn't she deserve just a teensy, tiny break?

She reached up to fist both hands into her hair, her *wet* hair, which reminded her how twenty minutes ago she'd tried—without any luck—to shower away all her cares and worries. The maneuver *usually* worked. Being out on the water, on her Catalina 34-foot sailing yacht nostalgically named *Summer Lovin'*, with none of the bullcrap day-to-day…*things* around her, save for the absolute bare necessities, she was *usually* able to find some clarity, some…peace.

But not tonight. Because either her ex-husband or her father or *both* were trying to kill her, and they'd apparently teamed up years ago to ensure she'd not only lost what little free will she had, but also completely annihilated any chance she had of making a life with the one and only guy she'd ever had the good fortune to love and…and…on top of all of that, an innocent man was *dead* because of their duplicity, because of *them*, because of *her*.

Blood running down a beer belly…Bearded mouth slightly open…Gray eyes glassy and dead…A red puddle of waning life steadily growing on the floor beneath a bar stool…

The images invaded her brain like a disease, and *shoot!* Now, she was going to lose it. She was *supposed* to have toughened up. She was *supposed* to have grown a set of brass ladyballs, but right now, despite her best efforts, everything was catching up with her, pressing down on her, pressing *in* on her. And she was going to lose it.

She bit her lip to try to hold it all back, but the sharp pain of her teeth sinking into the delicate pad didn't work. The world around her began to dissolve into a jumble of fuzzy shapes as tears welled in her eyes. *No, no, no...Don't do this. Don't—*

"Hey, hey," Billy padded over to her, throwing a heavy, damp arm around her shoulders. "It's no big deal. If I can just cut it away—"

"Y-you'll need m-my help," she sobbed, turning her face into his shoulder, breathing in the crisp smells of lake water and Billy. And it was official. The dam had broken. No, not broken. Exploded. Suddenly, she was shaking and bawling and probably working herself up to be a big ol' snot factory. But she couldn't help it. It felt like the entire world was out to get her, out to punish her for...for..."And I-I," she hiccupped, "I'm scared to go down there with you after," *hiccup*, "I nearly drowned!"

"You don't have to go down there with me. I can do it on my own, and—"

"Th-that's not *it*," she cried. "I'm n-n-not supposed to be scared of the water. It's my," *hiccup,* "my job!" Turning to wrap her arms around his neck, she choked on another sob when he immediately hugged her close. Hugged her up all tight and secure against his warm, solid chest, instinctively trying to sooth her, protect her. Being so nice. Being...Billy.

Oh, God! What had she *done*? Why hadn't she been tougher twelve years ago? Why hadn't she told her father to go screw himself when he kept after her about Blake? If she had, she'd have never betrayed

Billy and she wouldn't be in this mess right now. If she'd only remained strong, remained true, her whole life would be different.

What was that old chaos theory about a butterfly flapping its wings and setting into motion a series of events that resulted in a hurricane? Well, her decision to submit to her father's wishes was like the flapping of that butterfly's wings. And now she was experiencing the hurricane. She wished, oh, how she *wished* she could blame it on something or someone else, but it *had been* her decision, so this *was* all her fault...

And, *holy cow*, she was so tired. So tired. And so scared. And so unbelievably sorry for...for *everything*.

"Okay," Billy murmured next to her ear, his deep voice calm and capable-sounding. "You're not really scared of the water. You're just exhausted." She opened her mouth to refute his claim but snapped it shut when she realized he might be right. She was exhausted. Exhausted and defeated. "Which means you're going straight to bed."

"Wh-what about the rope?" she asked.

"In case you've forgotten, I'm a highly trained Navy SEAL. This little problem is exactly that. A *little* problem. And once I take care of it, *by myself*," he stressed, "everything will be perfectly fine."

Perfectly fine. Ha! Was he delusional? Nothing was perfectly fine. Everything was perfectly *wretched,* and *see!* Defeated. She was completely defeated. Which was...pathetic. And *so* not the kind of woman she'd been working hard to become.

Another wracking sob shook her shoulders

despite her best efforts to hold it back, and Billy held her tighter.

"Hey now," he crooned. "It's okay. I know things look really bad and everything feels really disastrous right now. But you just need some good, solid sleep. You'll feel better in the morning. Things *will* look better in the morning. I promise."

She tried to nod. Unfortunately the gesture just elicited a wet-sounding whimper.

You are such *a loser, Eve! A pathetic, wimpy, spineless, pathetic loser. Did I mention pathetic?*

"All right," he said. "I can see we've reached an impasse here. So, up you go." He bent to wrap an arm beneath her knees, then hoisted her up against his chest with the ease of the supremely fit.

"I can w-walk," she protested, her nose buried in the crook of this wonderfully solid shoulder.

"Shh," he murmured, turning sideways so he could squeeze them down the stairs leading to the small cabin. "I know you can walk, sweetheart. You can do whatever you set your mind to." No. No, she couldn't. Because she'd set her mind to winning him back, but so far she'd managed diddly-squat. Sure, he was being nice to her now, but that's only because she was having some sort of nervous breakdown and he was Billy. Loyal Billy. Courageous Billy. Trustworthy Billy. *Sweet* Billy. Kicking someone when they were down wasn't in his nature. But that didn't change the fact that her betrayal had cut him so deeply that even now, all these years later, he still had a hard time even agreeing to be her friend.

*Maybe...Someday...*The two words he'd mumbled back in BKI's onsite gym tumbled through her head like a couple of hot, thorny boulders, making her tears flow faster.

See? A loser! A sorry, pathetic loser!

"Come on, Eve," he begged. Peripherally she knew he was shuffling past the compact galley and the small table and booth toward the lone berth. "You've got to stop that. You're breaking my heart."

Oh, *great*. As if she hadn't done enough of that already!

"I'm s-s-sorry!" she wailed, now crying so hard her bones were rattling, so hard her lungs felt like they were trying to crawl out of her throat. "I never wanted to-to hurt you!"

"I know, sweetheart," he said, gently placing her on the mattress, dragging a pillow under her head and flipping one side of the blue and green coverlet over her. "I know you didn't. Just take a couple of breaths, okay? Can you do that for me?"

Could she do that for him? Was he serious? If asked her to jump off the John Hancock building, she'd happily pioneer unassisted human flight. But he wasn't asking her to jump off the John Hancock building, was he? He was only asking her to calm down, to take some breaths. Which she could do. Which she *would* do...

Fighting with everything she had, fighting for him like she should have fought for him years ago, she raked in a couple of ragged breaths through her stuffy nose. Then sucked in another through her mouth for good measure. It helped. Miraculously, her lungs once more settled into her chest. But when she raised her eyes to Billy's face, she had to bite her lip to keep from losing it all over again.

His intent brown eyes—his *beautiful* brown eyes—watched her with care and kindness and…and *sympathy*. Holy Mother Mary, a sob the size of Lake Michigan itself threatened to choke her. But she held it back.

"I-I'm okay," she sputtered, her stomach quivering so hard she thought she'd be sick. By the way he twisted his lips—his *beautiful* lips—it was obvious he didn't believe her. "Really," she assured him, her breath hitching only slightly this time. "R-really I am."

"You've always been a terrible liar," he told her, smiling gently. And his expression was so warm. So warm and understanding and…and his nearness… all that tan skin covered in all those star tattoos was overwhelmingly intoxicating, and—

"B-Billy, please," she begged him for…what? To take pity on her? To love her? To *make* love to her.

And just the thought had everything inside her screeching to a halt. Except for her heart. Her heart was pounding against her ribs so fiercely she was surprised her oversized T-shirt wasn't fluttering.

"That's better," he said, mistaking her stillness for calmness. Lord knew she was anything but calm. Because her grief and fear and sense of defeat had morphed into something else, something she'd been told grief and fear and defeat *often* morphed into, though she'd never experienced the phenomenon herself.

The French referred to it so eloquently as *convoitise de la chair*. But in the far more suburban English it was known simply as…*lust*…

And how was that possible? How could a mental switch just flip like that?

"I'm going to run up, cut that rope from the propeller, reset the auto-pilot, and then make us some PB and Js," he said, reaching forward to squeeze her knee. The touch of his big palm—his hands were rough from years loading and cleaning weapons, arming and disarming explosives, battle-hardened hands, if you will—set her on fire as surely as a lit match touching a pool of kerosene.

"O-okay," she told him, licking her suddenly dry lips.

"Okay," he repeated, offering her a wink that caused his thick lashes to cast a faint shadow on his cheek.

When he turned to shuffle back down the length of the cabin, she pushed up on one elbow to watch him go, her breaths coming short and fast. The muscles of his broad back bunched beside the deep divot of his spine, his big, sturdy shoulders rolled slightly with each step, and his butt? Well, not to put it too crudely, but his mama must've been a baker because holy smokes did she ever make the perfect set of buns!

Geez Louise and praise be to good genetics and squat thrusts!

Thrusts. *Gulp.* Just the word brought to mind carnal images. Images of Billy above her, pumping, straining, sweat dampening the hair on his brow and trickling down his temple, his warm eyes watching her as—

Okay. And that was it. She had to think of something else. Because the truth was, he may not know whether or not he could ever forgive her enough to call her a friend, but that didn't mean he didn't still want her. She *knew* he still wanted her from the ferocity of his kisses alone, not to mention the fact that there'd been no mistaking his erection when she'd been pressed against him both back at BKI and out in Delilah's parking lot.

He wanted her. Lord knew she wanted him. And if she was the sex-kitten-y type she might be tempted to give him the one and only thing he was still willing to take from her and, conversely, take from him the one and only thing he was still willing to offer. Unfortunately, she *wasn't* the sex-kitten-y type.

Then, seemingly from nowhere, a voice whispered through her head, *no more missed opportunities, Eve...*

Chapter Twenty

Despite her height, Eve looked very small and delicate in her oversized T-shirt and her bunched up tube socks as she lay propped against the bulkhead. But when Bill offered her a plate stacked with three peanut butter and jelly sandwiches, he came to the conclusion that she may *look* small, however, she was undoubtedly the *biggest* disaster of his entire life.

Because beyond all reason, beyond his better judgment, he felt himself falling. *Again*. Just ass over teakettle taking the dive, much like Jack after he'd gone up to the hill to fetch his pail of water. And okay, that just proved his point, because look how *that* had turned out. Then, if a person—namely *he*—wasn't inclined to learn any lessons from nursery rhymes, then said person—namely *he*—had only to take a long, hard look at history…

At what did history tell him, do you suppose?

Well, just that she'd betrayed him once. That she'd proven he couldn't trust her. That it'd been *her* decision to go out with Blake Parish that night after she'd pledged to remain true to him and only him—of course what'd happened afterward wasn't her fault, but the initial decision *had been hers*. So…falling for her again would be bad…asinine…the stupidest, craziest, most ridiculous thing he could do, right?

Right.

Unfortunately, he felt himself standing on the edge of a cliff, poised to do exactly that. Especially when she looked at him, all big doe-eyes and hero-worship and…*shit.*

He watched her pale, slender hand reach out to snag the top sandwich and just that one innocent move, that one silly, everyday occurrence felt somehow intimate. Suddenly, he was all about the *I'm the big, strong provider caring for my little woman. Jesus Christ,* it was pathetic.

"Thank you for taking care of the prop," she murmured softly.

"It was nothing a good, sharp knife couldn't handle," he assured her. "I didn't even need to come up for air." And to prove it, the boat's engine hummed happily beneath them, the autopilot directing them across Lake Michigan's smooth surface toward Ludington.

"I should've—"

"Shh," he interrupted her. "You should've done exactly what you did. Relax. It's been one hell of a day."

She nodded, swallowing. "O-okay. Thank you, Billy," she said. And inexplicably he was thrust back in time, back to a moment twelve years ago when they were hot and heavy in the backseat of his Camaro with the windows all steamed up, with his hand in her pants and her sweet, pale nipple in his mouth. She'd been soft sighs and hesitant, searching hands, but the minute he thrust his finger inside her tight, wet body, she'd tensed in his arms and he'd known. Despite the slow-as-molasses-in-winter route they'd been taking to the ultimate physical discovery of each other, despite her assurances that she was ready, he'd known.

She hadn't been ready.

So he stopped. It was the hardest thing he ever did, slowly removing his finger from her body while his balls pounded so hard he thought they might just explode. But he stopped, and he told her, "Let's wait a little while longer, okay? Let's just hold off until you're really, *really* ready."

He remembered her opening her mouth to protest, but he halted her with a kiss, a slow, thorough kiss. A kiss he tried his best to infuse with all sorts of promises. Then he remembered pulling back, resting his fevered forehead against hers. "We have all the time in the world," he said.

She'd searched his eyes then, her expression torn. And he'd known the horny teenager in her wanted to know what lay beyond that final hurdle, and, talk about a Charlie Foxtrot, because he'd *soooo* wanted to show her, had been *dying* to show her. But the scared young virgin in her hadn't been quite there yet. And she'd listened to that second part of herself that day. With a sigh that was one part regret and another part relief, she'd said, "Okay. Thank you, Billy."

And looking back on all of that now, knowing how it'd turned out, he didn't know whether he should give himself a medal for being a stand-up guy, or if he should just go ahead and dub himself Unluckiest Bastard on the Planet.

Blinking, he realized he'd kept the plate raised

toward her for a ridiculous length of time, and he snatched it back, surreptitiously watching as she took a delicate bite of the sandwich. She licked a dollop of grape jelly from the corner of her mouth and he thought, *Alrighty, then. It's time to vamoose yourself, Bill ol' boy, before you do something really stupid.*

Turning to head back to the small booth and table, her voice stopped him. "Don't go, Billy," she pleaded quietly. "Won't you…I…I'd like it if you sat with me."

On the bed. She didn't need to say those last three words. They were implied when she scooted over on the mattress, making room for him.

And talk about doing something really stupid…

For a moment he hesitated, glancing out the porthole on the starboard side, hoping…what? That there'd be a neon sign glowing out there, spelling out for him in no uncertain terms what he should do? But the only thing he could see outside the porthole was darkness, just a pitch-black void that gave him no help whatsoever.

Go figure. The universe was a total wad when it came to him, remember?

Which left him with no recourse but to swallow the lump of uncertainty in his throat before blowing out a covert breath and turning back to Eve. She sat looking at him, a combination of fear and hope in her eyes. Her usually sleek hair was still a little damp and a *lot* rumpled, and her red bikini bottoms were peeking out from where the hem of her T-shirt rode high on her hip. Her eyes were bruised and puffy, her nose was pink, and her left cheek sported a glistening tear trail. But even given all of that, she was still temptation personified, everything he'd ever wanted and knew for goddamned sure he *shouldn't*, because he refused to put himself out there again. Not when he didn't know if he could trust her. Not when it'd nearly killed him to have his trust in her, his faith in her broken the first time. Not when—

"It-it's okay," she said, tucking her chin and blinking rapidly as she hastily took another bite of the sandwich.

Damnit all to hell, and now he'd gone and made her cry again.

"Of course I'll sit with you," he said, promptly perching on the smallest edge of the bed, barely putting his weight down because…well, then he'd be on the bed. With Eve. He'd be on the bed with Eve and that could be very…stupid.

Shit. Had he covered this ground before? Eve plus bed equals stupid? Yeah, that sounded like an equation he'd already solved.

Giving her his back while he devoured one of the remaining two sandwiches in a couple of massive bites, the peanut butter and white bread stuck to the roof of his mouth and his tongue. He blamed them for the fact that he had a hard time swallowing.

Of course, the *real* reason his mouth was pulling the whole dry-as-the-desert-Southwest thing was because he could actually *feel* himself slipping closer and closer to the void with each passing second. Slipping closer and closer to that place where he threw caution to the wind and—

"I never did tell you how sorry I was about those pictures," she broke into his frantic thoughts, a catch in her voice.

He turned, cocking his head and frowning. "You can't blame yourself for those," he assured her. "Not after today."

"But I *do* blame myself," she insisted, staring down at the half-eaten sandwich in her hand. "If only I'd had the guts to tell my father to…to *shove* it. If…if only I'd stayed *true* to you, kept the promise I gave you, then none of this would've happened. None of this…" She trailed off, shaking her head. "I'm just really sorry, Billy."

A few months ago he would have been beyond thrilled to hear those words from her mouth. Now? Well, for some reason—probably because, in spite of everything, he just felt so friggin' *sorry* for her—they were about as rewarding as a cheap, plastic trophy.

And for a moment he considered holding his tongue, for a moment he thought perhaps it might be better for him, and for *her*, if he just accepted her apology and let it all go. But the question of *why* had been burning a hole in his brain since the day that wedding announcement arrived in the mail. And he knew if ever there was a time to face the facts about what'd happened, to get the explanation he'd always felt he so richly deserved, it was now. So, he sucked in a deep breath through his nose and blurted, "Why *did* you agree to go out with Blake?"

Her graceful throat worked over a swallow, her blue eyes filling with tears. Again he considered holding his tongue, calling back the question, letting her off the hook, but when he opened his mouth, instead of the words *forget it. It doesn't matter now. It's all water under the bridge...*Instead of *those* words coming out, he demanded instead, or maybe it was his ego that demanded, "Was it because he was handsome? Or rich? Or smart? Or suave? Was it because he came from the right family, or—"

She shook her head, two large teardrops spilling over her lower lids to run down her cheeks and drip from her trembling chin. His instinct was to reach forward to wipe at the glistening trails. Instead, he curled his fingers around the plate in his lap as his heart thudded viciously in his chest, as his blood hammered through his veins, as he remained as still as the hot, humid air outside. Not daring to move. Barely daring to breathe when she blew out a puff of breath that ruffled the hair around her face, causing one dark strand to stick to her tear-wet cheek.

"I was a coward," she said. Just those four words. And they explained so much, yet, at the same time, revealed so little. "My dad kept harping on me," she eventually continued, her face twisting with derision and self-disgust. "And I was too chicken-hearted to keep saying *no* to him. So, you know, I thought, *Hey, I'll just do it. I'll go out with Blake. That'll get my dad off by back, and Billy never has to know.*"

He bit the inside of his cheek, a thousand responses tumbling through his head. *But how could you think to deceive me like that? Why couldn't you have just stood up for me and the vows we made? Why didn't you tell me what your father was up to? Why didn't you—*

"But it was a betrayal," she cut in on his frothing thoughts. "I betrayed you the moment I agreed to that date. And for that I'm so very sorry. You have no idea how sorry I am."

"But why did—"

"And then afterward," she interrupted him, her eyes taking on a sad, faraway look that had him wondering if she'd even heard his attempt to ask a question, or if her mind had traveled back in time. "When you didn't—" She stopped herself abruptly, timidly meeting his gaze. "I don't know," she finally shrugged. "I suppose it was just…maybe *easy* is the word for it. I was disgusted with myself, depressed and withdrawn, and there was Blake, telling me he wanted me, telling me I was beautiful and desirable. He was handsome and charming. My father loved him. My friends loved him. He knew all the same people I knew, did all the same things I did, so when he asked me to marry him, I figured, why not? It seemed like the thing to do, the thing everyone *wanted* me to do. Of course, that was the rationale of a young and incredibly stupid mind. Obviously, right?" She snorted derisively, picking at the crust on her sandwich. "Considering how it all turned out?"

And it was finished. The explanation was finished. Finally. Finally, he knew why.

He should've felt better. He didn't…

Perhaps that's because there was still one thing that didn't make any sense. "Why did you send me that invitation?" The invitation that'd broken his fucking heart. The invitation that'd torn his entire world apart.

"That's the part I don't get. I never knew you to be intentionally cruel."

She cocked her head, her brow crinkling. "What invitation?"

"To your wedding. Did you send it to me thinking that it would be a sig—" he stopped himself when a series of emotions passed over her expressive face. First there was shock, quickly replaced by comprehension, morphing into unmistakable disgust mixed with more than a smidge of remorse.

His gut twisted, his ulcer burping up a cloud of stomach acid that warned him the peanut butter might've been a mistake. "You didn't know," he surmised, something inside him shifting, just a tiny bit. "It was your father."

Her soft lips pulled down into a deep frown. "I…I suppose he just wanted to make sure you knew which way the wind had blown."

He shook his head. "I guess I should've known." And, really, he probably *should* have. Because even though she'd disappointed him, even though she'd gone back on her word, and even though she'd admitted to being a coward and had chosen another man over him because it was *easier*, the fact remained, Eve could never be purposefully unkind.

"How could you have known? I'd already screwed you over so badly, how *could* you have known I wouldn't stoop to the next level?"

"You didn't—"

"Don't make any excuses for me, Billy," she interrupted, her expression suddenly stern, her blue eyes boring into him. "I won't be able to stand it if you start making excuses for me."

Okay. So he wouldn't make any excuses for her. At least not aloud. But inside himself he felt a categorical change, a shift in paradigm, in perception and—

"You should've been my first," she said abruptly.

What the—

His brain turned to mush and slid out through his ears. His ringing ears. They must be ringing, right? Because he couldn't have heard her correctly. "Huh?" It was the most astute question he could formulate.

"I've always regretted missing that chance." And what was that expression on her face? Confusion, doubt...*hope?* All of the above? For some reason, probably because his brain was puddled on the mattress and stars were spinning in front of his vision, he was having trouble processing.

"Huh?" And there he went again, being all witty and clever, but really. He couldn't think straight. Or crooked. Or any other way. He just couldn't think. Period. Because if he wasn't mistaken, Evelyn Rose Edens was propositioning him.

He must've been quiet for too long, because she rushed ahead. "I know how you feel about me. And I don't blame you. I wouldn't trust me either after what happened. So, I don't expect this to lead anywhere. But I'm okay with that. If...if you're okay with that, I mean. I...I just..." She stopped, rolled in her lips, and through the pinpoints of light dancing before his eyes, he could make out her imploring expression. "I just really want to see what it's like to be with you. Even if it's only this one time."

And what did a man say to something like that?

Well, even with only a partially intact cerebral cortex, and despite the fact he was pretty sure it would undoubtedly blow up in his face, he knew what to say. Because what was that line from *Catcher in the Rye*? Something like, *In my mind, I'm probably the biggest sex maniac you ever saw?*

Well, when it came to Eve, no truer words had ever been written. *So, yeah.* He knew what to say. One thing, and one thing only. "Okay."

Okay. Just that one word. *Okay.* Then, full stop.

Eve wasn't precisely sure what she'd expected from Billy. Perhaps a rebuff, or maybe a flying leap on top of her. But certainly not...*okay*. Just...*okay*.

What did that even mean? *Okay* to the way he felt about her? *Okay* to the part where she said she realized he could never trust her again? *Okay* to the sex? *Okay* to the sex not meaning anything?

Which part, dangit? Which part is okay?

"Uh...Billy?"

"Huh?"

Was it just her, or had his vocabulary shrunk? And, for Pete's sake, she could really use a little help here. Was he purposefully *trying* to humiliate her by just sitting there, brown eyes intent and blinking? *Sheesh!* Her cheeks were so hot she wouldn't be surprised to see flames shooting out of her face. "Wh-what do you mean by...um...by *okay*?"

And his response? *Blink. Blink.*

All right, that was it. She couldn't stand it a second longer. "Because I'm not really the sexpot, vixeny sort. I can't tell if that means, *okay*, you want the sex. Or *okay*, you know it'd be meaningless. Or *okay*, I'm right in that you won't be able to trust me again. When you say *okay*, do you—"

"Come here, Eve," he said, gently reaching to take the half-eaten sandwich from her nerveless fingers. She watched, breath lodged in her throat, as he placed it on top of the remaining PB and J. And after he bent to set the plate on the floor, he straightened and patted the mattress beside him.

Gulp.

All right, and she'd officially lost her nerve…

"Billy, I—"

"Come here, Eve," he commanded again. Yes, *commanded.* And silly, weak-willed woman that she was, that authoritative tone went all through her, zinging up her spine and fizzing through her heated blood. It was all about the *I'm the big, tough man, so you* will *obey me.*

She wasn't supposed to like that. She wasn't *supposed* to…

Heaven help her, in *this* situation, she did.

But she needed to know what he meant before she went and made an even bigger fool of herself than she already had. Swallowing, she bit her bottom lip and said, "So…so by *okay*, you meant—"

"Sweetheart." When he used that endearment, she felt like flying. "Come. Here."

The softly glowing lights overhead danced through

his chocolaty hair and highlighted his steely, stubbled jaw, and the gleam of determination and…was that *hunger* she saw in the depths of his eyes?

For some inexplicable reason, she thought of that sage bit of advice: *don't poke the bear*. Well, if she wasn't mistaken, she'd just poked. And for the life of her, she wasn't sure she could handle the beast once he'd been provoked.

"I…I th-think—" she sputtered.

He leaned back on one elbow, snagging her wrist and tugging her to the edge of the bed. The teakwood slats of the sailboat's flooring were cool beneath her socked feet when her legs dangled over the side of the mattress. But Billy's half-naked body was generating so much heat she felt a sheen of perspiration slick her skin. At six feet, he wasn't *that* much taller than she was. But he had the kind of shoulders, the kind of zero body fat muscles, that bespoke of his last dozen years as a hardened soldier, which meant, to put it simply, he was *big*.

Big and manly and delicious. And he made her feel dainty and womanly by comparison. He made her feel—

"Are you sure?" he asked, playing with her fingers. And even that small touch, that should've-been-nothing touch had desire igniting low in her belly.

"Uh…" When he looked at her like that, his dark eyes sparkling and discerning, his high cheekbones slightly flushed, and the muscle in the side of his jaw ticking, it made it hard to think. "Wh-what was the question again?" she managed. And who the heck had shoved a wad of cotton down her throat?

"Are you sure you want to do this?"

This? Did he mean the sex? Is that what his *okay* was supposed to convey?

"Y-yes," she said, although the word rose an octave at the end, making it sound more like a question than a statement.

"Okay," he nodded, and she was really beginning to hate that word. From this moment forward she was going to ban it from her own vocabulary and...and what had she been thinking?

She didn't know. Because Billy leaned forward until she could feel his warm exhalation whisper across her lips, until she could smell the peanut butter and jelly on his breath. "Well, come on then," he said. And she was left to close that last inch separating them.

Chapter Twenty-one

He wanted to plow her like a wheat field.

It was crude. But it was true.

Thankfully, good sense and good manners prevailed, and he managed to refrain from grabbing her shoulders and throwing her back on the mattress, tugging the leg of her bikini bottoms aside and plunging into her. But, *Jesus*, it was crazy how the mere smell of her, all that expensive lotion and fresh shampoo could make his head spin. Could make him instantly start to swell. Could make him picture the hot, wet place between her legs. Could make him imagine his fingers there…his tongue…his dick so deep inside of her and—

Okay, and now he hadn't just *started* to swell. He was swollen. Fully engorged. Throbbing and pounding and feeling as though he might just split his skin wide open. Which brought him back around to the part where he had to mentally and physically hold himself back from grabbing her shoulders and tossing her back on the mattress, tugging her bikini bottoms aside and…

But that would come later. Much later. Because Eve wanted him. And forgetting the fact that he wanted her too, the reality was there was a part of him that needed to show her what she'd missed when she'd chosen to cave to her father's wishes, when she'd chosen Blake over him. There was a part of him that'd spent the last twelve years waiting for this very day.

Which meant he had to make it good.

And to make it good, he had to take it slow. He knew enough about women to know Eve was the kind to like it slow. Slow and hot and a little bit dirty, which, praise be, just happened to be his specialty.

And maybe, *maybe* after he showed her what she'd missed, maybe after he got it out of his own system, he could begin to move on. Begin to break free of the past. Of her. Of his seesawing thoughts and feelings in regard to her.

Of course, when she leaned in close, opening her mouth to him—sonofabitch, she had the most amazing mouth, the softest lips he'd ever kissed—he stopped thinking altogether. Tentatively, she slipped her tongue between his teeth. And the taste of her—the taste of peanut butter and jelly and...*Eve*—went straight to his head.

Or his groin.

His erection was now aching like a bad tooth, hammering against the dampness of his swim trunks. And his blood was running so hot he was surprised steam wasn't billowing up from his crotch.

"Mmm," she purred in that way he'd grown to love that summer—in that way he'd missed every day since then. It was a husky little growl at the back of her throat. And when he sucked on her tongue, rolling his up and down, she moved toward him.

Just slightly.

But oh, she was sweet when she softly, carefully placed her hands on his shoulders, when she softly, carefully returned the favor and sucked on his tongue.

The carefulness was one-hundred-percent pure Eve, and, in a little while, it'd have to go. In a little bit he'd demand no-holds-barred abandon. But, for right now, he'd take her tentative exploration. He'd revel in her soft exhalations, and just imagine all the things he'd do to her, do to push past any reticence, to make that little purr turn into a full-on groan of pleasure…

Slipping one hand around the back of her neck, placing the other on her hip, he pulled her closer. Until they were hip-to-hip, thigh-to-thigh. Until he could feel her pressed so soft and graceful and…quintessentially *female* all along his side. He opened his mouth wider, pushed his tongue deeper, taking everything up one notch, and letting her know that, *yes*, she'd been right on the money about him still wanting her.

Want…

That didn't even begin to cover it. It was a *need*. A bone-deep, gut-wrenching, soul-shattering *need*. And it'd always been this way with her. Bigger. Heavier. Deeper. *Better* than with anyone else. And sweet Mother Mary, he hoped and prayed that after he'd satisfied that need, after he'd finally, *finally* quenched his thirst for her, he'd be able to move on. Because in all honesty, the sheer breadth of his desire frightened him. Frightened him now just like it'd frightened *her* all those years ago.

He wondered if it *still* frightened her…

So he was slow when he moved his hand from

her hip, softly sliding it around to her silky thigh. Carefully caressing his way underneath the hem of her T-shirt to the edge of her bikini bottoms. He was gentle when he fingered the elastic band, running his thumb along the perimeter of the lycra.

And she shivered. Just ever so slightly.

But it wasn't a shiver of fear. It was a shiver of desire. And that's all he needed to know.

That timid eighteen-year-old was gone, replaced by this woman whose blood ran as quickly and as hotly as his own. She knew where he was leading her this time around, and she was eager to get there. And, just like that, it was go time...

It was just like she remembered. And then again, it was so much better.

She wasn't scared this time. She wasn't nervous or thinking too much. She wasn't worried she'd do the wrong thing. There *was* no wrong thing. Because what lay between them was primal and basic. But, above all else, it was *real*. Real in a way it'd never been real with anybody else.

"Eve," he growled her name against her lips, nipping the bottom pad before releasing her mouth to leave a string of hot kisses across her jaw and back to her ear. He sucked the lobe into his searing mouth and her toes curled inside her socks.

"Billy," she sighed, palming the back of his head, tunneling her fingers through his warm hair. Desire didn't wash through her when he pulled back to tug her shirt over her head, it'd already pooled hot and heavy between her thighs. And when his gleaming eyes landed on her, garbed in nothing but that itsy-bitsy-teeny-weeny bikini, she was amazed her entire body didn't spontaneously combust. Just *poof!* A fireball of lust and passion.

"Sweet Jesus, you haven't changed a bit. You're perfect," he said, his low, guttural growl filled with masculine appreciation.

Perfect?

No. She was far from perfect. But she sure as heck wasn't going to point out the fact that, at thirty, she had cellulite at the top of her thighs that no amount of jogging managed to budge, or that her breasts weren't quite as perky as they'd once been. If he wanted to look at her and see that eighteen-year-old body, if he wanted to look at her and see perfection, far be it from her to disillusion him. Especially not when he hooked a hand behind her neck, dragging her forward for another mind-blowing kiss.

She didn't realize he'd untied the strings at her neck or the ones behind her back until she felt the cool cabin air brush across her nipples. Then...*oh, holy cow.*

Because Billy gently laid her back on the mattress, leaving a trail of wet, hot kisses down her throat and over to her right nipple. He thumbed it once, and it sprung to instant attention, pouting and puckering and begging.

"These haven't changed either, have they?" he grumbled appreciatively, the sound rumbling through his big chest. "Such a pretty, delicate pink, and so very easily aroused. Are they just as sensitive?" he asked, his eyes managing to be simultaneously laser-sharp and bedroom-lazy.

She bit her lip. "Why don't you find out?" she breathed.

And, okay, where the heck had *that* come from? She wasn't the sexpot, vixeny sort, remember? But that was exactly the type of thing a sexpot vixen would say.

It obviously shocked Billy as much as it shocked her, because he choked on a laugh, then instantly sobered, that muscle ticking in his jaw again. The look in his eyes was so hungry, so carnal, she shivered. "Don't mind if I do," he murmured then sucked her beaded nipple into his mouth, tonguing it slowly and languidly at first, then more quickly.

"Uhnnn," she moaned, digging her nails into his shoulders. "God, that feels good."

"Mmm," he hummed, doing some sort of simultaneous suck/flick thing that made her feel as if there was a string tying her nipple to her clitoris. Her sex throbbed heavily with each pull of his lips, with each wickedly erotic flicker of his tongue.

Oh, she *ached*. And when he turned slightly, gently pressing himself against her hip, it was like she was plugged into an electrical outlet. Because his erection was rock hard, sizzling hot, and so beautifully alive. Pulsing forcefully against her thigh. Burning her even through the damp fabric of his swim trunks.

She wanted to touch him. Palm the whole hot, rigid, silky flesh-covered length of him. Her fingers literally twitched with the need. But with his mouth still working on her breast, and his free hand gently tweaking her opposite nipple, she was a thing of pure feeling. Pure pleasure. Pure lust. And it was hard to get her mind to work, much less her muscles.

Somehow she managed, though. And her fingers fumbled with the tie at his waistband.

In just a second, she'd have him in her hands. In just a second, she'd once more know the feel of him, all throbbing and searing and undeniably *male.* In just a second, she'd—

"Cheese and rice, Billy!" she grumped. "Did you tie these things in a triple knot, or what?"

He growled against her nipple, like a dog refusing to give up its most-treasured bone. "I'm serious," she pushed at his shoulder. "Help me get your shorts off."

Her nipple popped free of his mouth—oh, she immediately missed the sensation of his tongue—as he leaned up on one elbow, looking down at her with one brow winged up his forehead. "Since when did you get so pushy?" he asked, his plump lower lip quirking.

"Since I stopped trying to please everybody else and started trying to please myself," she told him in a huff, ducking her chin to glare at the offending Houdini-worthy tie at his waistband.

"And taking off my trunks will please you?" he asked, his voice all low and sexy.

She remembered that voice. It was his Marvin-Gaye-Let's-Get-It-On voice. The difference now was that it wasn't just for show. Because they *were* going to get it on. She shivered in anticipation. Yes, they were going to get it on…if he would just take off his flippin' swim trunks…

"*Yes*," she scowled up at him. "Unless you can think of another way for me to touch your…um…" *Come on, Eve. You can do it. Be the sexpot vixen you've always dreamed of being.* "To touch your cock," she finished triumphantly.

And, damn her fair complexion! Her hot blush ruined the effect.

Obviously it still worked for Billy though, because his gaze sharpened and the skin across his cheekbones tightened. Then he growled, "You first."

Suddenly, he'd pushed up from the mattress. Standing at the end of the bed, he grabbed one of her ankles, pulling her leg up, and slowly, carefully removed her sock. He ducked his chin to kiss the arch of her foot—his beard stubble tickled and sent a zing of delight up her leg—then he positioned her ankle over his shoulder and reached for her opposite foot. The process repeated until both of her ankles were over his shoulders. Then he hooked his thumbs into the waistband of her bikini bottoms.

And the way he pulled them off her? So slowly, so incredibly, mind-bendingly slowly, as if he was savoring each new inch of skin that was revealed? It made goose bumps erupt all over her body despite the warmth of the air inside the cabin.

Then her bikini bottoms were gone, tossed over his shoulder without a second thought. She settled her heels on the mattress, squeezing her legs together, but he stopped her with his hands on her knees, gently forcing her to spread her thighs wide.

"Let me look at you, Eve," he breathed, his eyes even

darker than usual as his gaze settled on her naked sex. "I never got the chance to just *look* at you that summer."

Yep. Because the thought of him standing there, eyeing her bare, wide-open genitals would've mortified eighteen-year-old Eve. Heck, even thirty-year-old Eve had to fight to keep a hot blush from searing her from head to toe.

But then he said reverently, his voice all rough like he'd swallowed a spiky sea anemone, "My God. You're beautiful. So soft and pink. So delicate," and she forgot all about being embarrassed. It helped when he blew out a ragged breath, lifting one brow, adding, "and my regards to your bikini-waxer."

The ever-so-tiny, and impeccably sculpted landing-strip of inky-black hair covering her pubis had always baffled Eve. But her stylist had assured her, "It drives the men wild," and she hadn't had the heart to tell the woman, "Don't waste your time. You and I are the only ones who'll see it."

Now she was happy she'd held her tongue, seeing as how Billy's was nearly hanging out. Obviously, her stylist knew what she was talking about, and the woman was going to get a big tip—*huge*—the next time Eve had an appointment.

"Your turn," she insisted, her chest raising and falling rapidly, her hot blood racing through her body until her nerve-endings felt super-heated. "Take off your trunks."

Billy held her gaze, his eyes keeping her a prisoner. But her peripheral vision told her he reached for the tie at his waist.

"Your wish is my command," he said as his long, tan fingers slowly worked at the knot.

Then he pushed his trunks down his large, muscled thighs, and they hit the floorboards with a gentle *spllff*. She could no longer hold his gaze. Her eyes were drawn down the length of his body as if they were being pulled by anchors.

And talk about *gulp*.

She tilted her head, her stomach doing a series of quick backflips as a surge of blood gushed into her already engorged sex. "Are you..." she shook her head, licked her lips. "Have you *always* been th-that big?"

Because she didn't remember...but, *wow*. He was long and thick, the mushroom-cap head of him angrily red and massively swollen.

He chuckled, shaking his head. "No need to massage the ego, sweetheart," he said while bending to grab her ankles again. With a quick tug, he dragged her to the edge of the bed. "I'm pretty confident in that arena already."

And boy, oh boy, did he ever have reason to be. He was...*powerful*, she guessed was the best way to describe him. Powerful and unabashedly male. And she wanted to touch him more than she wanted her next breath.

He obviously had something else in mind, though. Because he positioned her heels on the very edge of the mattress, beside her bottom, which caused her legs to spread wide. Then he knelt at the foot of the bed.

Oh, geez. Oh, geez. Oh, g—

That's as far as she got. Because he used his thumbs to spread her plump, outer-labia wide, and then his mouth was on her. His tongue was sliding up and down the wet channel. And he was growling.

The rumble undulated all through her, better than any vibrator ever built, and her toes curled over the edge of the bed.

"Oh, Billy," she sighed, reaching between her legs to sink her fingers into his damp hair. He rewarded her by capturing her clitoris between his lips, sucking gently and laving softly with his tongue. Too soon she was teetering on the edge.

"You keep d-doing that," she told him breathlessly, "and you're going to make me—"

She didn't finish because he inserted one, then another finger inside her, pumping gently, moving them carefully in a come-hither motion, touching her in…Just. The. Right. Spot. And—

"Oohh, Goddd!" Her body spasmed. No, not spasmed. Exploded. Her sex clamped down on his fingers, pulsing so forcefully she couldn't tell if it was pleasure or pain. But whichever it was, she wanted it to go on forever. And Billy did his part as he continued to pump and suck, as the waves of her orgasm rolled endlessly through her.

It was so good. Wait. Good? No, no. It was better than good. It was transcendent. Like, for that brief moment, she thought maybe she could see through space and time. Scientists claimed all the elements on Earth, from the rocks to the atmosphere, from the smallest insect crawling through a log to the smartest man ever born, came from stardust. And that's what she felt like right now. Stardust. Elemental and at the same time so flippin' mystical and amazing.

But, all good things must come to an end. And, eventually, after what seemed like an eternity, her orgasm did. Which is when she realized she'd fisted Billy's hair in her hands. Slowly, she uncurled her fingers, and he looked up at her then.

Okay, so was there anything sexier than a man gazing up at a woman from between her legs after he'd just given her the most violently delicious orgasm ever? Well, if there was, Eve'd never seen it.

"Wow," she caught her bottom lip between her teeth, shaking her head in awe. "Just...*wow*."

He grinned, and it was arrogant and lazy and altogether too sexy. She didn't know how it was possible to want more after that Earth-shattering release. But she did. She wanted much more. She wanted Billy. She wanted to feel his hot, rigid flesh inside her. She wanted to slide her hands down his back, reveling in the power of his muscles as he thrust and thrust and thrust...

Her sex pulsed again, and she dug in her heels, pushing herself up on the mattress. Then she beckoned him with one crooked finger.

He stood, a series of movements that caused his tan muscles to ripple over his body. And there was his impressive penis again. Standing even higher than before...if that was possible. Looking even redder and more engorged.

"What now?" he asked, his grin going all lopsided

and indolent. Because he knew the answer. He just wanted to hear it from her lips.

And she obliged him. "Now we..." Was that her voice? All low and breathy? "...fuck like bunnies." *Sexpot vixen in the ha-yowse!* And if it wouldn't have ruined the moment, she'd have slapped herself a high-five.

"Yeah?" he asked as he lifted one leg, kneeling on the edge of the bed, depressing the mattress with his weight.

"Yes," she nodded, hoping her smile was sultry and seductive. She should've practiced in the mirror.

He lowered his hands to the bed, crawling up to her, crawling over her. His knees between her legs. His hands on either side of her shoulders. His handsome face and beautifully dark eyes looming above her.

Then all the air in her lungs escaped a giant *woosh* when he asked, "Condoms?" Because she didn't have any. Not one. Considering how long it'd been since she'd had sex—four years; that's right...four *long* years—that shouldn't have come as a surprise to her. But it did.

How the heck could she have purposefully set out to seduce him when she didn't have any flippin' condoms?

Eyes wide, mentally hitting herself in the forehead with an open palm while chanting *stupid, stupid, stupid*, she shook her head. But instead of frowning, Billy just smiled. His beard stubble looked particularly dark against his white teeth.

"Um," she scowled. "Correct me if I'm wrong, but

not having condoms at this particular juncture is nothing to grin about."

"I'm grinning," he said, still hanging above her, the heat from his big body seeping into her bones, "because if you don't have condoms handy, it means you haven't had a use for them. And call me a caveman, but I *like* the idea that you haven't had a use for them...until now."

"Well, that's all fine and good," she harrumphed, waving her hand around. It slapped into his very hot, very hard erection, and she tilted her chin down to see him dangling incredibly close to her pubic bone. Okay, and *that* was the sexiest thing she'd ever seen. Too bad it was all for naught. *We have no condoms!* "But that doesn't change the fact that now we can't... uh...fuck like bunnies."

Using the F-word made her blush. She couldn't help it.

"That's where you're wrong," Billy said, pushing up and away from her. Crawling to the edge of the bed, he stood and padded back toward the galley. She pressed up on one elbow to see him scrounging through the duffel bag he'd brought on board. He smiled at her triumphantly when he pulled out a length of condoms that unraveled accordion-style.

Well, obviously *he'd* had a use for them. She wasn't naïve enough to think he'd brought them along with him on the off chance he got to sleep with her. And as she watched him prowl back toward her, ripping into one foil packet with his teeth, she tried to feel some sort of animosity about that, about the fact that since they'd been reintroduced, it was no big secret that Billy was a total man-whore. But the sight of him stalking toward her, his erection bouncing between his bulky thighs, his six-pack abs flexing, made it difficult to feel anything other than explosive, volcanic lust.

And then, when he crawled up on the bed beside her, handing her the condom and presenting himself to her, saying, "Will you do the honors?" any hostility she felt toward his most recent bed partners vanished. She couldn't think about *them* when she was too busy thinking about *herself*. About the pleasure and satisfaction he was poised to give *her*.

Just as soon as she rolled on the condom, that is.

But, first…

She leaned forward on her elbow, swallowing the searing, weeping head of him without warning.

"Ughnnn," he made an inarticulate sound at the back of his throat, his hand tangling in her hair. She didn't know if he was begging her to take more of him—he tasted like man and sex and all things delicious and naughty—or if he was asking her to stop. And since she didn't know, she went with her own instincts, laving his plump head with her tongue, reveling in the way it caused his hips to thrust forward ever so slightly.

Suddenly, his hand was between her legs, his fingers gently delving between her slippery folds, searching for and finding her opening and pressing softly inside.

Ecstasy…

It was the only way to describe what they were doing to each other, giving and receiving pleasure in equal measures. And it ratcheted everything up another notch when he released her hair so he could find her aching, so-very-sensitive nipple. He tweaked it lightly, and she would swear she felt the sensation between her legs.

And speaking of…

The rough pad of his thumb landed on her clitoris, circling, circling, circling, and her whole body wound tight as a spring.

She ripped her mouth away from him so she could pant, "I don't want to…to come yet. I want to come with you inside me."

He obliged her by taking the condom from her fingers and deftly rolling it down his violent arousal. She watched the whole process with heavy-lidded, hungry eyes. Then he was between her legs, supporting himself on his arms. And as she looked up into his dear, beloved face, she knew two things without a doubt. First of all, she'd waited her whole life for this moment. And second, it wasn't going to be enough…

She'd been fooling herself, *lying* to herself, when she thought it would be. Because a lifetime in Billy's arms, in Billy's bed, wouldn't be enough.

But she couldn't think of that now. If she thought of that now, she'd start bawling her head off, and wouldn't that be just the thing to enhance the mood?

Um, no. Definitely not. There was nothing unsexier than a woman blowing a giant snot bubble.

Oh, suck it up, Eve, she admonished herself, *before you ruin it all. Take this one night. Take it for what it is, and then hold it in your heart forever. It's better than nothing.*

And that was good advice. Sage advice. So why did it make the need to cry even more overwhelming?

"Eve?" Billy must've seen something in her expression, because he was frowning down at her. And that wouldn't do. That wouldn't do at all.

If they only had this one night, she was bound and determined to make it perfect. To make the memory of it perfect.

"Kiss me, Billy," she breathed against his lips. "Kiss me and then take me."

Chapter Twenty-two

KISS ME AND THEN TAKE ME...

Were those the six sexiest words ever uttered from between soft, peachy lips, or what?

And Bill had always been good at taking orders. So he lowered his mouth to hers, and for one long, seemingly infinite moment, he kissed her. His tongue sliding into her mouth, tangling with hers as he let the taste of her, the amazing softness of her, melt into him, seep into his very bones.

Yeah, kiss her and then take her.

That was the plan. To take her higher, take her farther, take her deeper than she'd ever been taken before...

Breaking off the kiss, she moaned her disapproval, but he wanted to see. He wanted to watch himself slide into her. He wanted to witness his hard length pressing up and into her soft, pink body. He pushed up, sitting back on his heels as he grabbed her hips. Eve had slender hips, equipped with those soft divots on the inside of her pelvic bones that made perfect handholds whether grabbing her from the front or...*friggin'-A*...from behind.

Just the thought of slipping his fingers into those divots as he pumped into her from behind, her soft, pale ass slamming against his lower belly, had his cock jumping between his thighs. But that would come later. The dirty part of the slow, hot, dirty sex he figured Eve liked would come later. For now, he just wanted slow and hot.

The gentle glow of the overhead light danced over her black tresses, sparkled in her half-lidded eyes. And the smile she offered him was as warm and soft as the air inside the cabin.

"Are you ready?" he managed to ask through a throat that'd nearly swollen shut around a giant lump of lust.

"I-I've been ready for twelve years, Billy," she told him, her usually sweet-sounding voice all low and husky, and so damned sexy. He barely resisted the urge to plunge into her. No finesse. No skill. Just straight-up rutting.

But resist he did. Just enough to nod and drop his heated gaze so he could watch as he grabbed his dick and guided it toward her slick opening. He circled once, spreading her wetness onto himself, and then he gently, softly, oh-so-slowly pressed himself inside. Just the tip. The very tip of himself. And then he held still, his breaths shuddering from him, his chest working like bellows.

"More," she moaned, wiggling slightly, and he felt like the top of his head would blow off. Then he couldn't stand it any longer, he pressed into her. One long, wet, heated slide of hard flesh invading soft. And the sight of himself disappearing into her, the sight of her body swallowing him whole, was, hands down, the most erotic thing he'd ever seen. Because she was so tight, and so pink, and so plump, and so—

"Oh, God, yes," she moaned, tossing her head back on the pillow. She grabbed his shoulders to pull him down over the top of her and eagerly sought his mouth. He obliged, giving her a penetrating kiss.

And then he began to thrust. Slowly. Again and again. Long, slick slides out until only the head of him remained inside her, and then slow, forceful plunges that seated him to the hilt, that pressed his throbbing balls tight against her ass. And all the while she was kissing him like her life depended on it, like she drew breath only from him. Her tongue was halfway down his throat, her hands were skating over his shoulders and down his back to clutch his ass as her knees drew up higher on his hips. And every time he buried himself in her, she made that little purring sound at the back of her throat. *Jesus!* He swore he could feel that gentle vibration deep in his gut.

It was amazing.

Better than amazing. Because for this moment, the woman he'd been dreaming about for years was his to hold, his to touch and kiss and caress. The hot female flesh between her legs was his to quicken to pulsing, wet release. Unremitting lust fueled his thrusts, driving them faster until they were primal and persistent. And the friction produced by her sultry walls? It drove him to the brink.

And then he felt it. He felt her sex clamp down on him. Hard. She wrenched her mouth from his to scream, "Oohh, Billy! Oohh, Goddd!"

She strained around him, against him, digging her nails into his ass as she held him to her. And that was it. He followed her straight over the edge, pouring himself into her, pumping and thrusting and coming harder than he'd ever come before. And in that moment, as they hurtled over the brink together, he experienced the kind of rapture that managed to create an entire universe out of two intertwined bodies. The kind of rapture that only happened once in a lifetime…

He didn't know how long he lay atop her afterward, his heart thundering like he'd just cut the leads on an IED, his breath sawing from him in ragged gulps. But eventually, he became aware of her sweet softness beneath him, of the smell of her—and sex—all around him, of the sound of her gently breathing in his ear.

He reveled in it. In her. And then her inner muscles spasmed around him again, and he pushed up on one elbow to find her eyes half-closed and sleepy. *Spent.*

He knew just how she felt. Wonderfully, completely, fantastically *spent.*

"Eve?" he whispered her name as he bent to nuzzle her neck before opening his mouth over the bruises circling her throat. He gently pressed kisses there, until he moved back to suck on the soft spot just beneath her ear. She rewarded him by sliding her hands up his sweat-slicked back.

"Mmm?" she mumbled, that little purr sounding at the back of her throat.

"I'm going to want to take you again in about five minutes," he told her, nipping at her deliciously naked shoulder. The sweat from her skin had mixed with her lotion until she tasted salty-sweet.

"Mmm," she sighed dreamily, lifting her legs to hook her ankles together just above his ass. "I approve of this plan."

And right then he realized he'd been fooling himself. Having sex with Eve hadn't brought him any closer to some sort of closure where she was concerned. It hadn't taken the mystery or angst out of their history together. It certainly hadn't sated his hunger—because, if anything, he wanted her *more* now that he'd had her, and he wasn't sure that would go away even if he had her a thousand times again. And it definitely, most *definitely*, hadn't clarified his yo-yoing feelings about her.

Shit. What've I gotten myself into?

Although when her inner muscles squeezed his semi-erect penis, causing it to twitch as it once more filled with blood, he knew what he'd gotten himself into. He'd gotten himself into Eve. Into smart, beautiful, sexy Eve. And right at that moment, that's all that mattered. That's all he would *allow* to matter…

Somewhere on Lake Shore Drive
2:51 a.m.

He was leaning against the wall of his condo, sweating like some sort of blue-collar cretin as he listened to Devon Price's cultured voice ask, "Tell me, what do the police have on you?"

Sometimes it amazed him how *un*like the stereotypical gangbanger Devon was. The man had a degree in finance from Northwestern University, for Christ's sake. Yet instead of going to work on Wall Street or down at Chicago's Board of Trade, he'd taken his education back to the streets where he'd been raised. He'd taken his degree, combined it with his criminal genius, and built the most well-funded, well-disciplined, and well-insulated gang in Chicago.

The Black Apostles were untouchable, unbreakable, and…unrelenting. Which should've been enough to keep him from throwing in his lot with them. But he'd needed the money. *Damnit!* He *still* needed the money. Only now, he needed it to pay Devon back…

What a god-awful, unimaginable mess.

"Nothing," he assured Devon. "They don't have anything. And they *won't* have anything."

"Hmm," Devon murmured, a huge amount of skepticism evident in that one small utterance. He lifted a hand to wipe at his perspiring brow. *It should've never come to this. It should've never—* "You may be right," Devon cut into his rapid-fire thoughts. "But that doesn't solve our little problem now, does it? Eve Edens is still alive. You still owe me two million dollars. And I'm running out of patience."

The seed of fear that'd been planted in his belly when his last big gamble failed to pay off grew into a redwood of terror. "You c-can't kill me, Devon," he insisted, hating the fact that his voice sounded weak. He wasn't supposed to be weak. He was supposed to be a man of power. "You'll never get your money if you kill me."

"Yes," Devon hissed out the end of the word like a snake. "But it'll send a strong message to others that they shouldn't cross me unless they want to find themselves encased in a cement block at the bottom of Lake Michigan. And I find that scenario increasingly appealing."

"I didn't *cross* you, Devon," he insisted, his pulse racing out of control. "The deal went south and I—"

"I'm tired of listening to your excuses. This arrangement of ours has reached its conclusion, I think. And I—"

"No. No, I-I know where she is," he panted, sliding down the wall until his ass landed on the cold marble tiles. "I know how you can finally get her. I know how you can end this thing once and for all."

And *thank God* he'd managed to overhear that tidbit of conversation about the sailing trip to Ludington. If he hadn't, he had no doubt he'd be a dead man.

Silence on the other end of the line had his stomach jumping up to lodge in his throat. Then, finally, "I'm listening."

"She and one of those thick-necked bikers she hangs out with are sailing her boat to Ludington, Michigan. Tonight." That last part was a guess. He hadn't overheard exactly when she planned to make the trip, but he didn't want to give Devon a reason not to believe him. "You can send a couple of your men to meet them at the dock there. Then...then..." The plan was formulating in his head at the same time he was laying it all out. "If your guys have a second boat, like a rental, or hell they could just hotwire a boat there at the marina that they could tow behind the sailboat until they were in the middle of the lake, then they could kill Eve and the biker, sink the sailboat, and motor back to shore." And even though it was an on-the-spot plan, he figured it might just work. "No one need be the wiser. Ships go down on the Great Lakes all the time. I mean *all* the time, so it'd be just like we discussed. An accident. It'll be—"

"Shut up," Devon interrupted, his tone as sharp as a rapier. "I've heard enough."

He swallowed, licking his lips, looking with longing toward the decanter of scotch sitting by his favorite armchair. This fiasco was turning him into a goddamned drunk. And he hated drunks. His mother had been a drunk. And just look where that'd gotten *her*. And *him*, come to think of it…

"I agree with your plan," Devon said, and his heart leapt with hope.

"Good. That's good," he wheezed. "And you'll see, Devon. This will still work out."

"You're going to ensure it works out," Devon said, his tone just this side of malicious. "Because you're going to be the one to do it."

"What? But—"

"This scheme started out as yours, and you're going to be the one to finish it."

"But, the police…They may want to question me some more, and—"

"I'll supply you with a believable alibi," Devon said. "Chartreuse just loves to spin tales of her Johns. She'll come up with a great one for you."

Chartreuse…One of Devon's many gap-toothed whores. She was always meant to be his alibi if he came to need one. But he hadn't really thought he'd ever need one until now. Because the police *were* likely to demand another interview, and when they couldn't find him, he'd have to rely on Chartreuse to tell them he'd been with her the entire time. And considering the woman was about as skanky and rundown as the Southside project where she peddled her trade, it would absolutely ruin his reputation to be known as one of her clients.

Then again, if Devon killed him, he wouldn't have a reputation to ruin…

"Fine," he said through gritted teeth. "But I can't very well take my own car. I can't have traffic cameras catching me exiting the city."

"I'll supply you with a vehicle whose plates aren't in the system." Devon said and gave him the address where he could pick up the car. "It'll be there in thirty minutes."

He consulted the Rolex on his wrist; he had just enough time for one drink. So, he'd make it a big one.

"And one more thing," Devon said.

"Yeah?"

"This is your last chance. You fuck this up, and you're dead."

Lake Michigan
3:10 a.m.

Well, if this wasn't the sexiest, dirtiest, craziest thing she'd ever done—screwing Billy's brains out—she didn't know what was. And you know what? It felt divine. It was divinity. Like consecrated by the Gods or something…

Oh, sweet Lord in heaven…

She arched her back, biting the pillow beneath her cheek as Billy pumped into her from behind. His strokes were smooth and deep, his thighs rock hard against the backs of hers, his fingers doing something magical at the top of her sex where he had an arm wrapped around her.

The temperature inside the little cabin had jumped at least fifteen degrees since they'd started…well… *going at each other* she supposed was the best way to describe it. And, boy, oh boy, they should've done this years ago. She'd been an idiot to hold off. Because Billy was…well, he was *Billy*. Sexier, manlier, more physically inventive and more naturally talented than anybody she'd ever known. Yes, they should've done this…*Oh, God.*

She could no longer think. Because he was so deep inside her, pressing into her, now working her with short, hard thrusts, his middle and index fingers slipping over the bud of nerves at the top of her sex, and she was pushed up higher, pulled closer to the edge of the abyss. Then he lengthened his thrusts, stilled his fingers, and she moaned in frustration, shoving her butt back at him.

"Patience, sweetheart," he growled, reaching up to feather his fingers across her nipple. "I'll get you there."

Oh, would he ever. She had no doubt of that. He'd get her there and then he'd get her there again. And again. And again. And…

"Billy," she moaned his name when he leaned forward, his sweaty chest against her back, his hot breath whispering across her cheek as he murmured deliciously naughty things in her ear.

Billy…She glanced over her shoulder at the image

of their bodies pressed together. His skin was deeply tanned compared to her fair complexion, the hairs on his legs and arms black and crinkly. And he looked big. Compared to her, he *was* big. His muscles huge and bulging, the side of his wonderfully perfect butt hollowing slightly each time he thrust into her. And with each long, lazy stroke she sank deeper into the infinite gulf of sensation. Her fingers tightened on the pillow, her teeth sinking into the weave of the fabric.

And suddenly, her release was rushing toward her. Her breath hitched in her throat as she waited for it, shamelessly reveling in it when it rushed over her in a huge swell of pulsing, aching climax.

"Ah, hell," Billy cursed when her body clamped down on his. And it was obviously too much for him. He grabbed her hips, pumping into her violently until his own orgasm hit him, until he throbbed inside her. And then, together, they rode out the storm…

"You were supposed to wait," he breathed in her ear once they'd both stopped blowing like a couple of winded racehorses.

"Did you," she rasped, licking her lips and smiling at the weight of him along her back, pressing her into the mattress, "or did you not hear me when I said I'd stopped doing what other people tell me to do."

"Mmm." He rolled off her, and she muttered her disapproval as she heard the little *snap* as he pulled off the condom. She wasn't looking, but she assumed he tossed it toward the small metal trashcan to join its compatriot.

"Come here," he said, snaking an arm around her

waist, forcing her to roll onto her side and face him. She threw a thigh over his legs, an arm over his chest, and buried her nose against his neck, just under his ear, inhaling deeply.

"Are you...*sniffing* me?" he asked, his chest rumbling beneath her arm and against her breast.

"Mmm-hmm," she murmured. "Because you smell *good.*"

"I do?" he chuckled. "What do I smell like?"

She inhaled again, nipping his earlobe this time. He responded by rubbing a hand over her shoulder and down her arm, entwining their fingers. "You smell like Irish Spring soap. And leather. And sex. And...*you.*" Then she added, "And maybe a little bit like me."

He growled, playing with her fingers. "I like the sound of that. Because that means you probably smell a little bit like *me.*"

"I'm sure you're right," she agreed. "We've marked each other without all that pesky lifting of a leg and urinating business."

He snorted a laugh. "Well, whatever floats your boat, I guess."

"That does *not* float my boat," she assured him. "But speaking of markings," she released his fingers to trace one of the star tattoos on his arm, "what do your tattoos mean? If they mean anything at all," she was quick to add. "I totally understand if you got them just because they're pretty or—"

"First of all," he interrupted her, "my tattoos are *not* pretty." She begged to differ. In her eyes, they were very pretty. But she assumed that description might've pricked his male ego. "They're badass," he finished. And, yep, assumption proved. "And secondly, they *do* have a meaning. But now that I know you think they're...*pretty*," his nose wrinkled when he said the word, "I'm not sure you want to hear what they stand for."

"But I do," she assured him, moving her finger to trace another star. "I *do* want to know."

"The tale isn't *pretty*," he stressed the word.

"Oh, for Pete's sake," she huffed, slapping playfully at his shoulder. "I take it back. They're not pretty. They're hardcore, gangsta-hot, straight-up dope. Is that better?"

A laugh burst from him, all low and throaty. It sent a frisson of pleasure through her chest down to her belly. "Did you just utter the phrase *straight-up dope*? Where are we?" He glanced around the cabin. "1990?"

"Get to the point, Billy," she huffed.

"Yes, ma'am." He grinned at her when she pressed up on her elbow in order to scowl down at him. Too soon her expression smoothed. Because when Billy grinned like that, all playful and teasing, she could see remnants of that young petty officer she'd fallen in love with. She nipped his stubbled jaw for good measure before re-tucking her head beneath his chin so she could resume tracing his tattoos.

"Each of these tattoos represents an explosive device I successfully disarmed," he told her. Which only had her pressing up again, her eyes skimming over his right arm where at least twenty-five colorful, multi-sized star tattoos ran from his shoulder to just beneath his elbow. The opposite arm sported what appeared to be the same amount.

*Holy moly. Fifty times…*at least *fifty times, Billy put himself in the middle of an armed bomb…er explosive device, or whatever he calls them.* Her mouth dried at the thought, at the magnitude of the danger he'd lived through, at the extent of what he'd accomplished, and the untold lives he'd undoubtedly saved.

"Geez Louise, Billy," she breathed, searching his half-lidded, lazy eyes. "Were you—" She stopped herself, because the question she thought to pose sounded silly, even in her own head.

"Go ahead," he encouraged her. "Ask whatever you want."

"It's stupid," she assured him, shaking her head. "I already know the answer."

"The answer to what?" he smiled, cocking his head on the pillow.

"To whether or not you were scared."

"And was I?"

"Well, *of course*!" She threw a hand in the air. "You disarmed *bombs* for a living. A *lot* of bombs!" Her eyes flew over the myriad tattoos on his arms.

He grabbed her hand and flattened it against his chest. She could feel the steady beat of his heart. "You might be the only one who believes I was scared," he told her, and she frowned at him.

"How is that possible?"

"Well, I've been told that when I'm in the middle of a mission, or a bomb, or anything particularly hair-raising, I get really still. And really, *really* calm."

"Well, that just means you're internalizing your fear," she told him. "Which is undoubtedly why you're so good at what you do, steady hands and all, but it's also probably why you swill Pepto-Bismol like it's going out of style."

He barked a laugh. "Is that your official diagnosis, Dr. Phil?"

"Is it the wrong one?" she asked, lifting a brow.

"No," he admitted, a half-smile playing at his wonderful lips.

"Hmm." She nodded, once again tucking her head beneath his chin, reveling in the comforting sound of his heavy heartbeat. "And is that how you got your nickname? Wild Bill? Because you were crazy to have gone up against all those explosives?"

"Nah." The word rasped in his chest and in her ear. "I got that name before ever shipping out. It was a hold-over from my last few months of SEAL training."

"What do you mean?"

"I mean I went a little crazy there for a while. Drinking too much. Driving too fast. Pushing the boundaries with my superior officers. I was living on the wild side of life. Hence, the nickname."

"But why?" she asked, wondering if, perhaps, he'd started to regret his decision to be a Navy SEAL. If he'd started to second-guess—

"Why do you think, Eve?" His voice was suddenly quiet, subdued, and her breath hitched in her lungs like she'd run out of oxygen on a deep dive.

"B-because of *me*?" she asked, pressing up to stare down at him. But she already knew the truth in her heart.

And it killed her to think of the pain she'd caused him, to think of the career she *might* have caused him to lose had he ever stepped over the line as opposed to simply pushing it.

Well, that was just one more reason for her to hate herself for what she'd done…

When he opened his mouth to answer, she slapped her palm over his lips, shaking her head, tears pressing behind her eyes. "Don't answer that," she said. "I already know what you'll say. And I'm sorry, Billy. I'm so—"

"Eve." He moved her hand away. "Stop apologizing, okay?"

She shook her head. "Nope," she sniffled. "I don't think I can do that."

He sighed, pulling her down to press her cheek against his chest. "Well then," he said, "I'll just have to distract you."

"Distract me?" she asked, watching as he took her hand, curling all her fingers into a fist except for her pointer finger, which he straightened and used like a pencil, tracing one of the tattoos on the inside of his lean hip.

"Mmm-hmm," he murmured, dropping a kiss into her crown as his rough palm smoothed over her hip. "A man's got to do what a man's got to do."

"*The Grapes of Wrath*?" she asked distractedly when he released her hand so she could continue the tracing on her own. She caught her lips between her teeth as his manhood twitched and swelled to throbbing, violent life.

"A bastardized version of it," he whispered,

reaching up to thumb her nipple. It sprang to instant, aching attention.

And though there was a part of her that still felt close to tears, a part of her that felt that even if she apologized a thousand more times it still wouldn't be enough, there was another part of her that burned at the thought of Billy taking her again.

And he and John Steinbeck were certainly right about one thing. A man had to do what a man had to do. But a *woman* had to do what a *woman* had to do, too. So, lifting her head, she closed her mouth over his, breathing in his breath, reveling in his taste, letting herself get lost in him…

Chapter Twenty-three

Lake Michigan
7:15 a.m.

Kisses.

It was the most wonderful way to wake up. Sweet, delicate kisses drifting down Bill's stomach toward the erection that was straining beneath the covers...

When Eve got to his bellybutton, she stopped, dipping her tongue inside, and his toes curled. He threw back the comforter, pushed her inky hair away from her forehead, and the soft light filtering in through the portholes highlighted the glint in her gorgeous sapphire eyes as she looked up at him.

"Good morning," she breathed, catching her bottom lip between her teeth.

"Indeed it is," he told her, grinning, loving the half-smile pulling at one corner of her mouth. "And it'll be even better if you continue what you're doing."

"What I'm doing?" She lifted a brow, playing the coquette to perfection. "Oh, you mean this?" She opened her hot, wet mouth, and laved the tip of his erection with the soft, raspy pad of her tongue.

"Mmm-hmmm..." He fisted his hands in her hair, thrusting his hips upward just slightly. *Sweet Mother Mary, have mercy.* "That's exactly what I m-mean."

And just as he was about to settle in—because, come on, the only thing better than waking up to soft kisses on his stomach was waking up to a blow-job; he *was* a guy, after all—the softly rocking sailboat suddenly rolled violently to the port side, nearly tossing them off the bed. Then, the vessel heaved to the starboard, and this time Bill *did* slide off the mattress, slamming against the teakwood decking on his back.

"Holy crap!" Eve yelled. He pulled himself to his knees in time to watch her jump from the rumpled bed and grab onto the doorframe separating the berth from the rest of the small cabin. A sizzle of white light blazed through the portholes followed almost immediately by a deafening *crash* of thunder. "We've sailed into a thunderstorm!"

And yeah, he didn't need to be told. The fact that every hair on his body was standing on end pretty much made that a foregone conclusion. Talk about a total soft-on. For future reference, the best way to lose chub? Sail into a thunderstorm and get tossed off the bed onto your ass.

"I, uh, I forgot to check the NOAA weather forecast last night," he admitted as the boat heaved again. Scrambling to his feet, he grabbed his discarded swim trunks with one hand while steadying himself on the mattress with the other.

"We were a little busy," she said, turning, stumbling down the length of the cabin to retrieve her bikini bottoms as the vessel bucked again. The sky opened up and rain pounded against the hull, creating a constant, dull roar.

Yeah, busy. They'd certainly been that. And even with the vessel being tossed around like a cork on the ocean, he still took the time to appreciate the sight of Eve scrambling into those skimpy red bottoms while he hopped into his shorts. Shoving his cell phone into one Velcro pocket, he staggered out to the galley in time to see her slip an orange life vest over her T-shirt. Handing him a vest, he pulled it over his head just as the humming engine suddenly caught, choked, rumbled unsteadily for a bit, and finally sputtered and died.

"Shit," he cursed. "That can't be another rope. We *can't* be that unlucky."

Although, in all reality, considering how things had been going for Eve lately, he wouldn't lay down any money on that last statement.

"No." She shook her head, her eyes wide. "It's probably zebra mussels. With the water all churned up like this—"

"*What* kind of mussels?" he asked as the boat took another violent roll to the port side. He banged his hip against the table and caught Eve as she slammed against him.

"Hurry," she said, hastily pushing away, "we have to check the output port."

He followed her up the short cabin stairs. When she opened the door to the deck, the wind ripped the thing from her hands. It slammed against the side of the cabin—*crash!*—splintering the wood and cracking the porthole window. Rain immediately deluged them, soaking them to the bone and pelting against any exposed skin like tiny, sharp knives as the boat caught a wave broadside and tipped precariously. Frothing gray water rushed over the deck, pouring into the open cabin and freezing Bill's legs from the knees down as he struggled to retain his balance.

"The engine's cooling system's output port is on the aft, starboard side!" Eve shouted as she pushed up onto the deck, grabbing onto the railing to steady herself as the vicious wind tried to yank her from the boat.

Boom! Another flash of lightning blazed overhead, slicing through the violent sky, cleaving the angry, roiling clouds in two.

"Go check to see if there's a sooty residue near the port!" she yelled, stumbling toward the Harken roller that would unfurl the mainsail. "If there's not," he had to strain to hear her over the howling wind, over the rain drumming against the deck and the waves crashing against the hull, "then try to restart the engine! If there *is* residue, come back and help me with the mainsail!"

Shit, shit, *shit*...

Bill had been in some pretty hairy situations before, but usually he was the one who knew what steps to take. He wasn't used to relying on the expertise of another. Though, he had to admit, if he had to be caught out in the middle of Lake Michigan during a violent squall, he couldn't think of a better sailing partner than Eve.

The woman had been raised on the water. In fact, his sister had proudly informed him a couple of months ago that Eve was a five-time CYC Mackinac Island racing champ. At the time, he'd told Becky to stuff it, maintaining that he had no interest at all in Eve or her accomplishments. But, he had to admit as he stumbled across the heaving, bucking deck toward the rear of the vessel to check the cooling water output port—*please don't let it be sooty; please let us still have engine function*—right now he took comfort in the knowledge that she was a first-class yachtsman... er...yachtswoman? Was that even a word?

Sploosh! A giant gray wave rolled over the vessel behind him, and he turned to squint against the driving rain, his heart in his throat, half expecting to find Eve had been washed overboard. But she was hanging on to the main mast, wrestling with the forestay, the cable that ran from the top of the mast to the deck.

"Hurry, Billy!" she screamed when she caught him staring. It was all the impetus he needed. Clutching the railing in a tight fist, he shuffled forward on the slick deck until he reached the back of the vessel. Taking a firm handhold, he leaned over the side.

"Oh, fuck." His whispered words were caught and tossed away by the viciously howling wind. "Residue!" he yelled to Eve, turning to make his way back to her.

"Okay!" She nodded, finally defeating the stubborn forestay. "Come help me with the mainsail! It's blowing at least forty knots! These waves are coming every eight to ten seconds, and some are sixteen feet high! One more broadside could flip us! We have to get control! Now!"

And even though his breath was burning in his

lungs, even though his pulse was racing out of control, the way Eve was working, so quickly and so efficiently, gave him a modicum of…not comfort. There was nothing *comfortable* about their current situation. But knowing Eve, five-time CYC Mackinac Island racing-champ Eve, was in control made him feel as if the odds were stacked in their favor.

And in his line of work, anytime the odds were stacked in his favor he considered it a good day.

By the time he managed to shuffle back to the main mast, spreading his bare feet wide on the water-logged deck, she'd already begun the process of unfurling the mainsail. "We can't take it all the way up!" she instructed, her black hair plastered against her pale cheeks like long, dark fingers, her blue eyes bright with calculation. "We need it at about fifty percent to give us control!"

"Whatever you say, Captain!" he yelled, water filling his mouth and eyes as he tilted his head back to watch the mainsail climb toward the roiling sky, flapping violently with the wind, its cables clanging loudly against the mast.

When Eve was satisfied with the amount of woven sailcloth they'd unfurled, she instructed him. "Okay, let's move to the wheelhouse!"

Grabbing her hand, consoled by the feeling of her slim fingers laced with his, they shuffled around the cabin toward the covered cockpit. Ducking under the wheelhouse's roof was like stepping into a bass drum in the middle of the Rose Bowl parade. Rain hammered against the ceiling, roaring and pounding as towering waves continued to try to roll the boat. Then, Bill watched in amazement as Eve's hands grabbed the wheel. She turned it a bit, adjusted it a notch, then ducked her chin, water sheeting off her face, to watch the mainsail catch the wind and snap tight. The loud *pop* echoed even above the clamoring storm.

She nodded, blowing out a shaky breath as she maneuvered the boat into the waves until it was no longer rolling side to side but climbing each swell confidently before plunging down the other side.

"Sonofabitch," he breathed, holding onto the steering console, shaking his head. "I think I just shit enough bricks to replicate the Great Wall of China."

She reached up to scrub the water from her eyes. "You were in the Navy," she said, making a face. "Surely you've been in worse storms than this."

"Just because I was in the Navy, that doesn't mean I actually spent much time on a ship. And the ships I *have* been on were so big most storms didn't so much as make the vessel wobble."

"Well," she grinned, "welcome to the Wonderful World of Sailing. It's exciting here."

"Hot damn," he huffed in agreement, loving the way her eyes were bright with enthusiasm. Then, "Holy shit! You're actually having fun, aren't you?"

She laughed, shrugging one shoulder. Then her expression changed. Dimmed. Like someone had flipped a switch inside her. "Maybe not fun," she admitted, "but for a second there, I forget my father or my ex-husband or *both* were trying to kill me. For a second there, I forgot about what happened to Buzzard…"

And as wonderful as it'd been to see excitement in her eyes, it was just as awful to see such unremitting pain and guilt there. "Sweetheart," he tried to infuse his voice with understanding, "I told you, what happened to Buzzard wasn't—"

"I need to go out and reef the sail," she cut him off. "With the force of these winds, I think we're running too heavy."

"Let me—"

"No." She shook her head, her sopping hair swishing across the thick orange fabric of the life vest. "I'm the one who knows how much sail to bring in. You need to stay here and man the wheel." She pointed at the compass. "Try to keep it at this heading. That should ensure we're still going in the right direction for Ludington, but it will also keep up from sailing directly into the waves or having them hit us abeam."

"Eve, I—"

"You got this?" she asked, taking a step back, indicating he should take control of the vessel.

What could he say but, "Yeah, I got this."

When he grabbed the wheel, he was surprised by the way it bucked in his hand. It took strength to hold them on the correct course.

Strength…

Not something he'd ever really equated with Eve. But he was learning just how misguided and misinformed he was in that department. Still, the knowledge that she was one hell of a tough lady behind that delicate, fancy, cupcake exterior did nothing to mitigate his anxiety as she exited the wheelhouse and began inching her way across the slippery deck toward the mast. He realized he was holding his breath, trying to squint through the gray haze of rain to watch her every little movement, when his brain began to buzz.

Forcing himself to rake in much needed oxygen, he sent a prayer of thanks skyward when she quickly furled a tiny bit of sail before turning to make her way back to the cockpit.

Booooooommmm!

A blinding flash of bright white light accompanied a bone-rattling, ear-splitting crash that rocked the boat. The main mast lit up like a roman candle, and the hair on the top of Bill's head and the back of his neck lifted in warning. The metallic smell of electricity burned through the air and tasted like a new penny when he dragged in a harsh breath.

Jesus Christ! They'd been struck by lightning!

"Eve!" he yelled, turning toward the starboard side of the boat where he'd last seen her. But she was...*gone*.

Cold...

That was the first thing Eve noticed when she blinked open her eyes to find herself staring up into a frightening canopy of cruel, gray clouds. She was cold right down to the marrow of her bones. The second thing she noticed was a feeling of weightlessness, of being born up into the air and sinking back down again.

And then, suddenly, her stunned synapses began

firing, and she realized she was adrift. She was adrift in the lake and—

A huge cross-wave rolled over her head, filling her mouth with acrid-tasting water, trickling down into her lungs before her life vest bobbed her to the surface.

"Uhhhhh," she raked in a breath, coughing and sputtering, trying to orient herself in the water, trying to keep her head above the swells that lifted her aloft before slamming her down.

Oh, God. She was going to die. People set adrift in the vastness of Lake Michigan in the middle of a storm didn't survive. They just didn't.

Oh, God. Oh, God. Oh—

"Eve!"

At first she wasn't sure if she'd heard correctly. She thought it was the wind howling and screaming and playing trick on her ears.

"Eve!"

Okay, and that was no trick. She turned—struggling to tread water—just in time to see Billy throw an arm over her shoulder. He hooked his fingers into her opposite armpit in the traditional lifeguard's hold.

"B-Billy!" she choked, coughing up gritty water from her lungs. She'd never been so happy to feel the weight of another human pressing against her back as she was right at that very moment.

"Don't worry," he yelled, sputtering as a wave slapped him in the face. "I've got you!"

Yeah, he had her. But…but who had *him*?

And then she saw he was using his free hand to pull on the safety line he'd wrapped around himself, trying to haul them through the heaving waters back toward *Summer Lovin'*. The sailboat bobbed atop the waves some forty feet away.

Turning in his embrace, she grabbed the line. And, hand-over-hand, they managed to slowly, so frustratingly slowly, halve the distance to the boat as the wind and waves tossed them about like waterlogged scraps. In less than a minute, hypothermia was setting in. Eve could feel it in the stiffness of her muscles, in the numbness of her limbs, in the way her strength was ebbing, drifting out of her with each crashing wave.

"Hurry, B-Billy," she sputtered. "W-we..." Her teeth were chattering so hard, her jaw was locking down. "We h-have to get o-out of th-this water."

"I know," he coughed. "Wrap your arms around m-my neck and hang on. I can get us there f-faster—" Another wave rolled over their heads, filling their ears and mouths. And Eve wondered, as the frigid water swirled above her, whether or not they could actually make it. Any relief she'd felt upon seeing Billy beside her leaked from her to sink down to the pitch-black bottom of the lake. If he died while trying to save her, she'd never forgive herself...

Of course, she'd be dead, too. So yeah. There was that...

They bobbed to the surface, buoyed by their life vests, hacking up lake water. "I'll get us there f-faster on my own!" he yelled.

And though she hated the fact that he was right—because he *was* right—hated the fact that, in this instance, she really did need saving, her ego wasn't so big that she let it keep her from doing as he instructed. Releasing the lifeline, she wrapped her frozen, numb arms around his neck. In the next instant, they surged through the chop, his big shoulder muscles and sleek back muscles working beneath her as he pulled them through the turgid water toward the rolling boat.

She didn't know how long he worked as she did nothing but hang on. It felt like hours but could've only been a minute. And then, suddenly, *Summer Lovin'* rode the swell directly in front of them. And with a strength Eve would later marvel at, Billy hauled them the last few feet, managing to hook an arm around her waist and boost her up onto the swim ladder bolted to the back of the sailboat.

"Climb up!" he bellowed. And, yep, that should've been easy. There were just three measly rungs, after all. But her entire body was frozen.

He must've seen her trouble as she clung to the back of the boat, unable to move, unable to feel the fingers wrapped around the top wrung. With a curse, he grabbed the sides of the ladder when the boat sank into the bottom of another swell. Then, somehow he managed to climb over her and into the vessel. Hooking his hands under her armpits, with a grunt and mighty heave, he hauled her aboard.

And the only thing better than feeling Billy pressed against her in all that freezing water? Feeling the slick slats of the sailboat beneath her feet. Well, in all honestly she couldn't actually *feel* them. But when she glanced down at her pink, polished toenails, she knew they were there.

Holy moly! We actually made it!

She couldn't believe it!

"Come on!" Billy yelled, half dragging/half stumbling with her into the covered cockpit just as the rain picked up in intensity. "Sit!" he ordered, pushing her into the captain's chair and tossing a towel over her shoulders, chafing her arms until her skin began to sting. But that was a good thing, wasn't it? Stinging skin was reheating skin.

"W-w-what happened?" she asked through chattering, clenched teeth.

"The main mast was struck by lightning," he told her, moving his chafing to her sides. "The force of it knocked you off the deck into the water."

"Lightning?" She couldn't believe it. Boats weren't often struck, but when they were, it was usually catastrophic to the electronics on board.

"The navigation system?" she asked, and he moved slightly to the left so she could see the electrical panels on the console. The *dark* electrical panels. Not one light glowed on the entire vessel when she glanced around.

"The radio is shot, too," he informed her, raising his voice above the driving sound of the rain on the roof. "And I'm assuming…" He peeled up the Velcro on the pocket of his swim trunks and pulled out his iPhone. Pressing the power button, she didn't need to see the darkened screen to know the cell phone was a dead stick. The information was written all over Billy's scowling face. "We're on our own here," he muttered. Which was true. Because her phone was shoved in an evidence locker somewhere back in Chicago.

And though her mind should've been filled with all

sorts of logistics—like the tricky business of navigating the boat without the electronics, like the danger of riding out the storm when the waves and wind seemed to be getting worse and worse—she instead found herself occupied with one and only one thought. This was the *fifth* time she'd almost died in less than three months, and if things kept going like this, chances were pretty good she might not survive the sixth.

And she'd never told Billy she loved him.

It seemed such an easy thing to say, such an easy thing to admit, so why hadn't she? Was she still, deep down, that cowardly eighteen-year-old? Was she still—

"Hey." He pulled her into his arms, pressing her against his warm, wet chest, palming the back of her head. When she sucked a breath in through her nose—a deep breath that brought the crisp smell of lake water combined with the burnt rubber aroma of fried electrical wire casings—she realized her lips were trembling and hot, salty tears were pouring over her lower lids. "It's all right, now. We're going to be all right. I know you've been through hell, sweetheart. I know it must seem like the world is out to get you. But you just need to hold on for a little while longer, okay? Just hold on for a little while longer, and I promise you—"

"I've been holding on by sheer force of will these last f-few days," she whispered against his shoulder. "H-holding myself together, so you'd see I'm not that same cowardly girl from twelve years ago."

"Eve—"

"But I can't h-hold myself together anymore." She

talked over him, her voice rising with every word out of her mouth. Now that she'd started, she couldn't stop. "And I c-can't hold it in anymore. I love you, Billy. I've always loved you. And it's okay if you don't love me back. Because if these last few days have taught me anything, it's that I don't want to live with regrets anymore. And I *regret* not telling you right from the very start that I still love you. And I will *always* love you." She felt him still against her. The hands that'd been rubbing up and down her back stopped on her shoulders. "And it's a love with no strings attached. No expectations. Just a one-way love. F-freely given."

That's what she said. And she meant it when she said it. She really did. But, naturally, there was a part of her, a really big, really *hopeful* part of her, that wanted Billy to reiterate her words, to return her love. So when he gently pushed back, his brown eyes searching her face, his expression somewhere between anguish and sadness, a monster wave of grief threatened to overwhelm her as all that hope was washed away like the water washing over the hull of *Summer Lovin'*.

"Eve, I—"

"Shh." She pressed a cold finger over his lips. "You don't have to say anything."

"But, I—" Just then, the boat was pulled off course by the power of the current, the mainsail lost the wind, and the vessel rolled violently.

Cursing, Billy turned to grab the wheel.

She watched the muscles in his back and shoulders

bunch as he wrestled the vessel back into the face of the storm, as the mainsail once again snapped tight. Then she blew out a shaky breath and thought, *It's done.*

She'd gone all in. Put all her chips on the table. Played her last hand. Unfortunately, this time, the cards hadn't gone her way. Not that she should be surprised, really. The cards hadn't gone her way in a very long time.

But at least you had last night, a voice whispered through her head. *And at least you finally told him the truth...*

Yes. She could find comfort in those things, she supposed. She could find comfort in them because they were the only things she still had left to hold on to...

Chapter Twenty-four

Red Delilah's Biker Bar, Second Floor Apartment
8:34 a.m.

The notes of Neil Young's "Unknown Legend" woke Delilah from a deep sleep, and she fumbled for her cell phone on the cherrywood nightstand. She'd been too exhausted to scrub off her mascara in the shower last night, and in the intervening hours between then and now, it'd turned into some sort of industrial-strength adhesive. She had to use her thumb and forefinger to pry her left eyelid open. Blearily reading the number on her phone's screen, for a moment she forgot why Brenda, the office assistant extraordinaire at McClovern and Brown, would be calling her. Then, everything came back in a rush.

The shoot-out in the bar. Buzzard's death. That scene with Eve's father and ex-husband. The long minutes inside an interrogation room reliving it all. The coffee shop. Mac's refusal to take her to the chopper shop. And, finally, her decision to use her contacts at McClovern and Brown to see if she could find out anything about Keystone Property Development.

She'd shot off an email to Brenda last night before crawling into bed to cry herself silly—perhaps, along with her crusty mascara, her dried tears had a little to do with the whole eye-goop-glue thing she had going. Then, shockingly, because she hadn't really thought she would or could, she'd fallen into an exhausted, nearly catatonic sleep.

Unfortunately, instead of feeling better this morning, she just felt worse. Her limbs weighed a cool thousand pounds each. Her head was one giant throbbing ache. Her right nostril was completely clogged with…something she didn't want to think about. And, to top it all off, she'd forgotten to brush her teeth before bed. So now, her mouth tasted like a combo of used kitty litter and fresh road kill. *Blech…*

"Heh—" Okay, used kitty litter and fresh road kill all wrapped up in cotton, because she had to swallow twice, her dry throat sticking both times, before she could talk without sounding like Joe Cocker. "Hey, Brenda. That was quick." She blinked at the glowing red numbers on her digital alarm clock.

"When I got your email last night, I decided to head to the office early this morning. Personal business, eh?" Brenda's voice sounded perky, as always. And Delilah could *not* understand people who were cheerful in the morning. It's like they were aliens that came down from planet Bright Eyed and Bushy Tailed. "That sounds interesting. Although," Brenda's tone darkened, "if you're thinking of investing with these guys or something, I'd think twice. They're in it up to their eyeballs."

"No, no," Delilah assured the woman. "It's not that. It's—" And then she stopped herself. Because how the hell was she supposed to explain all of yesterday in two sentences? Which was really about the uppermost limit of any conversational energy she had in her. So, she finished lamely with, "It-it's something else."

"Mmm," Brenda purred. "More and more intriguing. Color me curious."

"I'll tell you all about it," Delilah promised, because she really *did* like Brenda despite the whole evil-alien-morning-person shtick. "But right now, I need to know what you found."

"The usual," Brenda said. "Three rich guys go into a highly speculative business together and then lose their pants."

"Wait..." Delilah sat up in the bed, throwing the autumnal-colored comforter aside and realizing she'd put her polka dot pajama bottoms on both inside out and backward. Maybe it was a good thing Mac hadn't let her go home with him. She'd obviously been a wreck last night, not fit for company. "*Three* rich guys? I thought the business was founded by two men, Patrick Edens and Blake Parish."

"Nope," Brenda said just as Delilah caught sight of her reflection in her dresser mirror. *Sonofa—* She looked like *she* was the fresh road kill. Lifting a hand, she tried unsuccessfully to pat some of her hair into place. "There was a third guy, a minor partner, and a silent one at that. I can't remember his name, but it's in the files I emailed you. I think it's spelled out somewhere in the articles of incorporation."

Another partner? Perhaps another man who'd have reason to see Eve dead? Delilah's hand halted mid-pat then she lowered it shakily to her throat.

"Brenda," her heart was a hammer in her chest, "I've got to go. But I owe you. Big time. Next time you come into the bar—" the bar where Buzzard had died, the bar she needed to get back up and running, the bar she *wasn't* going to think about right now, "—drinks are on me. All night."

"Deal," Brenda said, adding, "and toodles," before clicking off.

Delilah opened up her email account straight from her phone. Quickly scrolling through the files Brenda sent her, she stopped on the one titled "Articles of Incorporation." Her brain buzzing with curiosity and a weird sense of dread, she opened the document. One name jumped off the page.

"Oh, *shit*," she breathed, the room around her dissolving into a blur as she stared down at the email for one heartbeat, then two.

Then she shook herself, shook off the momentary shock, and dialed Information. After impatiently going through the rigmarole of saying what city and state she was in and which business's phone number she was looking for, she listened as the connection was made. A series of rings sounded. "Come on, Mac," she growled. "Pick up the damned phone."

No such luck. She was forwarded to a voice mail explaining that if she was interested in speaking to someone about a custom bike, she should email them at blah, blah, blah.

"Damnit!" She stabbed a finger onto her phone's screen, catapulting herself from bed and stumbling over to the dresser. Hopping out of her PJs, she wrenched open a drawer, dragged on a pair of jeans, shrugged into a sports bra, and pulled an old KISS T-shirt over her head. Slipping her feet—sans socks—into a grungy pair of red Converse sneakers, she hesitated in front of the mirror, contemplating whether to take the time to wash her face and comb her hair.

Whatever, she decided, waving a hand at her reflection before grabbing her purse and her keys. She wrenched open the back door only to run face-first into a curtain of driving rain. Cursing, she instinctively threw an arm over her head. But then she realized she was trying to protect…what? Her crazy, uncombed hair? Muttering obscenities to herself, she lowered her arm and raced down the metal stairway. Splashing through the puddles of water that'd gathered in the alley and the bar's tiny parking lot, she skidded to a stop at the corner, hand lifted in an attempt to hail a taxi.

And, praise be to the higher powers, if her rain-logged eyeballs weren't deceiving her, that was a red cab with a busted tailpipe pulling up to the curb. A mammoth bolt of lightning ripped open the sky, and a gust of wind blasted down the street between the buildings. Delilah's drenched hair plastered itself against her face as she heaved open the taxi's door. Sliding into the faux-leather seat, she gave the cabbie the address for Black Knights Inc. and finished with, "And there's an extra twenty in it for you if you get me there in under ten minutes."

Black Knights Inc. Headquarters
8:55 a.m.

"YO, ASSHOLE. GET UP."

Mac growled into the cushion of the shop's leather sofa, his face occupying the spot usually reserved for someone's ass. But he wasn't going to think about that. Not until after he'd had his first cup of coffee. And certainly not until after he'd gifted whichever Connelly brother was barking orders at him with a witty rebuttal that began with the word "fuck" and ended with the word "you."

Unfortunately, his witty rebuttal didn't quite have the *oomph* he was going for because it was muffled by the couch cushion. He flipped over to see Geralt Connelly scowling down at him. The Connelly brothers were the quartet of red-haired, freckled, built-like-linebacker native Chicagoans who took turns manning BKI's front gate. They were Irish Catholic to the core, rowdy as children, a slap-stick act when they all got together, and Mac usually liked them immensely. That is, when they weren't waking him up…he checked his watch…just *three* hours after he'd managed to *finally* fall asleep.

After he arrived home last night, thoughts of Delilah, thoughts of how he should've been kinder to her, should've *stayed* with her, had swirled around and around in his head until he'd damn near driven himself crazy. So, he'd worked on his cycle, cleaning the fuel lines, replacing the oil, polishing the chrome, until the wee hours of the morning when the previous day finally caught up with him and he passed out face-first on the sofa.

"Fuck *me?*" Geralt asked incredulously, his big, ruddy face wrinkling. "No, thank you. I don't go in for dick gymnastics."

"Come on now," Mac snorted a laugh. "I'm not even sure I know what that means."

"You know *exactly* what it means," Geralt replied in his thick Chicago accent. "Besides," the man reached up to scrub a huge mitt over his buzzed, carrot-top head. "I like redheads. In fact, I'm an easy mark for redheads. Especially busty ones."

Mac narrowed his eyes, pushing up into a sitting position. "And you're tellin' me this because..." He made a rolling motion with his hand, until it occurred to him that Geralt wasn't at his post. "Why the hell aren't you mannin' the gate? Did those goddamned reporters out there do somethin'?"

"Those goddamned reporters hightailed it home when this god-awful storm broke," Geralt said as a crash of lightning sizzled overhead. The resulting *boom* of thunder rattled the tall, leaded windows of the shop, and Mac suddenly realized the dull roar he'd been hearing wasn't a result of his own headache, but was, in fact, the sound of a deluge pounding on the roof of the warehouse. "And I'm not manning the gate because I couldn't get ahold of you." Geralt folded his arms over his massive chest, scowling fiercely. "Either your damned phone is off, or it's out of juice."

Mac dug in his hip pocket, pulled out his cell phone, and realized he was dealing with scenario *numero dos*. He usually plugged his phone into the charger on his nightstand before catching some Zs. Not the case last night.

He cursed, frowning up at Geralt. "So what did you need?" But as soon as he asked the question, Geralt's comment about being an easy mark for redheads, especially busty ones, had trepidation biting him in the ass like his father's cranky old ranch dog used to do.

And, yeah, just as he suspected..."The always lovely and terribly overripe Delilah Fairchild is here," Geralt announced gleefully, wiggling his nearly nonexistent eyebrows. Okay, so the dude's eyebrows weren't nonexistent. They were just so blond they *appeared* that way and—

And why the hell was he contemplating the color of Geralt's eyebrows? Holy shit fire, that didn't matter a hill of beans even on a *good* day! And this likely wasn't a good day because, first off, he'd napped with his face in a spot usually reserved for someone's *ass*. And secondly, Delilah was here. Which meant something was wrong. Something had happened. His heart crashed against his breastbone.

Unless of course, a soft voice of reason whispered, *she's here because she already has information on Keystone Property Development.*

A certified forensic accountant? Who'da thunk it? Because she didn't look like any accountant he'd ever known. Not by a long shot.

"Where is she?" he asked as another flash of lightning blazed through the windows. "At the gate?"

"She came by taxi," Geralt said, frowning down

at him like he was a few brain cells short of a fully functioning cerebral cortex. "And I couldn't very well leave her standing out in a thunderstorm. Although..." a devilish light entered Geralt's eyes, "...a wet T-shirt contest does sound—"

"Then *where* is she?" Mac cut in, wanting to hear the end of Geralt's sentence about as much as he wanted to schedule a colonoscopy.

"She's out in the courtyard," Geralt replied, now eyeing him curiously. When Mac pushed up from the sofa, Geralt stopped him from stomping toward the back door with a meaty hand on his chest. "You got a thing for her or something? Because I've known her for years, but I was thinking it might be time I try to get my swerve on, if you know what I mean. But if you've got dibs, then I—"

"No dibs," Mac informed him, though, for some reason he refused to contemplate, his blood pressure shot through the roof. He could actually feel the vein on the side of his neck pulse in warning.

"Good," Geralt said as he followed Mac down the long hallway toward the back door leading to the large, partially covered courtyard with its myriad outbuildings.

Before Mac pushed outside though, he quickly stepped to his left, glancing through one of the tall windows to see Delilah standing under the drooping, rain-heavy canopy with her arms crossed over her breasts, chafing her biceps like she was cold. And she probably *was* cold. You know, considering she was completely, deliciously, ball-swellingly drenched. Her hair was plastered down around her face and sticking to her pale cheeks. Her jeans—which always looked like they were painted on—now accentuated every tiny detail of her figure, like the fact that she had the cutest and most tempting little rolls right at the top of her thighs beneath her pert ass. And her T-shirt? Well, to put it simply, the damned thing should've been outlawed.

Wet T-shirt contest, indeed…

"If you're thinking about going back and trying to claim dibs," Geralt said from over his shoulder, "you can forget about it. You had your chance."

"I don't want your goddamned dibs," Mac harrumphed. Though he didn't know who he was trying to convince, Geralt or himself.

"Good." Geralt dipped his chin. "Then I'm headed back to the front gate."

"Good," Mac parroted, watching the carrot-topped giant lumber back down the long hall before wrenching open the heavy metal door. He stepped outside and a gust of warm, wet wind frisked him as efficiently as a well-trained field agent.

"Oh, thank God," Delilah breathed, taking a couple of steps forward to lay a hand on his arm. Her palm burned him. Actually *burned* him, and he had to resist the urge to yank out of her reach.

"What is it?" he demanded, trying, really *trying* not to look at her boobs in that wet T-shirt.

"It's not just Eve's father and ex-husband who are partners in Keystone Property Development." She lifted a hand to pull a lock of hair from where it'd blown across her mouth. Yessirree. Her nipples were hard. And okay, so he was looking at her boobs.

Goddamnit Mac, stop being such a shit-heel, he groused at himself. Himself immediately answered back with, *Yeah, easier said than done.*

"There's a third partner," she said, and *that* got his attention. "He invested less than Parish and Edens, so I suspect that means he has diluted voting power when it comes to business decisions. But he's still a partner."

"But Chief Washington said—"

"Chief Washington said his initial investigation was cursory at best."

Bill and the rest of the Knights claimed Mac had Spidey sense. He wasn't sure about that. But something inside him, something chilling, snaked up his spine, filling his brain with an icy blast of foreboding. And then he knew...

"Jeremy Buchanan," he muttered, the hairs on his arms standing straight as if in warning of another lightning strike. But the angry sky remained gray and unlit by electricity.

"Bingo." Delilah's green eyes were circled by mascara, but it did nothing to camouflage the fear in them. "And he knows where they're headed..."

"Give me your phone," Mac demanded, holding out his wide palm.

"Wh-what?" Delilah sputtered, looking down at his hand in confusion. "Didn't you just hear me say—"

"I heard you." The vein in Mac's temple pulsed, and his blue eyes glinted like the vodka bottles she kept on the third shelf back at her bar. The wind whipped his dark hair around his head. "Which is why I need your phone to call Bill. Mine's dead."

"Oh!" She dug into her purse. *Now, where's my damned phone when I...aha!*

She'd barely pulled her iPhone past her purse's top zipper before Mac snatched it out of her hand, thumbing it on and punching in a series of numbers with a rough finger. He held the device to his ear while she held her breath and waited. A second slid by, then another and another until Mac cursed, bellowing into the receiver, "Goddamnit, Will Bill! I hope you check your messages, because Jeremy Buchanan is mixed up in that mess with Eve's father and ex-husband, and he knows you're heading to Ludington. Call me!"

He jabbed a finger onto her phone's power button before handing it back at her. She curled her fingers around the device, holding it against her pounding chest, searching his impenetrable expression. "That's it?" she demanded. "We just sit here and hope he gets that message? What if he lost his phone? Or what if he—"

"Be quiet for a second," Mac said, his voice barely discernible above another *boom* of thunder. "I need to think."

"Well, think faster!" yelled.

He scowled at her. She scowled back. She hadn't gone through all this, through the hell of yesterday and last night and this morning, just so he could leave a freakin' *message!*

"The Coast Guard!" he snapped his fingers. "They can relay a communique to Bill via the sailboat's VHF radio." He turned to open the huge metal door with Delilah hot on his heels. He quickly swung back around, and she skidded to a stop, her Converse sneakers squeaking on the slate ground-covering.

"Don't you even think about leaving me out of this," she said, lifting her chin. "I'm in it. I've *been* in it. I have the right to see it through."

He stepped up close to her, his voice a low rumble. "Okay," he said, and the victorious smile that started to curl her lips turned down at the corners when he continued, "But before you set foot in this building, you need to understand something. You can't breathe a word about what you see inside." He hooked a thumb over his shoulder. "Not one word. Not to anybody. Or you could land all of us in hot water." The expression in his eyes was wary and worried…and perhaps a little bit beseeching. "Do you understand me?"

Her lungs froze in an instant, as did her heart. *Jesus, Mary, and Joseph, what are they* doing *in there?*

"Do you understand me?" he asked again, reaching up to grasp her bicep and give her a little shake. "I have to know I can trust you. There's more at stake here than you realize."

She swallowed, nodding jerkily. He searched her eyes for a second longer before turning to throw open the door. Following him inside, she quickly glanced around, expecting to see…she didn't know what, especially not after that speech he'd just given her. But to her utter relief and astonishment, the place looked rather ordinary. Rather like she'd expect a custom motorcycle shop to look. The exposed brick wall lining the right side of long hall he led her down was covered with old motorcycle license plates. And when they pushed out into the main body of the shop, she saw all the usual equipment. Bike lifts. Power tools. Blow torches. A big, precision water saw. The place smelled like burned coffee, hot metal, and old oil. It smelled just as she'd imagined it would smell and—

"This way," Mac motioned, turning to clomp up a set of metal stairs. She followed him, the sound of their footfalls on the treads echoing around the huge space, bouncing against the brick walls painted with massive, colorful caricatures of all the Black Knights. Yup. Nothing out of the ordinary there either. Bikers loved nothing better than to immortalize themselves in murals or in their own tattoos. Then she topped the last riser...

Uh...*okay.*

Because the lower floor might've looked like your typical custom chopper shop, but this second floor? Well, this second floor looked like what she imagined NORAD must look like. Stacked two-high against the far wall was a bank of massive computer screens, all blinking and buzzing, showing satellite images and real-time feeds from places that had to be on the other side of the globe. And sitting in front of that bank of computers, iPod earbuds shoved in his ears, head bobbing to whatever music he was listening to while tossing a pencil in the air, was Ace. The guy she'd been led to believe was the Black Knights' resident wiring expert. She immediately adjusted her thinking on that score. Especially when he turned and his jaw slung open like there was a two hundred-pound weight attached to his bottom teeth. He yanked the earbuds from his ears. "Delilah? Wh-what the hell are you doing here?"

She swallowed, shaking her head because she just couldn't take it all in. "M-me?" she finally sputtered. "The better question is what the hell are *you* guys doing here? What *is* this place?" She was starting to get the feeling she'd been a lot closer than she ever could've imagined with her earlier comparison to Area 51.

"No time for explanations," Mac cut in, stomping over to Ace. "We need to find the number for our contact in the Coast Guard."

"Why?" Ace asked him, though his astonished expression was still glued to Delilah's face.

As Bill filled him in, Delilah made sure she kept her eyes focused straight ahead. Not that the urge to look around wasn't intense, mind you. It was really, *really* intense. But if she wasn't mistaken, this place looked suspiciously like a secret government installation. And those unlucky civilians who stumbled upon secret government installations usually found themselves six feet under, didn't they? Well, they did in the movies—which was her only point of reference since she'd never seen the likes of anything like this in real life—so, yup, she'd just go with what she knew and focus on seeing as little as possible.

Holy shit. Holy, holy, *holy* shit!

A chill that had nothing to do with her wet clothes or the cool air of the warehouse slipped up her spine. With half an ear, she listened while Ace contacted the Coast Guard. With the other half, she concentrated on the pulsing sound of all her blood rushing to her head. She couldn't believe it. *The Black Knights are some kind of—*

"He says he can't raise the ship." Ace turned away from the computers, lowering his cell phone from his ear.

Delilah watched as the two men exchanged a look. "Call Washington," Mac instructed. "Let him know the situation. Tell him to alert the Ludington police." Then, Mac said four words she never thought she'd hear outside an AMC movie theater. "And get the chopper…"

Chapter Twenty-five

Harbor View Marina, Ludington, Michigan
9:27 a.m.

What the hell is the matter with me? Bill thought as he secured the last rope around a cleat on the weathered dock. Eve Edens had professed her love, her *no strings attached* love, almost two hours ago, and he'd yet to do or say anything in response.

And, yeah, yeah. So, they'd been a little busy fighting a raging storm that'd battered them unmercifully until it finally decided to blow itself out a mere five minutes before they pulled into port. But that was only a small part of the reason why it'd been Mum City inside the cramped wheelhouse. The truth was, he'd kept his mouth shut was because he didn't know *what* to say to something like that. A part of him gloried in her confession. She loved him! Everybody wanted to be loved, right? According to Lennon and McCartney, that's all you needed. On the other hand—*there's always another hand, isn't there?*—a part of him was—

"Your turn," Eve said, cutting his thought short. She'd emerged from the cabin after donning a dry T-shirt and a clean pair of jeans. Standing at the sailboat's rail, she was in the process of pulling her damp hair back into a ponytail. The way her arms were raised, he could see the faint outline of her erect nipples. Those sweet nipples. Those sensitive nipples. Those nipples he's sucked and laved and licked and…

Shit. Now was not the time to be thinking about her nipples. If he started thinking about her nipples, next thing you know he'd be thinking about getting her back into bed. And a man shouldn't think about getting a woman who'd just confessed her love for him back into bed unless he had something more than slack-jawed silence to offer her.

"I, uh…" He had a tough time meeting her gaze. Her eyes were too sad. Too hurt. Too…something he didn't want to acknowledge. "I think I'll go make sure Chris left his extra truck for us." Chris was an old high school friend who'd moved from the city to Ludington to become a fishing guide. Before they'd pulled away from the dock back at Belmont Harbor, Bill had called and asked the man to leave his spare truck in the parking lot. "Also, I need to stop at the yacht club, if it's open, to call back to BKI. Let the guys know we made it," he told her, shuffling his flip-flops against the slats of the dock. "Why don't you get everything secured on the boat, and after I've, uh, checked on everything, I'll come back and help you with the bags."

Silence met his suggestion. And he was forced to raise his eyes. She was just standing there at the rail staring at him, chewing on a hangnail. "Billy," she finally said, her voice barely above a whisper. "I didn't tell you that to make you—"

"I know," he cut her off, feeling like a complete ass-hat for fucking this thing up. And he *was* fucking it up.

But, goddamnit! He didn't know what to say to her! His feelings for her were...*confusing.*

Yeah, he mentally snorted. *Which is like saying advanced nuclear physics is confusing...*

"O-okay." She nodded, still chewing on that nail.

Blowing out a breath—he was quickly becoming disgusted with himself—he regarded her for a second more before turning to traipse up the dock. His flip-flops made a slapping sound that echoed out over the quiet harbor. For all the fury of the storm, its passing had brought on an eerie calm, made even more so by the fact that the marina was deserted.

Yeah, because no sane *person would be caught dead out on the lake on a day like this...*

Jesus Christ, what a morning! If he lived to be one hundred and eighty, he hoped he never had to experience another like it. When he closed his eyes, the image of Eve's orange life vest and black hair adrift out in the middle of all that frothing water blazed on the backs of his eyelids. It caused his heart to stutter, his ulcer to start complaining, and his brain to stumble over a series of questions—most of them along the vein of: *If you don't love her back, then why does that memory haunt you?*

Shit on a stick! What a morning, indeed...

He shook his head as he stepped off the end of the dock, traipsing up a small slope toward the large, empty parking lot. The air smelled crisp and clean, like wet evergreens and cool, clear water. It looked like his buddy Chris had come through for them. An old, beat-up, blue—well it *used* be blue, but now it was mostly rust—Chevy sat parked at the far end of the lot. He decided to pull it closer, so they wouldn't have as far to walk with the bags.

*I regret not telling you right from the very start that I still love you. And I will always love you...*Eve's words whispered through his mixed-up, mashed-up skull for about the thousandth time. And even though they caused warmth to pool in his chest and spread out through his limbs, he *still* didn't know how to respond to them.

Was he a coward? Had he been accusing Eve of being lily-livered when all this time *he* was the one who needed to man-up and grow some balls? Was he so afraid of being hurt again that he wasn't willing to risk—

The sound of squealing tires invaded his thoughts. He glanced up to see a dark SUV careening around the corner into the parking lot, and all his warrior's instincts sprang to life. But, it was too late...

Fuck! He was late!

Jeremy torqued the wheel of the big SUV, the *second* one he'd been forced to borrow from Devon Price since the first one had crapped out on him about two-thirds of the way to Ludington. And then because, you know, he couldn't exactly call AAA to come give him a tow since that would mean a paper trail, he'd been forced to sit on the side of the road for three *fucking* hours waiting for one of Devon's flunkies to deliver him a new vehicle.

Hence, he was late.

But not too late, he assured himself. Because if he wasn't mistaken, that was Bill Reichert standing in the middle of the parking lot, which meant Eve couldn't be too far behind. And if he could just get them both back out on the sailboat, maybe he could tie them up, which would give him time to hotwire a motorboat, and then everything could still go as planned.

Yeah, this thing can still work out...

Stepping on the brakes, his stomach sat where his heart should be and his heart throbbed in his throat, he flipped off the safety on the stupid, nickel-plated 1911 Devon had given him.

Why the hell gangbangers thought bright, shiny, nearly glow-in-the-dark guns were something to be coveted he'd never know. Then again, now was not the time to contemplate the idiocy of the thugs who made up the Black Apostles, because Reichert was lunging toward the ratty old truck parked fifteen feet away, and Jeremy couldn't let the man secure transportation. Shit would go downhill fast if he allowed that to happen.

Throwing open the driver's side door, he pointed the pistol straight at Reichert's bare chest and yelled, "Halt! Stop right there!"

But Reichert didn't listen to him. The idiotic sonofabitch just kept on racing for the truck, and Jeremy's plan went up in a puff of smoke. He was left with only two options. He could kill Bill and Eve right here in the parking lot, leaving behind a pile of evidence with the hope there wasn't enough to lead back to him, with the hope that with Devon's alibis and cars and weapons he could still slip the noose. Or he could give up and go home. In the first option, he stood a chance, a small chance, but still a chance of coming out of this thing on top. In the second option? Well, in the second option he'd be dead. Devon Price didn't make idle threats.

He went with door number one and squeezed off two rounds in quick succession…

Boom! Boom!

Eve froze, the hair on the back of her neck twanging upright.

She knew that sound. Ever since she'd begun taking shooting lessons, she knew that sound, sometimes even heard it in her sleep.

"Billy…" she whispered his name like a prayer before reality kicked in and she raced for the door to the cabin. Wrenching it open, she managed to pull it from its top hinge, and it slammed back against the side of the cabin with a loud *bang*. She didn't bother using the stairs as her heart grew wings and attempted to fly out of her mouth, she simply jumped down into the hold, stumbling when her foot caught on the last tread. Immediately righting herself, she reached for Billy's duffel in the small booth.

"Please, please, please…" It was a chant she breathed over and over as she dug through his gear and then… "Yes!"…Her hand landed on the hard outline of a handgun. She wrenched it from the bag, relieved to find it was a Glock 17, a pistol she'd trained with. Pulling out the clip, she wasn't surprised to find it full. Slamming it back into place with the edge of her palm, she turned to race up the stairs when something tucked into the mesh side compartment of Billy's bag caught her attention. It was the little snub-nosed Smith & Wesson she'd used at Dale's house. Quickly grabbing it, she shoved it into the waistband at the small of her back, before climbing the stairs, running across the deck, and taking a flying leap onto the dock.

Crack! The wood on the pier splintered beneath the force of her fall, and her right ankle and left wrist screamed out their objections. She ignored them both as she pushed up and ran. Ran like she'd never run before toward the end of the pier and up the small embankment that led to the parking lot. She topped the rise in time to see Billy dragging himself behind an old beat-up truck while someone with dark hair—it was too far away; she couldn't quite make him out—stalked toward Billy's position with his arms raised in such a way that there was no mistaking he held a gun.

With her heart and lungs pounding in time to the rapid slap of her sneakers against the parking lot, she lifted the Glock and squeezed the trigger. Again and again. And all the while she was screaming Billy's name…

~

He was in a world of hurt…

Not metaphorically. Literally. He was pretty sure the slug that'd plowed into his thigh hit bone. But that was nothing compared to the one that'd torn through the center of his chest, making it almost impossible to breathe. And the pain…it was like nothing he'd ever known. And he'd known pain before. Plenty of times before.

Fuck. He was a dead man. He knew it like he knew his name was William Wesley Reichert.

"Billy!" Between the loud buzzing in his ears and sucking sound his chest made anytime he attempted to take a breath, he heard his name echo across the parking lot. A series of loud pops followed, and he rolled himself over on the pavement, one hand pressed to the hole in his chest as blood poured hot and heavy between his fingers. The movement resulted in agony. A searing torture that, for a moment, precluded his ability to think. Then he saw Eve running toward him, slim legs eating up the distance, black ponytail flying out behind her, right hand raised and firing his Glock in steady bursts, and suddenly his brain kicked it.

And it was weird…

Because his first thought wasn't about the man who'd shot him, and why. Or even about the danger Eve was in, or the fact that his life was waning, leaking out of him and onto the craggy surface of the lot. No. His first thought, the first scintilla of cognition that darted though his head was that Eve Edens was beautiful when she ran. Absolutely, positively perfection in motion. All long legs and lean flanks, born and bred and built for speed. And then sanity and reality suddenly waylaid him, and he realized exactly what her speed was doing.

It was bringing her closer. To him. To the gunman who'd taken him out.

His heart, already laboring in his ruined chest, threatened to explode. *No, Eve. No!* He couldn't allow her to risk her life for him. He couldn't allow her to—

"Turn around! Run!" He meant to yell the words, but they came out as nothing more than a hoarse whisper. Coughing, he felt flecks of blood splatter his lips, and he raked in a shallow, sucking breath that burned like the fires of hell. "Turn around! Run!"

This time his words had some volume. Unfortunately, the volume cost him a series of deep, wracking coughs that filled his mouth with blood. Even so, he couldn't take his eyes off Eve. He couldn't take his eyes off the crazy, courageous—she was the goddamned bravest thing he'd ever seen—woman. He couldn't take his eyes off her because he was dying, and he knew the last thing he wanted to see was her. Eve. The woman he loved.

The realization hit him like a ton of bricks. He loved her. He'd never *stopped* loving her. And he'd been an *idiot* to hold something against her that she'd done over a dozen years ago, when she'd basically been nothing more than a scared, confused adolescent. And why the hell it took him shaking hands with the Reaper to finally admit as much he didn't know. Perhaps when faced with the great beyond, all other fears and reservations just disappeared. He loved her. And either she hadn't heard his warning shout, or she'd just chosen to ignore it, because her steps didn't falter. Not even once. And the insane, foolish, lionhearted woman was going to get herself killed trying to save a man who, for all intents and purposes, was already dead.

Boom! Boom! Boom!

As if to prove his point, the gunman returned a volley of rounds, and a bullet grazed Eve's shoulder, spinning her like a top and dropping her to the ground.

No!

He choked on his own blood, releasing the wound on his chest so he could use both hands to drag himself toward her. But it was futile. Because a split second later, she was up and running toward him again, returning fire like a battle-hardened soldier.

No! Turn around! Run! Save yourself!

Unfortunately, the words were only in his head. He could barely draw enough strength to mutter them, much less raise his voice to a level she could possibly hear. See, the mathematics for blood loss was real simple. The more you lost, the weaker you became. And that kind of arithmetic meant he had to act fast. While he still could. He had to draw the gunman's fire.

Pushing to his good knee, he reached up with a slick, blood-soaked hand to grab the truck's rusting side view mirror. His body was a giant, burning ball of agony. His heart skittered and missed beats. His punctured, bleeding lung struggled valiantly to rake in oxygen, all while his brain, deprived of said oxygen, grew dull and fuzzy.

But he couldn't give in yet. He couldn't give in until—

With a choking cry, he hauled himself to his feet. The world around him dimmed and flickered, then condensed down to nothing but that dark SUV and the gunman hiding behind the open door, peeking around to once again return fire.

"Over h—" *cough, cough, cough.* Hot blood poured down his chin and tasted like rusting iron on his tongue. He could smell it. Its metallic aroma tunneled into his nose, and he briefly flashed back to that time in Afghanistan when he arrived on the scene of a brutal roadside bombing to see bloody, shredded bodies littering the street. Death had been imminent then. Death was imminent now. But first…"Over here!" he finally managed to garble.

The gunman peeked his head out from behind the door, and blue eyes, *familiar* blue eyes, narrowed on Bill.

Jesus Christ! Buchanan? What the hell? *Why?*

He saw the shiny, silver gun in Buchanan's hand twitch, saw the evil black eye of the barrel focus on him. He squeezed his lids shut, waiting…waiting for the round that would take him out. But it wasn't a bullet that slammed into him, flattening him to the ground. It was Eve.

He was flat on his back on the hard pavement, pain wracking him from head to toe. Still, he had no trouble seeing Eve's beautiful, beloved face when she frantically pushed away, looming above him.

"Billy!" she cried when she saw the mess that was his chest. "Oh, God, Billy! Oh, God!"

She desperately pressed a hand over the gushing wound, but he knew it was useless. And if the terror on her face was anything to go by, she knew it was useless, too.

"Sh-shh," he soothed her, coughing wetly, struggling to breathe, struggling to tell her this last thing before death came to claim him. "L-listen to m-me." His voice was a garbled wreck, but she must've understood him because she quieted, her watery, red eyes intent on his face as her breath sawed from her lungs. "I love you, t-too."

"Don't you say that!" she wailed, bringing up her gun hand to wipe her runny nose on the back of her wrist. Then she whipped her T-shirt over her head, wadding it up and pressing it to the center of his chest. "You're only saying that because you think this is good-bye! It's not good-bye! Billy, it's not—"

"It's J-Jeremy," he gurgled, watching her face pale. Her eyes flew wide. She shook her head in denial. He nodded and saw her throat work over a hard sob as realization dawned. "It's Jeremy. He—"

Boom! Boom! Boom! Boom!

Bullets riddled the truck, and Eve jumped up to return fire. *Bam! Bam!* Then she squatted back down behind the wheel well, and he lamented the fact that he couldn't help her. He couldn't move. He'd used the last of his strength to stand and draw Buchanan's fire. But maybe—no, there was no maybe about it—he *would* hold on long enough to get her through this. To give her an edge…

"Get him to talk," he instructed through the blood that just kept filling his mouth over and over again no matter how much he swallowed or spit. She glanced down at him, her face so frightened, so very frightened, and oh, how he wished he could offer her some sort of comfort. But all he could offer her in these minutes, *his* last minutes, was his expertise, the hard lessons he'd learned from years on the battlefield.

"Get him t-to come out and—" He was nearly ripped apart by the next round of wet, ragged coughing, his mutilated lung struggling against all odds to continue to draw breath. The human body was amazing that way. It clung to life with sharp, jagged nails, fought for survival even in the midst of searing, mind-bending pain. "Get him to make a mistake," he was finally able to finish.

He saw her swallow and nod. Then she lifted her chin and cried, "J-Jeremy?" Her voice was a rough parody of itself.

Silence met her call. Then, Jeremy finally bellowed,

his tone that of a madman, "Why couldn't you just fucking die?"

Bill watched Eve's face cave in on itself, and for a brief moment he was afraid that the depth and breadth of her sorrow and betrayal might kill her quicker than any of Buchanan's bullets. Then she squeezed her lids closed and dragged in a couple of shuddering breaths before opening her eyes and calling, "Why? Why are you doing this? Did Dad and Blake put you up to it?"

"Ha!" Jeremy yelled back. "Your father and ex-husband wouldn't dare kill you. They fucking love you to pieces! *Everyone* fucking loves you to pieces! Even my own *mother* loved you best!"

"G-good," Bill sputtered, struggling to keep his buzzing brain on the conversation, waiting for the one piece of the puzzle that would give Eve the upper hand. "Keep g-going."

Eve nodded, rolling in her lips as tears streamed down her face. "Wh-what are you talking about, J-Jeremy?" she cried, her chest shuddering. "Your mother *adored* you!"

Even Bill could hear Buchanan's snort. "Yeah. She adored me so much she drank and gambled and flitted her entire goddamn inheritance away! She left me next to *nothing*, Eve! *Nothing!*"

"J-Jeremy, I—"

"Shut up!"

She snapped her mouth closed, sobbing uncontrollably as she tried to apply more pressure to the wound on Bill's chest. He wanted to tell her it was useless, not to worry about it. But he needed to save his breath and his words for more important things.

"T-tell him," he coughed. The pain was less. And while that *felt* good, in reality it was bad. Very, *very* bad. Pain equaled life in this little equation. "Tell him you'll give him your m-money," *cough*, "if he throws his weapon a-away." Each word was a struggle. Each syllable a goddamn uphill battle.

Eve nodded, tears streaming unchecked down her face. She lifted her chin to do as he instructed.

Buchanan's response was to riddle the truck with more bullets. Not that Bill should be surprised. Buchanan couldn't back down now. He'd killed Bill—was that a movie? His sluggish neurons appeared to be misfiring. Then, the tire beside Eve exploded with a loud *bloof* followed by a thin, high-pitched whistle. Eve lifted the Glock over her head, angled it over the hood of the truck, and blindly returned fire. *Bam! Bam! Click! Click!*

And those last two sounds, the sounds of an empty clip, stopped Bill's heart. *Oh, God, Eve! No! No!*

"Run!" he managed to garble. It was the only chance she had. Not a good chance. But still a chance.

"I won't leave you." She smiled sadly through her tears, scooting down until her back was supported by the blown tire and her long legs were stretched out in front of her. With gentle hands, she lifted his head into her lap.

"No." He swallowed more blood. Black spots invaded his vision. "Run."

"Shhh." She ran her fingers through his hair. He could barely feel it. Oh, how he *wished* he could feel it.

"You're out of ammo, Eve!" Buchanan called, tears

of hysteria tainting his voice, the sound of his footsteps coming closer. "But I promise you I'm going to make this quick. I *do* love you, you know?" And Bill still had just enough faculties left to realize the man was shithouse crazy. And one hell of an actor. He'd fooled them all. "But I have to look out for myself! I've always had to look out for myself! You wouldn't understand what it's like to—"

Bill stopped listening because he felt something cool press against his shoulder. He slid his eyes to the side. And even though his vision was almost completely shot, he recognized the outline of his snubbie.

He choked on a sob of relief. And then there was only one piece of advice he had left to give her. "Don't hesitate."

He felt her nod more than he saw it. And he heard her throat stick when she swallowed.

As the sound of footsteps loomed louder, closer, he tried not to cough, tried not to wheeze, tried to keep as quiet as possible so Eve could hear the instant Jeremy rounded the front of the truck.

And then, it happened. He felt Eve's arm jerk up, heard the subtle click of the trigger right before a shot echoed out over the parking lot. It was followed immediately by a second. Then, silence…

He couldn't see what had happened. There was nothing but blackness now. But, in the next instant, he heard Eve drop the pistol to the ground, felt her lean over him as she was wracked by hard, wet sobs, and he knew. It was over. She'd won.

Relief slid through him on a warm, golden wave. Relief and love and…acquiescence.

Shh, he wanted to tell her when her hot tears fell on his face, when her cries rang in his ears. *It's okay, now. I love you, and you're going to be okay.* But he'd lost the ability to speak. The Reaper was close now. He could feel the bastard. Could feel him pulling and tugging. And when the distant sound of sirens reached his ears, accompanied by the gentle mutter of an overhead helicopter, he knew she was safe.

So…he let go…

Chapter Twenty-six

Northwestern Memorial Hospital
Friday, 3:03 p.m.

He wasn't dead...

There were times since he first regained consciousness yesterday when the pain was so intense he wished he *was* dead. But then he'd look over at Eve in the armchair beside his bed—he'd been told by the night nurse that she hadn't left his side since the moment he came out of surgery—and he'd remember just how much he had to live for.

Eve...Beautiful, courageous, wonderful Eve...

She loved him, and he loved her, and as soon as he got out of this goddamned hospital bed, he was going to show her just how much he loved her. Show her again and again. In very inventive and enthusiastic ways. A smiled curved his lips just thinking of it. Because if *that* wasn't enough to have him happily suffering through the pain—if thoughts of getting Eve naked and sweaty wasn't reason enough to fight to heal—then he didn't know what was.

He glanced over now, expecting to find her curled up sleeping or reading. But she wasn't there. Instead his sister Becky was sitting cross-legged in the chair, frowning at the screen of her cell phone, her fingers fiddling with the end of the blonde ponytail draped over her shoulder. His eyes darted to the couch at the far end of the room. But Eve wasn't there either. It was his brother-in-law, the esteemed leader of BKI. Frank "Boss" Knight had stretched his significant bulk out on the sofa, his big biker boots were dangling over the arm, and he was flipping through the latest issue of *American Rider*.

Bill moved his hand, trying to get Becky's attention. Then he remembered, vaguely, through the hazy cloud of delicious, *delicious* pain meds, that he'd been taken off the ventilator earlier. So, he could actually talk. Licking his lips, he opened his mouth and asked, "Where's Eve?"

Or at least that's what he *tried* to say. In all reality, it sounded more like, "Wheh Eh?" followed by a series of painful, wheezing coughs.

And *damn* his throat hurt like he'd been swallowing glass, not to mention his mouth was so dry he wondered if they'd been packing the sucker with gauze for some inexplicable reason. Becky's head jerked up, and she jumped to her feet. Boss catapulted himself from the sofa with a grace that was shocking for such a big man.

"Billy!" Becky squealed, grabbing his hand. "My God! You're talking!"

Yeah, if two incomprehensible syllables counted as "talking." Naturally, he'd probably be able to do a little better if his mouth wasn't so goddamned dry. Licking his lips, he tried again. Only this time, he said, "Wah-tah."

He frowned, wondering if that was at all understandable. Then, he smiled in victory when Becky reached for a clear pitcher. She poured some water into a cup, inserted a straw, and held it to his lips. He sucked greedily. It was heaven. The water was cool and delicious, and it soothed his burning throat. When he'd downed the last of it, the straw made a slurping sound against the bottom of the cup, and he said, "More."

And this time—*yippee!*—the word actually came out sounding completely comprehensible.

"No," Becky told him, shaking her head, setting the cup aside. He looked at it with longing. "The doctor says you're not supposed to drink too fast or too much. I'll give you another cup in ten minutes. "

He shifted his gaze to her, scowling.

She scowled right back, planting her hands on her jean-clad hips, and sticking her tongue in her cheek. "And you can wipe that look right off your face, mister," she harrumphed. "You scared the shit out of me, out of all of us. So, my patience with you is at an all-time low."

He grinned, shaking his head against the pillow. "Love you," he croaked, and her expression softened. She brushed her fingers through his hair and bent to kiss his forehead. She smelled like she always smelled, a strange combination of woman and mechanic, all flowery with just a *hint* of motor oil. When she straightened away, he cleared his throat and glanced down at the foot of the bed.

Boss was standing there with a big ol' smile splitting his face. It caused the scar cutting up from the corner of his lips to pull tight. "Save your breath," Boss said. "I know you love me, too."

Bill chuckled, but it turned into a series of coughs that had Becky squeezing his fingers and going back on what she'd just said. She held the straw on a fresh cup of water to his lips. As he sucked the cool, soothing liquid down into his burning throat, he grinned up at her triumphantly.

"Don't go thinking you've found my weak spot. That trick will only work once," she told him, pursing her lips.

When the water was gone, he asked, "Where's Eve?"

"She needed to stretch her legs, so we sent her on a coffee run," Boss informed him. "She should be back soon."

And knowing she was going to come through that door at any minute sent warmth fizzing through his veins. Or maybe that was just the drugs. The delicious, *delicious* drugs. For a moment, he thought he drifted, then the memory of those last few seconds out in the parking lot at Harbor View Marina dragged him back to reality.

"Jeremy Buchanan?" he asked, glancing first at his sister, then at Boss.

Boss shook his head. "Dead on the scene. Two shots. Center mass."

Bill swallowed. "Is she…Is Eve okay?"

Neither Boss nor Becky answered him, and a hard lump of apprehension settled in the center of his chest. Then, Becky finally admitted, "She's handling it pretty well. But it's tough. Buchanan was like a brother to her."

He nodded against the pillow, still having trouble believing what'd happened, *why* it'd happened. Frowning, he posed the question aloud.

"It's a convoluted story from what the police have been able to piece together after scouring his condo from top to bottom," his sister grimaced. Boss mirrored her expression, his big, craggy face filled with disgust. "But the short version of the story goes something like this...His mother, Eve's aunt, was a bit of a party girl. She liked to spend money as opposed to investing it. Apparently, she blew through her inheritance and the portion of a trust fund her parents left her. So, when she died, Jeremy discovered he was a trust-fund baby minus one trust fund. Then," Becky sucked in a breath and continued, "when Eve's father started up his business with Blake, he invited Jeremy to come in as a junior partner. But Jeremy didn't have the capital to put down. So he borrowed the money from some big time gang lord he allegedly met while working vice. He promised the gangster a big payoff. But as you know, the business failed, and he was left owing a lot of money to one very nasty individual."

Becky reached into her hip pocket, pulled out an orange Dum-Dum lollipop, and peeled back the wrapper. Shoving the sucker in her cheek, she opened her mouth to continue, and Bill didn't know if it was drugs talking but all he could think was...*this is the* short *version of the story?*

"So unless Jeremy wanted to find his knee caps busted, or take a bullet to the brain, or get himself fitted for cement galoshes, or whatever it is gangsters do to their enemies," Becky talked around the head of the sucker, "he needed to find a way to pay the guy back. In comes *Eve's* portion of the family trust fund. The document apparently stipulates that if Eve dies without an heir..." She frowned. "Heir. I swear, every time I say that word or even *think* it, I feel like I should be twirling a parasol and having a spot of tea." Boss snorted, and she shook her head as if she needed the physical inducement to jangle her thoughts back in order. "Anyway, if Eve dies without offspring, her portion of the trust fund reverts back to her closest, living relative from her mother's side of the family. Jeremy." She blew out a breath. "And there you have it."

There he had it, indeed. His mind was *swimming*. It was like something from daytime soap opera. But there was something…missing. A misplaced piece of the puzzle that niggled at the back of his brain. He narrowed his eyes and tried to focus on it, but it flitted away. Then, in a flash, he had it.

"Wait." He had to clear his throat when the word croaked out of him like he was a friggin' bullfrog or something. "But how did he know Eve was at the bar? It was her *father* who called that night."

Becky made a face, crunching down on the sucker and chewing loudly while simultaneously answering. "Eve texted him. She'd forgotten about it what with all the hullabaloo surrounding her father and ex-husband. It wasn't until everything was coming out in the wash that she even remembered doing it."

"Which is why he made the point of telling Eve she needed to leave her phone as evidence," he mused aloud, remembering Buchanan's last words to Eve before they'd gone to confront her father. "He wanted to make sure he got his hands on it in order to delete the text."

"He had his hands on everything," Becky muttered, shaking her head. "He kept the police files so he'd know exactly what everyone was doing, what everyone knew. He rode CPD's asses so when something *did* finally happen to Eve he could say *I told you so* and keep speculation off himself. He was smart. He played everything and everyone just right."

"Except for one thing," Bill said, smiling at his sister.

"What's that?" She cocked her head.

"He underestimated Eve..."

Eve pressed herself against the wall beside the open door to Billy's hospital room. *Oh, thank you, God! He's talking*. And the sound of his voice was like music sent straight from heaven...

However, as much as she'd been looking forward to this moment, she'd been simultaneously dreading it. Because now that he was talking, she could no longer pretend that what he'd told her out there in that blood-soaked parking lot was true. He'd thought he was dying...

An image of him, thick blood leaking from his mouth, flashed before her eyes, followed immediately by the image of Mac and Delilah jumping from the fierce, black BKI helicopter. What happened next was mostly a blur. But she remembered Mac and Delilah helping her load Billy onto chopper. She remembered Ace at the throttle as the helicopter lifted from the surface of the lot. She remembered a crazy, five-minute flight to the nearest trauma center where dedicated medical staff worked hard to stabilize Billy before having him Life-Flighted straight to Chicago's prestigious Northwestern Memorial hospital. She'd called in every favor she could in order to get Billy in the operating room with one of the country's best cardiothoracic surgeons. Then, after about eight hours of surgery, a dozen pins and a steel rod inserted into his leg, what followed were two very stressful days where he remained unconsciousness and where every odd beep or strange blip of a monitor nearly caused her to stroke out.

Then, yesterday he turned the corner. And today he was *talking. Sweet Lord in heaven, he was talking!* Which meant very soon, she'd have to hear him tell her he hadn't really meant that *I love you.*

He thought he was *dying.* And he was Billy. Loyal Billy. Courageous Billy. Trustworthy Billy. *Sweet* Billy. So he tried, even in what he'd thought were his last moments, to give her comfort. To be…*kind.* And it was so beautiful. So like Billy.

But he didn't die. Thank *goodness.* Which meant now she had to let him off the hook. And she *would* let him off the hook. Just as soon as she could work up the courage to walk into that room…

A second passed. Then two. A nurse in bright blue scrubs walked by, cocking her head, and Eve realized she probably looked highly ridiculous, pressed there against the wall like her toes were curled over a twenty-story ledge, a cardboard carrier with three cups of coffee held tight against her chest.

Okay, Eve. You can do it. Ladyballs in the house, remember?

Then again, ladyballs were generally useless when dealing with matters of the heart…

Oh, for Pete's sake! Stop being a coward! Your love

is without strings, right? So, what does it matter that he doesn't really love you back?

Taking a deep breath, she pasted on what she hoped was a smile, then stepped into the room.

And there she was. Eve...

Billy's heart raced at the sight of her. Literally, the monotonous *beep, beep, beep* of some monitor he hadn't noticed until then picked up its cadence.

"Eve," he said her name and watched her eyes immediately fill with tears. Watched her lower lip tremble in the most adorable way.

"You're talking, Billy," she sniffed, barely sparing Boss a glance when he grabbed the cardboard coffee carrier out of her hands.

"I'm talking." He patted the bed beside him. Grinning when she bit her lip, hesitating. "Come on. I won't bite," he promised hoarsely.

"We're gonna leave you two alone for a bit," Boss said, to which Becky lifted a brow, frowning.

"We are?" Becky asked. "But why? I mean Billy just woke up and—"

"Clue in, woman!" Boss thundered, and Becky stuck out her chin, scowling. Boss just rolled his eyes, heaving a long-suffering sigh, and hooked an arm around her shoulders. She tried to backpeddle when he marched her toward the door. But then Boss bent down and whispered something in her ear. "Oh," she said, glancing over her shoulder at Eve, then, *"Oh!"* She nodded, smiling, and allowed Boss to escort her from the room.

Eve watched them go then turned back to him, her eyes searching and uncertain.

"*Now.*" He patted the mattress again. "Come. Here."

"Billy, I—"

"Are you really disobeying the wishes of a man who just had two bullets dug out of him?" The more he talked, the easier it became. That made him happy. Because there were a lot of things he wanted to say to Eve.

She shook her head and scurried toward him. Her hair was pulled back in a clip. Her face was free of makeup. She was wearing slim-fit jeans paired with a demure little pastel blouse that was guaranteed to raise his blood pressure on a better day. The bulk of the bandage on her upper arm where that round had grazed her—his stomach flipped just thinking about how close she'd come—showed through the flimsy material. And there were dark circles beneath her eyes from a combination of long, sleepless nights and the soul-deep sorrow of discovering who'd really been behind the attempts on her life.

Sonofabitch. He still had trouble believing it. Her own goddamned cousin. And then what she'd had to do…it was terrible. Unthinkable. And they'd have to deal with it. Probably for a long, *long* time to come. The psychological trauma of that kind of thing didn't just go away overnight.

But right now, he didn't want to think about Jeremy Buchanan. They had a lifetime to work through all of that. No. Right now, he wanted to think about *them*. Talk about *them*. About their future.

He frowned when she didn't sit on the bed beside him, instead choosing to stand there. And when she lifted a hand to start chewing on a hangnail, he cocked his head on the pillow. "Eve?"

"It's okay, Billy," she blurted. "I know you didn't r-really mean it. You're off the hook, okay?"

Huh?

He didn't realize he said the word aloud, until she swallowed and sputtered, "Y-you know. Out in the parking lot when you thought you were dying. I know you didn't mean it. I know you don't really love me. I know you can't ever trust me again after what I did. And it's okay. I understand. I—"

"Eve, stop."

She snapped her mouth closed and swallowed, staring at the baby blue coverlet on his bed as if it held the answers to man's greatest questions.

"Look at me," he commanded, and she swallowed again, gnawing furiously at her lower lip. But slowly, ever so slowly, she lifted her gaze. And the look on her face was a two-fisted punch in the gut. *Good God, she actually believes what she's saying. She actually believes she doesn't deserve forgiveness. That she doesn't deserve a second chance.* And because none of that was accurate. And because he didn't have the strength to argue or explain it all, he said the three truest words he could think of. And he said them with a conviction she couldn't mistake. "I love you."

Two fat tears spilled over her lower lids and streaked down her pale face. There was still a flicker of disbelief in her eyes, so he repeated himself. "I love you."

"B-But how?" she wailed, throwing her hands in the air. "After I betrayed you with B-Blake. After I broke my promise, broke my *vow*, how can you ever trust me again? How you just change your mind about that? About wanting me? What's different now?"

"Well..." He snagged her hand, and he tugged her forward. Or tried to, anyway. He was surprised and appalled by how weak he was. He had no more strength than a newborn. Still, she obliged him and perched on the edge of the mattress. "It's easy. I can trust you because I love you. And because I know you love me."

She searched his eyes. "But we loved each other back then, too."

"Yes we did," he smiled. "But we were also young and dumb. Hopefully we're not so much so anymore and—"

He was interrupted by a commotion outside the room. Boss's and Becky's voices rose angrily, and then right before Patrick Edens barged through the door, he heard the man say, "Dr. Fisher told me he was awake, and I need to see them, damnit! I have something for them!" Boss slapped a huge mitt on Edens's shoulder, ready to drag the man back through the door. "I have something they need to hear!" Edens roared, struggling ineffectually against Boss's meaty grip.

And as much as Bill hated the sight of the man's face, and even though he couldn't *possibly* imagine what Edens could have to say, he felt Eve stiffen beside him, felt her fingers instinctively curl around his. And he realized *she* might need to hear whatever it was her father was determined to convey. So, he said, "It's okay, Boss. Let him go."

Boss and Becky both eyed Edens like one might eye a pile of cow manure swarmed by flies and baking in the sun, and Bill couldn't help himself. One corner of his mouth twitched. Then, once Boss released him, Edens threw his haughty nose in the air, grabbed his lapels, and straightened his gray, pinstripe suit jacket, and Bill felt himself following Boss and Becky's lead. He opened his mouth to demand that Edens get on with whatever he'd come to say, but Eve beat him to it.

"Why are you here, Dad?" she asked. Her voice was steady though he could feel her fingers trembling.

Tough. His woman was one hundred percent, straight-up tough. And he was so goddamned proud of her.

Edens's eyes drifted over Bill, and to his utter astonishment, there seemed to be pain and…was that…? Hell, that looked suspiciously like remorse in the man's gaze. Then Edens turned to Eve and blurted, "He tried to call you." His voice was hoarse, but his words were clear.

"Wh-what?" Eve asked. And now there was a tremor in her vocal cords to match the one in her fingers.

Edens licked his lips, shaking his salt-and-pepper head. "Twelve years ago, after you had your cell phone turned off because the press got your number and started hounding you about the photographs, Reichert called the house. He left a dozen messages for you, asking you to call him to let him know what was going on. But I never gave you those messages."

Eve sucked in such a large breath Bill was shocked

there was any oxygen left in the room. Her hand flew to her throat, covering the bruises that'd turned from deep purple to a jaundiced-looking yellow. "H-how could you n—" she sputtered, but Edens cut her off.

"And she wrote to you, Reichert. Twice," he said, a muscle ticking in his jaw. He reached into his suit jacket, pulling out two envelopes that were yellowing around the edges. "In the first letter, she laid everything on the line. She sent the pictures and the articles. She begged you to forgive her and asked you to call her at her new phone number. In the second letter, she told you about Blake's proposal, asked if there was any chance you still loved her because she wouldn't go through with it if you did. But I intercepted the letters in the mailbox."

Edens hesitantly stepped forward, handing Bill the envelopes. And when Bill looked down at the things, he couldn't believe his eyes. He lifted the flap on one and out fell the pictures of Eve, those heartbreaking pictures, and the tabloid articles that'd run alongside them. And then there was the note. He'd recognize her handwriting anywhere because he'd *lived* for her letters, read and reread them thousands of times while he'd been in BUD/S training.

"I-I don't expect either of you to forgive me," Edens said, his nostrils flaring. "But after what you two have been through together, I realize I—" He stopped and cleared his throat, his chin sinking just a notch. "You may not be the kind of man I envisioned for my daughter. But you're the kind of man she needs. And I was…I was wrong to interfere."

He glanced at Eve one more time, his expression

softening, his mask of superiority slipping. "I really don't expect you to forgive me, Eve," he whispered again, and if Bill wasn't mistaken, the man's thin lips actually shook. "I just…" He turned and stared out the window at the building across the way. "I just wanted the *best* for you, and I thought Blake was the best, but you were so stubborn. You refused to…" He stopped, shaking his head. "So, I set out to sabotage the relationship you had with Reichert."

He turned back. There was real, honest-to-God regret reflected in his gaze, and Bill could hardly believe what he was seeing. The high and mighty Patrick Edens was actually admitting fault.

"But I was wrong," he continued. "What I did, *how* I did it, was wrong. And I *do* love you. And I'm so terribly sorry for not believing you were in danger. So terribly sorry for…everything."

And then, with only a second of hesitation, he turned and swept from the room. Eve watched him go, tears streaming unchecked down her face, her jaw hanging open.

Hell, Bill's jaw was damn near sitting on the bed beside him.

Boss and Becky exchanged a look before quickly following Edens from the room, softly closing the door behind them. And that's when Eve glanced down at him, hope and disbelief warring for supremacy in her eyes. "You t-tried to call me?" she asked at the same time he said, "You wrote me and tried to tell me what happened?"

"Yes," they answered in unison. And Bill couldn't

help it. He laughed. It hurt like hellfire, but he laughed all the same. Because good Lord, it'd been *Edens.* Edens and his goddamned machinations that'd kept them apart. All these years…it'd been Edens. And he didn't know if his laughter was caused by the joy of knowing Eve *had* tried to tell him, that she *had* loved him enough and been brave enough to try to fight for him, or if it was caused by a hysterical kind of fury brought on by the knowledge that her fucking father had almost cost them *everything*.

Then, he sobered, shaking his head. Because really, the only thing that mattered was that they loved each other. He could spend years railing against the way things had happened, looking back and lamenting what could have been. Or he could do the smart thing and look forward to what lay ahead…a lifetime of happiness and love. "I want to spend the rest of my life with you, Eve," he blurted.

Eve knew everything in her world had just changed. She knew from this moment forward things would be different. *She* would be different. Because Billy loved her. He'd *always* loved her. And twelve years ago, he hadn't rejected her or her apology. Heck, he hadn't even *known* about her apology. But even still, even thinking she'd never tried to contact him after the ordeal with Blake, even thinking she'd simply abandoned him with no word, he'd been willing to forgive her, willing to give her another chance.

And now, he was asking her to spend the rest of her life with him. Promising her love and support and partnership and sex and adventure. Promising her all the things she'd been missing her whole sorry life. And what did a girl say to something like that?

Well, she said the one only thing she could say. She said, "Yes! Oh, God, Billy! Yes!"

He smiled then. And it was the most wonderful smile. "Now, come here," he said, pulling on her hand. "Come crawl into this bed with me."

"I don't want to hurt you," she said, frowning at the tubes peeking from his hospital gown and the IVs in his hands.

"The only thing that's hurting me right now is not holding you in my arms," he assured her.

She turned her head, sticking her tongue in her cheek. "I'm telling you," she assured him, "getting in bed with you right now isn't a very good idea." She lifted his hand to her lips, grinning against his fingers.

"What? Why?"

"Because I've heard it's quite uncomfortable to get an erection while catheterized."

He barked out a laugh, and it was the most beautiful sound she'd ever heard. She realized then that all the bad things that happened to her over the last few months, even as terrible as they'd been—and, yes, she'd probably need to spend a lot of hours with a psychologist sorting them all out—were worth it. Because in the end, the bad things resulted in one good thing. One *wonderful* thing. The *best* thing, in fact. They resulted in her winning Billy back…